THE WAITING

THE
WAITING

A Ballard and Bosch Novel

MICHAEL
CONNELLY

LITTLE, BROWN AND COMPANY

New York Boston London

Little, Brown and Company
Hachette Book Group
1290 Avenue of the Americas, New York, NY 10104

Little, Brown and Company is a division of Hachette Book Group, Inc. The Little, Brown name and logo are trademarks of Hachette Book Group, Inc.

ISBN 9780316563796

Printed in the United States of America

To Mary "Meme" Mercer,
with many thanks

MONDAY, 7:28 A.M.

1

SHE LIKED WAITING for the wave more than riding the wave. Facing the cliffs, straddling the board, her hips finding the up-and-down rhythm of the surface. Riding it like a horse, making her think about Kaupo Boy when she was a child. There was a reverence to the moment before the next set came in and it was time to dig down and paddle.

She checked her watch. She could fit in one more. She'd ride it all the way in if she could. But she savored the moment of just floating, closing her eyes and tilting her head upward. The sun was just over the cliffs now and it warmed her face.

"Haven't seen you here before."

Ballard opened her eyes. It was the guy on the One World board. An OG with no wetsuit, no leash, his skin burnished to a dark cherrywood. She braced for what she knew would come next: territorial male posturing.

"I'm usually at Topanga," she said. "But there was nothing there this morning."

She didn't mention that she'd consulted a wave app. The OGs would never look at an app.

He was twenty feet to her left, riding the low rollers sideways so he could keep an eye on her. Women were unusual at Staircases. It was a big boy's break. Lots of rocks in the short tide. You had to know what you were doing, and Ballard did. She hadn't crossed anybody's tube, had not pulled out of a wave too soon. If this guy was going to try to school her, she would shut him down quick.

"I'm Van," he said.

"Renée," she said.

"So, you wanna get breakfast at Paradise Cove after?"

A little forward, but okay.

"Can't," she said. "Got one more set and then I got a job. But thanks."

"Maybe next time," Van said.

Before the conversation got more awkward, somebody farther down the line began paddling, aligning his board with an incoming wave. It was like a bird startling and jumping the whole flock into flight. Ballard checked over her shoulder and saw the next set coming in tall. She flipped forward and brought her legs up on the board. She started paddling. Deep strokes, fingers together to get speed. Digging down. She didn't want to miss the wave, not in front of Van.

She glanced to her left and saw him paddling stroke for stroke with her. He was going to press her, show her whose break it was.

Ballard paddled harder, feeling the burn in her shoulders. The board started to rise with the wave and she made her move, jumping up into a crouch on the center line. She put her left foot behind her and stood just as the wave crested. She pushed the nose down and began slicing down the face of the wave.

She heard Van's voice in the wake, calling her Goofy-foot.

She put her hands out for balance, heeled the board into a turn, and went up the wall before cutting it back down and taking it all the way in. For eight seconds everything about the world was gone. It was just her and the ocean. The water. Nothing else.

She was coasting on foam when she remembered Van and looked

back for him. He was nowhere in sight and then his head came up in the surf along with his red board. He raised his hand and Ballard nodded her goodbye. She stepped off, lifted her board, and walked out of the surf.

She had her wetsuit stripped down to her hips by the time she rounded the dunes and got to the parking lot. The combination of sun and wind was already drying her skin. She leaned her board against the side of the Defender and reached under the rear wheel well for her key box.

It was gone.

She crouched down and looked at the asphalt around the tire for the magnetic box.

It was not there.

She leaned in, looking up into the well, hoping she had set the box in the wrong spot.

But it was gone.

"Fuck."

She quickly got up and went to the door. She pulled the handle and the door opened, having been left unlocked.

"Fuck, fuck, fuck."

There was the key and the magnetic box on the driver's seat. She saw that the glove compartment was open. She leaned in, reached under the driver's seat, and swept her hand back and forth on the carpet.

Her phone, gun, wallet, and badge were gone. She swept her hand farther under the seat and pulled out her handcuffs and a seven-shot Ruger boot gun that the thief had apparently missed.

She stood up and looked around the parking lot. No one was there. Just the row of cars and campers belonging to the surfers still out on the water.

"Fuck me," she said.

2

WITH HER WALLET containing her ID card stolen, Ballard could not pass through the turnstile at the entrance to the LAPD's Ahmanson Center, so she drove into the overflow lot behind the massive training center and called Colleen Hatteras on her new phone. Hatteras answered with an urgent tone.

"Renée, where are you? Wasn't the unit meeting at nine?"

"I'm in the back lot. I want you to let me in the fire exit, Colleen."

"Are you sure? If the captain—"

"I'm sure. Just open the door and I'll deal with the captain. Is everyone still there?"

"Uh, yes. I think Anders went to the cafeteria but he didn't say anything about leaving."

"Okay, tell Tom or Paul to get him while you open the door for me. I'll be there in two."

"Well, what happened? You didn't call and didn't answer our calls. We were starting to get worried."

Ballard got out of the Defender and headed to the back door of the complex. She was already exasperated with Colleen and the day hadn't even started.

"Calm down, Colleen," she said. "Everything's fine. I lost my phone and wallet at the beach. I had to go home to get a credit card and then hit the Apple Store to get a new phone. So please just open the door. I'm almost there and I'm hanging up now."

She disconnected before Colleen could respond, which Ballard knew she would. She walked up to the fire exit, pulling her jacket closed so maybe it would not be obvious that she had no badge clipped to her belt.

Colleen opened the door and an ear-piercing alarm sounded. Ballard quickly stepped in and pulled the door closed, and the sound cut off.

"How did you lose your phone and wallet? Were they stolen?"

"It's a long story, Colleen. Is everyone here?"

"Tom went to get Anders."

"Good. We'll start as soon as they're back."

The fire exit was located behind the murder-book archive. Leading Colleen, Ballard walked the length of the back row of shelves and into the bullpen of the Open-Unsolved Unit. The center of this area was dominated by the "raft"—eight interconnected desks with privacy partitions between them. The side walls of the bullpen were lined with file cabinets and mounted whiteboards on which current investigations were tracked.

"Sorry I'm late," Ballard announced as she reached her desk at the end of the raft. "As soon as Tom and Anders are here, we'll start."

Ballard sat down and logged into her city computer terminal. She went through the department's password portal and pulled up the database containing crime reports from the entire county. She searched for reports on thefts from vehicles at county beaches and soon was looking at several occurrences. From this she was able to cull a list of thefts that had occurred at popular surfing beaches. From Trestles up to Dockweiler, Ballard had been surfing the Southern California coastline since she was sixteen years old. She knew every break and could see a pattern of BFMV—burglary from motor vehicle — reports occurring at places where she knew the parking facilities weren't visible from the ocean.

This told her three things. First, this was likely the same thief or group of thieves. Second, they were familiar with surfing and probably were surfers themselves. And third, because the thefts were spread out up and down the coast and across multiple police jurisdictions, the pattern had not been noticed by law enforcement. The thefts were seen as individual crimes.

Ballard started reading the summaries of the reports to see if any witnesses had seen anything helpful, if any suspects' fingerprints had been found, or if there was any follow-up to the initial reporting of the crimes. None of the thefts were large enough to warrant much interest from law enforcement. Wallets, phones, cash, and spare surfboards were the things most often stolen. Taken separately, Ballard knew, these cases likely died with the initial report. As protocol dictated, they would go to an auto-crimes desk somewhere, but without a description of a suspect, a fingerprint, or even a partial license plate of a getaway car, the reports would go into the great swirling maw of minor crimes that did not merit much attention from the criminal justice apparatus. It was the story of the modern age. Reports were taken largely for insurance purposes. As far as law enforcement went, it was a waste of paper.

Colleen stuck her head over the half wall separating Ballard's desk from her own. From her angle, she could not see Ballard's screen. "So, what are you working on?" she asked.

Ballard logged out of her search. "Just checking email," she said. "Is everybody ready?"

"Anders is here," Colleen said.

Ballard stood up to address the team.

3

OTHER THAN BALLARD, who was a full-time sworn officer, the members of the Open-Unsolved Unit were all volunteers. Two years ago, following a law enforcement trend that had budget-challenged police departments across the country using retired detectives to investigate cold cases, Ballard had been placed in charge of the LAPD's previously mothballed unit. She was also its chief recruiter, which meant that she had to convince people to contribute their skills to the noble effort at least one day a week, with fifty dollars a month to cover expenses. She had finally reached a point where she was happy with the squad she had curated.

Gathered at the raft were Tom Laffont, retired FBI; Lilia Aghzafi, who had done twenty years with Vegas Metro; and Paul Masser, formerly a prosecutor with the district attorney's office. Colleen Hatteras had never been a police officer. She had been a stay-at-home mom who got hooked on genetic genealogy and took online courses in its application to law enforcement. She was relentless at the keyboard — and at butting into the personal lives of the other members of the team, with a primary focus on Ballard. She was also a self-described empath who never shied away from expressing the feelings she picked up from people. Ballard reluctantly put up with this because of Colleen's case-related skills.

The newest member of the unit was Anders Persson, who was even more of an outlier than Hatteras. His law enforcement experience was limited to volunteer work with the Swedish Police Authority in his hometown of Stockholm. But Persson, just twenty-eight years old, now ran an L.A.-based software company by night and assisted the OU team by day. While Hatteras was the expert in hunting down family histories and genetic connections, Persson was the go-to guy when it came to navigating the internet and finding people who had gone to extreme lengths to avoid being found. Together, Hatteras and Persson were a formidable team that complemented those on the unit with real police and investigative experience. And while the unit and Ballard were still recovering from a major hit to their reputations, the result of an early case that had gone awry, Ballard felt the team was now humming like a well-tuned motor. The raft had room for two more volunteers, but Ballard was satisfied with what they were accomplishing. The unit cleared, on average, three cold-case murders a month. It was a drop in the bucket compared to the six thousand unsolved murder cases stored in the archive shelves behind the raft, but it was a solid start.

Ballard stepped over to the whiteboard wall to begin the meeting. Normally she would have left her suit jacket draped over her chair, but today she kept it on to hide the fact that she didn't have her badge.

Four side-by-side boards were used to track the cases that were in some level of play. Every Monday morning, the team gathered to discuss their progress. The first board listed all cases that contained evidence to be submitted for forensic and technological analyses. This primarily meant DNA, fingerprints, and, sometimes, ballistics. The application of DNA in criminal prosecutions had not been approved by the California courts until the early 1990s, and genetic analysis had taken major strides forward in recent years. This made unsolved cases from the last three decades of the previous century fertile ground for review. Additionally, fingerprint databases had greatly expanded. The ballistics databases lagged behind these advances and were not as useful, but in gun cases they couldn't be ignored.

What put sand in the gas tank of the unit's well-tuned motor was that many of the cases were so old that the killers the team identified were already dead or incarcerated. This brought answers to still grieving families, but it felt like justice that was too little too late. And the members of the Open-Unsolved team were denied what every investigator wanted and needed at the end of a case: the opportunity to confront the evil behind the murder. This was why so-called live cases — where the killer was believed to be living and still out there — were the investigations the team rallied behind. Though the archive contained records of unsolved cases going back to the early 1900s, Ballard directed the team to work only on cases recorded since 1975.

Ballard scanned the first board to see if any new cases had been added. When not working on a current investigation, every team member was charged with pulling cases from the archive and reviewing them for possible follow-up.

"Okay, anybody add anything new to our in-play list?" she asked.

After a round-robin of negative responses from the raft, Laffont raised his hand. "I think I'll have one to add this week," he said. "Expecting to hear something back from Darcy today — if I'm lucky."

Darcy Troy was the DNA tech who handled cases from the Open-Unsolved Unit. It was good to have a go-to person at the lab, but Troy was not assigned solely to OU cases. Current investigations were always a priority, and Troy had to handle DNA analysis from those cases ahead of anything that came in from the raft. Sometimes the wait was frustrating.

"What's the case?" Ballard asked.

"A sexual assault and murder from '91," Laffont said. "A bad one.

Not that there are any good ones, but the guy assaulted her several times before he strangled her. Ejaculated outside the body but left something behind on her clothes. Darcy took it. Last week she said she'd have something this week."

"Good," Ballard said. "What's the vic's name?"

"Shaquilla Washington," Laffont said. "A south-end case. Didn't get much attention in the day."

Ballard nodded. It went without saying that the archives were disproportionately heavy with cases that hadn't gotten much attention because they were from minority communities on the city's south and east sides. This could in part be due to the fact that there were more murders in these communities and the detective workloads there were the heaviest in the city. But it could also be explained by a lack of commitment to those communities and an absence of empathy for the victims. Ballard had noticed neither of those deficiencies in Laffont. When he had the time to go into the archives and pull cases for review, he often looked for reports from the south side. He was white and in his late fifties and had seldom worked on the south side as an FBI agent assigned to the Los Angeles field office. He saw his efforts now as a way to partly balance the scales. Ballard respected him for that.

"Hopefully Darcy comes through with something," Ballard said.

She continued reviewing the boards and the cases with her crew, eventually coming to the last board, which listed the cases that were most active in terms of pending arrests, prosecutions, or closures. The last case on the list belonged to Masser.

It involved the murder of a clerk at a Hollywood convenience store in 1997. A man in a ski mask entered the store, told the clerk to put all the cash in the register on the counter, and fired a shot into her chest, killing her instantly. The man then jumped into a waiting car and escaped. According to various witnesses from inside and outside the store, the getaway driver was a white woman with long black hair.

The car was described as a maroon sedan, and one witness provided the first two digits of its license plate.

There was a video camera inside the store, and a review of the tape revealed that the gun was fired while the suspect was gathering the cash the clerk had put on the counter. It appeared to be an accidental discharge that shocked even the gunman; he turned and ran out of the store, leaving half the cash behind.

The license plate digits and car description eventually led investigators through motor vehicle records to a man named Donald Russell, who owned a maroon Honda Accord with a license plate beginning with those two digits. Russell was unemployed and had a history of drug-related arrests. He lived with his wife, who also had a record of drug arrests. She, however, had short blond hair. Both were questioned but denied involvement in the robbery and killing. They provided an alibi that the investigators could neither prove nor disprove. The detectives took the case to the district attorney's office but prosecutors declined to file charges, saying there was not enough evidence to convince a jury and bring home a guilty verdict. But no further evidence was developed, and the case went cold—until Paul Masser of the Open-Unsolved Unit pulled the murder book off a shelf in the cold-case archive.

Masser reviewed the case and quickly learned that it didn't have the traditional kind of evidence that could jump-start a cold case. There were no fingerprints or DNA from the crime scene. The bullet had been collected from the fallen clerk's body, but it did not lend itself to modern ballistic technology because it had flattened when it hit the victim's spine, which made it useless for comparison with bullets in NIBIN, the national ballistics database. And no weapon had ever been recovered to compare the bullet to.

Masser located the suspects, still living in Los Angeles, and learned two things that could prove useful a quarter century after the killing. The first was that the couple were no longer a couple; they had divorced five years after the murder. The second, which he discovered through social media, was that the now ex-wife, Maxine Russell, was a recovering addict who had recently celebrated twenty years of sobriety, according to her Facebook page.

Masser, drawing on his experience as a prosecutor, knew that the couple's divorce meant that statutory spousal privilege was no longer in play. The rule held that a wife or husband could not testify against a spouse without that spouse's approval. But the protection was limited to the years of the marriage, which meant there was an opportunity to pit the ex-wife against her former husband. Masser, drawing on his experience with an addicted family member in recovery, also knew that most rehab programs encouraged participants to keep journals as part of their steps toward sobriety.

With information gathered in the original investigation, Masser drew up a search warrant for the apartment where Maxine Russell now lived and convinced a judge to sign it. The warrant included all journals and documents written by the suspect as well as family photos that showed Maxine with long dark hair. On a shelf in the living room, Masser found several journals Maxine had kept over the years of her sobriety. One entry described the robbery gone wrong and another expressed Maxine's guilt at having been involved in the taking of a life, even though she claimed it had been an accident. Additionally, a photo album found in a closet contained photos of Maxine going back to when she was a child. In many, she had long dark hair.

Maxine had been arrested two weeks ago and was still in jail, unable to afford a bond on bail set at two million dollars. The department low-keyed the arrest and it had so far escaped media attention. It was now time for Masser to move forward with the second part of the case strategy.

"I'm going to meet with John this afternoon," Masser told the group. "We're going to go to Maxine's lawyer and see if she wants to deal. After two weeks, she is probably getting the idea that incarceration is not how she wants to spend the rest of her life."

John was John Lewin, the deputy DA assigned to prosecute cases from the Open-Unsolved Unit. In the news coverage that solved cold cases often brought, the local media had dubbed him "the King of Cold Cases."

"Has she called her ex-husband from the jail?" Ballard asked.

"Not on the recorded lines," Masser said. "I doubt he knows she's been arrested."

"What's John going to offer her?" Laffont asked.

"I don't know where he'll start but he told me he'll go to full immunity," Masser said, "if she delivers the ex."

"And you think she'll go for it?" Laffont said.

"Yeah, I do," Masser said. "I tried to pull the divorce file but it's sealed. But twice since the divorce, she's asked for a restraining order against him. It doesn't look like she has a whole lot of love for him anymore. She's going to flip."

"Hope so," Ballard said. "Let me know when you know."

"Roger that," Masser said.

"Okay, then, that's it," Ballard said. "Sorry I was late and I appreciate everybody sticking around. Let's dig down and make cases."

Ballard always ended the weekly meeting with the same message, taken from a Muse song she loved: "Dig Down." The words were on a sign on the wall of her pod. It was her code when it came to both life and cases.

4

BACK AT HER desk, Ballard pulled up one of the crime reports she had reviewed earlier. This one was for a car burglary that had occurred at the Topanga break a few months ago. What drew her back to it was the officer's note in the summary that there had been a fruit vendor in the parking lot where the theft occurred. The vendor said he had seen nothing, but the officer had taken down his name and phone number for follow-up. Ballard copied the information about the fruit vendor and the victim of the theft into a small notebook. The victim was named Seth Dawson. He reported that in addition to his brand-new iPhone 15, a Breitling watch worth three thousand dollars, a gift from his father, had been taken. Those two items pushed the crime beyond petty theft and well into felony territory.

As she was putting the notebook back in her jacket pocket, Colleen poked her head up over the partition wall again.

"Did you forget something today?" she asked.

Ballard immediately thought about the staff meeting and wondered what she had possibly missed covering. "I don't think so," she said. "Like what?"

Colleen lowered her voice to a conspiratorial whisper. "Like your badge, for example."

Ballard dropped her hand to her right hip as if to feel for the badge on her belt.

"Shit, you're right," she said. "It's in my car under the seat. I'll get it when I go out. Thanks for noticing, Colleen."

"Anytime," Hatteras said.

One of the two lines on Ballard's desk phone started flashing. "Can you get that?" she asked Colleen.

"Sure," Hatteras said.

She dropped from sight and answered the phone. Then she spoke to Ballard without poking her head over the partition. "It's Darcy Troy on line one," she said. "She said it's important."

Ballard punched the button and picked up the phone.

"Darcy, let me guess. Shaquilla Washington?"

"Shaquilla Wa—? No, it's about something else. We just got a hot shot on the Pillowcase Rapist."

Ballard said nothing as a cold finger slid down her spine.

"Renée?"

"Yeah, sorry, I'm here. Where do they have him?"

"They don't have him. It was a hit on the familial search you put in last year."

"Tell me about it."

"A guy was arrested by West Valley Division on a felony domestic. His swab was taken and we sent it up to DOJ. It came back as a familial match in the Abby Sinclair case."

It was one of the first cases Ballard had submitted for comparative genetic analysis after restarting the unit two years ago. The Pillowcase Rapist had terrorized the city for five years beginning at the turn of the century. Dozens of women were assaulted in their homes. Each had been sleeping and woke up as a pillowcase was pulled over her head, blinding her to her attacker. After the rape, he choked each victim into unconsciousness, hog-tied her with plastic snap ties, and escaped.

A task force was formed but no arrests were ever made. The reign of terror culminated in the murder of Abby Sinclair, the last known victim, in 2005. He went too far with Sinclair, choking her to death after the sexual assault. Following that, the attacks stopped, and the Pillowcase Rapist went dark.

"So it was a familial match," Ballard said. "How close?"

"Very," Troy said. "This guy who was arrested, he's likely the Pillowcase Rapist's son."

Ballard nodded. She could feel her heart rate rising as adrenaline ticked into her blood. "How long ago was the arrest on the domestic?"

"Nine weeks ago."

"Wow."

"That's how long it takes to process the arrest swabs and put them into the DOJ bank. These don't get priority like DNA from crime scenes. Thank God you had that familial search in place."

Ballard had joined the department and was in the academy and later in uniform patrol during the years that the Pillowcase Rapist had terrorized the city. She and her partner had been first on scene on the murder of Abby Sinclair. It was the first murder scene Ballard had ever been to, and although many followed, the image of Abby Sinclair's naked body in her bed, the pillowcase pulled over her head, had stuck with her. It was the first case she'd pulled off the shelf in the library of lost souls — the murder-book archive.

"Okay, Darcy," she said. "Give me what you've got on the domestic."

Ballard wrote the information down, thanked Troy for the call, and hung up. She stood to see who was left on the raft. While the Monday-morning staff meetings were mandatory, the investigators were required to work only one day a week, and they often cleared out after the meeting, choosing to fulfill their commitment on other days. Ballard saw only Hatteras and Persson. She knew Aghzafi liked to work Thursdays or Fridays, and Masser had probably left to meet with the prosecutor and defense attorney on the Maxine Russell case. Laffont was nowhere to be seen, but Ballard hoped he had just stepped out for coffee or to go to the restroom, because she was going to need him.

"Okay, Anders, Colleen, listen up," she said. "We've got a hot shot here I want to go full-court press on."

She referred to her notes before continuing.

"I want you to run down a Nicholas Purcell, DOB January twenty-nine, 2000. He was arrested on a felony domestic about nine weeks ago in West Valley. I want to know everything about him: where he lives, where he works, the domestic, everything."

"What's the case?" Persson asked.

"About twenty years ago, there was a serial offender called the Pillowcase Rapist," Ballard said. "He assaulted several women over a five-year run. I'm talking dozens of victims. He finally killed one and then dropped out of sight. He was never caught. That murder — that's our case."

"But wait," Hatteras said. "If Nicholas Purcell was born in 2000, then he — "

"Can't be our guy," Ballard said. "That's right, he's not. It's his father. We got a familial match. Purcell's father is the Pillowcase Rapist. Through his son, we find him, get his DNA, and go from there."

"Groovy," Persson said.

Ballard looked at him for a moment, not sure what part of this the Swede thought was groovy. She chalked it up to English being his second language. She nodded and then started toward the archives, listening as she went to Hatteras and Persson discussing the division of labor on their assignment.

The cases in the archives were organized first by year and then alphabetically by the victims' last names. Ballard had to crank the shelves open to access the 2005 cases. The Abby Sinclair murder book was actually a murder box. It contained records of the murder investigation and the forty-six sexual assaults that had begun in 2000. It was a cardboard box with handles. Ballard pulled it off the shelf and lugged it back to her desk.

Hatteras and Persson were both turned in their seats and waiting for her when she came out of the archives. Ballard could not yet read Persson as well as she could Hatteras after two years of working together. And her read of Hatteras now was that something was wrong.

"What?" she asked.

"Well, we found Nicholas Purcell," Hatteras said. "We also think we have his father."

"That was quick. What's the issue?"

"Take a look." Hatteras stood up to give Ballard access to her screen. Ballard put the murder box down on the seat and leaned on it to look at the screen. It was a photo on Nick Purcell's Facebook page of a family gathered around a birthday cake.

"I scrolled back three years to find this," Hatteras said.

"Okay, what am I looking at?" Ballard said.

"Read the caption," Hatteras said. "This is Nick's twenty-first birthday. That's his father on the right."

Ballard studied the father. She was hit with a slight glint of recognition, but she didn't know where she would have known him from. He looked to be a fit fifty with a ruddy face and a full head of dark hair. He wore a striped golf shirt with sleeves stretched tight around his biceps.

"Who is he?" Ballard said.

"He's a judge," Persson blurted out, beating Hatteras to the punch.

"He's the *presiding* judge of the Los Angeles Superior Court," Hatteras said. "The Honorable Jonathan Purcell."

Now Ballard realized how she knew him.

"Did you pull up the report on the domestic?" she asked.

"Have it right here," Persson said. "But I must tell you now, it was never filed."

"Declined by the DA's office," Hatteras said. "Maybe the judge got to them."

Ballard gave her a look that warned that things like that were dangerous to say.

She stepped over to Persson's desk and leaned down to read his screen. Persson got up and she sat down to scroll through the summary written by the arresting officer. She was looking for the details of the alleged assault and what had bumped it up to a felony. The victim was identified as twenty-one-year-old Sara Santana, who said her boyfriend Nicholas Purcell got angry and choked her into unconsciousness when she was late coming home from work. Ballard scrolled farther down to see what evidence, if any, had been collected. It said the officer had taken photos of the victim's neck and of her left hand because she said she'd broken two fingernails while struggling to pry Purcell's hands off her neck.

"The photos are not in the report?" she asked.

"No photos," Persson said.

"Should they be in there?" Hatteras asked.

"If the officer took them with his phone, they should be attached," Ballard said. "It's part of the protocol on domestic calls."

"I wonder if he did and if the DA saw them," Hatteras said.

"That's the question," Ballard said. She got up, went to the murder box, lifted it, and headed to her desk. "So, listen to me," she said. "Neither of you talk about this case outside of this room. No one else knows about the case or the judge or any of it. Understand?"

Hatteras and Persson nodded somberly.

"Good," Ballard said. "Anders, send me that report."

She put the box down on her desk and lifted the top off. It contained six plastic binders, placed in the box spine up, with the dates marked and in order. She remembered from her first look at the box two years ago that the first five binders were task force reports on the series of assaults attributed to the Pillowcase Rapist. The sixth binder was dedicated to the last case, the killing of Abby Sinclair. She pulled this binder out of the box and sat down to get reacquainted with the murder investigation.

But before she opened the binder, she opened the contacts list on her cell and called Laffont.

"What's up, Renée?"

"Did you leave?"

"Yeah, I thought we were done. Meeting a friend for lunch. I was planning to come back when I hear from Darcy on my case. I'll get my hours in after that."

"I need you back here after your lunch. We just got a hot shot that I want to move on today."

"Uh, sure. I could also come back now. I'm only ten minutes away. I stopped to shoot the shit with Captain LaBrava. He saw me in the parking lot and asked about our door alarm this morning."

LaBrava was the commander of operations at the Ahmanson Center. That put him in charge of the building but not of the Open-Unsolved Unit, which fell under the command of the Robbery-Homicide Division downtown.

"Jesus, this guy and that back door," Ballard said. "Doesn't he have more important things to worry about?"

"He should," Laffont said. "But I think I smoothed it over. I said we had a lizard in the archives we were trying to save by getting it outside the quickest way we could."

"A lizard? And he bought it?"

"I don't know, but it gave him a reason to drop it. I don't think he'll bring it up again."

"We'll see."

"So, what's the hot shot?"

Ballard told him that one of the first cases she, as head of the unit, had sent to the lab for familial DNA comparison had just produced a hit. And that hit led to the presiding judge of the Los Angeles Superior Court.

Laffont whistled, loud enough that Ballard had to pull her cell away from her ear.

"Did you ever appear before Purcell?" he asked.

"Not that I remember," Ballard said. "I think he was mostly in civil. And now he's the chief judge, but that's primarily an administrative position."

"Too bad he's not in court. I'd like to get a look at him."

"Well, you will. I want to get some DNA off him as soon as possible."

"Surreptitiously?"

"Unless you know another way. I don't think going to the courthouse, knocking on the door of his chambers, and saying, 'Hey, Judge, mind if we take a swab?' is going to work."

"Nah, I don't think so either. So what are you thinking?"

With a solid lead in a very big unsolved case, Ballard did not want to delay the investigation for a day, an hour, or even a minute. This was a case she had prioritized from the day she'd rebooted the unit. "Well, I haven't thought too much about it, but judges get to park in a garage under the CCB. I'm thinking we pick him up as he's coming out at the end of the day and go from there."

"Sounds like a plan. You sure I can keep my lunch date and come back after? We won't need to get downtown till four or so, right?"

"Yes, but I want you to be familiar with the case. I just pulled the box."

"I'll be back by two, how's that?"

"Good. I have a lunch scheduled too. See you this afternoon."

"We aren't going to do this by ourselves, are we?"

"No, I'll try to get Paul and Lilia to come back in."

"Good. See you at two."

"Right."

Ballard disconnected and checked her watch. She had a half hour before she had to leave for her appointment. She opened her laptop and went online to check recent purchases on the credit cards that had been in her wallet. She was hoping that at least one card had been used and she'd be able to track that purchase back to the thief, but there'd been no new activity on either.

She leaned back and thought about this. Usually stolen cards and their numbers were sold off quickly by thieves to a second tier of criminals who worked furiously in a race against time before the victim of the theft canceled the cards. That apparently had not happened yet. Disappointed, she considered the possible reasons for this and wondered whether she should cancel the cards or leave them live with the potential of generating a clue trail.

Hatteras popped her head up over the divider but didn't say anything.

"What is it, Colleen?"

"Just wondering if there's anything you need me to do."

"No, I'm going out for an appointment. You don't need to stay."

"You sure?"

"I'm sure."

"Okay, then."

Ballard looked back at the screen and started the procedure for reporting her credit cards stolen and requesting new ones.

5

DR. CATHY ELINGBURG'S office was north of the airport in Playa Vista, an area known as Silicon Beach because of all the tech companies and start-ups located there. Elingburg's practice was largely made up of young tech types with competition paranoia and sleep disorders. As far as Ballard knew, she was the only law enforcement officer on Elingburg's roster of clients, and that was how Ballard preferred it. She wanted no one with a badge to possibly know she was seeing a therapist on a weekly basis. It might be well into the twenty-first century, but a cop seeing a therapist was still viewed by other cops as a sign of weakness.

She arrived early and sat in the waiting room, studying the framed diplomas from UNC Chapel Hill and Elon. Both were awarded to Helen Catherine Sharpe, an indication that Elingburg was a surname she took through marriage. In the eight or so months Ballard had been seeing her, she had not gotten around to asking how someone who had been schooled in North Carolina ended up in Silicon Beach.

At noon, Ballard heard the exit door from the office open and close. The office was designed so that a departing client did not pass through the waiting room where the next client was sitting. It was a privacy that Ballard appreciated.

Moments later, the door to the office opened and the doctor welcomed Ballard into the rectangular space. To the left was a desk; to the right was a seating area that looked like a basic living room, with two couches, one on either side of a coffee table, and solo seats on the ends. Their habit was to sit across from each other on the couches, and Ballard took her usual spot.

"Water?" Elingburg asked. "Coffee?"

"No, I'm fine," Ballard said.

Elingburg started with a discussion about the next Monday being Presidents' Day and a holiday. She told Ballard that she wouldn't be seeing clients in the office that day, and they could either move their standing appointment to a different day or do it by Zoom with Elingburg connecting from her home. They decided on an office appointment on the following Tuesday and then got to work.

"So, let's begin. How is your day going?"

"Well, it didn't start out well. I mean, at first it was good—I was on the water—but then it went to shit."

"What happened? Work?"

"No, work is actually okay. But I got ripped off when I was on the water. I went up to Staircases because the apps said that was the break that was happening. But up there, you park behind the bluffs. You can't see your car from the water, and somebody was there watching. Had to be. They saw me hide my key. When I got back from the water, my badge, my wallet with my credit cards and police ID, and my gun were gone."

"Oh my gosh."

"Oh, yeah, and my phone. I spent part of the morning at the Apple Store. So not a good start."

"What happens now? You tell your boss and they investigate?"

"I haven't told anyone. I'm supposed to report it, but if I do that, I could lose my job."

"What? It was not your fault."

"Doesn't matter. If I were a man and I reported it, they might put a ding in my jacket for being careless. But for me, I'm not so sure. Like we've talked about before, I'm on thin ice downtown. There are people just waiting for me to fuck up so they can transfer me to the boondocks or get rid of me altogether. The job I have right now is where I need to be. It's where I know I make a difference. So I can't report this because it might be the thing that drives them to say, 'You know what, we're going to make a change.'"

"But you can't go around without a badge or a gun."

"I have a backup weapon and a boot gun the thief somehow missed in the car." Ballard opened her jacket to show her backup holstered on her hip.

"What about the badge?"

"Well, I have to get it back."

"How?"

"I'm going to track down whoever the fuck took it."

Elingburg just nodded as if considering whether that was a good plan or not.

"Anyway, things got better after that," Ballard said. "We got a good case going."

"What is a good case?" Elingburg asked.

"Mostly a case where the suspect has a pulse. And also is out there living his life and thinking he got away with it. Somebody you get to put the cuffs on."

"You get a good charge from that."

"Fucking A right, I do. It's what it's all about."

Elingburg nodded again and changed the subject. "Anything new on your mother?"

"No. Nothing."

The last Ballard heard about her mother, she was living somewhere in Maui, the Hawaiian island where Renée had been abandoned at age fourteen — until Tutu had found her and taken her to California.

Maui had been ravaged by wildfires six months ago. The town of Lahaina was destroyed and the remains of nearly a hundred people had been recovered so far in the ash. Many were unidentified. Makani Ballard was believed to have lived on the east side of the island, away from the fires, but she likely frequented Lahaina to shop and seek work. At the moment, she was listed among the missing.

"I called Dan, my contact in Maui, last week but they don't have anything new," Ballard said. "They still have so many UBs that it's going to go on for months."

"UBs?"

"Unidentified bodies."

"Oh."

"We shorten everything in the cop world. My guy over there works for something called the MINT."

"Which means what?"

"Morgue Identification and Notification Task Force. That's a horrible name so we shorten it, give it a catchy acronym."

"Understandable. This not knowing about your mother, whether she's even alive — has it softened your feelings about her at all?"

There were shelves lining the wall behind Elingburg's couch that were filled with books and small statues and other knickknacks. There was also a framed mirror on a stand that Elingburg had previously told Ballard was used in therapy sessions with clients who had body-image problems. Ballard could see herself in the mirror now as she considered Elingburg's question. She saw the stress in her dark eyes and realized that she had been so preoccupied with the theft of her badge and gun that morning that she had forgotten to pull her sun-streaked hair into a ponytail for work. It fell, unbrushed and straggly, to her shoulders.

"Softened my feelings..." Ballard said. "No, not really. I feel like if she's gone, I've missed my chance to get an answer from her."

"Answer to what?" Elingburg asked.

"You know, why she fucking went off into the hills and left me like that."

"Abandoned you, you mean."

Ballard nodded. "I guess it's kind of hard to say that when it's your own mother," she said.

"That's the self-blame we've been talking about since you came to me," Elingburg said. "It's not on you, Renée. Your mother did this to you. And you did nothing to deserve it."

"But I don't get why she didn't see enough in me to stick around. I mean, we had a home, we had the water, we had a horse. She had me, but somehow... it wasn't enough for her."

Elingburg kept a notebook and pen on the coffee table. For the first time during the session, she picked them up and wrote something down.

"What did you write?"

"'Vicarious trauma.'"

"Which means what?"

"It's when you share someone else's trauma. People with jobs where they see tragedy and trauma all the time — police, firefighters, ER workers, soldiers — it has a second-tier effect on them."

"What about therapists? Do they get it?"

"They can, yes."

"What's it got to do with my mother?"

"Well... I think maybe subconsciously you have masked the trauma of losing your father and being abandoned by your mother with vicarious trauma from your work. Taking on the pain of others camouflages your own. And that was your shield for many years, until the death of your grandmother left you with no one but your lost mother somewhere out there. It's bubbling up to the surface, and that's what causes your insomnia. It's all coming to the conscious mind."

Ballard thought about this. It was true that she had felt the need to talk to someone shortly after Tutu passed. It was ironic that she had been telling Elingburg about her mother in weekly installments when the fires swept through Maui and possibly took her life. It was almost as if the anger and hurt she'd spewed out in the sessions had ignited the flames.

"So," Ballard finally said, "what do I do about it?"

"Well, as I've been saying all along, you have to stop blaming yourself for your mother's choices," Elingburg said. "You have to remember that both of you were abandoned by your father. His—"

"Wait a minute. He drowned. He didn't abandon us."

"You're right. It wasn't an intentional abandonment. It wasn't a choice, like your mother's. He drowned. But he died pursuing a lifestyle that he knew could be dangerous. So his leaving was like an abandonment of you both. She handled it poorly, but, you know, some people are not as strong as others. You are strong, Renée. So you have shouldered this weight in your mind, but sometimes the mind grows tired and drops its defenses, and things come forward."

Ballard was silent as she considered this. She had come to Elingburg a month after Tutu had peacefully slipped away in hospice. The insomnia had begun soon after her death, and a Google search had produced Elingburg as a sleep-disturbance expert.

"And I know today was bad with your things getting stolen at the beach," Elingburg said. "But don't let that deter you from going. The water is your salvation. You need to get out on the water as much as you can."

"Don't worry. I will."

6

AT FIVE P.M. Ballard was posted in her Defender in front of the PAB—the Police Administration Building—on First Street. She had a clear view up the slight incline of Spring Street at the exit gate from the garage beneath the Criminal Courts Building. Tom Laffont was in his personal car at the top of the incline at Spring and Temple. Paul Masser was positioned in one of the pink chairs in Grand Park next to the courthouse. This put him closest to the exit from the garage where the building's judges parked. His angle would allow him to see the license plates on the vehicles leaving the garage. They were looking for a Mercedes C 300 Coupe that belonged to Judge Jonathan Purcell. It was as black as a judge's robe, according to Anders Persson, who'd gotten the registration from the Department of Motor Vehicles.

Lilia Aghzafi was posted in her car on Temple so she could swing around the corner and pick up Masser once Purcell's car was spotted and surveillance ensued.

Ballard picked up her rover and pressed the send button. "Everybody got their eyes open?"

She received a mic click from each of the others. Satisfied, she picked up her cell phone and called a number she had written in her notebook. She put the phone on speaker so she wouldn't have to take her eyes off the courthouse garage exit.

The call went immediately to voicemail.

"This message is for Seth Dawson," Ballard said. "This is Detective Renée Ballard with the Los Angeles Police Department. I'm following up on the car burglary that occurred on the Pacific Coast Highway at Topanga in November. I have some questions I'd like to ask you. I can be reached anytime at this number. I would appreciate a call back."

She disconnected and reviewed her words. Dawson would have a recording of her talking about an investigation that was not hers to conduct, which could be problematic should things blow up in her face. But the way she had worded the message gave her a plausible out, because she'd never said that she was conducting an investigation, only that she wanted to ask him questions.

The rover crackled with Masser's voice.

"Black Mercedes coming up the ramp."

Ballard grabbed the binoculars from the center console and trained them on the garage exit onto Spring. The black Mercedes soon appeared and held still as its driver waited to make the turn. It was a one-way street. The driver had to go right and come toward Ballard's position.

Ballard grew impatient waiting for Masser to report. Without taking her eyes from the binocs, she grabbed the rover.

"Do we have the plate?"

She waited and then turned her focus slightly left to pick up Masser. She saw him walking out of the park and talking into his sleeve, but she was not hearing him on the rover.

"Is anyone getting audio from Paul?" she barked into the rover. "He's talking but I can't hear him."

"No audio from Paul," Laffont said.

"Can't hear him," Aghzafi reported.

Ballard had to think quickly. The Mercedes had turned onto Spring and was coming to the traffic signal at First Street. The fact that Masser had walked out of Grand Park and was out on the sidewalk indicated that the black Mercedes was the one they were looking for. She keyed the mic. "Lilia, go get Paul and let us know about the plate. Copy?"

"Copy."

At First Street the Mercedes turned right and headed up to Broadway. Ballard pulled the Defender away from the curb and moved into the left lane. She had to make a U-turn, and the five o'clock traffic was thick with oncoming vehicles. She brought the rover back up to her mouth. "Tom, are you on the move?"

"No, waiting on orders."

"Damn it, go. I'm stuck. He went north on First toward Broadway. Go."

"On my way."

Ballard saw an opening in the traffic and dropped the rover into the center console so she could use two hands to yank the wheel into a U-turn. She headed toward the intersection at Spring, looking a block ahead for the Mercedes. She saw it moving on Broadway. Her guess was that it was going to the 101 freeway entrance. From there, the freeway quickly reached an interchange where Purcell could go in any direction and be lost to them.

Ballard had to hit the brakes when the car in front of her stopped early on a yellow. She slapped the steering wheel. "You asshole!"

But then she saw Laffont's white Ioniq make the turn and head toward Broadway. It was followed by Aghzafi's Volvo. She grabbed the rover again. "Lilia, did Paul confirm the plate?" She waited.

"Yes, confirmed."

Ballard nodded to herself.

"Okay. Tom, you have the target? I caught a light."

"Affirmative. Locked on."

The light turned green and Ballard waited for the car in front of her to get moving. Lilia's voice came up on the rover.

"And we are right behind. Have target in sight," she said.

"Okay, keep spacing," Ballard said. "I think we're heading to the freeway."

She jockeyed the Defender around the slow mover in front of her and made the turn onto Broadway. Laffont began a play-by-play on the rover.

"Okay, we're on the freeway roundabout. Turning north at the moment."

Ballard cursed as she caught the light at Temple. She figured that the Mercedes was on the freeway merging lanes and quickly approaching the 110 interchange.

"Tom, which way are we going?" she radioed.

"One-ten north," Laffont responded. "Looks like Pasadena."

Not so fast, Ballard thought. The 110 north fed to both the Glendale and Golden State Freeways. At this point Purcell—if it was Purcell they were following—could be going anywhere. She keyed her mic.

"Has anybody been able to see the driver? Have we confirmed the target?" She waited.

Lilia must have given her rover to Masser because Ballard heard him say, "It's him. I saw him when he had his window down to talk to the guard at the garage. Sorry about my handset."

They had photos of Purcell from his son's Facebook page and a profile Hatteras had found online. It had run in the *Los Angeles Legal Journal* when he was appointed presiding judge of the superior court. The profile gave some details about the judge but did not reveal where he lived. They had no photo or home address from his driver's license because the DMV had a security block on these. This was a common practice with law enforcement officers and the judiciary. Even the car registration that they were able to access had a post office box for an address.

Ballard finally got on the freeway and started working her way ahead. Eventually, she saw Aghzafi's Volvo. She was about to tell the others that she had caught up when her phone rang. It was Hatteras. "Colleen, what's up?"

"How are you guys doing?"

"We're in the middle of it. What do you need?"

"I just wanted you to know I started working on the DNA heritage pattern for Purcell."

"Okay, what does that mean?"

"It's a genetic family tree."

"Okay . . . anything good yet?"

"I'm just starting."

"Well, then, how about you let me know if you find something we can use as an investigative lead?"

"Of course. I will. Are you guys following the judge now? I can hear you're in the car."

"Yes, we are, and I really need to focus on this, Colleen. So if there isn't anything else, I'm going to let you go."

"Okay, good luck. Let me know how it goes."

"Are you coming in tomorrow?"

"Of course. I want to keep building this tree."

"Then we'll talk tomorrow."

Ballard finally disconnected. Hatteras had the ability to push her patience to its limit. Yet she was good at what she did—if she just maintained focus and did it. More than once, Ballard had thought about telling Hatteras it wasn't going to work out and that she was off the team. But investigative genetic genealogy was where cold cases often went, and all the things that made Hatteras annoying— the woo-woo vibes, asking too many questions, crossing boundaries, sticking her nose into things—were what made her good at IGG work. So Ballard put up with her because the payoffs were worth it.

She also had a soft spot for Hatteras because she knew why her cold-case work meant so much to her. She'd packed the second of her two children off to college in September, and her husband of twenty-three years had promptly moved out and filed for divorce. As Colleen told it, this was not exactly a surprise move, as their marriage had stopped functioning years before and was mostly a front for their children. But the dramatic drop in activity at home resulted in her increased activity at the Ahmanson Center.

Purcell stayed on the 110, passing exits for the Glendale and Golden State Freeways, all the way to the Orange Grove exit in Pasadena. Laffont, who maintained lead car in the surveillance, reported the exit, and all the unit's cars followed. Since it was rush hour, there were so many cars on the road that Ballard wasn't worried that Purcell would realize he was being tailed. Their efforts were also camouflaged by the falling of night. If Purcell checked his mirrors, he'd see headlights behind him but no identifiable vehicles.

After exiting, Purcell took a couple of right turns and soon was on Arroyo Drive cruising north through an old and well-to-do neighborhood with homes on the right and the Arroyo Seco wash on the left. There was little traffic now, and Ballard instructed her team to slow down and spread out. A minute later Laffont reported over the radio that Purcell had pulled into a driveway at the corner of Hermosa. "I kept going," he said.

Ballard thought of a plan and put it into the rover. "Tom, pull over. Double back on foot on the west side. Lilia, you go right on Hermosa and post up. Tom, I'll get to you in a minute."

As she was finishing her orders, she saw Lilia's right turn signal a half block ahead. The Volvo made the turn onto Hermosa. Ballard continued on straight, and as she passed the house on the corner, she saw an open and lit-up garage at the end of the driveway. The black

Mercedes was in the left bay next to an SUV, and Purcell was getting out with a briefcase in hand.

She kept driving until she saw Laffont's car parked at the curb three houses down. She pulled in behind it in front of a Craftsman with no lights on and a real estate sign on the lawn that said IN ESCROW. She got out and crossed the street to the Arroyo Seco side. There was a footpath through the trees that ran along the upper slope of the wash. She didn't see Laffont until she was almost back to Hermosa, and she startled as he stepped out of the shadows.

"Are you trying to scare me?" Ballard asked.

"Uh, no," Laffont said. "Just trying to be inconspicuous."

They spoke in whispers even though they were more than a hundred feet away from the Purcell house.

"Did you see him?" Ballard asked.

"Not after he closed the garage. Lights were already on in the house. What do you think? He's in for the night?"

"Possibly. I don't know." Ballard had her rover in her hand. She whispered into it. "Lilia, what's your angle? You see any activity?"

She turned the volume knob down before there was a response. When Aghzafi's voice came back, she held the rover up, and she and Laffont tilted their heads toward it to hear.

"We have an angle on some rear windows. Looks like the kitchen. Two people in there talking, a man and a woman."

Ballard looked at Laffont. She was beginning to think the surveillance was a bust.

"Making dinner?" he said.

"Probably," Ballard said. "Look, if they're tucked in, we might be doing this again tomorrow, so I'm going to send you and Lilia home. I'll keep Paul and stay a little bit longer."

"I don't mind staying. Why not send them both home? They're already in the same car."

"No—just in case, I want Paul here."

What was unsaid but had been established in the team's previous surreptitious DNA captures was that Masser, a former prosecutor who knew the rules of evidence, was the better witness for testifying about DNA collection. He could stand up to any challenge from a defense attorney about the procedures followed in gathering and preserving genetic evidence.

Ballard used the rover to instruct Lilia to drop Masser at Ballard's car and head home after giving him her rover. Laffont left shortly after that, telling Ballard to call him back if the judge decided to go out.

Ballard and Masser stood in the shadows of the woods across the street from the Purcell house. Twice during their vigil, a neighborhood resident came by walking a dog and gave them suspicious glances. But no one challenged them on what they were doing there.

"We're going to give it another half hour and then call it," Ballard said. "It's a Monday night. People don't go out on Monday nights in Pasadena."

Masser pointed across the street. "Don't be so sure," he said.

She followed his finger and saw that the garage door was rising and the light inside had come on. She saw two sets of legs, and when the door finished going up, Purcell was in full view, holding open the passenger door of the Mercedes for a woman in a purple pantsuit.

"Hot nights in Pasadena, I guess," she said. "I'm going to get the wheels. You stay here to see which way they go."

"You got it," Masser said.

7

FIFTEEN MINUTES LATER they had followed the Mercedes
through the Old Town district of Pasadena to a restaurant called the
Parkway Grill, where a valet took the Mercedes, and the couple from
it went inside. Ballard had pulled to a stop at a red curb where they
had an angle on the front door of the restaurant.

"What do you think?" she asked.

"It will be a DNA-rich environment," Masser said. "The question
is how do we make the capture without notice."

"Right. So let's go in, see what we see."

"You sure?"

"If it's not good, we start fresh tomorrow."

"Reinforcements?"

Ballard thought about bringing back Laffont and Aghzafi and
decided against it. "I think we can handle it."

"Your call."

Ballard pulled away from the curb and moved the Defender into
the valet lane at the restaurant. Valets approached the car on either
side and opened the doors. Ballard told the man holding her door that
she had to get something out of the back. From a plastic carton, she
grabbed two plastic evidence bags and stuffed them into the pocket of

her blazer. She knew that there might be more than one opportunity to capture Purcell's DNA inside the restaurant. From another box she pulled latex gloves and put them in her other pocket.

They entered the restaurant. There was a bar to the right and a crowded dining room to the left. Ballard saw Purcell and the woman she assumed was his wife being led to a table in the front of the room. A team of young women in sleek black dresses stood behind the check-in stand. One of them asked how she could help, though she said it in a tone that conveyed her supreme power in the granting of tables for dinner.

"Do you have a table for two?" Ballard asked.

"Do you have a reservation?" the hostess responded.

"No, we don't."

"Our wait right now for a table without reservations is forty-five minutes. I can seat you at the bar, which is first come, first served. We offer the full menu there."

"Perfect."

They went into the bar and found two seats together on the end closest to the dining room. From there, Ballard could see the Purcell table clearly in the mirror behind the bar's display of bottles of various bourbons.

"Well, do we order?" Masser asked.

"Might as well," Ballard said. "They're going to eat and we might be conspicuous if we don't."

They studied the menus. When the bartender came over, Ballard ordered the branzino and a tonic with a lime and a splash of cranberry juice, which she knew would pass for an alcoholic drink. Masser ordered the same. In the mirror they watched the Purcell table, where a bottle of wine was produced and decanted. Ballard settled in for what could be a long night. She hoped the food was good. She'd heard of the restaurant but rarely ventured to Pasadena to eat.

"You okay with this?" Ballard asked. "How's your wife doing?"

"She's fine," Masser said. "I texted her."

They sipped the nonalcoholic drinks the bartender put down and Ballard started thinking about the case. "Colleen said she's already building a genetic family tree."

"Why? If this is the guy, we won't need a tree."

"True, but it will keep her busy."

Masser laughed. "There's that," he said. "Hey, look."

Ballard checked the mirror. The woman—possibly the mother of Nicholas Purcell—had gotten up from the table and was walking toward the bar.

"We've been made," Masser said, a panicked tone in his whisper. "What do we do?"

"Just hold on," Ballard said. "Let's see what—" She saw the woman make a turn at the end of the bar and go down a hallway to the left.

"She's going to the restroom," Ballard said.

"That was close," Masser said.

"You keep your eye on him. I'm going to follow her."

"You sure?"

"I'm sure."

She got up, leaving her napkin on her seat, went down the hall, and pushed through the door to the restroom. There were four stalls and two sinks. Three of the stall doors were slightly open, and the fourth was closed. Ballard could see the cuffs of the purple pantsuit beneath the closed door. She went to one of the side-by-side sinks, buttoned her jacket to avoid exposing her weapon, pulled a tissue from a box, and leaned over the sink toward the mirror.

She waited.

The toilet in the fourth stall flushed.

Ballard started dabbing at her left eye with the tissue. The door to the stall opened and the woman from Judge Purcell's table emerged and went to the other sink. Ballard continued dabbing and the woman started washing her hands.

"I hope he pays for it," the woman said.

"Excuse me?" Ballard said.

"Whoever just broke your heart. I hope he gets his broken worse."

"Oh. No, I'm just trying to fix my contact."

"Oh, my mistake."

"No worries."

The woman finished washing and turned off the water. She pulled paper towels from a dispenser, dried her hands on them, and tossed them into a trash hole cut into the countertop. She reached into a pocket of the pantsuit, produced a lipstick in a gold case, and touched up her lips, then took a tissue from the box. After dabbing her lips with it, she dropped the tissue through the counter hole.

Ballard stepped back from the sink and fluffed her hair while looking in the mirror. The woman turned toward the door.

"Have a good night," she said.

"You too," Ballard said.

When she got back to the bar two minutes later, her branzino was waiting. Masser was already eating his.

"Sorry, I couldn't wait—it looked so good. What happened in the restroom?"

"I got a tissue with her lipstick on it," Ballard said. She patted her jacket pocket.

"But why?"

"Because I don't know who she is."

"What's that mean?"

"I had the opportunity. We don't know who she is. Is she Nicholas Purcell's mother? A stepmother? We need to know who the players are, and I had two evidence bags. The question is, are we going to get to use the second one?"

"Well...guess what, they're leaving."

Ballard checked the mirror. "That was fast," she said. "Did they even get food?"

"Just appetizers and soup," Masser said. "Then the judge got a call on his cell and they asked for the check."

"Something must have happened."

"Looks like it."

Watching in the bar mirror, Ballard saw a server go to the Purcell table and give the judge a to-go bag.

She took the second genetic-evidence bag out of her pocket and handed it to Paul under the bar. "You have gloves?" she asked.

"Got one already on," Masser said.

"Good. What are you going to go for?"

"Before he got the call, he had the soup. I'll go for the spoon."

Ballard nodded. Masser started to get off his stool. Ballard put her hand on his arm to stop him. "Not yet," she said. "Wait. Let them get out the door."

"But they might clear the table," Masser said. "There's people waiting."

Ballard kept her hand on his arm. In the mirror she watched the couple moving toward the door. She glanced over at their empty table with the judge's napkin balled up on top of it. She swiveled on her stool to watch them leave.

But they didn't.

The judge stopped in front of the trio of young hostesses to engage in conversation. He was probably a regular and was explaining his reason for departing early. Each hostess made a face of faux empathy and understanding. Ballard checked the table. A waiter hovered over it for a moment, then picked up the check folder the judge had left behind.

Ballard looked back at the judge. He was still talking.

"We've got to do this," Masser urged.

"Shit," Ballard said. "Okay, go. Try not to be seen."

"Yeah, right."

"You know what I mean."

Masser headed into the dining room just as a busboy was moving toward the judge's table. Masser pulled his phone from his pocket with his ungloved hand and walked with his head down, looking at its screen. He and the busboy converged at the table, and Masser tripped and lurched into it, his upper body leaning over the judge's former seat. He pulled back and apologized, holding his phone up in explanation—and to draw the busboy's attention from his other hand.

Masser returned to the bar and sat down.

"You learn that move in magic school?" Ballard asked.

"Oh, yeah," Masser said. "One hand distracts while the other hides the rabbit."

Ballard looked down and saw Masser had the evidence bag open between his legs and was placing the soupspoon in it. She checked the mirror and saw the judge and his wife finally pushing through the door. Ballard waved to the bartender and signaled for the check.

Ballard looked down at her uneaten dinner. The branzino was brushed with a beurre blanc sauce and looked like it had been perfectly grilled.

"We got what we need," Masser said. "You're not thinking of leaving this food behind, are you?"

"I want to see why they left without eating theirs," Ballard said.

"Then give me the valet ticket. You take a few bites while I get the car."

Ballard reached into a pocket and handed over the ticket. The bartender brought the check and she put down cash to cover it. Then she ate three bites of fish—it was delicious—and went out the door to her waiting car.

They followed the judge's Mercedes and were surprised when he went back to the house on Arroyo. There was a car sitting on the street outside the house. Its lights were on, and exhaust from its tailpipe steamed the crisp night air. It was a car Ballard immediately recognized as a city plain-wrap—a detective's car. As they approached, the doors opened and two men started getting out. The headlights of the Defender splashed across them and Ballard recognized the man on the driver's side.

"Keep going," she said.

"Well, I wasn't exactly planning to stop and say, 'How y'all doin'?'" Masser said.

"Sorry."

"No worries. Who are they?"

"RHD."

"Robbery-Homicide? Why would they call him away from dinner?"

"Search warrant. Must be a case that can't wait."

"So what do we do?"

"I think we call it a night. He'll probably stay in after this and we got what we came for."

"Up to you."

"Yep."

"You recognized those two guys, didn't you?"

"One of them. Gil Perado. He's an old bull."

"You have a history with him?"

Ballard didn't answer, so Masser did.

"That's right. You have a history with everybody."

"Used to. Let's head back downtown. To your car. I want you to take the samples to Darcy Troy first thing tomorrow."

"Okay. But you usually do that."

"I have something to do in the morning. And I want no delays in getting that to the lab. I'll call Darcy. She'll be ready for it."

"You got it."

"After that, I need you to run down Nicholas Purcell's birth certificate. We need to cover all bases, make damn sure he's the judge's son. You might have to go down to Norwalk for that. We'll need the date the birth certificate was filed to be sure."

The main offices of the county registrar were down in Norwalk in the south county. While Ballard knew from prior cases that it was difficult and time-consuming to break through the seal on adoption records, the date that a birth certificate was filed with the registrar — meaning how many days after the birth — was a strong indicator of whether an adoption had occurred.

"Sure, I'll go straight there from the lab," Masser said.

"Thanks," Ballard said. "I might not be in till later, but let me know what you get."

"Of course."

TUESDAY, 12:14 A.M.

8

BALLARD WOKE TO the sound of her phone buzzing on the bedside table. She checked the number but didn't recognize it. She answered anyway.

"Ballard."

"This is Seth."

"Okay. Seth who?"

"Dawson. You left me a message, said call anytime. I just got off work."

Ballard put it together.

"Oh, right, yes. Sorry, I leave a lot of messages for a lot of people. Anyway, I wanted to ask a few questions about the burg —"

"Did you catch them?"

"Uh, no, we didn't. But why do you say 'them'?" Ballard pivoted to a sitting position, put her feet on the floor. She turned on the bed-table light and reached for her notebook next to it.

"Had to be more than one," Dawson said. "To hit all of those cars that morning. At least, that's what the cop said."

"Wait a minute," Ballard said. "There was more than one auto burglary? I only have your report."

"Yeah, see, I was the only one who waited around for the cops to show up. It took them like an hour. But I had insurance, so I needed a police report. I knew that. The other guys got tired of waiting and took off."

"How many others got ripped off?"

"There was four of us, including me."

"Do you recall what was taken from the other cars?"

"I think just phones, maybe a little bit of cash."

"Do you know the other three?"

"Not really. I mean, I saw them on the water, but we didn't really talk. Just stayed out of each other's way, mostly."

"Okay, Seth. The police report says you live in Venice. Do you go up to Topanga often?"

"Hardly ever. And after that shit, never again, man. My insurance had a five-hundred-dollar deductible, so that cost me."

"I understand. You lost a phone and a watch?"

"Yeah, the Breitling was from my dad. He spent three grand on it."

"I'm sure it was of great sentimental value to you."

"It was."

"So, if you hardly ever went up to the Topanga break, how come you went there that morning?"

"It was like glass down by me in Venice. So I checked the app and it said that was where the waves were that morning. I went."

"Which app do you use?"

"I used to use Dawn Patrol but then I switched to Surf's Up. I think, if I remember . . . yeah, I had switched by then. It woulda been Surf's Up."

It was the same app that Ballard used and that had led her to Staircases yesterday morning. She wrote it down in her notebook even though she knew she wouldn't forget. It was a solid lead. If the thieves were using a surf app to determine which breaks were hot and drawing surfers, she could do the same thing in her search for who-ever had stolen her badge and gun.

"You said you just got off work," she said. "Where do you work, Seth?"

"The FedEx at the airport," he said. "I'm a cargo coordinator. I make sure the right packages go to the right planes going to the right airports. It's just a job."

"You work nights to keep your days for surfing?"

"Exactly."

"I know the drill. Listen, I'd appreciate it if you kept this conver-sation between us. It's an active investigation, so it would be better if people didn't know what we're doing."

"Okay."

"Thank you for your time. I'll be in touch when we get these guys."

"Cool."

Ballard disconnected and thought about things for a moment. She was energized by the lead regarding the surf app. She lay back down on the bed. It took her only thirty seconds to know sleep was not happening. She got up to take a shower.

9

SURF'S UP REPORTED that for a second straight day, the break at Staircases was where the juiciest waves in the Southland were rolling in. While Ballard didn't believe the thieves she was looking for were the smartest criminals she had ever hunted, she did think that they were probably wise enough not to return to the same spot a day after stealing a police officer's badge and gun. But she headed up the Pacific Coast Highway anyway, just to scope it out through eyes that had a better understanding of the setup.

She had spent a good part of the night working online, matching theft reports against the wave history on the Surf's Up app. With only one exception, every theft reported by a surfer in the previous twelve months had occurred at the break where the app said the best waves were to be found. It was clear when her analysis was completed that the thieves—and she, too, was convinced it was more than one culprit—were using the Surf's Up app to plot their crimes.

And now she was driving in predawn darkness toward Staircases on the off chance that the thieves were not as smart as she'd assumed.

It was still dark when she got there. The parking area behind the bluffs was empty. She got out and walked the length of the lot, looking at the ridgeline that ran behind it. There had to be an observation point where both the water and the parking area could be seen. This would allow the thieves to watch their intended victims hide their vehicle keys and know exactly when they were out on the water so they could make their move.

The bluff between the parking lot and the water was at its highest point at the north end of the lot. Ballard instinctively knew that it would be the best observation spot. She turned on a mini-flashlight she had retrieved from her equipment bag and trudged up the sandy incline. At the top she found a small clearing in the seagrass where the parking area and the beach were easily viewed. The litter of cans and bottles and other trash seemed to be proof that she was right.

Most of the debris was discarded willy-nilly on the sand or in the seagrass rimming it. But one can of Red Bull stood upright. Ashes around the pop-top hole indicated that it had been used as an ashtray. This seemed unusual to Ballard, considering that the spot was out in the open, and ashes could easily be flicked into the wind.

She snapped on latex gloves and picked up the can by the rim using two fingers so as not to smudge any prints on the barrel. She gently shook the can, and it seemed empty of liquid, but there was something inside. She guessed it was a cigarette butt or the end of a joint. She pulled an evidence bag out of her pocket and put the can in it. It was possible that the can had been handled by the thieves who ripped her off, but it was a long shot. Still, she had learned over the years to follow her hunches. Sometimes they paid off.

Looking out across the beach to the water, she saw one surfer already out there in the early light of dawn. He wore no wetsuit, and Ballard knew it was her breakfast suitor, Van.

Ballard wished she were out there, not standing on a bluff with an evidence bag in her hand. She wondered if there would ever come a time when she didn't carry latex gloves and evidence bags in her pockets.

She walked back down to the parking lot and saw that there was now another vehicle there, a vintage VW van painted light blue with white trim. Windows all around, and surf racks on the roof. It had to be Van's van, and she wondered if Van was really his name or a nickname he'd picked up because of the VW. Either way, she liked him better for what he drove and its connection to the surf culture of the past.

She got back in the Defender and took the Pacific Coast Highway to the 10 freeway, which would take her through downtown and out to Cal State L.A., where the department's forensics lab was located.

On the way she stopped at the beach at Topanga and looked around, but there were no surfers and not much action on the break. She looked for the fruit vendor mentioned in the Dawson police report but he was nowhere in sight, and Ballard wasn't going to wait to see if he showed. The Red Bull can in the evidence bag on the seat next to her was front of mind and she wanted to get it to the lab without further delay.

The PCH curved east through the tunnel in Santa Monica and transitioned to the 10 freeway. Twenty minutes later she was through downtown and taking the exit for the lab complex the LAPD shared with the sheriff's department. The latent-prints unit was on the first floor, and as it did in the DNA lab three floors above, the Open-Unsolved Unit had a go-to tech there assigned to handle its print requests. But criminalist Federico Beltran was not as accommodating as Darcy Troy. Ballard was hoping that by coming in person to deliver a piece of evidence for examination, she could avoid delay.

After parking, she pulled her phone and called Paul Masser. She didn't want to run into him in the building and have to explain what the Red Bull can was all about. When he answered, she could tell he was in a moving car.

"Hey, did you get to the lab yet?" she asked.

"Just left. Darcy said she'd put the samples through today."

"Samples?"

"I gave her both. As you said last night, it would be good to identify the woman and get her genetic signature."

Ballard nodded, though she knew he couldn't see her. "Okay, but will it slow Darcy down, having two samples to send to DOJ?"

"I don't see how it could, but if you want me to call her back and say hold off on the lipstick, I will."

"No, never mind. I'm overthinking it."

"She said she'd be quick."

"Good. Where are you headed now?"

"Norwalk to pull Nicholas Purcell's birth certificate — if he was born here in the county. After that, back to the barn."

"Okay, I'll see you there later. I've got an errand to run this morning. Tell Colleen not to panic if I'm late."

"I'm sure she will anyway."

Ballard disconnected and realized she had a problem: She needed her ID to get inside the building. She had been to the lab so many times during her career that she knew every one of the security officers who manned the front entrance. More than once, she had been waved through without showing her ID, but she always had it with her. It would be just her luck if a new guard was on post today and asked her for it.

She thought about possible solutions for a few moments and then got out and opened the back door of the Defender. She had a plastic carton there that contained her crime scene equipment — overalls, booties, rubber boots, gloves, hats, crime scene markers, extra notebooks, and a camera. She hadn't needed most of it during her time in the Open-Unsolved Unit because the crime scenes in those cases were long gone. But she needed it now. She put the bag containing the Red Bull can on top of the carton, kicked the door of the Defender closed, and carried the whole thing to the building.

As she went through the automatic doors, Ballard exaggerated the weight of the carton and tried to hurry by the check-in desk, where a security guard sat. She recognized him, but he was fairly new and might not recognize her. She quickly read his nameplate — Eastwood — as she moved by, and it prompted her to remember his obvious nickname.

"Hey, Clint," she said. "Ballard, Open-Unsolved, going to see Rico in Latents. Can you put me down?"

"Sure thing," Eastwood said. "Badge number?"

"Seven-six-five-eight."

"All you need is a nine."

"What?"

"To make a straight."

Ballard threw out a fake laugh. "Oh, yeah, right. Can you hit the door?"

"Sure can. You need help with that? Looks heavy."

"No, I got it. Thanks."

Eastwood buzzed the automatic door and it opened. Ballard was in. She walked down the hall to the latent-prints section and put the crime scene carton down next to the door. She went in with the evidence bag containing the can.

Federico Beltran was already in his cubicle looking at side-by-side fingerprints on a large computer screen. Ballard knew this was the last step in making a print match. The computer pulled matches from all databases the department subscribed to around the country, and it was the tech's job to eyeball the matches for accuracy and make the call.

"Rico, my favorite print man," Ballard said. "How are you this fine morning?"

Beltran looked up at her; she was leaning on the half wall to the right of his screen. "Ballard," he said. "I'm busy this fine morning."

"Well, I'm going to have to add to your plate," Ballard said. She raised her hand from behind the wall so he could see the evidence bag containing the can. Beltran groaned like Ballard had known he would.

"Come on, now," she said. "Cheer up. I'm only laying one item on you. It could be a lot worse."

"Leave it on the desk and I'll get to it," Beltran said.

"Actually, I need this on a priority, Federico. I'm going to wait on this one."

"You can't. I'm in the middle of a case here."

"And I can see you're at the end of it, so finish that and run with mine. You're our guy and the key to solving this case. You could be a hero, and we won't forget to mention you in the press release."

"Right. We never get the kudos. You people hog all the glory."

"But not this time. I just need you to vape this can and see what you get. Two hours tops, and if there's any kudos to hand out, your name's first on the list."

"Yeah, I've heard that before and I think it was from you."

But Beltran turned away from his screen and took the bag from Ballard. She knew she had him.

"What's the case number?" he asked. "I'll have to see if a vaper is free."

The vaper was the glass case where small objects were exposed to vaporized cyanoacrylate, which crystallized on the ridges of fingerprints, raising them and turning them white. They could then be collected by tape or photographed and compared to other prints in the databases.

But whether or not the vaper was free was not Ballard's immediate problem. All work submitted to the latent-prints section for processing and comparison had to be filed under a case number. The problem was that Ballard had no case number because there was no official investigation into the theft of her badge, gun, and other property. Ballard had to be careful about which legitimate case number to give. If she gave Beltran a case that was solved someday, her request for a print run would become part of discovery during a prosecution and could hand a defense attorney all that was needed to question the integrity of the case.

This was why Ballard was prepared with a murder case that would never be solved. She gave Beltran the number, 88-0394, and the name, Jeffrey Haskell. Beltran wrote the information down and realized the case was more than three decades old.

"Eighty-eight?" he said. "How can this be a priority?"

"I'll tell you how," Ballard said. "Because that Red Bull can was touched by a suspect we watched yesterday, and I need to know his identity and see if he connects to any other cases."

The truth was that the 1988 case had been reviewed by members of the Open-Unsolved Unit earlier in the year and Ballard had signed off on their assessment that it was not solvable using any contemporary forensic tools. There was no DNA. There were no ballistics. There were no fingerprints. There weren't any witnesses, and there was no murder weapon. The case was the murder of a twenty-two-year-old Malibu kid named Jeffrey Haskell who had driven into a crime-ridden area of South Central to buy drugs in a housing project. Instead of scoring, he was robbed, stabbed with an unknown instrument, and left to bleed out in the car he had borrowed from his mother after telling her he was going to a bookstore. Thirty-plus years later, there were no leads to follow and no suspects. It was a cold case that was destined to forever be on a shelf in the murder archives.

Not every case could be solved. Ballard knew this but also knew the value of a case number and name that could be used to get lab work done on items that were not part of an active investigation. She had committed Jeffrey Haskell's name and his case number to memory. She knew she would never be able to get justice for Haskell, but in a way only she knew about, he might help solve another crime.

"Okay," Beltran said. "I have your cell. I'll call you if I get anything."

"No, I'm staying," Ballard said. "That way I know you won't back-burner it the minute I walk out the door."

"I'm not going to do that."

"So you say."

"Okay, fine. Stay as long as you like. I'm going to go fume it."

He stood up, took the evidence bag, and headed to the lab doors at the back of the room. Ballard knew she couldn't follow him. There were strict protocols in place to ensure that evidence in the lab was not contaminated or tainted by nonessential personnel.

"Okay, so you'll let me know when you have something?" she called after him. She hated how her tone verged on pleading.

"I said I would," Beltran said without breaking stride or turning back to her.

Ballard watched him go through the doors and then checked the time on her phone. It was only 8:20, and if she left now, she could be to the Ahmanson Center before anyone — other than Colleen Hatteras — realized she was late.

10

HATTERAS LET BALLARD into the unit through the emergency door, and Ballard went right to the phone at her desk at the end of the raft. Beltran had not answered a call from her on the drive out to the west side and Ballard believed it was because he knew her cell number and chose to ignore her when he saw it on the caller ID screen.

She dialed his direct line now and tried to slow her breathing. She was frustrated with Beltran but knew this was not the time to confront him. This was an off-the-books investigation that she did not want to draw any attention to. As she'd expected, Beltran picked up on the first ring. Ballard swallowed her frustration and went with her routine-casework voice.

"Rico, it's Ballard. Just checking to see if you've got something for me."

"Yeah, what I got, Ballard, is a complete waste of my time."

"Yeah? How so?"

"There's no way this is your guy from that '88 case. He wasn't even born in '88."

Ballard realized that she'd told Beltran that the Red Bull can had been handled by a suspect in the case. That was a misstep. She tried to cover the discrepancy with a quick comeback question. "Well, then, who is he?" she asked.

"The prints on that can came back to a Dean Delsey, age twenty-fucking-two. You can't pull me off the important shit on my plate to run down these long shots that are a complete waste of time."

Ballard did a slow burn in silence.

"Ballard, you there?"

"Yeah, I'm here. Give me his DOB and anything else you came up with."

Beltran grudgingly gave her Delsey's birth date and added that he had a record of arrests for minor crimes and assaults. No prison time but he was currently on probation for an auto-theft conviction.

"Thank you," Ballard said with zero sincerity. "What I'll do is talk to Doreen and ask her to put Open-Unsolved cases with a different print tech from now on."

Even though this was an off-the-books investigation, Ballard felt she had to draw a line with Beltran because his attitude could hinder her unit's legitimate investigations. Doreen was Doreen Hudson, the longtime director of the LAPD crime lab and a woman who had undoubtedly put up with her share of obstructive male tactics in her rise from an entry-level criminalist nearly four decades before. By referring to her by her first name, Ballard was signaling that she knew Hudson well and that the sisterhood was not to be fucked with. The truth was that she didn't know Hudson well enough to call her directly and complain about Beltran or ask for a new tech to be assigned. She was counting on Beltran's not knowing that.

"Oh, well, you don't have to do that," Beltran said quickly. "We can —"

"It's not a problem," Ballard said sweetly, cutting him off. "If you think what we're doing out here is a complete waste of time, then that's not a great fit and I'll take care of it. Have a good one!"

Before Beltran could respond, Ballard pushed the button to disconnect the call.

"Whoa, who was that?" Hatteras said.

Ballard glanced up to see Hatteras looking over the partition, as usual.

"Never mind, Colleen," Ballard said. "Just some jerk. Is Paul back yet?"

"Here," Masser said.

Ballard turned in her chair and saw him walking in. He held up a document and came right to Ballard's station.

"Got a copy of the birth certificate," he said.

He put the document on her desk and pointed to the date of birth for Nicholas Purcell and then to a second date in a box marked RECORDED. The birth certificate had been recorded two days after his birth at St. Joseph's Medical Center in Burbank.

"What's it mean?" Hatteras asked.

"It means Nicholas Purcell was not adopted," Masser said. "To adopt, a judge issues a decree, and a new birth certificate is created. The giveaway is that it's usually weeks between the date of birth and the date of recording at the county registrar. Two days between dates means no adoption. Nicholas is the son of Jonathan and Vivian Purcell."

"So that means . . . the judge is definitely our guy?" Hatteras said.

Masser nodded. "Looks like it," he said.

"But we stick with protocol," Ballard said. "We wait for the DNA confirmation."

"And we should have that by Friday," Masser said.

"Then we make our move," Ballard said.

They fell into a solemn silence for a long moment, the gravity of knowing they were going after a superior court judge weighing on them. Masser finally broke the silence, but only to add more weight to their thoughts.

"The repercussions will be massive," he said. "Any case he ruled on will be vulnerable to appeal. I guess it's lucky he's always been on the civil side. But still, the appeals that come out of this will clog things up for years."

"That's not our concern," Ballard said. "If he's the guy, he's the guy, and we take him down."

"Absolutely," Masser said.

Hatteras cleared her throat to draw Ballard's attention.

"What is it, Colleen?"

"Well, one thing you should know is that I've been building a heritage pattern using—"

"You mean a family tree?"

"Yes, the genetic tree, starting with the DNA sequence we got from Darcy."

"Nicholas's DNA."

"Right. And what's strange is that I'm not connecting anything to the judge so far."

"What are you saying? We might be barking up the wrong family tree?"

"Funny, but yes, something doesn't fit. I feel like I should be making connections, and so far they're not there."

"Well, keep at it, Colleen. It will probably be Friday before we know anything for sure about the DNA."

"Okay, boss."

"And don't call me that."

"Okay, Renée."

"Better."

Hatteras dropped down behind the partition to go back to work, and Masser went to his module as well. Ballard looked at the info she had written down during the call with Beltran.

She opened up the DMV link and typed in Dean Delsey's name and DOB. She knew she was creating a DMV search record that could be found should her off-the-books investigation blow up in her face. Unlike the crime report searches she'd conducted during the night, the department assiduously monitored DMV searches because of past abuses involving officers taking cash to conduct such searches for private investigators and lawyers. But Delsey was Ballard's only lead at the moment and she was willing to risk it. She felt confident that should she be questioned, she'd be able to come up with an adequate cover story.

The address Delsey had on his driver's license was on Park Court right off Speedway in Venice. That fit the profile she was building in her mind for the people who had ripped her off. Delsey was a small-time criminal living close to the beach and the surfing culture he was preying on. The photo on his driver's license supported this as well. He was white, with the sun-bleached hair and ruddy complexion of a surfer.

The fact that Delsey's fingerprints were on a can that was found in a small clearing on a bluff overlooking a prime surfing beach was evidence of nothing. But Ballard instinctively believed she was closing in on her target.

She thought of something and picked up the desk phone, then thought better of it and used her cell. This would be a test. She called Beltran's direct line, and this time he picked up the call from her cell immediately.

"Hey, Detective, I think we got cut off before."

"No, actually, I hung up."

"Oh. Did you already talk to the director?"

"No, not yet. I'll do it later. But I forgot to ask before—did you figure out what was in the Red Bull can?"

"Yes, I was just writing up the report for you. There were two cigarette butts and the tip of a cannabis joint. I preserved it all. You need me to pack it all up and send it over to genetics?"

"No, just hold everything there and I'll be by at some point to grab it."

"I'll have it here when you need it."

"Thanks, Rico."

She disconnected. She wasn't sure whether she preferred the old resentful Rico or the new obsequious Rico, but confirming that there was a joint in the Red Bull can was helpful intel for when she confronted Delsey.

"Paul?" she called without looking over the wall.

Masser appeared above the partition. "Yes?"

"Thanks for everything this morning. Can you mind the store for a while? I'm going to run an errand."

"Not a problem. I want to do more legal vetting on Judge Purcell."

"Meaning what?"

"You know, look at the trials he's handled, how he's ruled. I mean, I'm fascinated. What a double life — assuming he's our guy. You know he was appointed to the bench the same year Pillowcase went inactive on the rapes?"

"Yeah, I saw that."

"Anyway, I want to know everything there is to know about him."

"Good. When you're ready, we'll do an all-hands meeting to talk about what you got."

"Good by me."

Ballard stood up. "Okay, I'll be back."

She was about to step away when the desk phone buzzed. She reached down and answered it. "Open-Unsolved."

"Landry at the front desk. You've got a visitor. An Officer Bosch."

Ballard froze for a moment.

"A female Bosch?" she asked.

"Female," Landry confirmed. "Madeline Bosch. Should I send her back?"

"Uh, no, I'll come out."

"I'll tell her."

Ballard disconnected and for a moment just stared at the phone.

"What is it?" Hatteras said. She'd stood up again. "You look like you've seen a ghost."

Ballard shook her head. "No, I'm fine," Ballard said.

She walked away toward the entrance to the unit, trepidation building with every step. Once she exited, she walked down the long central hallway of the complex to the front, where there was a reception desk and a row of chairs. The Ahmanson Center was the LAPD's main training center, and most days many of those chairs were occupied by applicants who wanted to wear the badge.

Maddie Bosch was there in street clothes. There appeared to be no stress or sadness on her face.

"Maddie, is Harry all right?" Ballard asked.

Maddie stood up. "Uh, yeah, as far as I know," she said. "I haven't talked to him in a couple of days. Did you hear something?"

"No," Ballard said. "I just thought that if you came to see me in person, there might be something—"

"No. Sorry if I scared you—that's not why I'm here. As far as I know, Dad's fine. He's Harry."

"Okay, good."

Harry Bosch had been a mentor of sorts to Ballard and had worked with the Open-Unsolved Unit at its start. He was now battling cancer and Ballard had not gotten an update recently.

"I'm here because I want to volunteer," Maddie said.

Ballard was not expecting that. "What, you mean for the unit?" she asked.

"Yes, the unit," Maddie said. "I'm on a four-on-three-off schedule at Hollywood Division, and they have me working PM watch Friday to Monday. It gives me a lot of free time during the week and I thought this might be good, you know? I want to be a detective one day and this can give me some experience."

"Did you talk to Harry about it?"

"No. Harry's retired and I make my own decisions."

"Right. Sorry. I didn't mean to—"

"It's okay. I just don't need his permission. I'd like to volunteer. Can we talk about it? Do you have time?"

"Yes, of course. Let's go to the cafeteria so we can sit down and talk a little more privately. There's not a lot of privacy in the bullpen here."

They walked down the main hall and turned right to a smaller hallway that led to the cafeteria. Ballard got a coffee and Maddie a hot tea. The place was largely deserted because it was between the breakfast and lunch rushes. There was a sea of empty tables and they took one that would afford the most privacy for their conversation.

"I haven't been back here since I was in the academy," Maddie said.

"I trained in the old place in Chavez Ravine," Ballard said.

"I almost never go there."

"So, I take it you know what we do here."

"Well, you work cold cases. Murders mostly. From what I understand, you have all the murder books right here. You review them to see if modern forensic technology can be used to identify suspects and bring closure to families that lost people."

"We close cases but I'm not sure we ever bring closure to the families. We give answers, but answers don't end the grief people carry."

"Harry always said the same thing."

"Then you know. A lot of the people who want to volunteer for the unit come with a specific case in mind. Like a friend or a family member, someone from the neighborhood where they grew up. Is there a case like that with you?"

"Not really, no."

"Okay, well, I know I could talk to Harry about a recommendation and —"

"I'd rather you didn't. I'd really like to do this on my own."

"I understand that, but Harry's my friend and I think it would be odd if I didn't at least tell him we're going to work together."

"Can you do that after you decide? I brought a sheet with me." She took a printed sheet of paper from her pocket and unfolded it.

"This has the names and numbers of my supervisors," she said. "Has my TO on there, though I'm no longer a boot. But she could tell you what a quick learner I am and how I react under pressure."

Ballard took the paper and looked at it. She didn't recognize any of the names, even though, until just a few years ago, she had been assigned to Hollywood Division as the midnight-shift detective.

"Man, it looks like a complete turnover of command staff since I was there," she said.

"Yeah, just about everybody is new," Maddie said.

Ballard nodded and continued to stare at the paper.

"So, what do you think?" Maddie prompted.

Ballard looked up at her. "Well, a couple of things I want you to know first," she said. "I expect members of the unit to put in one day a week. I prefer two but I'll take one. They don't have to be eight-hour shifts, but I want to see you in here at least once a week. Will that be a problem?"

"No, not at all," Maddie said. "Like I said, I have a lot of free time. The only thing that might be a scheduling conflict is if I have court. But that doesn't happen a lot. What else?"

"If you're running with a case, you stick with it or hand it off. And if you're not running down a case, I want you pulling cases and reviewing them to see if there's a shot at getting something done. We have a whole protocol for determining that. But there are six thousand unsolved cases going back to 1960. Right now the sweet spot is the eighties and early nineties. The cases are recent enough that there might be a live suspect out there, and those cases were originally worked before DNA was part of the landscape."

"Okay."

"Do you have any questions?"

"Um, the cases here, they go back only to 1960?"

"No, we've got cases from way earlier than that, but our cutoff point is currently 1975. With anything before that, it's unlikely that anyone involved would be alive — suspects or immediate family."

"Oh, right. I get it."

"Yeah. So, anything else I can answer?"

"Not really...except when will you decide if you'll take me on?"

"Well, I have to do a couple of things first. I have to talk to my captain and see if he'll approve taking on someone who's already full-time in the department. That hasn't happened before. But I'll tell you, and I'll tell him: It would be really good to have someone else in the unit with a badge. It would take a lot of stuff off my shoulders. A lot of things come up that only a badge can do, like make arrests and testify in court. And I'm the only one. It would be nice to have you in the unit. Real nice, in fact."

"Well, good. I hope you can convince the captain."

"Me too."

Ballard held out the paper she had been given. "Do these people know that I might call them?" she asked.

"Not really," Maddie said. "Should I tell them?"

"Uh, no, it will be better if I call them cold. Do you want to see the unit and where you'll be if this works out? A couple of the other volunteers are here today."

"Sure."

"Okay, let's go."

11

BALLARD PARKED ON Speedway in front of a garage door at the rear of a walled residence. Three signs on the shabby gray door warned of the consequences of blocking it. But Ballard wasn't planning on leaving her vehicle. The spot gave her a prime view of Dean Delsey's second-floor apartment in a run-down complex that had been built seventy-five years ago and designed to look like a boat. The windows in the complex were round like portholes, and the exterior front corner of the retaining wall surrounding the property had anchors attached to it as if it were the prow of a ship. Before settling in to watch, Ballard had done a walk around the apartment complex and had determined that Delsey's DL address corresponded with the apartment at the east end of the second floor.

The apartment had a balcony that overlooked Speedway. Stacked against its side wall were three or four surfboards. Ballard could see that the sliding door to the apartment was open, and faint, unidentifiable music was floating through.

Someone was home.

Ballard settled in for what she knew could be an hours-long surveillance. She wasn't sure what her next move would be but she hoped at a minimum to get a look at Delsey before she called it a day.

She thought of something she should have done before leaving the office and decided to risk drawing Hatteras into her off-the-books actions. She called her on her cell.

"Renée, you all right?"

"I'm fine. But I need you to do something for me."

"Sure."

"All right, go over to my terminal. I should still be signed in."

"You got it."

Ballard waited until Colleen said she was in place and that Ballard was still signed in to the department network. Ballard then walked her through accessing the DMV database and putting Delsey's address into the search engine to see if the same address happened to be on anyone else's driver's license.

"Two names come up," Hatteras said.

"One is Dean Delsey," Ballard said. "Give me the other one."

"Robert Delsey. Must be his brother. Or, wait, no, this may be his father. He's older."

"What's his DOB?"

Hatteras gave a birth date in 1981, making Robert twice Dean's age. It also doubled Ballard's interest in the pair. Another father-and-son case, the second in two days. Ballard did not put much stock in so-called coincidences — Harry Bosch had taught her that — but she thought this one must be a genuine one.

She directed Hatteras to open a search on the department's criminal records index. Hatteras reported that Robert Delsey had a criminal history much longer than Dean's. It included a nine-year stretch in prison for assault with a deadly weapon. Nine years meant it was no bar fight or skirmish over surf territory. It told Ballard that he had probably come close to killing someone, and that meant he was a dangerous man.

She asked Hatteras to use her cell phone to take a photo of Robert Delsey off the computer screen and text it to her.

"What are you up to?" Hatteras asked.

"Just an old case I worked before I came to the unit," Ballard said, ready with her answer. "Nothing you have to worry about. Send me that photo, and thank you, Colleen." Ballard disconnected before another question could come.

The photo arrived on her text app and Ballard studied Robert Delsey. The genetic connection to Dean Delsey was evident. They were most likely father and son. Robert's face and skin were worn by more years in the sun and salt. Ballard thought of her own father and the deeply tanned wrinkles etched into the corners of his black-brown eyes — he had eyes like his favorite actor, Charles Bronson.

Ballard sat for twenty minutes with a decision she had to make before finally picking up the phone and calling a name on her favorites list. Harry Bosch answered with his usual greeting.

"Everything okay?"

"Everything's fine. How about you?"

"No complaints."

"Staying busy?"

"Not too much. Been bingeing *The Lincoln Lawyer,* if you can believe it."

"You still working with the real Lincoln Lawyer?"

"Here and there — when he needs me."

"And how is your health, Harry?"

"I'm hanging in. My last scans were clean."

"That's good to hear."

"So what's up with you?"

"Just checking in. Hadn't heard from you, and there's something I need to talk to you about."

"Sure."

"It's about Maddie and it's a bit awkward."

"What's going on?"

"Well, Maddie came in and volunteered for the squad."

"Open-Unsolved?"

"Yeah, my squad."

"Okay. What's the awkward part?"

"Well, she didn't want me to tell you because she's, you know, asserting her independence and she's probably not sure how you'd take it. But it puts me in an awkward spot because it's not something I would keep from you. I don't want to get in the middle of you two. I'm sure she'll tell you. If she's approved by the captain, I mean."

"Did she say why she wants to do this?"

"Well, I think it's kind of obvious. She wants to be like you, Harry. She wants to be a detective, and this won't hurt her cause. It could even fast-track it."

Bosch went silent and Ballard imagined him sitting in his house up on the hill, thinking about his daughter.

"You still there, Harry?"

"I'm here. What do you think about this? Do you want her on the unit? She's young. She doesn't know what she doesn't know."

"There's that, but, selfishly, I want her. I've been telling the captain for months that I need another badge on the squad. I have to do too much of the legal stuff. The Mirandas, the testifying, the search warrants. It takes too much of my time. So, yeah, I'd take her. But I'll kill it right here if you want me to, Harry."

Bosch hesitated, but only for a moment.

"No, it's not my choice. It's hers. She's got to follow her star. Isn't that what the kids say?"

"As long as you're sure."

"I'm sure. Just watch over her, Renée. Keep her safe. And I'm not talking about from bullets. From all the other stuff. From going into the darkness. It's there in those cold cases you work."

"I know and I will, Harry."

"Thank you."

There was an awkward pause.

MICHAEL CONNELLY

"So, you're sure you're doing okay?" Ballard asked.

"A hundred percent," Bosch replied.

"Okay, then let's get a dinner or a lunch soon."

"You got it."

Ballard disconnected. She knew that Bosch in his own way had tried to keep his daughter safe from the darkness that had gotten inside him at times. But it was a never-ending battle. She thought about what Dr. Elingburg had said about vicarious trauma. Sometimes it wasn't vicarious. Sometimes it was right in your face.

As soon as she dropped her phone into a cupholder, it buzzed. She thought it might be Bosch calling back about something but the screen showed that it was her boss at RHD, Captain Gandle. For a few seconds she considered not answering, but she knew that whatever he wanted, she'd inevitably have to deal with it. She took the call.

"Captain."

"Ballard, what the fuck? You followed the presiding judge of the superior court to get a DNA sample?"

"Who told you that?"

"Doesn't matter who told me. You didn't think to ask my permission to do this?"

"Captain, I have a mandate from you to follow cases where they lead. Do you remember telling me that?"

"Yeah, but not to put the presiding judge under surveillance without at least notifying your CO about what you were doing. Do you have any idea what kind of shit will come down on us if this goes sideways?"

"He's a primary suspect in a murder and several rapes. It's not going to go sideways. If the DNA matches, we're going to take him down, and I don't care who he is."

"Ballard..." Gandle went silent.

Ballard needed to know how he'd gotten his information. If she had a leak in the unit, she had to shut it down.

"Look," she said, "I don't know what you were told but we got a familial hit on the Pillowcase Rapist. I'm sure you remember the case—a serial rapist that ended up murdering a woman. Two months ago a man was arrested on a domestic-violence call. He was swabbed, and the genetics eventually went into CODIS and pointed to his father as the Pillowcase Rapist. We have the son's birth certificate, and the judge is his father. No adoption. So what were we supposed to do? Not follow through? No fucking way."

"No, you were supposed to call me and say, 'Captain, we have a delicate situation here.' We—you and I—would have then decided what to do from there."

"There was no deciding what to do. He's a suspect, and just because he's a judge doesn't mean he wasn't a rapist and murderer twenty years ago or isn't one now. We did exactly what we should have done—we got his DNA and we'll know by Friday if he's confirmed as the guy. What I want to know now is who told you about this."

"Why do you care?"

"Because I need to know who to trust in my unit with need-to-know information. If this gets out of the department and to the judge before Friday, we're going to have a problem."

"It was Kelly Latham, okay?"

The head of the DNA lab and Darcy Troy's boss. Ballard immediately knew that Paul Masser had given Troy too much information when he dropped the DNA samples at the lab. It made Ballard breathe a little easier. She doubted that Masser realized the background detail he had given Troy would end up with her boss and then make the jump to the captain overseeing the Open-Unsolved Unit.

"You really fucked me, Renée," Gandle said. "I have this information that I wish I didn't have. Because I should turn around and inform the tenth floor about this right now."

The tenth floor of the PAB was where the offices of the chief of police and most of the department's command staff were located. One of the things Ballard liked most about her job was that, at the Ahmanson Center, she was away from all that. She had only one commander to worry about there, and he was more concerned with back-door alarms than anything else.

"Do what you need to do, Captain," she said. "But if I were you, I would wait until we hear from the DOJ, because when we get the match, we're going to have to come up with an arrest plan and that's when you can bring the tenth floor into it."

Gandle hesitated. "By Friday, you think?" he asked.

"Our lab liaison put a rush on it," Ballard said, deciding not to mention Darcy Troy's name.

"Okay, but I want to be informed of every move you make between now and then."

"Well, that's easy. We're not making any moves until we get the results back. My IGG person is building a genetic tree, but that's internet work. We're not out there knocking on any doors."

"That's Hatteras? Tell her to stop the IGG. Do nothing more until the results are in. Understood?"

"Yes, understood."

"What are you doing right now?"

"I'm sitting in my car making calls about a prospective volunteer. I'll let you know if she pans out and I want to bring her on."

"A she—that's good. Just make sure she can kick a door open."

"I already know that she can, Captain."

"Good. Let me know."

He disconnected and Ballard sat there staring through the windshield, reviewing the call and hoping she had headed off a problem with the captain. It was a long moment before she realized that there was a man standing on the balcony of the Delsey apartment.

She grabbed the binoculars from the center console and focused on him.

It was Dean. He was wearing a blue-and-white Hawaiian shirt. He looked older than his license photo, and his hair was shorter now, but he was definitely in his twenties, not his forties. He was holding a bottle of beer and smoking a joint, blowing the smoke out across Speedway. Ballard watched, waiting to see if he was joined on the balcony by his father or someone else from the apartment. But no one came out.

Dean Delsey finished smoking and flicked what was left of the joint down onto Speedway. He then disappeared back inside.

Ballard did some quick detective math. It appeared that Dean Delsey was alone in the apartment. If the father and son were responsible for the string of thefts, it stood to reason that between the two, the son would be the one she had the better chance of breaking. He had an arrest record but had repeatedly been given second chances by the system. The father had done hard time. Dean was on probation; Robert was on parole. Dean was the weak link.

Ballard reached under her seat and grabbed her handcuffs, then lowered the front visor and got out of the car.

12

BALLARD STEALTHILY APPROACHED the door to apartment 211, then leaned her right ear toward the jamb. She heard music playing inside but again couldn't identify it.

She took a step back and checked for a peephole or a Ring camera. There was none. She used the side of her fist to pound loudly on the door.

"Parole, open up!"

She leaned forward again but heard no movement inside — no toilet flushing, no footsteps of someone rushing around trying to hide contraband. She pounded on the door again, this time harder.

"Department of Parole. Open the door or we'll kick it in."

Now she heard the music cut off and footsteps approaching. She unholstered her weapon and held it down at her side.

The door opened and the man from the balcony stood there.

"He's not here," he said.

"Step back," Ballard said.

Dean Delsey saw the gun at her side and raised his hands as he stepped back.

"Whoa, no need for that," he said. "Bobby's not here."

"Are you Dean Delsey?" Ballard asked.

"That's me but—"

"Against the wall. Now."

"Okay, okay."

Delsey turned, spread his hands at shoulder height, and put them on the wall, a move he had clearly made in the past. Ballard used a foot to kick his legs farther apart. She holstered her gun, then placed one hand on his back to keep him in position while using the other to pat him down for weapons.

"Where's your father?"

"I don't know. He went out, didn't tell me where."

"When's he coming back?"

"He didn't say."

"Give me your right hand behind your back."

"Look, you don't need—"

"Right hand behind your back. Now."

He complied. She took the handcuffs out of the waistband at the back of her pants and snapped one around his wrist.

"Now the left."

Delsey complied again, but not without complaint. "I'm just saying, if you're here for him, you don't have to hook me up," he said.

"Who said I'm here for him?" Ballard said. "Move."

She pulled him away from the wall and walked him to the center of the apartment's living room. There was a threadbare couch, a beat-up La-Z-Boy chair with its faux leather cracked and split on the armrests, and a flat-screen TV tuned to a muted music channel.

"On your knees," Ballard said.

"Aw, come on," Delsey said.

"Knees."

"Fuck it."

Delsey dropped to his knees on the uncarpeted terrazzo floor. Ballard grabbed the chain between the cuffs with one hand and the back collar of his Hawaiian shirt with the other.

"Okay, I'm going to lower you onto your belly now. This is for my safety and yours."

"Yeah, bullshit."

Ballard pushed him forward and he went down easily.

"Okay, what is this?" Delsey protested. "Are you here for me or him?"

"For you, Dino," Ballard said. "And I could violate you right now and put you in the pen. I watched you drinking and toking on the balcony ten minutes ago."

"I got news for you: I'm over twenty-one, and recreational use of marijuana is legal."

"And I got news for you: Read the terms of your probation. No alcohol and no drugs, even legal ones, without permission of the court. You want to show me your court permission to get high?"

She waited. Delsey was silent.

"I didn't think so. You are fucked, my friend. I own you."

"Fuck this. I want to see some ID right the fuck now."

"That's funny. I want to see some ID too. My ID. But you took it."

Delsey strained to look up at Ballard standing over him. She saw that he recognized her from the LAPD ID card stolen from her car.

"Yeah, it didn't take me long," Ballard said. "I found your ass."

"I don't know what you're talking about," Delsey said.

"Sure you do. But you know what? This is your lucky day, Dino. If you make it right, you can stay out of jail. Otherwise, we wait here for dear old Dad to come home and see if he wants to make a deal instead. He still has five years on his parole tail. You have eighteen months on your suspended sentence. I'm guessing he'll throw you under the bus to avoid going back to Soledad for the full nickel."

Delsey was silent. Ballard waited.

"What do you want?" he finally said.

Ballard moved over, sat on the couch, and leaned down toward him. His face was on the terrazzo, turned to the side.

"I want my shit back," she said. "All of it."

"Impossible," Delsey said.

"Why is that?"

"Because we don't keep it, okay? I mean, I've still got the wallet and ID card but everything else is long gone, so you're out of luck, Officer."

"If that's the case, then you're the one who's out of luck. You've got one shot here, Dino. Tell me where it went and I cut you loose. Nobody needs to know, not even your father."

Delsey thought about it. After a moment Ballard prodded him.

"The clock is ticking," she said. "All bets are off the minute Daddy comes through that door. What's it going to be, Dino?"

"I hate that," Delsey said. "Would you stop fucking calling me that?"

"Fine. What's it going to be, *Dean*? I take off the cuffs or I take you to jail? I'm running out of goodwill here."

"Fuck."

"Yeah, I get it. Life's a bitch. But it is what it is, Dean. So decide."

"All right. We take everything to a guy down the beach. He gives us cash. That's it."

"What guy?"

"His name's Lionel but he calls himself the Lion. I don't know his last name. He's connected to some serious people. My dad knew his dad up at Soledad."

"Where is he exactly?"

"The Eldorado. He lives in one room and does business in another across the hall."

Ballard knew of the Eldorado. It was a dump hotel about ten blocks up Speedway. "How do you reach out to him?" she asked.

"My dad texts him when we have stuff," Delsey said. "That's it."

"You brought him stuff yesterday after ripping me off at Staircases?"

"Bobby did, yeah."

"What kind of security does the Lion have?"

"I think there's a guy there. But I don't know for sure. My dad always goes."

"What's his number?"

"I don't know. I've never texted him."

"Then I guess we're going to have to wait here for Bobby to show up. But then he'll know that you snitched. Is that going to be a problem?"

"Look, I don't know the number because it changes all the time. But I know where yesterday's number is."

"Where?"

"In Bo — uh, my father's room. There's a night table next to the bed. He's got a pad in the drawer there and he scratches off the old number and writes the new one down every time."

"And you said you still had my wallet with my ID card. Where is it?"

"My room. There's a table in the same spot."

Most criminals were not smart. Ballard knew that it was usually a criminal's stupidity rather than a detective's great work that led to solving cases. Delsey and son were not shining examples of the criminal mind.

Ballard looked around and saw a bottle of Corona on a pass-through counter to the kitchen. She grabbed it and took it back to the living room. She carefully placed it on Delsey's back between his shoulder blades.

"You move, I'll know it," she said. "You won't want that."

She walked into a short hall that led to two bedrooms with a bathroom between them. In the first bedroom, she found her wallet with her ID card in the top drawer of the bedside table. She was surprised by how relieved she felt at recovering it. The badge was the main thing and that was still out there somewhere, but the ID card got her through security at all city facilities. She could go back to using the front entrance at the Ahmanson Center. All the credit cards that had been in the wallet were gone, but her driver's license was still behind the plastic window. She got another mood lift from that.

Ballard checked the living room to make sure Delsey had not moved, then went into the other bedroom, opened the bedside table drawer, and found the scratch pad. Bobby Delsey had written down seven phone numbers; six of them were crossed out. As Ballard typed the seventh number into her phone, she wondered how long the Delsey duo had been ripping off surfers and fencing the goods through the Lion. She tore the page off the pad and stuffed it in her pocket, hoping it would cut off communication between the Lion and the Delsey duo.

When she put the pad back in the drawer, she noticed a watch with a metal band; it had been hidden behind the scratch pad. She lifted it out and studied the face. There was a brand mark: Breitling. She realized it was probably the watch stolen from Seth Dawson. The watch his father had given him. She turned it over and checked the back. There was an inscription: *To Seth from Dad 12-25-21.*

She pushed it over her hand and onto her wrist.

When she returned to the living room, she saw the beer bottle still in place between Delsey's shoulder blades.

"You and your father were using the Surf's Up app to pick your locations," she said.

"Is that a question?" Delsey asked.

"Not really. I'm just telling you I'm onto your game. Is there any code used when texting the Lion?"

"I don't know. My dad always did it."

"Don't move." She put one foot on either side of his body and used a key to remove the handcuffs.

"You should have reached farther under the seat," she said. "You would have gotten my cuffs."

"It wasn't me," Delsey said. "It was my dad. I was just lookout."

"What a team. My guess is you actually knew some of the surfers you ripped off."

Delsey said nothing. Perhaps he felt guilty, but Ballard doubted it.

"Don't tell your dad or anyone else about me. You warn the Lion and I'll fucking come back and find you. You won't want that."

"I'm not going to say anything."

"And I'll tell the Lion it was you who snitched him off. You and Bobby won't want that either."

"I told you, I'm not going to say anything."

"And you're not going to rip off any more surfers. I'll be reading the crime reports every day. One more rip-off at a surf beach and I'll put together a case on you myself."

"How do I tell my dad we have to stop without telling him about you?"

"Just say your probation officer came by and asked questions about the thefts. Convince your dad it's time to move on."

"Easy for you to say."

"I'm a little short on sympathy for you, Dino. In fact, I want to put you and your fucking father in jail and throw away the key. But you got lucky this time. It won't happen with me again."

Ballard went out the door. She was halfway down the stairs when she heard the glass beer bottle rattle and then roll across the apartment's terrazzo floor.

When she got back to Speedway and headed toward her car, she saw a tow truck parked in front of it; the hook was being lowered. A man with white hair pulled into a ponytail stood between the car and the garage door it was blocking. He wore sunglasses and had his arms folded across his chest as he watched the tow truck operator lower the hook. Ballard trotted over before her Defender got attached.

"Hey, hold on!" she yelled over the sound of the truck. "I'm moving it."

"You're too late!" the man with the folded arms yelled back. "It's clearly marked 'No Parking.' Why do people ignore the signs?"

Ballard walked into the channel between the garage and the car. The man unfolded his arms and held his hands up as if to stop her forward progress.

"I'm sorry," he said. "You ignored the warnings and you'll have to pay Venice Tow if you want it back."

Ballard held up her newly returned ID card. "I was on police business," she said. "Talk about signs—you didn't see the sign on the visor?"

"Uh, what sign?" the man asked.

"Go look."

"I will."

He went all the way around the Defender to get to the front and had to crane his neck to see the OFFICIAL LAPD BUSINESS sign attached to the visor. Ballard followed him and used the key fob to unlock the car.

"That's too small," the man said. "Nobody would notice that."

She opened the driver's-side door, and the man put his hand on her arm to stop her from getting in. Ballard reacted quickly, mostly out of instinct and partly out of the anger she felt at having to let the Delsey duo off the hook. She grabbed the man's wrist with her left hand, seized his elbow with her right, and spun him hard into the passenger door of the Defender.

"Do you want to go to jail for assaulting a police officer?"

"Assault? That was no assault. *You* assaulted *me*."

"You touched me. It was unwanted. That's assault."

"Look, you—"

"No, you look. Go back inside and set your parking trap for somebody else."

The man's mouth dropped open.

"That's right," Ballard said. "I know. You get a nice kickback from the tow yard."

She let him loose. The man turned and silently walked over to the tow truck operator, shaking his head.

Ballard got in the Defender and started it up.

13

BALLARD HAD A view of the entrance to the Eldorado from a spot at a red curb at Paloma and Speedway. There was a lot of pedestrian traffic in and out of the one-star hotel, mostly young people. Ballard guessed that there were other businesses besides the Lion's being run out of the Eldorado. If the Lion was paying cash for stolen goods, there was probably a place to spend that money nearby. The likely products for sale were drugs and sex.

She couldn't get a sense of the security arrangements from outside. She knew she would have to go in blind, and for the first time she started second-guessing her off-the-books maneuvering to get her badge and gun back. She thought maybe it might have been better to just report the thefts and take the heat.

Now it was too late.

She watched a skinny white teenage boy go into the hotel, carrying a laptop case. Ballard guessed it belonged to one of the kid's parents and he would trade it for pennies on the dollar to get a hit of fentanyl or crystal meth. The Eldorado was at the low end of nowhere.

She opened her phone's text app and composed a text to the Lion.

Lion, it's Bobby D. New phone. I'm sending my girlfriend to you. We hit it big 2day—iPhone 15 and GoPro Hero 12. Brand-new shit. Stupid german touristas. She's on her way. What room should she go to?

She waited to see if there would be a response. It came two minutes later.

If this is Bobby, what did you give me last time?

The Lion was no chump. Ballard just had to hope that the Delsey duo hadn't cashed in anything else after the theft at Staircases. She typed in what she knew.

Badge and Glock.

She waited again for the go-ahead and it came a minute later.

Room 11. Bring the iP, no on the gopro. Got too many.

Ballard took that to mean she had passed the test. She got out of the front seat of the car and into the back seat. She had a box there filled with clothing she used on surveillances and surreptitious DNA captures. Sometimes she had to change clothes while on a tail to avoid being made by the target.

The back windows of the Defender were darkly tinted and she changed without worrying about being seen by passersby. She put on ripped jeans and a peasant shirt with Mexican embroidery around the neckline. She pulled on a pair of Old Gringo boots that were wide in the calf and made her look slightly bowlegged, but the extra space left room for her Ruger. She knew she would probably be searched by the Lion's security, but she might get the boot gun through.

She finished her new look with a sun-bleached Dodgers hat. Before getting out of the car she called Tom Laffont. He picked up right away.

"What's happening?"

"I need you to do me a favor."

"Okay."

"Take down this address. If you don't get a call from me in thirty minutes, I want you to call Pacific Division and send backup."

"Okay. You want backup right now? I can be there in thirty minutes."

"No, it's just a precaution. I gotta do an interview on an RHD case from before. Kind of a dicey no-tell hotel but I should be fine. In and out in thirty."

"You sure?"

"I'm sure."

She gave him the address of the Eldorado along with the room number supplied by the Lion. After hanging up, she set the timer on her phone for twenty-nine minutes. She knew that Laffont would be precise and would call Pacific Division at the exact thirty-minute mark if Ballard did not get back to him first.

She got out of the car, locked it, and proceeded to the entrance of the hotel.

The lobby of the Eldorado was not meant for loitering. There were no chairs or benches or even counters to lean on. The front desk was enclosed behind glass with a push-through slot for credit cards and cash. The man at the desk was reading a book and seemed to take no notice of Ballard as she entered.

Ballard saw a single elevator to the left and a hallway to the right. A placard on the wall between them told her that rooms 1 through 12 were down the hall. She headed that way but had to step aside when the boy she had seen earlier with the laptop passed by, now empty-handed. He had made his deal.

The corridor was dimly lit; the room numbers rose as she walked. Ballard saw a man sitting on a chair at the end of the hall. She judged that he was sitting between rooms 11 and 12. He stood up before she got there. He was Black, six feet–plus, thick in the middle, and dressed completely in black. There was a handgun holstered on his hip and in plain view of all who approached.

"Here to see the Lion," Ballard said.

The security man flipped his hands up, signaling her to raise her arms. She complied and he patted her down with no deference to her gender. He ran his hands down both her legs but half-assed it over her boots because it was difficult for him to bend over his stomach and get his hands down there. When he was finished, he knocked on the door of room 11 and stepped aside.

The door opened and a smiling white man stood there. He was rail-thin with dyed blond hair braided into cornrows. He looked like he couldn't be more than twenty-five years old. He wore a Dodgers uniform top with Ohtani's number on it, board shorts, white socks, and black slides. Around his neck on a thick gold chain was an over-size medallion of a lion's head with emerald eyes.

"You're Bobby D.'s girl?" he said. "I'm the Lion."

"All right if I come in?" Ballard asked.

"Sure. Make yourself at home."

Ballard entered what looked like a basic fourteen-by-fourteen hotel room adapted for an unintended use. The bed was turned up and leaning against the back wall to make room for the folding tables on which the week's take was stacked. There were phones, laptops, cameras, electronic game consoles, and plastic tubs filled with various items. One held prescription bottles. Another had a closed top, but the shapes of handguns were visible through the white plastic. One table held designer handbags and jeans in piles, price tags still attached. The room was clearly the destination for goods stolen and shoplifted from across the city.

The Lion closed the door behind Ballard and she heard the lock click.

"See anything you like," he said, "it's yours. Gratis."

Ballard turned and looked at him. He held out his arm like a game-show host, presenting the treasure on the tables. His shirt came up on his right hip and Ballard saw the pearl handle of a gun protruding from the waistband of his shorts.

"I'm sure we could come to an understanding, you and me," he said. "I don't think Bobby would mind too much, do you? I mean, I love older women. They know just what a guy needs."

"Uh, he told me to just make a deal," Ballard said.

The Lion spread both arms wide and ran his eyes down Ballard's body.

"Well, now, I only see one thing you got with you to trade, darlin'. So how 'bout we go across the hall to my private crib for a little of that afternoon delight?"

"I think I just want to make a deal. I've got the phone Bobby gave me in my boot."

Ballard reached down and pulled up the leg of her jeans.

"Hey, wait," the Lion said, sensing danger.

But it was too late. Lion went for his gun, but Ballard came up with her gun in hand and pushed the barrel into his neck.

"Don't do it," Ballard said.

The Lion started raising his hands. Ballard saw fear creep into his eyes.

"Okay, okay, now," he said. "Be easy."

"Shut up," she said. "You make a sound, it'll get you killed." She reached her free hand to his waist and pulled his gun.

"Hey, come on," he said. "Let's just be friends."

Ballard stepped back and pointed the big and small guns at his chest.

"On the floor," she said. "Now."

Keeping his hands up, the Lion got down on one knee and then the other.

"Lionel, huh?" Ballard said. "What's your last name?"

"Why do you care?" the Lion said. "What do you want?"

"Good question. Bobby D. brought you a gun and a badge yesterday. Where are they?"

The Lion's eyes widened.

"Oh, shit! That was you! That was your badge! Bobby told me they took it off a surfer chick who was a cop."

He gave a short, high-pitched laugh. Anger flooded Ballard and she rushed forward into him, knocking him backward to the floor. She was on top of him then and this time she pushed the barrel of his own gun into his neck.

"I asked you a question, Lionel. You want to get out of this room alive, you better start telling me what I — "

"Okay, okay, okay. Take it easy. We can deal, we can deal."

"I'm not interested in a deal. Where is the badge? Where is the gun?"

She pulled back from him and dragged the barrel of his gun down his torso to his thigh, where she held it.

"Talk," she said. "Or you're going to lose a leg."

"Okay, okay, the gun is in the gun box," he said. "Right behind you. Just take it, it's yours."

"The badge."

"Uh, I, uh, already sold the badge. But we can get it back."

"Sold it to who?"

"Just a guy. A customer buys guns from me. He'd been telling me he was looking for a badge and so I hit him when one came in."

"What did he want the badge for?"

"I don't know. It's not my business. He probably wanted to rip off drug dealers, you know? Pull 'em over, take their shit."

Ballard stood up and signaled the Lion back up to his knees. "Stay right there," she said.

She backed up to the gun box and flipped off the top. She looked through the guns inside it until she saw a blue-steel Glock 17. She put her boot gun down on the table and lifted out the Glock. She checked the slide and found her initials there, etched at the academy gun shop the day she took possession of the weapon.

She used the gun to signal the Lion to turn around. "Face the wall, Lionel," she said.

The Lion didn't move. "Why?" he said. "You're not going to do me. You're a cop."

"I said face the fucking wall," Ballard said. "Now."

"Okay, okay, okay."

"Then do it."

He turned on his knees and faced the wall. But she had been too loud. There was a sharp knock on the door and then the muffled voice of the Lion's security man.

"Everything all right in there, boss?" he said.

"Tell him you're fine," Ballard whispered.

"Everything's fine," Lionel called. "We're good."

Ballard put his weapon in the box, then popped the cartridge on her Glock. It was a full clip, and she reloaded the weapon.

"You said you know how to get the badge back," she asked. "How?"

"Easy," the Lion said. "The guy who wanted the badge also told me he was looking for a SIG mini."

"Which is what?"

"SIG Sauer MPX. A mini machine gun. Uses thirty-round clips and can do some heavy damage."

"He needs that to rip off drug dealers?"

"That was just a guess. I don't know what he wants it for. It's not my business."

Ballard instinctively knew that whoever had her badge was planning something bigger than carjacking drug dealers. Chasing down her stolen property had led her into the middle of something—something she couldn't leave alone.

Ballard made a decision.

She walked over to the table with the designer handbags and chose an over-the-shoulder Prada bag. She checked Lionel's position before touching it.

"Put your forehead against that wall, Lionel," she said. "Right now."

He complied. She unzipped the Prada bag and pulled out all the tissue stuffing. She slipped the strap over her shoulder, put her gun into the bag, and kept her hand on it.

"Okay, we're going to go now," she said.

"What?" Lionel said.

"You and me, we're going to walk out of here and you're going to tell your guy out there that everything's cool and he needs to mind the store till you're back. You say anything else and somebody's going to get shot, Lionel, and it won't be me."

"Why don't you just go? I'll make sure he doesn't try to stop you."

"That would be nice but I'm going to need you once we get outside."

"For what?"

"We'll talk about that when we get there. You have your phone on you?"

"I got it."

"Good. Let's go. You lead the way. Tell your guy you're just walking me out."

"Whatever."

He opened the door and immediately his security man stood up from his chair in the hall.

"Be right back, big man," he said. "Just walking the lady out."

Lionel headed up the hall. Ballard smiled at the security man and followed. The walk to the end of the hall seemed to take forever, but she knew that turning around and checking on the security man might tip him off that something was wrong.

They made it through the lobby and out to the street.

"Now what?" Lionel said.

"I got something in my car I want to show you," Ballard said. "It's over here."

They walked up Speedway, to where the Defender was parked. Ballard opened the driver's door, pulled the gun from the handbag, and held it free. She leaned into the car, threw the bag in, and reached under the driver's seat for her handcuffs. She turned to Lionel, and his eyes went wide when he saw the cuffs.

"What the fuck?"

"Put your hands on the car."

"Wait, you're arresting me? I'm trying to help you here."

He turned to run, but Ballard was ready for the move. She grabbed the back of his collar and the thick gold chain around his neck. She yanked him backward and spun him to the ground. Putting a knee on his spine, she shoved her gun into the waistband of her jeans. She pulled his right arm behind his back, cuffed it, and then went for the left.

"What are the charges?" Lionel yelled.

Ballard couldn't help but laugh.

"You really need to ask?" Ballard said. "Let's start with possession of stolen property. That Prada bag still has a Nordstrom price tag on it. Two grand, Lionel. That puts you into a felony and a cell."

Ballard checked his pockets and pulled out a set of keys, a roll of cash, and his phone. She needed that phone for her plan to work.

"Now we're going to get up," she said. "If you help me, you'll be able to make all of this go away."

"Fuck you," Lionel said. "I ain't fucking helping you do shit."

"We'll see if you change your mind after a night in a cell."

"I got a lawyer. He'll get me out in an hour. You heard of the Lincoln Lawyer, bitch?"

"Yeah, I've heard of him. But the thing about lawyers is that they have to be able to find you to get you out."

The Lion didn't have a comeback for that.

"Let's go," Ballard said. "Get up."

14

BALLARD KNOCKED ON the door of the house on Woodrow Wilson. It was dark but the lights were on behind the windows. She was raising her fist to knock a second time when the door opened and there stood Harry Bosch.

"Renée, you all right?"

"I am now. I need help, Harry. And I think you're the only one I can trust."

"Is this about Maddie?"

"No, nothing to do with Maddie."

"Come in."

He stepped back and Ballard entered.

WEDNESDAY, 11:15 A.M.

15

THE BADGE BUYER was fifteen minutes late. Ballard was getting anxious. She checked on Bosch through her binoculars once again. She could see him in the Cherokee, drumming his fingers on the steering wheel. He was anxious too. If the badge buyer didn't show, they had no plan B.

The Cherokee was parked in an open area in the vast beach lot off Ocean Park in Santa Monica. On an overcast Wednesday morning, the spot drew only a handful of beach enthusiasts. The parking lot was so empty that a local roller-hockey club was able to set up their nets, delineate boundaries with orange cones, and play a game at the far end of the lot.

Ballard saw the door of the Cherokee open. Bosch climbed out and was careful not to glance in her direction. She was parked up on Ocean Boulevard with a down-angle view on the beach lot. They had chosen the meeting spot for this vantage point and because there was only one entrance and exit to the lot.

Bosch was holding the burner cell they had used to contact the unnamed badge buyer. Lionel Boden had provided the number after deciding his best move was to cooperate. Bosch leaned back against his car, hiked one leg up, and put his heel against the front wheel. He started typing on the phone. Ballard understood that he had gotten out of the car so she would see what he was doing: texting the badge buyer, probably to ask where the hell he was.

But before Bosch finished typing the message, Ballard saw a white Ford panel van cruise across the white lines on the empty asphalt and directly toward Bosch. It had not entered the lot just now — it had been there, parked near the scattering of vehicles belonging to the roller-hockey players. Ballard had thought it was the group's equipment van, but now it was in the open and heading toward Bosch's position.

Ballard kept the binoculars up and watched as the van made a circle around Bosch's car and stopped in front of him. There were no markings on the van's panels and she had gotten only a fleeting glance at its license plate. She noted the plate was bright yellow with a red design or lettering on it. But her view of it disappeared quickly when the van made the loop around Bosch and his car. New Mexico was the only state she could recall with bright yellow plates.

The visors on the van were down and Ballard could see only the driver's bearded jaw from her angle. He stayed in the van and spoke to Bosch through an open window.

Bosch responded to the driver by opening his army-green field jacket to show his T-shirt — which advertised an organization engaged in preventing veteran suicides. He had chosen it based on a guess that the badge buyer was a veteran experienced with weapons. Bosch then pulled the shirt up, exposing his torso to show he was not wired or carrying a weapon. Through the binoculars, Ballard could see Bosch's ribs and realized how much weight he had lost during his cancer treatment. She felt an immediate pang of guilt for drawing him into her problem.

The conversation in the parking lot continued briefly before Bosch pushed himself off his car and took a step toward the van.

"Don't get in the van, Harry," Ballard said out loud.

Bosch held his phone up to the van's driver, and Ballard let out her breath. He was only showing the photos of machine guns they had downloaded to the phone for what they believed would be the play with the badge buyer. Bosch even offered the phone to the van driver so he could swipe through the photos. It was a move to possibly get fingerprints, but the driver was either too smart for that or had seen enough photos. He demurred.

The conversation soon ended. Through the binoculars, Ballard saw Bosch nod to the driver. It was the signal to Ballard that they were going to make a deal.

The van drove off with Bosch standing there. He turned back to his Cherokee. Ballard pushed the ignition button and put the Defender in drive. She was ready to follow the van once it left through the parking lot's exit. Bosch would be on the move as well but he would hang far back, since the van's driver had already seen his thirty-year-old car.

Ballard had a Bluetooth earbud in and wore her hair down, covering it. When Bosch called, she answered without taking her eyes off the van.

"How'd it go?" she asked.

"He said he wants to deal," Bosch said. "He wants four. But he could have been just bullshitting. Said he'd set up a meet for tomorrow for the exchange."

"Did you get a look inside the van? Was he alone?"

"I didn't want to be obvious. But I think he was alone."

"I saw you tried to get his prints."

"Yeah, that didn't work."

The white van exited the parking lot and turned left on Ocean. Ballard waited for traffic to clear and then pulled away from the curb, made a U-turn, and followed.

"So, what was he like?" Ballard asked. "I mean, formidable? Is he a player?"

"Uh...maybe," Bosch said. "Forty, forty-five, white, thick beard. He seemed fit, no paunch, but he could've had a wheelchair in the back of the van for all I could see. He stayed behind the wheel."

"He say his name?"

"No, no names."

"I saw you delay when he drove away. Did you get the plate?"

"There is no plate. He's got a Gadsden flag on there. Rattlesnake, the whole bit."

"'Don't tread on me.'"

"Right."

This told Ballard that the badge buyer was either claiming to be a sovereign citizen or posing as one. She knew from FBI bulletins and LAPD intel alerts that sovereigns were considered anti-government extremists who did not recognize any taxing, licensing, or law enforcement authority. The last alert she remembered stated that the number of sovereigns in the country had grown markedly since the twin ideological earthquakes of the COVID pandemic and the failed insurrection at the U.S. Capitol. The alert had concluded with the warning that all sovereigns should be considered armed and that law enforcement should approach with extreme caution. Because of this, most cops looked the other way when noticing the fake plates.

Ballard checked the van ahead and goosed the Defender to catch up and not be left behind at a traffic light.

"He has a bumper sticker on there too," Bosch said. "'Your Vaccine Is a Bioweapon.'"

"Nice," Ballard said.

"These nutters like to stockpile weapons and they talk a good game, but they're usually guys who just don't want to pay taxes, whether it's on income, property, or cars."

"Not the case here, I don't think. He's up to something."

"You sure?"

"No, but why buy guns illegally when you don't have to? Why would a guy who supposedly doesn't recognize the police as a legit authority buy a police badge?"

"There's that."

Both were quiet for a long moment as they contemplated the badge buyer and what he might be planning. Bosch finally spoke.

"I'm out of the lot now. I'll hang back, but which way are you going?"

"North on Ocean. Coming up on Broadway now."

"Okay, I'm five behind and will cut it to two."

"Sounds good. Keeping the line open."

Ballard kept her eyes on the white van, which was now about two blocks ahead of her in moderate traffic. She was watching the crosswalk countdowns and maintaining a pace that would keep her from getting stopped by a traffic signal.

She saw the van glide into the left-turn lane ahead and she prepared to follow suit. "Harry, he's going down the California Incline."

"Got it."

Cars stacked up in the turning lane and Ballard ended up only three cars behind the van. She caught a glimpse of the badge buyer in the van's rectangular side-view mirror. He was wearing sunglasses.

The arrow turned green and the van made the turn. Ballard followed, keeping the three-car separation. The traffic dropped down and the road merged with the Pacific Coast Highway. The van moved to the inner lane, indicating to Ballard that the guy would not be turning off anytime soon.

"On PCH, heading toward Malibu."

"I missed the light at the Incline. You got him for now."

"Not a problem."

She thought about where the badge buyer might be headed. She knew that the sovereigns fit in nicely with most of the other extremist groups nowadays, from Aryan Nation to the Oath Keepers to the grab bag of other groups that had charged the Capitol three years before. That didn't quite fit with Malibu, but beyond Malibu was Ventura County and towns like Oxnard and Fillmore, where such groups were known to have roots.

But the badge buyer stopped well short of Ventura County or even Malibu. Just past Sunset Beach, still within the city limits of Los Angeles, the van pulled to the side of the road across the coast highway from the beach at Castle Rock. The van eased into a spot behind a large RV that was parked in a line of other RVs, smaller campers, and vans below the cliff facings of the Pacific Palisades.

To Ballard, it looked like someone had been waiting there for the van and had moved an orange cone that had been used to reserve the spot so the badge buyer could slip into it.

Ballard drove by to avoid notice.

"Harry, he just pulled over on the east side at Castle Rock. I drove by and I'll figure out a way to double back."

"Got it. I'll find a place to pull over short of there. Give me a meetup point when you've got one."

Ballard pulled into the left-turn lane and cut quickly through an opening in the oncoming traffic into the parking lot on the beach side of the PCH. She worked her way through the lot and found a spot with an angle on the white van across the four lanes of highway.

"I went into the lot on the beach side," she said. "I have eyes on the van but not the guy."

Bosch didn't respond but Ballard assumed he was maneuvering and wanted his hands free. He wasn't a Bluetooth-and-earbuds kind of guy.

She took up the binoculars and tried to see into the van through its windshield, but there were curtains hanging down behind the front seats. She hadn't noticed them earlier and thought the badge buyer might have gone into the back of the van and pulled the privacy curtains closed behind him.

"Harry, what's your twenty?"

His answer was a knock on her front passenger window. Ballard unlocked the door and he climbed in.

"You see him?" he asked.

"No, I think he's in the back of the van," Ballard said. "There are curtains behind the front seats. Did you see that when you talked to him?"

"I didn't notice."

"The other thing was that it was like he knew that spot. Like it was waiting for him."

"You see anybody else talk to him?"

"I think somebody moved a cone blocking the spot out of the way for him. But then I had to drive by and didn't get a look."

"So, is that reserved camper parking over there?"

"I don't think so. Probably just unregulated mobile homeless people."

The city was not enforcing most laws that were designed to help curtail the number of people living on the streets. Despite curfews and laws about sidewalk obstruction, encampments proliferated. Unenforced overnight-parking regulations had created a population of homeless people who lived in vans and campers that lined public streets at night.

"Great," Bosch said. "Now we have homeless terrorists."

"You really think that's what he is?" Ballard asked. "A terrorist?"

"I wouldn't bet against it. If he's downloaded the sovereign bullshit, that could be exactly what he is. A lot of people like that stormed the Capitol."

Ballard said nothing. She continued to stare across the street, her view of the van repeatedly interrupted by passing cars.

"So, what do you think?" Bosch asked.

"I think there's a good chance that my badge is in that van," Ballard said, "waiting for me to come get it."

16

IT WAS FOUR hours before the badge buyer emerged through the curtains of his van and opened the door to step out. In the interim, Ballard checked the webcam of the pet day-care center where she left her dog, Pinto, when she was at work, and she dealt with calls from Colleen Hatteras, Tom Laffont, and Maddie Bosch. She told Hatteras and Laffont that she was working on non-cold-case matters and they should not expect to see her in the office until Thursday. She told Maddie Bosch that she had been cleared to begin work with the OU team the following day. She was welcome to come to the bullpen, take the desk her father had used the year before, and start looking at cases.

Ballard was careful not to call Maddie a volunteer, because she wasn't. Ballard had received the green light from Captain Gandle to take the younger Bosch onto the team if the police union gave its approval. This was the most difficult step because the union, which represented the rank and file of the department, was not in the business of allowing its members to do unpaid police work and objected to such a precedent. Ballard handled that by agreeing to pay Madeline Bosch four hours of overtime per week as a member of the unit. If she chose to work more than those four hours, that was between her and the union. Ballard knew she could cover the overtime with money from a National Institute of Justice grant she had received to review cold cases. It was money she could use at her discretion and she decided that having Maddie Bosch and her sworn law enforcement powers on the unit was worth it. She could pay Maddie for four hours a week for at least five years before the grant money ran out.

"He changed clothes," Bosch said.

He was watching through Ballard's binoculars.

"He probably had a nice nap too," Ballard said. "What's he doing?"

"Talking to the guy from the RV in front of the van," Bosch said. "They look like they're very familiar with each other."

"Why not? They're neighbors. They've probably been camped out there for months, nobody from the city doing a thing about it."

"What do you think the average house on the beach here goes for? A couple million?"

"Easy. Probably double that."

"It must make them so happy to have these people out here."

"Harry, that's a heartless way to describe the unhoused."

"I guess I'm not woke."

"You, not woke? Shocking."

Ballard knew Bosch wasn't heartless. But like many in Los Angeles, he was losing patience and empathy as he watched the city he loved slide into chaos because of a problem the government and its citizens seemingly had no solutions for.

They lapsed into an uneasy silence as Ballard thought about the price of the double-wide she had bought a block off the beach in Paradise Cove last year. She had needed all of the inheritance from her grandmother and the proceeds from the sale of her house in Ventura to buy into what was known as the most expensive trailer park in the world.

Still, she didn't regret it. The sunsets alone were worth the price of admission.

"So what's the plan?" Bosch finally asked.

"No plan," Ballard said. "I'm going to watch and wait. If I get a shot at that van, I'll take it. But this is my thing. You don't have to stay, Harry. Thank you for your help."

"No, I'm cool. I want to know what this guy's up to. I just thought you might have to bail for a hot date and I was going to say I would stay on watch."

"A hot date?"

"It's Valentine's Day. I thought maybe —"

"Uh, no, no hot date. You're my date if you're staying."

"Happy to. I wish I had flowers."

An hour of intermittent banter went by. Ballard checked on Pinto again and sent a message to the day-care center informing them that he would likely be staying overnight.

The sun dropped behind the ocean. The badge buyer was seen in and out of the van, mingling with people from the other vehicles parked along the street. Ballard and Bosch took turns using the public restrooms on the beach, and eventually their cover became strained as beachgoers left with the sun. Soon the Defender stood out as one of the last few cars in the lot.

"We gotta move," Ballard said. "We're sitting out here in plain sight."

"Where to?" Bosch asked.

"That's the thing. I don't see a better angle on the van. We could cross the street and park, but we wouldn't have eyes on it."

"So maybe we stick here."

Ballard considered not moving.

"Tell you what," she said. "I'm going to take a walk over there, see what I can see and hear."

"You sure?" Bosch asked. "If he sees you, you're burned as far as any walk-bys tomorrow or after."

"I got some things here that will help with that. I'm going to go."

"Your call."

Bosch's tone suggested he thought she was making the wrong call, but Ballard got out and opened the back door of the car to get to her disguise box. She took off her jacket and pulled on an old gray hoodie. She added the Dodgers cap with the frayed edge to its bill that she had worn into the Eldorado and pulled the hood up over it. She took the Glock and its holster off her hip and put it in the box.

"You're going naked?" Bosch asked.

"I've got my boot gun," Ballard said. "I'm going to go a block north, then cut across and come back down like I've been walking. I've got my earbud in and I'll call you on approach."

"Got it. Be careful."

"Always."

Ballard walked to the north end of the parking lot, which was at least a hundred yards away from the badge buyer's van. She waited a solid five minutes before there was enough of a break in the traffic for her to cross. She then walked south toward the line of parked vehicles. She kept her head down and her hands in the front pockets of the hoodie, one of them holding her phone.

As she approached, she pulled out her phone and called Bosch. He picked up right away.

"I see you," he said. "It took you long enough."

"Had to wait to cross," Ballard said. "You see our guy anywhere?"

"The van is dark. I think he's in one of the big RVs."

"I'll see what I can see."

Ballard could see through the front windshields of the parked motor homes, giving her a limited angle on activities inside. She passed two campers and a large RV, and each was dark. The next RV had its interior lights on but appeared to be vacant.

Then she saw where everybody was. Two more vehicles down, an RV was parked in a spot where the cliff was concave enough to offer space for a circle of folding chairs around a flaming grill. The firelight shone on the faces of several men and women in the chairs, including a bearded man who Ballard believed was the badge buyer.

She reported all this to Bosch in a low voice as she approached the circle.

"They've got themselves a bonfire on the other side of one of the RVs," she said. "I think our guy is in the circle."

"Okay," Bosch said. "What are you going to do?"

"Pick my way by and see if the van's unlocked."

"I don't think that's a good idea."

Ballard was now too close to the fire circle to risk speaking to Bosch. She kept her head down and worked her way around the circle. There was no sidewalk. She had to go between the line of campers and the cliff; otherwise she'd be in the traffic lanes. She counted five men and two women sitting around the flaming grill. They weren't cooking anything, just warming themselves. One of the men called out to her as she passed.

"Hey, sweetie, you want a beer?" he said.

Ballard couldn't tell which one had said it. "No, thanks," she said. She kept going, not turning toward the group.

"Then how about a ride?" the voice called.

Ballard didn't respond.

"On my lap," the man added.

This was met with raucous laughter from the circle. Even the women joined in, one issuing a high-pitched cackle that rose above the noise of traffic off the highway.

Ballard passed two more pickups with camper shells plastered with bumper stickers. Most had catchy slogans that derided liberal ideologies or the sitting president or both. She passed a thirty-five-foot-long RV with a name painted in script on the side: *Road Warrior.* She laughed to herself, remembering a game she played as a teenager with Tutu when they'd driven on a freeway. They would put the word *anal* in front of the RVs' names.

"What's so funny?" Bosch asked.

"Nothing, really," Ballard said. "I'm passing by the Anal Road Warrior."

"What?"

"Never mind. I'll tell you later. I'm going to check out the van."

Ballard cut in front of the RV and started walking down the other side of the string of vehicles. This put her only a few feet from traffic and in the blinding glare of the headlights of cars whizzing by.

She got to the white van and saw that it was completely dark inside. She went to the driver's door and tried the handle.

"It's unlocked," she said. "I'm going in. You got me?"

"I see you," Bosch said. "But I don't think it's a good idea."

"He can't see me from there and we need to know what he's up to."

"Still don't think it's a good idea."

"Come on, Harry. You know you'd be in here if it were you."

Ballard climbed into the driver's seat and cautiously looked through the windshield in the direction of the circle. From this angle, she could see only one of the seated people, a woman in a folding chair with a built-in cupholder for her beer.

Ballard took a quick look through the glove box and storage areas in the front. She did not find her badge, but in a cupholder there was a key ring with two keys and a chip fob on it. It said YOU-STORE-IT on the fob and provided an address on Lincoln Boulevard in Santa Monica. The numbers 22 and 23 were stamped on the keys.

Ballard split the curtains behind the front seats and ducked into the back. The rear windows were blacked out and the interior was pitch-dark. Ballard's face immediately came into contact with something wet and spongy.

"Shit."

She struggled to get the light on her phone on.

"What is it?" Bosch said. "What's wrong?"

She turned her light on. There was a damp beach towel hanging from a makeshift clothesline strung diagonally from the back corner of the van across its interior. The wet weight of the gray-and-white-striped towel made the line droop in the middle.

"Renée, what's wrong?" Bosch repeated, his voice rising.

"Nothing," Ballard said. "I walked into a wet towel on, like, a clothesline. It's gross. But I'm in the back and I've got my phone light on. Let me know if you see it through the curtains."

She did a quick sweep with the light across the rear of the van. "Anything?" she asked.

"Not really," Bosch said. "But I'm a lot farther away than the people in the fire circle."

"I'll be quick."

"What do you see?"

She swept the light across the space slowly.

"Queen-size mattress at the back," she said. "Looks like it's on top of a built-in box. A large plywood box for storage. The bed's not made. There are clothes and other shit hanging in nets on the side walls."

She moved toward the back. There was a sheet hanging off the unmade mattress and over the edge of the wooden box. Ballard swiped the sheet away to see if there was a latch or handle for opening the box.

There was a padlock.

"Shit," she said.

"What?" Bosch responded, panic in his voice.

"The bed sits on this built-in storage unit. But it's got a lock on it."

"Did you bring picks with you?"

"No, but it's a combo."

"You see any hinges?"

"Hold on."

She put the phone down on the carpeted floor of the van and

moved to the bed. The mattress was no more than four inches thick. It was easy for her to push up and roll back so she could examine the top of the wooden box.

There was a seam halfway back on the top of the box and two metal hinges. She put the light close to one and saw three screws holding each side of the hinge.

"Two hinges, three screws each," she said. "I need a Phillips-head."

"That'll take too long," Bosch said. "Just get out of there. We'll figure something else out."

Ballard swept the light across the full rear compartment of the van. On the floor under the back of the driver's seat there was a red metal box that was either for tools or first aid. She crawled over, pulled the box out, and flipped the lid open. The box contained tools, and there was a Phillips-head screwdriver clipped to the top of it.

"I have a screwdriver right here, courtesy of our badge buyer."

"Just be quick, Renée, okay? I'm going to change position to see if I can get a direct look at the circle jerks."

Ballard smiled. "I've got six screws to remove," she said. "I'll be as fast as I can."

She moved back to the box and went to work. It was a homemade job, and the screws anchoring the hinges to the plywood had loosened over time from the repeated opening and closing of the lid. They turned easily and Ballard had all six out in less than five minutes.

"How are we doing?" she asked. "Screws are out and I'm going to open the lid."

"I've got eyes on the circle," Bosch said. "I can't see everybody, but I'll be able to see if anybody moves toward the van."

"Good."

"But don't waste time. See what's there and get the hell out."

Ballard didn't respond. She held her phone light up with one hand and raised the lid with the other. She folded it down over the padlock.

The box was filled to the top with haphazardly folded clothing. She swept the light across. There were several pairs of jeans, jackets, and shoes. Still holding the light up, she started grabbing clothes and pulling them out of the box, digging down to the bottom.

Soon she saw the glint of metal and began uncovering weapons. There were rifles, handguns, boxes of ammo, combat knives, and more.

"There are enough weapons here to start a little war," Ballard said, "but he still needs four machine guns. This guy's — "

She stopped talking when she flipped over an assault vest with metal plates and saw LAPD stenciled across the front and back.

"What?" Bosch said. "I lost you."

"He's got an LAPD SWAT vest. What the fuck is this guy up to?"

"We'll figure it out. What about your badge?"

"Not here, as far as I can tell."

"Okay, then, why don't you get the hell out of there. Now, Renée."

"I can't just leave it like this. He'll know we're onto his ass. I need to put everything back like I found it."

"You're going to give me a heart attack here."

"I'm fine, Harry."

"For now. Just hurry it up."

"Yes, Dad."

She put the phone down next to her knee so she could put everything back into the box. She had to carefully refold some of the clothes so they would look the way she had found them. She closed the lid and started screwing the hinges back into place.

She had just moved to the second hinge when she heard Bosch's voice in her earbud.

"Renée, listen to me. He's coming to the van. He and another guy. It's too late to get out. You need to hide."

"Hide? It's a van, Harry."

"I know, but they're right there. Hide. *Now.*"

Ballard abandoned the hinge and flipped the mattress back down. She grabbed her phone and killed the light, then climbed onto the mattress, bunched an insulated blanket into a ball, and propped the two pillows on either side of it. She slid down between the pile and the back doors of the van. In the darkness she looked for a handle she could use to open the back doors if she needed to escape, but she saw nothing. The handle was beneath the level of the built-in storage box.

She reached down, slid the left leg of her jeans up, and pulled her Ruger out of her ankle holster.

She heard the voices of two men outside the van. The front doors opened and the men got in.

17

IF THE TWO men in the front of the van knew that Ballard was hiding in the back, they didn't give any sign of it. Neither opened the curtain to look. The engine started, and Ballard felt the van jerk into motion. The driver pulled out onto the coast highway and started heading north. Ballard heard Bosch's panicked voice in her ears.

"Renée, I'm right behind you in the Defender," he said. "Can you speak? Probably not. What about text—can you text? I need some kind of a signal from you or I gotta stop this. I'll figure out how to do it. If I don't get something from you in three minutes, I'm going to stop the van, even if I have to run it off the road."

Ballard raised her head slightly and looked over the pile of bedding to the front of the van. The curtains were still closed, and judging from the banter between the driver and passenger, they didn't know of her presence. She pulled her phone out of her pocket and checked that it was set to silent mode, then texted Bosch an all-clear message.

Code 4. Don't stop the van.

She waited for Bosch to acknowledge.

"Okay, I got your text," he said. "But if you say my name, that will be the signal for me to make a move. Anything goes sideways, just say my name. I don't know if you can see where they're going, but right now it's north — actually, I guess it's more west now — on PCH through Malibu."

Ballard knew what he meant. Most of Malibu's coast had a southern exposure as the coastline jutted out. It was what made several of its beaches good surfing breaks.

She thought of something and sent Bosch another text.

**I can hear them when they talk. Send him
a text about the SIGs, get them talking.**

Bosch acknowledged verbally and she waited for his text to land. Soon she heard a phone ping, and the men up front started talking.

"Read this, I'm driving. It's from the gun guy."

"He says, 'I've got another offer. You still need four?' Fucking guy, just trying to jack up the price."

"Doesn't matter, we're not going to pay for them. Tell him, yeah, we need four, and we can make the deal tomorrow. Tell him we also need shoulder slings and reload mags."

There was silence; Ballard presumed the passenger was typing the text. Soon Bosch told her that they had responded and wanted to make the deal for four mini machine guns the next day.

"They want slings and extra magazines," he said. "I don't know what they're up to but it sounds like they're going to be carrying multiple weapons and lots of ammo."

The van stopped and Ballard froze, wondering if they had heard something from the back.

"You're at a traffic light," Bosch said. "Las Flores Canyon."

Ballard could picture it. She drove this road every day to and from work and when heading south to surf. They were at La Costa Beach and then it would be Carbon followed by the pier and then Malibu Lagoon.

The van took off again. Ballard thought about what she had heard and understood that if they were not going to pay for the mini machine guns, that meant they were going to either rob or kill the seller. But with the integrity of their plan — whatever it was — at stake, it seemed unlikely that they would only rob him.

Soon the van slowed and then jogged to the right and stopped. Ballard guessed that they had slipped into a parking space.

"It'll be nice and crowded Monday," the driver said.

"Perfect," the other man said.

"Go back?"

"Let's hit up Mickey D's on the way."

The van started moving again and almost immediately made a U-turn. Ballard wasn't ready for it, and the centrifugal force threw her against the back of the van with a thud. She froze and then let her breath out slowly, trying to deflate her body, make it as low as possible behind the pile of bedding and pillows.

The light in the rear compartment changed and she knew that someone was looking through the curtain. Then the darkness returned.

"You gotta tie your shit down, man."

"I do. I think it's the spare. It's underneath and it gets loose."

Less than a minute later, the van made a ninety-degree turn and Bosch whispered in Ballard's ear that they were in the drive-through lane of a McDonald's.

Ballard listened while they ordered seven combo meals. They paid and waited for their order to be handed through the window. Ballard couldn't see it but she could picture it. Then the men up front spoke.

"This will make that thing in Vegas look like child's play," one said. "The precision of it, you know?"

"Oh, yeah," said the other.

Soon they had their food and were on the move again; they exited the drive-through and turned left onto the PCH. The smell of McDonald's filled the van, and Bosch's voice came to Ballard through her earbud.

"Looks like they're heading back to the caravan with the food," he said.

But Ballard barely heard him. She was concentrating on what she had heard from the front of the van and what it meant.

Ten minutes later there was another U-turn and the van parked. Ballard knew that they had returned to the original place in the line of campers. The hot food saved her from discovery as the men got out of the van without further investigating the sound they had heard from the back.

"Am I clear?" she whispered.

"They're going back to the grill fire with the food," Bosch said. "Get out of there."

"Not yet. I have to finish putting the hinges back on."

"Then hurry. Luck is a fluid thing, and you've been lucky so far."

"I get it."

Ballard rolled the mattress back to access the top of the box and the hinges. She had left the screwdriver and the screws there, and the mattress had held them in place. It took her less than five minutes to re-anchor the last hinge and put everything back.

"How does it look outside the van?" she asked.

"You're clear," Bosch said. "Use the driver's-side door and they won't have an angle on you."

"Got it," she said. "Where are you?"

"Back in the lot across the street."

"On my way."

Five minutes later Ballard was safely across the street. Bosch was still behind the wheel of her Defender, so she took the passenger seat.

"Before they made the first U-turn and went to the McDonald's, they pulled over for a minute or so," she said. "Where were we?"

"Yeah, I had to drive by them," Bosch said. "They were in front of a vacant business. It looked like it used to be, like, a chicken-in-a-bucket place."

The description didn't match anything in Ballard's memory. "What was across the street?" she asked.

"The Malibu pier," Bosch said.

"Shit."

"What?"

"They talked about how crowded it would be on Monday."

"Monday's a holiday. Presidents' Day. A lot of people go to the beach if it's warm enough. And the pier — they've got two restaurants there. What are they going to do?"

"Whatever it is, they said it would 'make that thing in Vegas look like child's play.'"

"The mass shooting at the concert?"

"I assume that's what they meant. They already have an arsenal and now they want machine guns and extra ammo? Has to be something like that. They talked about 'the precision' of it. I assume that means it'll be a close assault, not sniping from a faraway structure like in Vegas."

Bosch was shocked into silence.

"At least we know when they're planning to do it," Ballard said.

"There's that," Bosch said.

He was staring across the street at the row of vehicles he called the caravan.

The biggest RV shielded their view of the grill fire but the glow from it climbed up the rock face of the cliff above the motor home.

"How many of them are involved in this, you think?" he asked.

"I don't know," Ballard said. "They ordered seven combo meals at McDonald's. When I walked by their bonfire, they all looked like they were pretty tight. It was five men and two women. Maybe they're all in it, or maybe it's just the two in the van."

Bosch nodded.

"They want the guns," he said. "All four. Maybe that's where we set up a takedown."

"They talked about that after you texted," Ballard said. "And they aren't planning to pay for the guns."

Bosch nodded again. He knew what that meant.

"This has gotten too big," Ballard said. "It started with me looking for a pissant car burglar and my badge, and now we're talking about possible domestic terrorism. We can't sit on this."

"The bigger this thing is, the bigger the consequences for you," Bosch said. "If the media gets hold of it and finds out that your badge ended up with terrorists who were going to shoot up the pier —"

"I know, I know, I'll be lucky if they put me back on the late show in Hollywood."

"You'll be lucky if they put you back on patrol in Devonshire."

"Thanks for being so supportive, Harry."

"I'm sorry, but I don't support career suicide. Not when it's your career."

"Then what do you suggest?"

"I don't know, but the good thing is that we have some time. You heard them yourself. Monday is the day. That gives us four days to come up with a plan."

"And what if we don't?"

"Then, fine, you call in the troops."

Ballard nodded. "Okay," she said. "But I'm not waiting till Sunday night. Two days, Harry. We figure this out in two days or I take it to CTSOB and the sheriff's department."

The Counter-Terrorism and Special Operations Bureau handled all organized threats to public safety. The sheriff's department had jurisdiction over Malibu and the pier.

"I'm good with that," Bosch said.

"So what's our next move?" Ballard asked.

He pointed across the street at the caravan. "We try to find out who these people are," he said. "And why they needed a badge."

Ballard nodded.

"I know a place we might want to start," she said. "There was a key ring in the van with keys to a You-Store-It in Santa Monica. I think our badge buyer has a couple storage lockers there. There were numbers on the keys."

"Sounds like a lead," Bosch said. "Let's go check it out."

18

THE YOU-STORE-IT WAS on Lincoln a block from the east-bound entrance to the 10 freeway in Santa Monica. The office was long closed for the night by the time Ballard and Bosch arrived, but the facility offered those who rented storage space twenty-four-hour access. All that was needed to enter through its glass doors was the fob that came with every rental unit. But there was a pickup truck parked near the entrance and a man was standing at its open tailgate unloading five-gallon buckets of paint onto a dolly. It gave Bosch an idea.

"What tools do you have?" he asked.

"You mean here in the car?" Ballard asked.

"Yes, what tools?"

"Uh, none, really."

"You don't have a jack?"

"Yes, there's a jack. I thought you meant like a toolbox."

"Get me the crowbar from the jack and I'll need that hat and hoodie."

"What are you going to do?"

"I'm going to follow that painter in, so let's hurry."

They both got out and went to the back of the Defender. The

spare tire and tire-changing tools were underneath the flooring of the rear compartment. Ballard had to take out her crime scene kit and the plastic tub containing surfing equipment to access it. In the meantime, Bosch put the disguise box on the ground and started looking through its contents.

"I don't know what your plan is but there are going to be cameras in there," Ballard said.

"I know," Bosch said. "That's why I need your hat and hoodie."

She lifted the flooring and grabbed a rolled leather satchel containing tire-changing tools.

"Let me see it," he said.

Ballard slid the tire iron out of the satchel and handed it to him. It was eighteen inches long with a bend near one end. That end had a socket that would fit the lug nuts of the car's wheels, and the other end tapered to a flat edge that could be used as a wedge for popping off wheel covers.

"Perfect," Bosch said. "Give me the hat and hoodie."

He put the tire iron into the disguise box and accepted the Dodgers hat from Ballard. He put it on and pulled the brim down low over his forehead. He glanced over at the pickup, and Ballard followed his eyes. The man was closing the tailgate. The dolly was fully loaded with buckets of paint ready to go into storage until the next job.

"Hurry, put the hoodie in the box," Bosch said.

Ballard pulled it off and threw it into the box.

"Okay, what were the numbers on the keys you saw?" Bosch asked.

"Twenty-two and twenty-three," Ballard said. "What are you —"

"Perfect. I gotta go."

He walked off, carrying the box with both hands.

"Wait, what do you want me to do?" Ballard said.

"Just stay there," Bosch said. "I'll call you when I'm ready."

"Ready for what?"

Bosch didn't answer. He picked up his pace and followed behind the man pushing the dolly toward the glass doors. Ballard watched as the man raised his hand and held a fob to an electronic reader at the side of the entrance.

The double doors split and slid open. The man started pushing the dolly again, and Bosch fell into step behind him.

"Hold the doors," he said. He raised the box up so it blocked the lower half of his face when the man turned to see who had spoken.

The man showed no alarm. He even took one hand off the dolly's push bar and signaled Bosch in.

Ballard smiled. It reminded her of her move to get into the lab earlier. "Fucking A," she said to herself.

The automatic doors closed and Bosch disappeared inside. Ballard saw the interior lights of the facility, most likely on motion-activated circuits, illuminate.

Ballard closed the back of the car and walked to the front, leaned against the fender, and waited. Several minutes went by. When she saw the automatic doors open again, it was the man from the pickup who came out. She watched him get in his truck and drive out of the storage facility's parking lot. That left only Bosch inside, and Ballard began to worry. She pulled her phone and called him but got no answer.

She called twice more with the same outcome and started to worry that the physical exertion of the day had caught up with Bosch. She knew she couldn't leave him there but she wasn't sure what to do. On the fourth call she even left a message: "Harry, what is going on? Call me back."

She was no longer leaning nonchalantly on the fender. She began pacing, head down, thinking about how to call in the emergency to the Santa Monica police. No matter how she played it out, bringing the cops in didn't end well for her or Bosch.

She had her back to the automatic doors when she finally heard

Bosch calling her. She whipped around to see him standing in the open doorway, waving her in.

Ballard walked briskly toward the entrance but slowed as she got close.

"It's clear," he said. "You can come in."

She entered slowly. "What about—"

"The cameras are taken care of."

He pointed overhead as he stepped into a central hallway that fronted several tributary aisles of storage rooms. Ballard looked up and saw her Dodgers cap draped over a mounted camera at the top of the wall.

"This way," Bosch said.

She followed him until he turned left and headed down an aisle without hesitation. Ballard entered behind him and saw the hood of her hoodie draped over another camera.

"Twenty-two and twenty-three are down at the end," Bosch said.

As she followed, Ballard noted that each of the storage units they passed had a roll-down steel door that was locked with a padlock through a hasp bolted to the concrete floor. When she caught up to Bosch at the end of the aisle, he was standing by two side-by-side open doors. The tire iron was on the ground next to one of two broken hasps that had been pried out of their concrete moorings.

"Harry, what did you do?"

"We wanted to see what the guy had. Now we can."

"But whoever runs this place will probably call him tomorrow and then he'll know somebody's onto him."

"No, because they'll tell him his was one of several units that got hit."

He pointed to the other side of the aisle. Ballard saw that three other units' padlocks and corresponding hasps had been pried out of the concrete. She turned back to Bosch and noticed the sweat on his forehead and cheeks. It had taken some muscle to break the security of the storage rooms.

"We probably shouldn't waste time," he said.

"No," Ballard said. "We shouldn't."

"You take twenty-two and I'll take twenty-three. Be quick."

"Got it."

They both disappeared into their respective units. Unit 22 was the size of a modest walk-in closet or a prison cell. It was stacked on both sides with cardboard boxes, each helpfully marked with a list of its contents. Ballard moved down the stacks, looking for a box that could be of importance to the investigation and also be a test of the reliability of the listed contents.

She came across one at the top of a four-box stack that was marked *Taxes 2012–2022*. She pulled the box down to the floor. It was heavy. When she took off the top, she saw that it was filled end to end with files with different years marked on the tabs. She took out the last file, marked *2022*, opened it, and found a photocopy of an IRS tax return.

"I've got tax records here," Ballard called out.

"What's the name?" Bosch called back.

"Thomas Dehaven."

"I've got that name on a couple of things over here. He must be the badge buyer."

"Get this. I'm looking at an IRS return for last year. If this is our badge buyer, then the sovereign plate and all of that is bullshit. He's a poseur."

"What's the address?"

"Uh, Coeur d'Alene, Idaho."

"Take a photo and let's keep going. We can't stay here all night."

"Got it. Luck is fluid."

"That's right."

Ballard used her phone to take a photo of the tax return. She replaced the file and put the top back on the box. Standing up, she counted the boxes in the small room. There were sixteen along one side and another thirteen on the opposite wall. The majority were marked *Books* followed by a classification of fiction or nonfiction. She went through all of these first, opening them to find in each a row of books spine out. Thomas Dehaven favored contemporary mystery and horror. Ballard saw the names of several authors she recognized, including some she had even read: Child, Coben, Carson, Burke, Crumley, Grafton, Koryta, Goldberg, Wambaugh, and many others.

"Guy doesn't read Chandler," she said.

"What do you mean?" Bosch said.

"There's a book collection over here, mostly mystery and true crime. But no Chandler."

"His loss."

"What do you have over there?"

"A lot of junk. Clothes, ski equipment, fishing poles, and —"

His report was cut short by the sound of the automated doors at the front of the facility opening and closing. Someone had entered.

Ballard stepped out of unit 22 and into the aisle. Bosch was already there. They stood listening and heard muffled voices. More than one person was inside. Bosch held his hand out as if to stop Ballard from speaking even though she knew to be quiet.

There was a metallic bang and then the harsh sound of a metal door being rolled up. Whoever had come in had gone down one of the other aisles to a storage unit.

"Luck is fluid," Ballard whispered.

"How much more time do you need?" Bosch whispered.

"I have four boxes left."

"I have about the same. Let's get it done."

"Quietly."

They returned to their respective units. Ballard went quickly through the last four boxes in hers. They contained household items like pots and pans, cooking utensils, dishware, and knickknacks that might have come off shelves in a kitchen: Thanksgiving salt- and pepper shakers that looked like pilgrims, a coffee cup with the previous president's booking photo and the words *Presidential Mug* on it, and four ceramic coasters that said *Keep Calm and Carry* above the silhouette of a gun, a different gun on each.

Ballard heard the roll-down door from the other aisle shut with a bang. She stepped out of the storage unit and listened. She again heard muffled voices as whoever had entered earlier made their way back to the exit.

Bosch stood on the threshold of unit 23 listening as well. When he heard the automatic doors at the front open and then close, he nodded to Ballard and went back to work. Ballard followed him into 23. It was not as neatly kept as 22, though Ballard could not tell whether that was because of Bosch's search or because it had been that way when he found it.

"Anything in twenty-two?" he asked.

"Not since I found the tax records in the first box I opened," Ballard said. "What about here?"

"No, just that." He pointed to a stack of three cardboard boxes.

Sitting on top of it was a white jewelry box. Ballard stepped over and opened it. The inside of the lid was a mirror. Below it were felt-lined sections containing gold and silver bracelets and earrings. Ballard rarely wore jewelry and was not equipped to judge the value of what she was looking at.

"Why do you have this out?" she asked.

"Because we need to take something if we're going to convince him that this was a random burglary," Bosch said.

"Come on. It's one thing to break in here, but I don't want to take anything. That's a line I don't think I can cross."

"You don't have to. I will."

"Harry, we—"

"Look, these assholes — they're up to something. Something big. An hour ago you said so yourself. Something that's going to require four machine guns. So I'll cross whatever line I have to if it stops whatever it is from happening. And I won't second-guess myself for one minute."

Ballard understood and nodded.

"Okay," she said.

"So, I'm done in here," Bosch said. "No badge."

"No, no badge."

"I'm beginning to think I know where it is."

"Where?"

Bosch closed the jewelry box and put it under his arm, ready to go. He kicked the stack of boxes over.

"Clipped to his belt or on a chain around his neck," he said. "It might be part of their plan, but it's also his get-out-of-jail-free card."

"How so?" Ballard asked.

"If he gets pulled over or stopped anywhere, he shows the badge," Bosch said. "You know, says he's working, maybe claims to be under-cover. He uses it to talk his way out of getting his ass cuffed up."

Ballard thought there had to be a bigger purpose for wanting the badge.

"Maybe," she said.

"I know a way to test it out," Bosch said.

"How?"

"Let's get out of here and I'll tell you."

THURSDAY, 8:39 A.M.

19

BALLARD AND BOSCH were squeezed into one side of a booth at Mary and Robbs Café in Westwood. The other side was empty.

Bosch checked his watch. "You sure this guy's going to show?"

"He's never stood me up before. He's probably walking over."

"You mean, like, stood you up for a date? That sort of thing?"

"No, Harry. It's strictly a professional relationship."

"You trust him?"

"I wouldn't have called him if I didn't trust him. Gordon is a good guy. He's helped the unit on a lot of cases. The FBI obviously moves a lot faster on out-of-state warrants than we do because they've got agents everywhere. And it's a fact that people who think they've gotten away with murder tend not to hang around. They split, and having a go-to guy in the Bureau is gold. I know your relationship with the FBI was...fraught, but that was then and this is now."

"'Fraught.' Yeah, I think that might be a bit of an understatement."

The waiter brought a mug of coffee for Ballard and black tea for Bosch.

"What's with the tea?" Ballard asked. "You were always a black-coffee guy."

"I don't know," Bosch said, shrugging. "People change."

She nodded and watched him over the rim of her cup as she sipped. He looked beat, and once again she felt guilty for enlisting him in whatever this was.

"You doing okay, Harry?"

"I'm fine."

"You look tired. Maybe we should—"

"I told you, I'm good. If I wasn't, I'd say so. So what's the plan here? We just hand this off to the guy and walk away from it?"

"We'll see how he wants to handle it. But he's got to promise me about the badge or it's a no-go and he gets nothing. You good with that?"

"I'm good with it. I just thought that if there's a way for you to get some credit for bagging this guy, that would help ... you know, secure your position inside the department."

Ballard shook her head. "You'd think, right?" she said. "But probably the exact opposite would happen. They'd ding me for going out of my lane."

Ballard had a view of the front door but knew there was a back way into the restaurant that would be on a direct walking route from the FBI's field office three blocks over on Wilshire Boulevard.

She flipped open the file folder on the table and looked at the photo of Thomas Dehaven she had pulled from Idaho DMV records. She closed the file when she looked up and saw Gordon Olmstead approaching the booth. She wasn't sure which way he had come in.

Before he sat down, Olmstead held out his right hand to Renée.

"Happy New Year," he said.

She shook his hand.

"Happy New Year to you, Gordon," she said. "This is Harry Bosch, who I told you about. Harry, Agent Gordon Olmstead with the Bureau."

The two men shook hands and Olmstead sat down across from them. He was a seasoned agent, a few years away from retirement.

He worked in the fugitives division after a long career of postings in almost all sections in the Los Angeles field office.

"I have to say, I'm very intrigued," Olmstead said. "We don't get many of the insurrectionists out this way."

That was how Ballard had baited him. She'd told him she could deliver a man wanted on a federal warrant for his activities during the attack on the U.S. Capitol in 2021.

Ballard now slid the folder across the table to him. It was bad timing. Just as Olmstead started to open it, the waiter came to the table to ask if he wanted coffee. Olmstead declined any drink and waited for the server to walk away before opening the file.

There were two printouts inside. The top was a photocopy of Thomas Dehaven's driver's license issued four years earlier in Idaho. He had been thirty-nine at the time and clean-shaven. But Bosch had confirmed the ID. Dehaven was the man who had met Bosch in the beach parking lot to talk about machine guns.

Olmstead studied it briefly and then went to the second sheet, which was a printout of the FBI's wanted poster for Dehaven. He was charged with murder, sedition, and assault on a law enforcement officer. The poster prominently featured the same photo from the Idaho driver's license plus two other shots of Dehaven inside the U.S. Capitol Building on January 6, 2021. One photo showed him posing at the speaker's podium in the chamber of the House of Representatives. The other shot was a candid taken at the Capitol's entrance that showed Dehaven in a highlighted circle spraying a chemical under the helmet shield of a Capitol Police officer.

"You're telling me this guy is here in L.A.?" Olmstead said.

"Yes," Ballard said.

"And you can lead me to him?"

"Yes."

Olmstead studied the summary of crimes on the wanted poster.

"You guys want him bad," Bosch said. "He killed his ex-wife because she called the FBI after seeing him on TV at the Capitol."

"Somehow he found out," Ballard said. "Killed her and has been in the wind ever since."

"And how did you come across him?" Olmstead asked.

"You probably wouldn't believe me if I told you," Ballard said.

"If I'm going to do anything with this, then I need to know," Olmstead said.

Ballard turned to Bosch to make sure he was still with her. He nodded without hesitation.

"I could and should give this to LAPD counterterrorism," she said. "So if I give it to you, I need two assurances."

"Let's hear them," Olmstead said.

"First, my name is nowhere near it," Ballard said. "You got this from a CI or a concerned citizen who saw the guy's picture in a post office or online or something."

"I can do that, but why?" Olmstead said.

"Because of condition number two," Ballard said. "Dehaven has my badge. You arrest him, you get it, and you give it back to me. It does not get mentioned in any report."

"Wait, what?" Olmstead said. "He's got your badge? How?"

"That's the story you wouldn't believe if I told you," Ballard said.

"Well, I think you'd better tell me anyway," Olmstead said.

"My badge was stolen Monday while I was surfing up near Dock-weiler Beach," Ballard said. "There's a surfing break called Staircases. While I was on the water, a couple of assholes broke into my car. I tracked them down but not before they got rid of the badge. They sold it to a fence, who then sold it to Dehaven."

"You didn't report it?" Olmstead asked. "It can't be that big a deal, can it?"

"For me it would be," Ballard said. "Suffice it to say there are people in the department who would use it against me. It would be my ticket to a transfer and freeway therapy. The bottom line is I love my job, Gordon, and I'm good at it. I want to keep it."

"Okay, I get it," Olmstead said. "And I know firsthand that you're good at your job. Where does Dehaven have your badge?"

"On him, we think," Ballard said.

"Why do you think that?" Olmstead asked.

Ballard glanced at Bosch. She wasn't going to reveal any of the lines she had crossed, no matter how much she trusted Olmstead.

"We just do," she said. "It will be on him or nearby. That's all you need to know."

Olmstead looked from Ballard to Bosch and then back to Ballard.

"Okay, we won't go there," he said. "But let me see if I've got this clear. I'm supposed to take this guy down, get the badge, and turn it over to you. That would be evidence I'm handing over."

"Not evidence of anything he's charged with," Ballard said. "But there is something else. Dehaven wanted the badge because he's planning something. He has guns and he's looking to buy more — machine guns."

"What is he planning?" Olmstead asked.

"We're not sure," Bosch said. "But we're four days out from Presidents' Day and he and one of his pals have been casing the Malibu pier. In their words, on Monday they're going to 'make that thing in Vegas look like child's play.'"

"You mean a mass shooting," Olmstead said.

Bosch and Ballard both nodded.

"Jesus Christ, you actually heard this said?" Olmstead asked.

They nodded again.

"And I'll be your confidential informant," Bosch said.

The skin around Olmstead's eyes tightened as the weight of everything they had told him landed.

"Okay, where is Thomas Dehaven right now?" Olmstead asked.

"You don't need to know that," Bosch said. "What you need to know is that he wants to buy machine guns from me. I set up the meet, and that's where you take him. Before Monday."

"Wait, no," Ballard said.

That had not been part of the plan she and Bosch discussed before she contacted Olmstead. The plan was to tell the agent about the caravan out on the coast highway.

"That's way too dangerous, Harry," she said. "We need to set up a controlled takedown where he—"

"You want your badge, right?" Bosch said. "He'll have it when he comes for the guns. He'll use it to rip me off. He'll pull it, say he's LAPD, and take the minis."

Ballard realized that Bosch might have solved the riddle of why Dehaven needed a badge. The moment he said it, she knew that it fit and that his plan was the best way to recover the badge and take down Dehaven.

"Harry, are you sure?" she asked.

"Yes, it's going to work," Bosch said.

"Okay, fine," Ballard said, looking hard at Olmstead. "But this has got to be somewhere out in the open, somewhere safe, where nothing goes wrong."

"We can do that," Olmstead said.

"Can you get us four SIG Sauer MPX mini machine guns with the firing pins removed?" Bosch asked.

Olmstead paused a moment on that question.

"Come on, you're the FBI," Bosch prompted.

"No promises," Olmstead said. "But we can try."

20

LILIA AGHZAFI, PAUL Masser, and Colleen Hatteras were in their places on the raft when Ballard arrived at the unit. Ballard felt compelled to explain her long absences during the week, though without revealing what she had actually been up to. She stood at the end of the raft and addressed the group.

"Hey, everybody," she began. "I just want to say that I have not been here a lot this week because I've been involved in a case that doesn't come out of this unit. I got pulled into it and it's about to wrap up and things should get back to normal."

"What's the case?" Hatteras asked. "Maybe we can help."

"It's a sensitive case, Colleen, so I can't really talk about it," Ballard said. "Basically, I got a tip from a CI who'd fed me intel before we started the unit. I had to run with it but now it's been handed off and I'm back here. And speaking of being here, we have a new team member who was supposed to come in today. Has anybody seen Maddie Bosch?"

"She's here," Masser said. "She's in the lockdown room looking at the old cases."

The lockdown room was what they called the interview room that had been converted to a storage room for murder books and evidence from sensitive cases. It was locked but everyone in the unit knew where Ballard hid the key — beneath the calendar on her desk.

"Who let her in there?" Ballard asked.

"She wanted to see the old cases," Hatteras said. "I thought it would be okay, so I gave her the key."

"That's fine," Ballard said. "Why don't you go get her, Colleen, and we'll go over the boards. I know it's not Monday but we won't be meeting Monday because of the holiday and I think it will be good for Maddie to see how we track cases."

Ballard knew that it was also a way for her to spend time with the unit, make everyone feel like it was business as usual, when her mind was elsewhere and business was anything but usual.

Hatteras went to get Maddie. Ballard turned her attention to Masser. "Paul, I don't suppose we've heard anything from Darcy or the DOJ?" she asked.

"Not yet," Masser said. "Hopefully tomorrow. It's like that old Tom Petty song."

"What song?"

"'The Waiting.' You know, the bit about it being the hardest part."

He sang the lyrics but Ballard shook her head like she didn't recognize it.

"Oh, come on," Masser said. "It was a huge hit."

He sang some more, then stopped when he realized Ballard was playing him.

"Ah, fuck you," he said.

Ballard and Aghzafi started laughing.

"You know they have an all-unit talent show every year in the auditorium at the PAB," Ballard said. "I think you'd have a shot at a trophy."

"Like I said, F you," Masser said.

His face was turning red and Ballard decided to lay off and change the subject.

"I was talking to this guy on the Maui fire task force," she said. "You know, about the fires and all the unidentified dead they have. He told me they have this mobile DNA lab that they take into the fields of ash that is all that's left of Lahaina. They put in what they can find of the human remains and they get DNA comparisons done in ninety minutes."

"Oh, wow," Masser said.

"And here we are, and it takes days or weeks to get anything done," Ballard said. "I'm going to apply for a grant to get one of those labs to use right here."

"That would be cool," Aghzafi said. "We'd really start kicking ass."

"Well, I think we already do kick ass," Masser said.

Ballard nodded as she realized that Masser probably wanted to ask her about why she was talking to an investigator in Maui. He was the only one in the unit she had confided in about her missing mother.

The awkward moment ended when Hatteras returned with Maddie.

"Hey, Maddie," Ballard said. "Welcome to the unit."

"Glad to be here," Maddie said. "Exciting."

"You see anything in the lockdown room you can solve?"

"Uh, not yet."

"Okay, well, did you pick a desk yet? We've got two openings on the raft."

"Uh, not yet. The raft?"

Ballard pointed to the interconnected desk modules. "That's what we call the setup here," she said. "All the desks joined together like a raft."

"Floating on a sea of cold cases," Masser said.

Ballard walked Maddie around to the side of the raft where there were two unused desks.

"Either one of these," she said. "Your dad used this one when he was here. You'd be across from Colleen, who is going to teach you the IGG work we do."

"Okay," Maddie said.

She looked down at the two chairs and hesitated. Ballard understood what that was about and pointed to the desk that Harry had not used.

"Why don't you start your own path?" she said.

Maddie nodded, and the decision was made. She stepped into the pod and pulled the chair back so she could sit down.

"The terminal is old but basically the same program you use at Hollywood Station," Ballard said. "Use the same password. In these first few weeks, coordinate with Colleen on when you'll both be in so she can start you with the IGG procedures. I think having two people with those skills, especially one with a badge, will be great."

"Good," Maddie said. "Um, I also wanted to ask you about something."

"Sure."

"Well, I was just in the lockdown room and I noticed that the Elizabeth Short case has its own file cabinet but it's locked."

Ballard smiled and nodded. It wasn't the first time a member of the unit had asked about the Black Dahlia case. The savage 1947 murder of Elizabeth Short was the most famous unsolved murder in the history of Los Angeles.

"Yeah, it's locked because those cabinets are almost empty," Ballard said. "Over the years a lot of the files have disappeared. Most of the evidence is gone too. I guess it doesn't matter. That one will never be solved."

"The evidence is gone how?" Maddie asked.

"Pilfered by cops who had access to the files. The original letters, witness statements — they're all gone. No physical evidence except the suitcase in there that was hers — she kept it in a locker at the bus station. But you can find most of the missing information on the internet. More there than what's in that file cabinet."

"Oh."

"If you still want to look, I'll give you the key. But be prepared for disappointment."

"I'll take a look anyway. I've always been fascinated by that case. My dad has too."

"Really? Harry never mentioned it."

"I think it sort of reminds him of his mother."

"Got it. I should have thought about that."

An awkward silence ensued as Maddie realized she had overshared about her father in front of the group. Ballard broke it.

"Well, we're going to start going over our active cases," she said. "I thought it might be good for you to see how we do it. Usually we do it on Mondays, but you're here for the first time and this coming Monday is a holiday, so I thought we'd do it now."

"Sounds good," Maddie said.

Ballard took her position in front of the whiteboards and started the review of the cases the team was working on. They brought Maddie up to date on the Pillowcase Rapist case, but after that there was not much new to report, largely because Ballard's pursuit of her stolen badge had hijacked most of the week. The one high point of the round-robin came from Masser.

"I just heard from John Lewin at the DA's office, and Maxine Russell's lawyer has reached out," Masser said. "She wants to deal."

"And she'll give up her ex on the convenience-store shooting?" Ballard asked.

"I assume so," Masser said. "There's no deal if she doesn't. They're meeting tomorrow morning."

"Good," Ballard said. "Let us know."

The rest of the review went quickly after that. "We're expecting results from the DOJ tomorrow on our DNA capture from Monday," Ballard said. "If it goes the way we expect it to, we're going to have to set up a surveillance on the judge while I go to the PAB and get the okay for an arrest. Who's coming in?"

All hands rose in response. Everybody wanted to be in on the kill, so to speak. Even Maddie Bosch raised a hand, although she would be working her patrol shift Friday night. Ballard appreciated the team's enthusiasm but told them that it was highly unlikely that they would be involved in the arrest.

"For something like this—big case and big suspect—they'll tell us to stand down, and SIS will come in, take over surveillance, and make the arrest," she said.

That got a round of boos. SIS was the Special Investigation Section, which handled major-case arrests.

"Don't worry, we'll still get the credit for it," Ballard said. "It's still our case."

She went on to thank the team for their dedication and hard work. As the meeting broke up, she invited Maddie to have a cup of coffee.

The cafeteria was largely empty except for a table full of men Ballard knew were academy instructors. Ballard got a coffee and Maddie got a bottle of sparkling water.

"Your dad is switching from coffee to tea," Ballard said.

"Really?" Maddie said. "You saw him recently?"

Ballard realized her mistake.

"Uh, yeah, I asked him for some help on a case," she said. "Advice. Did you tell him about joining the unit?"

"Not yet," Maddie said. "Now that it's official, I'll call him."

"Good. You should. But I sort of sense that there's something else going on with you. Something in play you haven't told me about. And so I just wanted to give you the chance to tell me now rather than later."

"Wow. I guess you can really read people."

"Comes with the territory. So what's going on, Maddie?"

"Well — you have to hear me out, because this is going to sound ... weird, I guess. And don't laugh, but I think I might have solved the Black Dahlia case."

Ballard had no urge to laugh at all. The fervency with which Maddie had said this told her that she was deadly serious.

"Tell me about it," Ballard said.

21

BALLARD WAS EARLY pulling into the parking lot of Echo Park Storage. She thought about her activities at the You-Store-It in Santa Monica. The coincidence of it was not lost on her. Unrelated but similar things seemed to be happening in twos.

She parked and left the car running while she made another call to the number Gordon Olmstead had told her was his direct line. As before, it went straight to voicemail.

"It's Renée," Ballard said. "Again. Just wondering what's happening. Give me a call."

She disconnected. She wondered if her tone sounded too pleading. There was a hollow feeling building in her chest as she second-guessed herself for bringing Olmstead and the FBI into the Thomas Dehaven investigation. She tried to push the feeling aside by calling Harry.

He answered right away.

"Just checking to see if you've heard anything from Olmstead."

"Yeah, he called a little while ago. He said they want to set up the gun buy for Saturday morning."

Ballard was immediately annoyed that Bosch was in the loop but she wasn't. At the same time, she understood that Bosch had to be in the loop since he would be the tethered goat they'd use as bait in taking down Dehaven.

"Are you good with that?" she asked.

"The sooner the better, as far as I'm concerned," Bosch said. "But they need the time to set it all up and pick their spots."

"Where is it going down?"

"They want the same place the first meeting was at, the parking lot at the beach. I told them Saturday morning, that lot will fill up fast. It's a beach day for people. But they like that because, you know, they can get their people in there in cars and whatnot."

"I get it. So have you texted the arrangements to Dehaven?"

"No, Olmstead and the Bureau people have sort of hijacked the texting. There's a way they can do it without my phone."

"Right. So when was the last time you talked to Olmstead or anybody with the Bureau?"

"Olmstead told me all of this a couple hours ago. He'll probably call you once they have it set up."

"Are they getting the plugged minis for you?"

"He said they'll have them. They want the deal to go down because it will be an added case against him. Dehaven will never breathe free air again."

"You'd think killing his ex would be enough for that, but I get it. They want more federal charges. They want to bury him in that supermax out in Colorado."

Ballard saw a car glide into the open space next to her. It was Maddie Bosch.

"Okay, well, it looks like Olmstead doesn't have me on the need-to-know list," Ballard said. "So let me know what you know."

"I will," Bosch said. "This is your case whether you want credit for it or not."

"Not anymore. But that's the way it goes. Talk to you later, Harry."

"Wait. I was going to call you. Did Maddie start with the unit today?"

"She did, yeah. It was good. I think she's going to fit right in."

"Okay. Good."

"She told me she was going to call you today to tell you."

"She hasn't yet, but good."

"Yeah. See ya, Harry."

"Bye."

Bosch clicked off and Ballard killed the engine. She put her phone in her pocket as she got out. Maddie was waiting behind her car, checking her phone.

"So," Ballard said. "*Storage Wars,* huh? I would have had you down as a Kardashians girl."

"What? Kardashians? *No.* And I don't think I've ever watched *Storage Wars* either."

Storage Wars was a reality-television show in which people bid at auction on storage units whose renters were more than three months delinquent in their payments. Under California law, the contents of these storage units could be discarded or put up for auction by the business owner. The show was basically a treasure hunt, with winning bidders hoping to find valuable contents in the storage units they bought.

Maddie had explained to Ballard that she had a unit at Echo Park Storage that she'd rented when she moved into her boyfriend's apartment and had to store the furniture and other belongings from her place. She wanted to keep her furniture in case the relationship didn't work out. One day while on her way to work, she had stopped by her unit to retrieve a lamp she wanted to bring to her new home. She was not in uniform but had her badge on her belt. The manager saw the badge and told her he was cleaning out a storage unit that was delinquent on payments and had found some disturbing things inside. He wanted Maddie to take a look. What Maddie found in the unit made her rent it on the spot and pay the manager five hundred dollars for its contents. Maddie had been going through those contents in her spare time. She decided to volunteer for the Open-Unsolved Unit after opening a file labeled *Betty*.

"Well," Ballard said. "Let's see what you've got."

The storage facility was an old brick warehouse that had somehow withstood the test of time and earthquakes. Ballard guessed that it had once been a manufacturing plant of some kind. She could see where windows had been removed and walled, creating a hodgepodge facade of cinder block, concrete, and brick.

"How old is this place?" Ballard asked.

"Built almost a hundred years ago," Maddie said. "I asked the guy who runs it — Mr. Waxman. He said they originally made parts here for the Ford plant that was down on Terminal Island. In the sixties they moved in all these old shipping containers, and it became a storage facility. Most of the containers have separating walls inside, so you get half a container. There are doors on both ends."

"The guy who rented the unit we're talking about — how long did he have it?"

"Since the sixties — he supposedly got it then and kept it."

"And what happened to him?"

"He died, like, seven years ago but the rent had always been paid through a trust fund. It was in his will to keep it going, and it paid for the year ahead every November first. But I guess the money ran out, and last November no payment came. After three months, Mr. Waxman went in to clean it out and I happened to come by that day."

Another coincidence, Ballard thought. They entered through a garage door that had been rolled open. Inside, the large space once used for manufacturing was filled with freestanding rows of shipping containers with an office at the front of one of the rows. Lights hung from the rafters above, but there was not enough illumination to keep back the shadows. The place felt eerie to Ballard. Ominous.

"It's back here," Maddie said. As they passed the office, Maddie waved through a window to a man sitting behind a desk.

"Is that the guy who told you about it?" Ballard asked.

"Yeah, Mr. Waxman," Maddie said.

"He's not the owner?"

"No, he's just the manager. The owner is an old lady who lives up by the Greek. He told me she might remember the guy who rented it."

"Aren't you creeped out by this place?"

"Definitely. But it's close by and cheap. I don't spend much time here—I mean, I didn't before this thing came up."

"Tell me about the guy who rented the unit."

"Emmitt Thawyer. I ran him through our databases and got nothing."

"Sawyer?"

"No, it's like *Sawyer* but with a *T-h.* Not a lot of Thawyers out there. I googled him but couldn't find anything. Mr. Waxman says Mrs. Porter—she's the owner—ran the place before she hired him and probably met Emmitt Thawyer. Back in the day, he was some kind of photographer."

The individual storage units had not been updated in years. Rather than roll-up metal doors like they had at the You-Store-It in Santa Monica, these units had the original shipping container double doors secured with locking bars and padlocks. Maddie stopped in front of a door marked 17 and pulled a key ring off her belt.

"This is it," she said.

Maddie removed a thick padlock, pulled the locking bar up, and swung open the heavy metal doors. The container was pitch-black inside. Maddie reached in and flipped a switch, and a line of caged bulbs down the center of the ceiling lit the space. Ballard was expecting a hoarder's pile of junk and debris, but the container was neatly ordered with a row of metal file cabinets on one side and old photography equipment on the other. There were light stands and wooden-legged tripods. At the back of the space was a worktable on which stood pans, beakers, and other film-developing equipment.

"At first I thought it was like a meth lab or something," Maddie said. "But it's a photo lab. And these file cabinets are full of negatives and photos, contracts for jobs, and invoices. It looks like he did a lot of work for catalogs, shooting products and things like that. It's all legit work except for what's in the last cabinet. That was the one Mr. Waxman opened."

"Let's see."

"It's pretty bad."

Maddie reached down to the bottom drawer of a file cabinet but Ballard stopped her.

"Wait," she said. "Did you wear gloves when you went through this place before?"

"Uh, no," Maddie said. "Sorry."

"That's okay. You didn't know what you'd find. Here." Ballard reached into her pocket for latex gloves. "I only have one pair," she said. "Let's each put a glove on."

They did, and then Maddie opened the file drawer. It made a sharp screech, which somehow seemed appropriate to Ballard.

The drawer was filled with hanging files with the names of women on the tabs. They were alphabetized and the first one said *Betty*. Maddie pulled it out with a gloved hand and gave it to Ballard, who opened it on the worktable.

The file contained eight black-and-white photos, several showing the body of a woman who had been horribly tortured and killed. In an instant Ballard recognized Elizabeth Short, the Black Dahlia.

"Oh my God," she said under her breath.

"Yeah," Maddie said.

22

"IS IT HER?" Maddie asked.

"Sure looks like it," Ballard said.

She stacked two film-development pans to make room to spread out the eight photos on the worktable. Their white borders were yellowed despite having been in a file cabinet for decades. They depicted various stages of the defilement, torture, and murder of a young woman. They had not been in chronological order but Ballard was able to put them in order on the table by the appearance of injuries and wounds. The first photo showed the woman before she realized what was about to befall her. She was sitting on a stool, a come-hither smile on her lips, wearing just a bra and panties. The next shot was a close-up of her face, both cheeks slashed from the corners of her mouth, her eyes wild with fear and pain.

It got worse from there. The seventh photo showed her full body lying bloody on a concrete floor next to a drain. She was clearly dead. The injuries to the body matched the autopsy photo long ago stolen from the Black Dahlia files and posted on the internet, an image Ballard had seen online and that was seared into her memory. In the last photo, the body on the concrete had been cleanly severed across the abdomen, blood flowing into the drain.

Nausea hit Ballard, and she put both hands on the worktable and leaned down.

"Are you all right?" Maddie asked.

Ballard didn't answer. She closed her eyes and waited for the feeling to pass.

She finally found her voice. "You see things on this job and can't understand how they could happen," she said.

She straightened up and looked at Maddie.

"Are the other files in there . . ." she began.

"Yes," Maddie said. "Not as bad, but bad."

"How many?"

"Seven."

"Who the hell was this guy?"

"A monster."

Ballard shook off the fog of horror and put her game face on. "All right, we need to pull those files and take them back to the raft," she said. "We seal this place for now."

"Okay," Maddie said.

"Let's go talk to Mr. Waxman."

Maddie gathered the other file folders from the cabinet. They stepped out of the container, and Maddie handed Ballard the files while she locked the door. Ballard reluctantly leafed through them, seeing photos of the other women in life and death, all of them having met agonizing ends. Ballard was still grappling with the idea that the most famous and hideous killing in Los Angeles history was not a one-time-only crime. The Black Dahlia was just one flower in a black bouquet of murder.

They walked silently to the office, where the man Ballard had seen before was sitting behind a desk stacked with paperwork.

"Mr. Waxman, this is Detective Ballard," Maddie said.

He nodded at the files Ballard held. "Are they real?" Waxman asked.

"You mean the photos?" Maddie asked.

"We're not sure yet," Ballard said quickly. "We'll have them ana-lyzed. But we would like to see any records you have on the person who rented that storage unit."

"Emmitt Thawyer was his name," Waxman said. "But he's dead."

"You must have a file with contact information, billing, things like that," Ballard said.

"Yes, but he didn't pay," Waxman said. "He had a trust fund that paid. I hope it's Hollywood stuff, you know. Fake stuff from the movies."

Ballard realized he might not have recognized the woman in the first file as Elizabeth Short, the Black Dahlia.

"Possibly," she said. "Hopefully. But you must have records of the payments from the trust fund. Can we see those?"

"Okay. I have to go back to storage to get it," Waxman said.

"We can wait," Ballard said.

Waxman stood up and left the office.

"Who did you say owned this place?" Ballard asked.

"Nancy Porter," Maddie said.

"We'll need an address for her too."

"I already have it."

"From Waxman?"

"Yes, I thought I — we — might need it, so I got it from him after he showed me the storage unit."

"That was smart. Maybe we'll go see her after this. If you have time."

"I'm in. This is so much more interesting than patrol."

For a moment Ballard considered warning her about vicarious trauma but decided not to get into it now.

Waxman came back a few minutes later with a file; he handed it to Ballard and went back behind his desk. The file contained several documents, starting with a yellowed information sheet apparently filled out by Emmitt Thawyer and dated November 1, 1966. It listed a home address on Kellam Avenue.

"Kellam Avenue," Maddie said. "That's in Angeleno Heights. I remember when I was a kid, my dad and I used to drive around in there and look at the old houses. I love that neighborhood."

"Well, it looks like a serial killer might have lived there," Ballard said.

"He was probably there when we drove by his house."

"Maybe."

The information sheet also included Thawyer's driver's license number and a birth date of January 7, 1924.

"He just had a birthday last month," Ballard said. "He'd be a hundred years old."

Ballard did the math and determined that Thawyer would have been twenty-three when Elizabeth Short was abducted and murdered. It was a little young for a serial killer, but maybe she was his first victim.

"You think he did that on purpose?" Maddie said. "Put enough money in his trust fund to pay for storage till he was a hundred?"

"Who knows," Ballard said. "But I like the way you're thinking."

Ballard didn't know if telling Maddie she reminded her of her father would be taken as a compliment or not. She kept it to herself and went back to the documents in hand.

The rest of the pages in the file were annual invoices stamped PAID with a handwritten date of payment. All the dates were in late October or the first day of November, corresponding with when Thawyer first rented the storage unit.

"Mr. Waxman, we're going to need to keep this file for a while," Ballard said.

"It's yours," Waxman said. "I'm done with it."

"Do you speak to Mrs. Porter often?"

"No, we don't need to speak. I run the business for her and she's happy being hands-off."

"How old is she?"

"I don't know. Very old. She inherited this business from her father. He did what I do—ran the business. She did too, but then she got tired and turned to me."

"Did you tell her about this—what you saw in the unit?"

"I told her, yes."

"Did she remember Mr. Thawyer?"

"She wasn't sure. She said the name was familiar but she couldn't remember the man."

"How about you, Mr. Waxman. Do you remember him?"

"I don't believe we ever met."

"Did you tell anyone else about what you saw in that storage container?"

"Only Mrs. Porter."

"Please tell no one else, Mr. Waxman."

"Believe me, it's not a story I would enjoy sharing. I saw the photos. I'll never forget them. Horrible."

Outside, as they walked to their cars, Ballard carried the files. Her phone buzzed. It was Olmstead finally calling back.

"I need to take this in private," she said to Maddie. "Let's go to Kellam first. I'll meet you in front of the house where Thawyer lived."

"See you there," Maddie said.

Ballard took the call as she slipped behind the wheel of the Defender and put the files on the seat next to her.

"Gordon, where you been?"

"Sorry I haven't been able to call back till now. Have you talked to Bosch?"

Ballard knew she would get more information if she acted like she had none. "No, what's going on?" she said.

"We're set for Saturday," Olmstead said.

"Where?"

"Same place Bosch met the guy before."

"You'll have it squared away?"

"Totally. We already have a tactical team on Dehaven. We'll be watching every move he makes till the exchange."

"What about Harry?"

"What about him?"

"I'm worried that he's not an agent."

"What's that mean?"

"He can't get hurt, Gordon. He's not expendable."

"I should be offended you'd say that, but I'll let it go. I know he's not expendable, Renée. But we've got it covered. He'll be fine."

"You're not making him wear a wire, right?" It was the most dangerous part of undercover work. Things could easily go wrong with a wire.

"Not a body wire. We'll rig his car. He'll have the guns in the back, and that's where the bug will be. If he senses danger, he's got a go word. But he'll be fine."

"I told you they're not planning to pay for the guns."

"We know that. But this will be in a busy parking lot. They won't want to make a scene."

"How can you be sure? I don't like this, Gordon. You have Dehaven on murder and sedition. You don't need more charges."

"Look, Renée, it's not about the charges on him. He's not in this alone if he needs four machine guns. We let him take the guns back to the group, then we get the group. You know how it works. The weapons are like ant bait. He takes it back and poisons the nest. We grab him and all the others involved."

Ballard knew the strategy and knew it was right, but too many things could go wrong.

"I still don't like it," she said.

"Well, Bosch does," Olmstead said. "He's agreed and he's ready to go. He wanted to go tomorrow, in fact, but we need another day for the setup. We're going to have cameras hidden all over that lot. We'll have snipers on the roof of the condo across from it. Bosch says the word and they'll drop Dehaven in his tracks."

"Where will you be?"

"We'll have a command post up on Ocean. A van. It looks like an Amazon delivery van."

"I'll be there too."

"Renée, you can't do that."

"I'm there or I'm parking in the lot where I can put eyes on Bosch. Your choice."

"You want this to go down, right? You want your badge back?"

"Fuck my badge. I don't want Bosch to get hurt and I don't think you guys really care about him."

"And, what, you being in the command post is going to keep him safe? Your logic doesn't add — "

"I'll be able to make sure you guys don't screw up."

There was a long silence, and when Olmstead's voice came back, it was angry but tight and controlled.

"Fine," he said. "We'll make room in the CP for you."

"Thank you, Gordon," Ballard said. "What time?"

"We set the meet for oh-eight-hundred. Before the parking lot gets too crowded with civilians but still busy enough to get our cars and people in there. We'll be on-site at six."

"Then so will I. Have you picked up Lionel Boden?"

Olmstead had said that Boden had to be taken out of circulation to ensure he didn't reach out to Dehaven and warn him. After using Boden's phone to set up the initial meeting between Dehaven and Bosch, Ballard had deleted the contact from the device and allowed Boden to return to the Eldorado. She knew it would be bad for business and his personal safety for him to warn Dehaven, since it was Boden who had snitched him off. But Olmstead had said that wasn't good enough for operational integrity. Boden had to be kept under wraps.

"Yes, we quietly picked him up and moved him to our luxurious accommodations downtown," Olmstead said. "We'll keep him till this goes down. And probably then some."

"Good," Ballard said. "What else?"

"You covered it all. But one other thing."

"What?"

"Thank you for dropping this in my lap. After we take these guys down, are you sure you don't want to be there when we hold the press conference? We're happy to share the credit."

"I appreciate that, Gordon, but no, thanks. I'll just see you Saturday at six."

"You got it."

Ballard disconnected and started the engine.

23

FROM THE WAREHOUSE, Ballard took Sunset Boulevard over to Angeleno Heights. The two neighborhoods were five minutes apart by car and a century apart in design. Atop a steep hill at the edge of downtown, Angeleno Heights was the oldest unchanged neighborhood in Los Angeles. Only Bunker Hill was older, but that was all glass and concrete now, the future having plowed the past under.

Angeleno Heights was the same as it ever was. The neighborhood had long been designated a historic preservation zone by the city, so the place was frozen in time, its streets lined with pristine examples of the evolving architectures of early Los Angeles. Queen Anne and Victorian homes 150 years old stood side by side with turn-of-the-twentieth-century Craftsman and bungalow masterpieces. Ballard was counting on nothing having changed because of the strict rules regarding any modifications to homes in the neighborhood. She pulled in behind Maddie Bosch's car in front of the house at the Kellam Avenue address Emmitt Thawyer had given, a one-story Craftsman with a driveway running down the left side to a garage in the back.

Maddie was leaning against her car, checking messages on her phone. She put the phone away when Ballard got out.

"You've already done some good detective work," Ballard said. "Let's keep it going. You do the door knock, show your badge, see if you can talk our way in."

"Really?" Maddie said. "But you're the real detective."

"I'll back you up. If needed."

"So, we're looking for information on the man who used to live here, but we're not sure when he moved."

"That's a start. We want to get in, look around, see if anybody knew or remembers Thawyer. And I want to get into the garage in the back."

"The garage? Why?"

"To see if there's a drain."

"Oh. Got it."

As they went up the steps to the wide porch that ran the length of the front of the house, Ballard pulled her phone and opened the Zillow app. She had used the real estate database when looking for her place in Malibu. She plugged in the address of the Kellam Avenue house and scrolled down to the sales history. It showed that the house had not changed hands since 1996. The app did not provide the identity of current or previous owners.

Maddie knocked forcefully on the front door's glass.

"The owner's had it since '96," Ballard said, showing Maddie her phone.

"Got it," Maddie said.

Through the glass they could see a woman slowly approaching. Maddie held up her badge. The woman cautiously opened the door. She was at least eighty, with gray hair, and she was wearing a baggy housedress.

"Yes?" she said.

"Hello, ma'am, we're investigators with the LAPD," Maddie said. "Can we ask you a few questions?"

"Did something happen?"

"Uh, no. We're investigating an old case, a crime that may have happened in this neighborhood. Have you lived here very long?"

"Almost thirty years."

"That's a long time. Did you buy this house?"

"My husband did. He's dead now."

"I'm sorry to hear that. Do you happen —"

"It was a long time ago."

"I see. Uh, do you happen to know who the previous owner was?"

"Uh... I used to but I can't remember. It's been too long."

"Does the name Emmitt Thawyer sound familiar?"

"Yes, that's it. I remember because we got his mail for a long time after that. My husband used to take it to him."

"Where was that?"

"The retirement home."

"Do you remember which one?"

"I don't know if I ever knew. I remember he'd go over to Boyle Heights to deliver the mail."

"Can I get your name, ma'am?"

"Sally Barnes. My husband was Bruce."

Ballard recognized the name and thought Sally Barnes might have been a midlevel actress at one time. She also thought that Maddie was doing well, but they weren't inside yet. It was doubtful anything would be gained by that, but Ballard wanted to get a sense of the place and maybe learn some information about its previous occupant.

"Do you know if Mr. Thawyer had a family when he lived here?" Maddie asked.

"No, he lived alone," Sally said. "He was a photographer and he traveled for work. It wasn't good for a family."

"Did your husband ever say anything about him after he dropped off the mail?"

"He just said Mr. Thawyer was grateful but said that we didn't need to do it. He said we could throw his mail away. Eventually, we did. I need to get to my chair. Standing isn't good for me. I fall."

"Well, let me help you to your chair."

"You don't have to. I'll be fine. I could move into the motion picture home in the Valley but it's too hot up there. I won't go there till I have to."

"If it's all right with you, can we come in? Our captain tells us that whenever we do a home visit, we should offer to do a security check of the house."

"Well...sure, okay. Can't be too careful these days with all the follow-home robberies you see on the news."

"Exactly."

Sally stepped back and they entered the house. To the right was a living room with a large stone fireplace, to the left a dining room. Bosch put her hand on the old lady's elbow and led her to a chair in the living room.

"Okay, we'll take a look around now," Bosch said.

Ballard and Bosch split up and checked the windows and locks in each of the front rooms as Sally Barnes sat watching.

"What kind of crime was it?" she asked.

"A homicide," Ballard said.

"Here, in this house?" Sally asked.

"We're not sure, but probably not."

"Emmitt Thawyer's dead — if he's your man."

"Yes, we know. How did you know?"

"I think it was Mr. Mann from the historical society who told me. But that was many years ago."

"You don't seem shocked or surprised that Thawyer might be our suspect. Why?"

"Oh, the neighbors. When we first moved in, they told us they were happy to have a regular couple here. They said Mr. Thawyer was a strange man with his cameras and lights. He kept odd hours, sometimes worked all night. They'd see the flashes from the camera, you see."

"From inside the house?"

"Well, of course. I'm going to move back to the kitchen, where I have my work."

"Do you need help?"

"No, I'm fine."

"Okay, and we'll finish our security survey. We won't take long."

Ballard and Bosch quickly moved through the house, checking doors and windows, finally ending up in the kitchen, where Sally Barnes sat at a table with a spread of eight-by-ten glossy black-and-white photos. She was signing them with a felt-tip pen. Ballard stepped over and recognized a much younger Sally Barnes in the photos. They were old publicity shots.

"I thought I recognized you," she said. "Were you in the movies?"

"Television," Barnes said. "I was on *Police Woman* in a recurring role. I did *Baretta, Rockford Files, Barnaby Jones, McMillan & Wife,* all of them."

"*Police Woman* — that's where I recognized you from. I went back and watched that whole series recently. Angie Dickinson kicked butt."

"In more ways than one. I played a prostitute and I was her snitch. I got killed by my pimp when Angie thought I was getting too much fan mail. Written out."

"Wow, that wasn't fair."

"Hollywood was never meant to be fair. Bruce wrote for TV, and when we got married, I retired. I became like that joke about the blonde who married the writer. But Bruce did well in TV and took good care of us. He bought this place with his residuals. We raised two sons here."

Ballard nodded and gestured toward the photos on the table. "Well, people obviously remember you."

"They do. And I thank them for it. I only charge for postage and handling."

"Those neighbors who said Emmitt Thawyer was strange—are any of them still around?"

"No, they all died or moved away."

Ballard nodded again and Maddie joined them in the kitchen. She shook her head, telling Ballard that she had noticed nothing of import. Ballard looked back at Sally.

"Well, Mrs. Barnes, your house is pretty solid," Ballard said. "You've done a good job of keeping it secure. All right if we check your garage? Then we'll get out of your hair."

"Go ahead," Sally said. "I don't keep a car anymore. My eyes are bad."

"Is there an automatic opener?" Maddie asked.

"There's a button by the back door," Sally said.

Ballard and Maddie found the button by the door and pressed it. They went out and crossed a small sunburned lawn as the double-wide garage door creaked open. The space was mostly bare. No car, no workbench. Just cardboard boxes marked CHRISTMAS stacked in the middle of one of the bays.

Ballard scanned the concrete floor but saw no drain. She went over to the boxes and shoved the stack aside to see if they were covering one; they weren't.

"Damn," Ballard said. "And this was looking so good too."

"Well, maybe he had an office or a lab somewhere," Maddie suggested.

"With a concrete floor and an iron-grated drain? I doubt it."

"Well, shit."

"Yeah. Go back in and tell the old lady thanks. Remind her to keep her doors locked. I'll meet you on the street."

"Okay."

They split up; Maddie went to the back door while Ballard

walked down the driveway toward the street. She pulled her phone to check for messages. There were none. As she put the phone away she noticed the three trash cans lined up between the house and the driveway. Behind them she saw a casement window. Her first thought was that a flash from there could have been seen by the neighbors next door.

Ballard turned and trotted around the corner to the back of the house. The door was already locked but she saw Maddie in the kitchen talking to Mrs. Barnes. She knocked rapidly on the glass. Maddie opened the door.

"There's a basement," Ballard said. "Mrs. Barnes, where are the stairs to the basement?"

Sally looked up from her autographing.

"Right behind you," she said.

Ballard and Maddie turned. The wall behind them was composed of floor-to-ceiling cabinets. Ballard reached out and pulled on the handle of one of the cabinet doors. It was a false front. The whole assembly opened, top to bottom, revealing a doorway and a set of stairs going down into murky darkness.

24

BALLARD REACHED THROUGH the doorway and swept her hand up and down to find a light.

"I forgot to mention the basement," Sally said. "The light is on the left."

Ballard switched sides and found the light, and the stairs down were illuminated.

"Did you and your husband put in this cabinet?" Maddie asked.

"Oh, no, it came that way with the house," Sally said. "Mr. Thawyer built that, and Bruce thought it was pretty unique, so we kept it. Not many houses in Los Angeles have basements, you know."

"Almost none," Ballard said.

"I can't do the stairs anymore," Sally said. "Watch for spiderwebs down there."

"We will," Maddie said.

Ballard locked eyes with Maddie, and they shared a look of excitement and dread. Then Ballard started down the steps with Maddie right behind her.

Some of the lights attached to the rafters were dead. Gray light came in at angles from four casement windows, two on the driveway side, two on the opposite side. There were pull-down shades that were rolled up. The basement was wide open, no partitions or storage rooms. Four thick oak pillars supported the main crossbeams of the house.

The floor was concrete, poured and smoothed at a barely discernible down angle toward an iron-grated drain in the middle.

"Maddie, go back to my car and get those files," Ballard said. "Here." She handed over her key fob. Maddie turned and headed up the steps without a word.

"Also, in the back of my car, there's a crime scene kit that has a pump bottle with luminol in it. Says it on the label. Bring that too."

"You got it," Maddie said.

Left alone, Ballard crouched next to the drain. She believed that horrible things had happened here. It was a long time ago but there were ghosts here, waiting for someone — waiting for her — to set them free.

She felt a solemn duty to them. As with the library of lost souls in the archives at Ahmanson, she carried the burden.

Maddie was soon back with the files and luminol. Ballard opened the file marked *Betty* and held the photos up under a bulb to compare them to the room they were in. The drain grate was a match. The rough surface of the concrete and the sweep patterns left by a trowel were a match.

"No doubt," Maddie said. "Those were shot down here."

"Can you go up the steps and turn off the lights?" Ballard asked. "And be careful coming back down in the dark."

While Maddie went up the stairs, Ballard went to one of the casement windows and pulled the string knot on a long-furled shade. The string broke; the shade unrolled and fell over the glass as a cloud of dust descended on Ballard. She waved her hand and coughed. Then she went to the next shade as the overhead lights went off.

After all the shades were down, Ballard took the spray bottle of luminol from Maddie and tried to use her nails to break through the plastic seal.

"Will it work after so many years?" Maddie asked.

"I don't know," Ballard said. "I had a case once where it showed blood on concrete twenty-three years after the murder. The tech who did the test said the older the blood, the more intense the reaction. But I don't think he was talking about a seventy-seven-year-old case."

She started peeling the plastic collar from the bottle. "The problem is the cleanup," she said.

"The cleanup?" Maddie said.

Ballard dropped to a crouch again.

"The luminol reacts with phosphors in blood — the iron in hemoglobin. But bleach contains some chemicals that will light up as well. If Elizabeth Short was cut in half on this floor, there would have been a lot of blood, and that would mean a lot of cleanup, most likely with bleach."

Ballard started working the pump, sending a fine mist of the chemical over the concrete around the floor drain.

"Don't we need an ultraviolet light?" Maddie asked.

"Only on TV," Ballard said.

She stopped spraying and waited, eyes down on the concrete. A bluish-white glow began to spread across the floor. She heard Maddie's breath catch. She started working the pump again.

The glow around the drain was too spread out and too uniform to be from a blood trail.

"He mopped with bleach," Ballard said.

"Wait, look how intense it's getting," Maddie said. "You're saying that was from mopping with bleach?"

"Exactly. Probably."

"Well, shit."

"It doesn't help us, but it also doesn't hurt us. Luminol is just a presumptive test. In and of itself, signs that someone mopped up blood from the concrete floor in a basement are just as suspicious as blood spatter. But wait. Sometimes it takes a while."

Ballard waved her arm in a straight line, putting down another layer of luminol mist, then started to lock down the pump.

"What about this side of the drain?" Maddie pointed to an area Ballard had not sprayed.

"I don't want to cover the floor in case we come back for DNA," Ballard said.

"There's DNA from the Black Dahlia available?" Maddie asked.

"Not in evidence. But you never know. If it becomes important, we could conceivably exhume her body to get it. She's buried up in Oakland."

"How do you know that? I mean, where she's buried."

"Because it was one of the first cases I reviewed when I started the unit. Like you, I guess, I was fascinated by the case and I had to see why it had never been solved. Since there was no DNA in evidence in 1947—DNA hadn't even been discovered yet—I researched where Elizabeth Short was buried. Mountain View Cemetery. People still put flowers on her grave."

"You went there?"

"Yeah. I had to go up that way for a meeting at the DOJ in Sacramento. I flew into Oakland and checked it out before driving up."

The chemical reaction on the concrete continued, and a deeper shade of blue manifested on the floor. It was a long, thin shape that looked like a meandering stream on a map.

"Turn on your phone light," Ballard said. She opened the Betty file. The final picture of the body was on top of the stack. Maddie put the light on it, and Ballard compared the flow of blood to the drain in the photo to the meandering stream of deep blue on the floor. It was almost an exact match.

"It's the same," Maddie said excitedly.

"It's close," Ballard said. "Give me the other files and go hit the lights."

Ballard waited as Maddie trudged up the steps again and flicked on the lights. She then flipped through the files to the one marked *Cecily*. As with the photo chronology in the Betty file, the Cecily file contained eight glossy eight-by-tens that ranged from a shot of a fully clothed woman they assumed was Cecily to a pair of tasteful, unrevealing nudes to photos of the woman's degradation, torture, and death. In the final photo, the victim was sitting on a concrete floor, her back to a square wooden post. Like the Dahlia's, her cheeks were slashed open from the corners of her mouth. It was the commonality in the photos of all the victims: the horrible clown smile cut into the skin.

Cecily's arms were tied behind the post, and a length of rope with a slipknot was around her neck and the post. Cecily had been slowly strangled by the makeshift garrote.

Maddie came down the stairs and rejoined Renée.

"Look at this," Ballard said.

She ran her finger up the wooden post in the photo. "It's been painted but you can still see the grain pattern," she said. "There's a knot in the wood."

"I see it," Maddie said. "We can find it."

They separated, and each went to one of the four posts supporting the house's primary crossbeams. Using their phone lights, they studied the graining of the wood at about the three-foot mark, moving around the post to check all four sides.

"Here we go," Maddie said.

Ballard walked over and confirmed by comparison to the photo that this was the spot where Cecily had been murdered.

"This place," Maddie said. "He killed them all here."

"Maybe," Ballard said. "Let's go through the rest of the files."

It took a half hour to do the comparison of photos from the other files—Elyse, Sandy, Debra, Willa, Siobhan, and Lorraine—to physical markers in the basement.

They were on the Lorraine file when Mrs. Barnes called from the top of the stairs, "Are you two all right?"

"We're fine, Mrs. Barnes," Ballard said. "We're just about finished. Thank you for your patience."

"I don't know what you could be doing down there," Mrs. Barnes responded.

"When we come up, we'll explain everything," Ballard said.

In the death photos, Lorraine's body was propped against a concrete-block wall. Her throat had been cut, and the killer had used her blood to paint the letters *BDA* across her abdomen. Working together, Ballard and Maddie were able to match inconsistencies in the concrete blocks and grouting in the photo to a spot below one of the casement windows.

"That's all eight," Ballard said.

Her tone was somber; she no longer sounded excited by what the discoveries in the basement meant. It was a grim discovery from grim work. Ballard wanted to get out of the house and into the sunshine. She wanted to be on her board in the water, waiting for the next set.

"*BDA*," Maddie said. "What do you think it means?"

"Black Dahlia Avenger," Ballard said. "That's what he called himself in one of the letters he sent to the newspapers back in the day. It's actually a key piece of the picture he gave us."

"How so?"

"It means that Lorraine, at least, came after Betty. I would have pegged the Black Dahlia as last because of the heightened brutality and figured the other deaths were steps toward that kind of hatred, mutilation—all of it. But his putting *BDA* on Lorraine says otherwise. Maybe Elizabeth Short was the first and the others followed, with him controlling his rage better."

"Elizabeth Short got so much attention," Maddie said. "Maybe he refined his kill patterns because he was afraid of getting caught."

Ballard nodded, impressed by Maddie's thinking.

"So, do we call in FSD?" Maddie asked.

Ballard knew that the techs from the Forensic Science Division would be able to process the basement and come up with confirmations of what the luminol and photos indicated, but she was reluctant to go wide with the investigation.

"Not yet. There's still work to do. We'll bring them here when we know more."

"Then what do we do?"

"We find out more about Emmitt Thawyer. We take the Betty file to somebody who can verify it's Elizabeth Short. And we try to put full names to the other women in the files."

"What about Nancy Porter?"

"Yes. Let's go see her."

FRIDAY, 9:21 A.M.

25

BALLARD WAS TWENTY-ONE minutes late to the all-hands meeting that she had called for the night before. Everybody else was already there.

"Sorry I'm late, everyone," she said as she put her bag down on her desk and stayed standing. "I had to go to the lab this morning, and everybody knows what a shitshow the traffic is from there to here. Thank you all for getting here. This could be a big day. We have two things in play. Most of you know about one of them, so let's start there. Paul, anything on the DNA from the judge yet? Is he Nick Purcell's biological father?"

Masser cleared his throat. "I talked to Darcy a few minutes ago and she's still waiting on Sacramento," he said.

There was a groan from Laffont.

"DOJ, man," he said. "Taking their sweet-ass time. 'Delay of Justice' is what they should be called."

"Darcy said she would call up there if she didn't hear anything by ten," Masser said.

"Guys, it's only been three days," Ballard said. "If it carries over to Monday, we'll be fine."

"Monday's a holiday," Hatteras said.

"Then Tuesday," Ballard said. "So, until we hear from Darcy, we move on. We have another case I need you all on. But before we discuss it, I want to stress that what we talk about here does not leave this room. Not until we have this thing tied up in a bow. You don't even tell your wife or your husband what you're working on. Everybody get that?"

Ballard swept the room with her eyes, making sure she saw a nod of agreement from everyone on the squad.

"Maddie Bosch brought this case to us," she said. "So I'm going to let her brief you."

Maddie stood up and started at the beginning, with Mr. Waxman calling her into the storage unit that had belonged to Emmitt Thawyer. The others paid rapt attention to the story. There was no one in L.A. law enforcement who didn't know about the Black Dahlia. Even among the public, there were very few citizens who had not heard of the woman who had been cut in two and found in an empty lot in Leimert Park.

Maddie finished by summarizing their findings in the basement of the house on Kellam Avenue. She then handed the briefing back to Ballard.

"We also attempted to talk to Nancy Porter, the owner of the storage facility," Ballard said. "But no one was at her home when we checked last night. We'll follow up with her when we can."

She opened her bag on her desk and started removing the files taken from the Thawyer storage unit.

"Can we see these photos you found of the Black Dahlia?" Laffont asked.

"You can, but not at the moment," Ballard said. "I gave most of them to the digital analysis team this morning so they can confirm my visual identification of the victim as Elizabeth Short. I also gave a couple of pictures to the photo lab to see if they can determine the age of the Kodak paper they were printed on. Over the years there have been hoaxes related to the Black Dahlia—false confessions and peo-ple claiming their father, son, brother, stepbrother, even their mother was the killer. We don't go out with this until we nail down every aspect of it, and then Carol Plovc makes the final call."

Plovc was a deputy district attorney. Although John Lewin was the unit's assigned DA, he handled live cases—cases where there were suspects who could still be prosecuted, whether they were already incarcerated or not. Plovc handled dead cases. She had the final sign-off on closing and clearing cases in which the alleged cul-prit was beyond prosecution because he or she was deceased. It was LAPD policy not to close a case without the approval of the district attorney's office.

"As soon as I get the photos back, I will share," Ballard said. "But I warn you, they are graphic and horrible. They will stay with you."

"If real," Laffont said.

"If real," Ballard agreed. "So, meantime, I've got the files with the photos of the other women here. I want everyone to take a file—a victim—and work it. You start with a first name and a photo, because that's all we've got. Try to find out who she was, when she went miss-ing, and if a body was ever found."

"You're talking about going back seventy-plus years?" Laffont said.

"That's right, and there won't be any records to go to unless they're right here in our homicide archives," Ballard said. "I checked with records this morn—"

"Um, there aren't any in our archives," Maddie interrupted.

"How do you know?" Ballard asked.

"I came in early and went through all the pre-1960 books," Mad-die said. "I checked all female victims against our list of first names. There was only one match, a victim named Elyse, but she was Black and our photo is of a white victim. So, no, nothing in archives."

"Good initiative," Ballard said. "That supports the theory that these women came after Elizabeth Short. He changed his MO. Rather than leave the victims on display, he hid them."

"To avoid media and police attention," Masser said.

"They're probably buried in that basement," Laffont said. "Like Gacy did in Chicago."

"When we bring the crime scene techs into this, I'm sure they'll look at that," Ballard said. "But as I was about to say, our missing persons files don't go back this far. What's that leave us?"

"Newspaper archives," Hatteras said.

"Definitely," Ballard said. "That's a starting point. What else?"

"There are many sites online that track missing women," Persson said. "The question will be how far they go back."

"Right," Ballard said. "I remember seeing something in the *Times* about a privately funded site that tracked missing people in L.A. I forget the name."

"Lost Angels," Aghzafi said. "I used them on a case in Vegas. Unidentified DB we thought might be a guy from L.A. They were quite helpful but we never matched him up."

"Any idea how far back they went with missing persons?" Laffont asked.

"I don't remember," Aghzafi said. "It was funded by some tech billionaire who was looking for his mother who disappeared when he was a kid."

"That's the story I remember from the *Times*," Ballard said. "That may be a useful site."

Hatteras stood and came around the raft to Ballard.

"Colleen?" Ballard asked.

"Can I pick one?" Hatteras responded.

Ballard gave Hatteras the stack of files. But rather than looking through them to make her choice, Hatteras hugged the stack to her chest. She closed her eyes and held still for a long moment.

"Colleen?" Ballard said. "You told me you wouldn't do this."

"I know, I know," Hatteras said. "But these women have waited so long for justice. I want to connect. It could help us."

"Look, we talked about this. Just pick a file and pass the stack. Now."

"Okay, this one. Willa." She separated the Willa file from the others and held it up as if to the heavens. "God bless this young woman," she said.

"It might be a little late for that," Laffont said.

Seemingly annoyed by Laffont's sarcasm, Hatteras walked past him and gave the remaining files to Masser.

"Just so you all know, I have edited the files," Ballard said. "Each contains two photos. One in life, one in death. For now, you don't need to see what happened in between. Another thing: The files don't leave the raft. As I said before, nothing is discussed outside this room. Everybody good with that?"

She got a round of nods. The files were handed around the raft, with one coming back to Ballard. She checked the tab and saw that she had the Cecily file—the woman who had been strangled against the basement post. Ballard checked the two photos in the file. The victim's eyes were open and staring down at the concrete floor between her legs. Ballard could see the hemorrhaging around the eyes. Cecily had died horribly, and Ballard knew that there was no one left alive to punish for it. Yet she felt a sense of duty to find out who Cecily was and make her story known.

26

IT WAS AFTER two p.m. when they got word about the judge's DNA from Darcy Troy. By then the Open-Unsolved team had come up with two identifications of the women in the Thawyer files. Willa Kenyon was reported missing in 1950; her case was one of the oldest in the Lost-Angels.net database. And Elyse Ford was identified through a keyword search on the Library of Congress newspaper database. While her 1949 disappearance had apparently gotten no ink from the newspapers in Los Angeles, it had in her hometown. A search of the database using the words *Elyse, missing,* and *Los Angeles* produced three stories that had run in the *Wichita Eagle.* It was a familiar story: *Young woman from the Midwest went to Hollywood to seek fame and fortune, and now she's missing without leaving a clue. The L.A. police are not too interested in chasing another one of these, but her parents back in Kechi are worried sick.* Still, even the Wichita paper dropped the story after four months and three articles.

Both the newspaper accounts and the Lost Angels site provided photos of the missing women that clearly matched two of the women in the photos in Thawyer's files. Ballard was convinced by her own comparison and believed that her team of volunteer investigators were close to having enough evidence to take to Carol

Plovc at the DA's office and ask for clearance and closure in those two cases.

But she put those thoughts aside when she saw Darcy Troy's name on her cell phone.

"It's her," Ballard said.

She immediately drew an audience; Hatteras and Masser got up and came to her pod as she answered.

"Hey, Darcy, give me the good word."

"Well, I don't have good news. Purcell's father, the Pillowcase Rapist, is not the judge. I'm sorry."

Ballard was stunned. "I don't — how can that be?"

"I don't know what to tell you other than it's no match. The woman is wrong too. No match. She's not the mother. Obviously, it was an adoption."

"No. We pulled the birth certificate. It was filed too fast for an adoption."

"Then I don't know what to tell you, Renée. The science is the science."

"It couldn't be a screwup on the DOJ end, right?"

"Don't go there. Highly unlikely."

"Okay. I'm just..."

"Let me know what else I can do."

"Sure. I will."

Ballard disconnected and looked up. Now the whole team was gathered around her end of the raft.

"No match," she said. "Nick Purcell isn't related to the judge or his wife."

"Fuck!" Persson yelled.

Masser snapped his head back and spun away from the group as if shot.

"I knew it," Hatteras said.

"You knew it?" Laffont said. "Why didn't you say so?"

"I did—nobody listened," Hatteras insisted. "I said the genetic tree I was building didn't connect in any way to the judge."

"Yeah, whatever," Laffont said.

"It's the truth," Hatteras said. "But it doesn't matter. What matters is what do we do now?"

"All right, let's just calm down," Ballard said. "I know this isn't what we expected. But let's think."

Ballard knew that something had gone wrong as they built their case against the judge. That had started with the birth certificate indicating no adoption had taken place.

"Paul, can we take another look at the birth certificate?" she asked.

"Right here," Masser said.

He grabbed a printout of the birth record off his desk and handed it over the wall to Ballard. She confirmed what she already knew: The birth certificate was filed with the county two days after the birth. Then she noticed a detail she had not seen the first time.

"Nicholas Purcell was born at County-USC," Ballard said. "Maybe their birth records will tell a different story."

"Not without a court order," Masser said. "It's a dead end."

"But wait," Ballard said. "The judge wasn't a judge yet when the kid was born, but he must've been doing well, right? I mean, well enough to get appointed or elected judge."

"I would say so," Masser said. "Successful enough financially or reputation-wise or both to get a slot on the superior court."

"So, County-USC back then or even now is not one of your high-end hospitals. It's a public facility. It even provides indigent care. Is it the kind of hospital where the wife of up-and-coming lawyer, soon to be judge Jonathan Purcell would want to give birth to their child?"

"I should have seen this," Masser said. He looked mortified at not noticing the inconsistency earlier.

"So what do we do?" Hatteras asked.

"Well, for the moment, I want you all to go back to what you were doing," Ballard said. "Let's try to run down more of the names from the Thawyer files. When you're needed on Purcell, I'll let you know. Maddie, when's your roll call for tonight?"

"Five," Maddie said.

"Okay, well, you should cut out, then," Ballard said. "Get ready for your shift."

Maddie looked crestfallen, like she was being cut out of her own case, and Ballard read it in her expression.

"Don't worry," she said. "You're still lead on this. It's your case. We won't make a move on it without you."

"Let me know when you need me," Maddie said.

As people reluctantly returned to their spots on the raft, Ballard stood up from her desk.

"Paul, let's go get a coffee," she said.

Ballard turned and headed toward the exit before any of the others could react to being left out of whatever discussion Ballard was about to have. She didn't speak to Masser until they were in the cafeteria and sitting down at a table with to-go coffee cups in front of them. Before Ballard could begin, Masser spit out an apology.

"I am so sorry," he said. "If I had put together the incongruity of the hospital, we'd be two days into a new direction."

"Not necessarily," Ballard said. "And I didn't buy you coffee to set up an apology."

"Then why did we come up here? The others think you took me to the woodshed."

"I don't care what they think. We need to figure out our next move on this. I'm already taking heat for putting the judge under surveillance. Now that it's not him, this could really turn bad for the unit."

"Well, I think it's obvious. We have to go to the judge."

Ballard nodded. "I was thinking that too. But he could blow us out of the water, especially if we tell him we collected his DNA."

"His *and* his wife's. He may blow a gasket, but he might also see that we had no choice. We did what we had to do."

"Hopefully. But how are we going to get him to talk if he was involved in some sort of shady deal getting the kid?"

"You mean like a black-market baby?"

"Maybe. I still don't see how the birth was recorded so quickly. That means somebody at the hospital was somehow involved in making this work."

"There's something we don't know here. Even if we could get into adoption records, I have a feeling there wouldn't be any for Nicholas Purcell."

"So when do we go to the judge?"

"That's your call. That's why you get a salary and we don't."

"Right."

Ballard went silent as she mulled the question. Intruding into these thoughts was the reminder that Captain Gandle had directly ordered her to keep him in the loop. She knew she should inform him of the DOJ results and the plan to brace the judge. But by doing so she risked Gandle telling her to stand down until he got clarity from the tenth floor. That move could take days and maybe even weeks. Ballard was not interested in stalling the case while the command staff considered the political gain or fallout from asking the presiding judge of the superior court questions about the possibly illegal adoption of his son.

"What are you thinking?" Masser finally asked.

"I'm thinking if we left now, we could get to the CCB before the judge takes off for the weekend," Ballard said.

"So you want to do it today?"

"Why not?"

"Because if the judge gets mad and throws us in jail, we probably won't get out till Monday."

"More like Tuesday because of the holiday."

"Yes, Tuesday."

"Fuck it. Let's go."

"I'll drive. My keys are on my desk."

"Let's not tell the others what we're doing. I don't want Colleen calling every ten minutes."

"She'll do that whether she knows what we're doing or not."

"I'll meet you in the parking lot. Go get your keys."

As Ballard walked out of the building toward the row of parking spaces assigned to the unit, she pulled her phone to call Captain Gandle. Then she thought better of it. Calling him now before the hour's drive into downtown was too risky. He could shut down her plan before it even started.

Instead, she used the phone to google a phone number for the clerk of the superior court. By the time Masser showed up at his car with the keys, she had already called the courthouse and been transferred to Purcell's clerk, who confirmed that the judge was still working.

"Purcell's still in chambers," Ballard said.

"Good," Masser said. "I think."

27

BALLARD AND MASSER parked in the garage at the PAB and walked the block up Spring Street to the courthouse. Along the way, Ballard pulled her phone and called Ashley Fellows, who was one of the last friends she had in the Robbery-Homicide Division.

"Hey, girl, whatcha doin'?" Fellows said.

"Biding my time till it's time," Ballard said.

It was their routine greeting.

"You still in the same desk over there?" Ballard asked.

"Sure am," Fellows said. "What's up?"

"You've got eyes on the captain's office, right?"

"I do."

"Is he in there at the moment?"

"No, but he's right outside it talking to Broom-Hilda."

That was the name they used for Captain Gandle's bully of an adjutant, who sat at a desk outside the captain's glass-walled office and guarded it like it was Checkpoint Charlie. Her name was actually Hildy McManus.

"I need to call him but I don't want him to answer," Ballard said.

"One of those," Fellows said. "Well, he asked me this morning for an update on a case I'm working. I told him to give me a few hours. I could call him over to look at what I got spread all over my desk. But you still got Hilda to worry about. She could pick up."

"He gave me his direct line once. I think she doesn't have that on her phone."

"Then give me three minutes before you call. I'll get him over here."

"Thanks, Ash." Ballard disconnected.

"What was that about?" Masser asked.

"If we confront the judge without approval from the captain, there could be hell to pay. But I don't want to wait for him to take it to command staff. So I'm going to call him and leave a message to cover my ass."

They got up to Temple Street, and Ballard made the call. She held her breath until it went through to voicemail.

"Captain, it's Renée. The analysis on the judge's DNA came back negative — Nick Purcell's not a match to him or his wife. That leaves us no alternative but to talk to the judge about his son. I need to do that before he goes off for a three-day weekend. Heading to the CCB now. Just keeping you in the loop like you asked."

She disconnected, hoping that her casual tone implied that this was a routine interview, even though she knew there was nothing routine about an interview with the presiding judge of Los Angeles Superior Court.

In the Criminal Courts Building, they took the law enforcement–only elevator up to save time. Purcell's courtroom was on the sixth floor in Division 101. The courtroom was literally dark when Ballard and Masser entered. There was one overhead light on and it was shining down on the clerk's corral, where a woman with short brown hair sat. She looked up when she heard them enter.

"We're dark today," she said. "Can I help you?"

"We're with the LAPD Open-Unsolved Unit," Ballard said. "We'd like to talk to Judge Purcell."

"He's on a deadline writing orders before the weekend," the clerk said. "You need an appointment, and he has no room on his calendar this afternoon. If you need a search warrant signed, I would suggest that you go see Judge Coen for that. He handles criminal matters."

"It's about his son, Nicholas," Ballard said. "I think you should ask him if he wants to see us."

Without responding to Ballard, the clerk picked up a phone, hit one button, and then whispered behind a hand cupped around her mouth. Ballard made out the word *Nicholas* but otherwise could not pick up on the conversation. The clerk put down the phone and got up. She walked to a half door in the corral and pulled it open.

"The judge will see you," she said. "Come through here and then go through that door and down the hallway. His chambers are the first door on the right."

Ballard led the way. The clerk's directions were not needed because the judge was standing in the doorway of his chambers. He was wearing a white shirt and tie but no jacket or robe. Ballard watched his eyes for any hint of recognition of Masser or herself from the surveillance at the Parkway Grill.

She saw nothing.

They followed Purcell into the office. He sat down behind a desk covered with legal documents. He pointed to the two chairs across from him, and Ballard and Masser sat.

"Thank you for seeing us, Judge," Ballard began.

"Never mind that," Purcell asked. "What's my son done this time?"

"Uh, nothing, sir. As far as we know."

"Then if this is about the DA dropping those charges against him, I had nothing to do with that. I didn't even make a call."

"It's not about that, sir."

"Then why are you here on a Friday afternoon before a holiday weekend? What is so important about my son?"

"Well, sir, we are from the Open-Unsolved Unit and we think your son is key to identifying and arresting a serial rapist and murderer."

Purcell drew his head back as if he'd been slapped.

"What the fuck are you talking about?" he said. "Nick's had his difficulties but nothing that even approaches an involvement in —"

"We are not suggesting he is in any way involved, Judge," Ballard said quickly. "It's his father we're looking for. His real father. His biological father."

That stunned the judge into silence. Ballard studied him for any sign that he knew about the Pillowcase Rapist's connection to Nicholas Purcell. She saw none.

Ballard felt her phone buzz in her pocket. She guessed it was Captain Gandle calling her back, probably to tell her not to approach the judge without the command staff's approval. But she had a perfect excuse not to answer. You didn't take calls when you were talking to the presiding judge of the superior court. You didn't even look to see who was calling.

"What do you mean, his real father?" Purcell said.

Ballard nodded. This was the moment.

"Judge, do you remember the Pillowcase Rapist case?" she asked.

"Of course," Purcell said. "But that was before my son was even born."

"Not quite, but that's the case we're working. And I need you to know that that is all we're interested in. We don't care about anything else, what you may have done in adopting your son or —"

"Are you suggesting that Nicholas is not my son?"

"Judge, we *know* he's not your son."

"This is incredible. How could you —"

He stopped mid-sentence as a thought occurred to him.

"You talked to my wife?" he said. "You talked to Vivian?"

"No, sir, we didn't," Ballard said. "We got your DNA from a spoon you left on a table at a restaurant."

In her peripheral vision, Ballard saw Masser turn toward her, questioning her decision to reveal to the judge that they had followed him. Ballard kept her eyes on Purcell, who seemed incredulous as he grasped what had gone down.

"You thought it was me," he said. "You thought I was the Pillowcase Rapist?"

"Judge, when your son was arrested last year, his DNA was collected and sent to the state's Department of Justice database. That produced a familial match to DNA collected from several crime scenes involving the Pillowcase Rapist. The science told us that Nicholas Purcell's father was the rapist. We pulled his birth certificate, and you and your wife are listed as the birth parents. You can understand why we then placed you under surveillance so we could make a surreptitious DNA capture. We did that at the Parkway Grill on Monday night. We got DNA from your wife too and sent the samples through our lab to the DOJ. We received results today that confirm that neither of you are birth parents of Nicholas Purcell."

Ballard stopped there to let Purcell digest what had happened. The skin around his eyes darkened, and she suspected his blood pressure was rising.

"Were these actions approved by your superiors?" he asked, his voice tightly controlled.

"I run the unit, sir," Ballard said. "We like to say the cases go where they go. I did not need approval, though I did make my captain aware of it."

"I should jail you both for contempt of court," Purcell said. "That you would—"

"You could do that, Judge, but it would get messy and very public," Ballard said. "I didn't think you'd want that for your son, your family. There is a way for us to keep Nicholas out of this, especially when it hits the media. But that would entail you cooperating with us and explaining how he became your son."

It hit Purcell then, the threat of public exposure. Nicholas could be branded as the son of a rapist-murderer.

Ballard waited, stealing a quick glance at Masser. Color was just coming back to Masser's face after the threat of jail from the judge had bleached it printer-paper white. She realized that she should have let him in on how she was going to play it.

"We tried to have children of our own," the judge said. "It wasn't happening. Then an opportunity presented itself."

He stopped there. Ballard sensed that he needed to be prompted to continue revealing a secret he had kept for almost twenty-five years.

"You were offered a baby?" Ballard asked.

"Not exactly," Purcell said. "There was a girl in the neighborhood. A high school girl. She got pregnant. The family — her family — they were very religious. They believed she had to have the child. And her parents, they knew us from down the street. They knew about … our struggles. We were open about it. They came and said there was a way for — you see, they didn't want their daughter's life to be forever changed by this. They had an unwanted child coming and we wanted a child so very badly …"

"You agreed to take the child."

Purcell nodded.

"Did you know who the real father was?" Ballard asked.

Purcell shook his head. "No, she never told her parents or us," he said. "She was protecting him. I wanted to know so we could protect ourselves, you understand. I wanted everyone's approval … but she wouldn't tell."

"How did you register the birth so quickly?" Ballard asked.

"That wasn't a problem. I had a former client in a divorce case who worked in the registrar's office take care of it. I didn't want there to be any kind of stigma, you know? For the boy to grow up with that, knowing he was adopted, not knowing who his father was."

"And the mother, she was never involved?"

"No, not after the birth. The family had a place in the desert. Out at Smoke Tree. They moved to that house. Kept the house on Arroyo, but the whole family started over out there. It worked. No one ever knew about the baby ... except us. Till now."

"We need to reach out to her, Judge. What's her name?"

"You can't. It's too late. She killed herself a year after. Took a lot of pills, sat in a car in the garage, and started the engine. It was a terribly sad thing. We thought that, having lost their daughter, the parents would come to us for the child. We were prepared — legally — to fight it. But it never came to that."

Ballard glanced at Masser. The DNA door they thought had swung open for them was now swinging shut. She saw her own dismay playing on Masser's face.

She looked back at the judge.

"Judge, what about those parents?" she asked. "Are they still around?"

"Robin is," Purcell said. "Edward passed, and now she's selling the place on Arroyo."

Ballard thought about the house with the IN ESCROW sign she had parked in front of while following the judge Monday night.

"What is Robin's last name?" she asked.

"Richardson," Purcell said. "Robin Richardson."

"Do you have a phone number or an email for her?"

"Vivian has that. I can get it."

"One last thing. What was the daughter's name?"

"Mallory. She was a great kid. One mistake changed all of that. Like I said, it was sad. Very sad."

Ballard nodded and realized she had one last question. "What school did she go to when she lived on Arroyo?"

"That would have been St. Vincent's in South Pasadena. That was their church too. We also sent Nick to St. Vincent's for a few years."

"Thank you, Judge. If you can get us Robin Richardson's contact info, we'll let you get back to work."

Purcell looked at her with worried eyes.

"Keep Nick out of this. He's a good kid. If he knew who...where he came from, he wouldn't take it well."

"We understand, sir," Ballard said. "We'll do our best."

SATURDAY, 7:22 A.M.

28

BALLARD SAT IN the second row of folding chairs, behind Gordon Olmstead and another agent, Spencer, who was wearing an Amazon delivery uniform as cover because he was the driver of the command-post van. The van was parked on Ocean Boulevard, a block away from the parking lot displayed on the four screens attached to the inside wall.

Olmstead sat in front of a stick microphone and was in constant contact with all agents involved in the operation. Speakers mounted below the screens allowed Ballard to hear the play-by-play on the comms. The only one of the team not transmitting was Bosch. He had previously declined to wear an earpiece. His car was wired for sound but he didn't want to speak; if he was being watched by a Dehaven confederate, it might tip him off.

At 7:25 the agents watching the caravan on the PCH where Dehaven parked his van overnight reported that Dehaven and another man were in the van and pulling into traffic. They were on their way.

Olmstead shook his head and keyed his mic. "They're already breaking the rules," he said. "Subject was to arrive solo. Everybody stay sharp. We are off script."

Tension in the van ratcheted up a notch. Ballard watched the screens and saw Bosch open the door of his Cherokee.

"He's getting out," Ballard said. "Why's he getting out?"

"It's part of the plan, Renée," Olmstead said. "Cool your jets."

Ballard was annoyed by his tone and by the fact that she had been left out of the planning, but she knew this wasn't the time to go to war over it. She watched as Bosch went to the back of the Cherokee and lifted the rear hatch. He was wearing an old army camo jacket that looked bulky.

"Is he wearing plates?" she asked.

"No," Spencer said. "He refused a vest, plates, anything that would look like he might be law enforcement."

Bosch sat on the back bumper and folded his arms across his chest. Next to him in the rear cargo space of the Cherokee were two beach bags with straps. They looked like they were filled with striped beach towels, but Olmstead explained that the towels concealed the mini machine guns, two in each bag, with ineffective firing pins.

"We wanted two bags so Dehaven would have to carry them with two hands," he said.

Ballard nodded, knowing that the two-handed carry would hinder an effort to draw a weapon.

Minute-by-minute updates on Dehaven's progress on the coast highway were radioed to the command post.

"He's going to be early, people," Olmstead said. "Be ready."

"Is there any way to get that message to Bosch?" Ballard asked.

"Not unless we break position," Olmstead said. "We don't want to do that and Bosch knows to be ready for anything. Early arrival, late arrival—doesn't matter."

Ballard nodded. She knew that Bosch was ready. She had checked with him earlier that morning and given him every opportunity to back out of the operation, but he refused. He told her that the situation went beyond recovering her badge. He wanted to be part of the team that took Dehaven down.

At 7:46 the follow team reported that Dehaven's van was on the California Incline and three to five minutes from the beach parking lot. The tension in Ballard's chest tightened and she pushed her chair back and stood. It was the only way to deal with the adrenaline hit. She started shifting her weight from one foot to another, her eyes intent on the screens.

"Renée, you're jumpy," Olmstead said. "You need to relax. Everything is in hand."

"I can't relax," Ballard said. "Not till this thing is over and he's safe. I pulled him into this."

She studied the screens that showed four images of Bosch from four different camera angles. He was still sitting, arms crossed, on the back bumper. He certainly seemed calm even if she wasn't.

"I need to be down there with him," she said.

"Too dangerous," Olmstead said. "You can't even get out of the van at this point. We don't know what other eyes are out there."

"I know, I know. Are all of these frames fixed? They're too tight. You can't see what's happening in the lot."

"Hold on."

Olmstead made a radio call to one of the lot surveillance teams and told them to widen their camera's angle. It was the camera on the southwest corner of the lot that offered a view over the right side of the Cherokee and Bosch's left shoulder. The angle widened and Ballard could see the entire lot, including the roller-hockey game being played on the north end.

"That better for you?" Olmstead asked.

"Better," Ballard said. "But you let them play hockey with this going down?"

"They play every Saturday morning. We don't know if Dehaven

knows that. We cancel it and it could be a tell. It could blow the whole operation. Nothing is going to happen here. We're going to follow them back to the nest, remember?"

"I remember. It's just that plans don't always go as intended."

Almost as soon as she said it, she saw the van she recognized as Dehaven's drive down the ramp off Ocean and into the parking lot. Because it was so early and the lot was largely empty, the van cut across the painted lines of the parking rows, heading directly toward Bosch.

Ballard watched Harry push off the bumper and stand up to meet it.

"Here we go," Olmstead said.

29

THE VAN PULLED up at an angle to the left rear side of the Cherokee. On one of the screens, Ballard could see that Dehaven was in the passenger seat. The camera positions and a light reflection off the windshield did not allow a clear view of the driver. Bosch walked directly to the passenger window to confront Dehaven. His back was to the open hatch of the Cherokee, and his words were partially muffled by his body and the limited reach of the bug. Ballard leaned over Olmstead's shoulder to get closer to the speaker.

"You...alone," Bosch said.

"Relax," Dehaven said. "He's..."

Bosch pointed into the van at the driver.

"He...the van," he said.

"Okay, not a..." Dehaven said. "Just take...cool."

Bosch turned back to the Cherokee, his voice now directed at the bug.

"I'll be cool as long as he stays in the fucking van," he said.

Dehaven opened his door and got out behind him. Bosch walked to a position under the hatch where he knew his words would be clear and recorded.

Ballard checked all corners of the screens for a red dot or other indicator. "You are recording this, right?" she asked.

Olmstead said nothing. Spencer said nothing.

"What the fuck?" Ballard said. "You're not recording this?"

Her voice obscured something Bosch said.

"Ballard, be quiet," Olmstead barked. "We need to hear. Yes, it's recorded."

Ballard didn't believe him. And she knew there was only one reason not to record the takedown.

"If Bosch gets hurt, I won't keep my mouth shut about this," she said.

Olmstead held his hand up for silence.

On the screen, the deal was about to go down. Dehaven was at the back of the Cherokee next to Bosch and was pulling towels out of one of the beach bags. He held the towels under one arm while looking into the bag. He reached down to inspect the weapons without lifting them out of the bag. Seemingly satisfied, Dehaven stuffed the towels back in that bag and moved on to the second one. This time when he removed the towels, he dropped them next to the bag, leaving both hands free.

"No slings?" he said. "Dude, I ordered slings."

"You gave me short notice on that," Bosch said. "I can get 'em Tuesday or Wednesday for you."

"That'll be too late."

"For what?"

"What?"

"Too late for what?"

"Too late for none of your fucking business."

"You're right. I don't want to know your business. I just want to finish ours. Where's the money?"

"In the pocket of the guy you told to stay in the van. He's the buyer. I'm just the go-between."

"Then you can go get the money from him."

"I sure can."

Dehaven picked the two beach bags up by the straps, one in each hand, and turned from the Cherokee.

"No, they stay here till you bring me the cash," Bosch said.

"Oh, come on, man," Dehaven said. "You'll get your money."

He attempted to walk past Bosch to the van, but Bosch put his hand in front of Dehaven's chest. Dehaven shrank back from it.

"Don't touch me, man," he said.

"You want the guns, you pay for the guns," Bosch said.

Ballard could feel the mounting tension between the two men. They stood there staring at each other for a long moment before Dehaven dropped the bags to the ground.

"Fine, tough guy," he said. "I'll get you your money."

He walked past Bosch to the van. He reached in through the open passenger window, and it appeared to Ballard that he took something from the driver, though the hand-pass was below the window line.

Dehaven turned toward Bosch as he took his hand out of the window. The move was smooth and quick. While making the pivot, he dropped his hand to his side, guarding it from Bosch's view.

Ballard's eyes jumped from one screen to another as she looked for an angle on Dehaven's left hand. Olmstead beat her to it.

"Gun!" he yelled into the microphone. "Blue, blue, blue!"

Blue was the go word. In the command post, Ballard didn't hear the shots, but almost immediately after Olmstead yelled the word into his mic, she saw Dehaven's body jerk from the impacts of at least two sniper hits. He collapsed to his knees and then fell backward to the asphalt, a handgun next to his left hand.

Ballard saw Bosch drop to the ground and crawl to the side of the Cherokee for cover.

The van started forward and she saw the flash of gunfire from inside as the driver shot at Bosch through the open passenger-side window. But Bosch got to a safety point against the rear tire of his car.

Then came the explosion of glass as sniper shots pierced the van's windshield and took out the driver. The van kept moving for twenty-five yards and drove directly into one of the concrete pedestals of the parking lot's light poles. It stopped and Ballard saw no movement from inside.

"Clear the van!" Olmstead barked. "Clear the van!"

On the wide screen, Ballard saw FBI cars race across the lot to the van. She saw Bosch crawl back to Dehaven. He shoved the gun away and put a hand to Dehaven's neck to check for a pulse. He bent over the body and turned an ear to listen for breath.

He straightened up and looked directly at one of the cameras.

"Dehaven's down for good," he said.

Agents wearing black assault gear were now on foot and moving in on the van, their weapons trained on the driver's position. One agent got to the door and opened it. The driver tumbled out to the ground. Another agent opened the side door while a third covered. They moved in weapons-first and in a moment backed out.

Ballard heard the all-clear call on the radio.

"Spencer, get us over there," Olmstead said.

Spencer jumped up and went through a curtain to the front cab of the van. Olmstead followed him and took the front passenger seat. The engine roared to life and took off with such a jerk that Ballard was thrown into the back doors. They popped open and she fell to the street.

The van didn't stop. From the ground, she watched it drive away.

30

BY THE TIME Ballard got to the parking lot, agents were already stringing yellow tape around the shooting scene, using the light poles as the corners of a huge restricted area. People, including many of the roller-hockey players, gathered at the perimeter. Ballard was attempting to lift the tape and walk under when an agent in bad-ass black commando clothes and gear stopped her. She identified herself, but he would not let her into the crime scene without permission from his superiors.

"Then call Olmstead," she said. "Tell him Ballard wants in."

While the agent whispered into a wire-thin microphone attached to his earpiece, Ballard massaged her shoulder, which she had landed on hard when she fell out of the van.

"He said he's coming," the agent said.

"When?" Ballard demanded.

"Now."

She saw Olmstead break away from a huddle of agents near the Cherokee and head toward her.

"Why'd you jump out of the van?" he asked.

"I didn't," Ballard said.

"What? We got here and you were gone."

"Whatever. Can you tell this guy to let me in?"

"You don't want to be here, Renée. This went sideways and the media is going to be all over it. Helicopters, cameras — you don't want to be on video."

She knew he was right but she didn't want to leave.

"Then I want to talk to Bosch. Send him out here."

"He's being debriefed."

"I don't care. You'll be talking to him for hours. I just need five minutes to make sure he's okay."

"All right, five minutes, then you get away from here."

He turned to walk back to the scene but then pivoted and returned to the yellow tape. "So far, no badge," he said. "We checked the body. We still need to go through the van."

"Fine. Let me know."

"Will do."

He walked away and Ballard watched as he was immediately intercepted by another agent holding a clipboard. They started discussing something and Ballard thought he was going to forget to send Bosch to her. But once he signed something on the clipboard, he went directly to the command-post van, opened the back door that Ballard had fallen through, and signaled Bosch out. Once Harry was out of the van, he was pointed to Ballard, and he headed her way.

"Harry, you okay?" Ballard asked as he approached.

"I'm okay," he said.

"You sure? You don't have to talk to them right now if you're — "

"Renée, I'm okay."

Ballard nodded. "Jesus, that was close."

"Yeah, well...they were ready for it."

"How's your car?"

"It took a few shots, I think. I haven't really checked."

"Maybe time to get something new."

"I just got that after the last one got shot up."

Ballard looked up at the sound of a helicopter and saw a blue chopper banking over the beach. It said FOX in white letters on the side.

"The media's already getting here," she said.

"That's SkyFox," Bosch said. "Stu Mundel."

"You actually know the pilots of the news choppers?"

"I know him. He's good. I like watching those live freeway chases. Helps me go to sleep at night."

"Harry Bosch, a man of mystery. Anyway, I shouldn't be here, so I'm going to go. But will you call me as soon as they cut you loose? Maybe we can meet up."

"I'll call you as soon as I'm out," Bosch said.

He walked up to the yellow tape and reached an arm across to hug her. Ballard was surprised by the move from the usually undemonstrative Harry Bosch but took a step forward and put her arms around him. She patted his back and felt a twinge of pain in her shoulder.

"I'm glad you're okay, Harry," she said.

"Me too," he said.

They separated.

"Check your pocket when you get to your car," Bosch said.

"Uh...okay," Ballard said.

But she put her hands into the pockets of her jacket without waiting and her right hand closed around what she knew was her badge. She nodded.

"When you bent over him listening for breath," she said.

Bosch nodded. "He was dead," he said. "But I knew he had the badge around his neck when he wouldn't let me touch his chest. I guess it's lucky for you they didn't put a bullet through it."

"Yeah, lucky all right," Ballard said. "Thanks, Harry."

He nodded and turned back toward the crime scene. Ballard walked away, keeping her head down as the news helicopter circled above.

SUNDAY, 1:00 P.M.

31

THE RIDE OUT to the desert took two hours. Masser did the driving while Ballard typed a case summary on her laptop. She was far behind on the digital paperwork on the Pillowcase Rapist investigation and knew if she got something filed by the end of the day, it would buy her time with Captain Gandle. Once she was finished, they stopped for a quick lunch at an In-N-Out in Cabazon — Ballard had gone back to eating meat after being vegetarian for some time. They sat in the car, and while Ballard ate her hamburger, she pulled up the *L.A. Times* website on her phone and checked the news stories on the shootout in Santa Monica the day before.

The violent takedown of two men, Thomas Dehaven and Frederic Standard, and the arrest of four of their coconspirators quickly became national news Saturday when the FBI announced that the group had been planning a mass shooting on Presidents' Day at the Malibu pier. But so far Ballard had received no inquiries from the media, so Olmstead must have been keeping his promise. Ballard held an ace in that Olmstead knew that if he leaked any information and she was dragged into the media frenzy, she could reveal things that were not consistent with the narrative the feds were spinning publicly.

She looked at the top stories on the site and saw that there were already two follow-up reports on the events of the day before. One was a profile of Thomas Dehaven, the ringleader of the group that had come to Los Angeles in a caravan of vans and RVs.

TERROR SUSPECT ROAMED COUNTRY FINDING RECRUITS

By Scott Anderson, Times Staff Writer

The wanted man shot dead Saturday by the FBI while allegedly buying machine guns for a terrorist act had roamed the country over the past two years, avoiding capture and recruiting fellow extremists to his cause, according to federal sources.

Thomas Dehaven, 46, of Coeur d'Alene, Idaho, was being sought in the death of his ex-wife and on charges of sedition in regard to the attack on the U.S. Capitol on Jan. 6, 2021. According to the FBI, Dehaven fled from Idaho in March of 2021 after allegedly shooting his ex-wife, Kimberly Boyle, when he learned from their son that she had helped the FBI identify him in videos taken during the violent siege at the Capitol.

Dehaven then began a monthslong odyssey that first took him through the South, where he met and recruited Frederic Standard, 31, in Mobile, Alabama, in a scheme to make a violent statement in California. FBI agents are piecing together the path he took and have been contacted by several individuals in Louisiana, Texas, and Arizona who said they heard Dehaven's pitch but did not join the scheme.

"Most of these people didn't take him seriously," Agent Gordon Olmstead said in an interview. "They shined him on, thought he was a bit out there. But we know that others believed in his plan and joined him or gave him money and equipment."

One of those was Tracy Bell, 39, of Shreveport, Louisiana, who joined Dehaven and offered him her camper van, which he was using on Saturday when he and Standard met with an FBI informant to purchase four machine guns. The guns were allegedly going to be used by Dehaven and Standard to fire on people on the crowded Malibu pier during the national holiday on Monday.

Ballard stopped reading.

"*Allegedly*," she said. "They always use the word *allegedly*."

"You talking about that thing in Santa Monica yesterday?" Masser said.

Ballard realized that she had almost revealed that she knew more about the incident than she should.

"Yes," she said. "Seems from what I've read like there was nothing *alleged* about their plan to shoot up the pier."

"Yeah, true believers," Masser said. "They'll be martyrs for the cause now, like that woman who got shot at the Capitol."

After finishing their food, they got out of the car and switched seats so Ballard could give Masser a break. They got back on the road into the Coachella Valley.

Smoke Tree Ranch was a small private enclave of mostly historic desert homes passed down from generation to generation by moneyed East Coast, Midwest, and Southern California families. Its best-known resident over the century of its existence was undoubtedly Walt Disney, who had had a home on the ranch until he sold it to raise money to build an amusement park that would be called Disneyland. After the success of the park, Disney came back to the ranch and built a new house. Following a long-held tradition, residents of the ranch referred to themselves as colonists.

Ballard had traced Robin Richardson through DMV records to a home on San Jacinto Trail on the back perimeter of the ranch. The street ran alongside the Palm Canyon Creek wash below the majestic San Jacinto mountain range. There was a guard gate at the ranch's entrance and Ballard used her recovered badge to convince the uniformed security officer to let them through. Ballard didn't mention Robin Richardson. There were guest cabins on the property and she told the guard that they had police business at the management office.

Once they were through the gate, however, they quickly discovered that the Richardson home was difficult to find because there were no street signs or house numbers on the ranch. The only markers were numbers painted on large white rocks at each corner. It was only with the help of a woman walking a dog that Ballard and Masser located the home:

"Robin's house is on rock seventeen, fourth house on your right."

With those directions they found the house and pulled into the gravel driveway. Like almost every home they had passed in the private enclave, it was a sprawling ranch house surrounded by desert landscape and cacti. Its wood siding had been burned gray over the years by the unrelenting sun.

The desert air was crisp and Ballard and Masser put on their jackets after getting out of the car. Ballard's knock on the front door was answered by a diminutive woman in her mid-sixties. Her long gray hair was in a braid. She wore rimless glasses and had the deep tan of a full-time desert resident.

"Mrs. Richardson?" Ballard asked.

"Yes, that's me," she said. "How did you get into the ranch?"

Ballard once again showed her badge. "We're police officers, ma'am," she said. "From Los Angeles. We'd like to ask you a few questions."

"About what?"

"Well, we'd rather not talk about it here on the doorstep. Could we come in and sit down with you?"

"Not until you tell me what this is all about."

"It's about your daughter, ma'am. Mallory."

If Richardson had been tipped off to their impending arrival by Judge Purcell, she did a masterful job of covering and looking surprised, then apprehensive. Ballard read the reaction as legit. Richardson opened the door all the way and invited them in.

She led them into a living room with a mid-century design to the furnishings. Richardson took a seat on a couch while Ballard and Masser sat across a glass-topped coffee table in two cushioned chairs.

"We work cold cases for the LAPD," Ballard began. "We were given your name by Judge Purcell, who was your neighbor when you lived in Pasadena."

"Why would he give you my name?" Richardson said. "What is this about?"

"It's about an old case involving sexual assault and murder. We went to Judge Purcell because of his son, Nick. A familial DNA match in our case indicated that Nick's father is our suspect. Only it turns out, Judge Purcell is not Nick's father. And his wife is not Nick's mother. When we found out that Nick was adopted, the judge told us that his biological mother was Mallory."

"You're saying that the son my daughter gave up is a killer?"

"No, not at all. We believe his father is the man we're looking for. We came out here to ask you who that was."

"There must be a mistake. How could this be?"

"The DNA analysis confirms it. Do you know who the father was, Mrs. Richardson? Did your daughter ever tell you?"

"She didn't, because she was afraid."

"Afraid of what?"

"What my husband might do to him."

"Why? Did someone hurt your daughter, Mrs. Richardson?"

"I don't like talking about this. You're bringing up the worst part of my life."

"I understand and I apologize. But the person we're looking for may still be out there hurting women. We need to find him and I'm sure you want to help. Do you remember anything at all from that time that could tell us who the father might have been?"

"You have to understand that I've blocked so much of it out. Those years — they were the worst years of our lives for my husband and me. And now suddenly you come here and . . . I don't know anything that can help you."

Ballard leaned in. She knew the next part of her questioning would be especially difficult.

"We understand that your daughter took her own life, Mrs. Richardson. We are very sorry for your loss. Did she leave behind anything that might help us identify the father of her child?"

Richardson's eyes were not focused on anything in front of her. She was time-traveling back to those difficult years. She slowly shook her head. "She was never the same, you know," Richardson said. "After giving up the baby, she wasn't the same. She used my pills. She didn't leave a note."

Ballard nodded. She was aware that she had upended this woman's fragile existence with just a few questions, and she didn't think pushing her further would yield anything useful. It had been a long drive to another dead end.

"Can I ask a question?" Masser said. "Mallory went to school at St. Vincent's, right?"

"That was our church too," Richardson said.

"Was it possible that the father was a boy — a student — from the school? Was she dating anyone at the time?"

"She didn't have a boyfriend. That year a boy asked her to the senior prom and she went, but they weren't dating."

"Do you remember his name?"

"It was Rodney."

"Do you remember a last name?"

She shook her head.

"That's okay," Masser said. "The name Rodney helps us. Was he a senior?"

"Yes, he must have been," Richardson said.

"Did your daughter by any chance have any yearbooks from St. Vincent's?"

"There's one. From when she was in tenth grade. I kept it because she is so beautiful in the photos."

Ballard nodded. She said nothing. Masser was connecting and making headway.

"Do you think we could borrow the yearbook?" Masser said. "I guarantee I will personally get it back to you."

"I can go see if I can find it in the library," Richardson said.

"Thank you, that would be very helpful."

Richardson stood up and left the room. Ballard looked at Masser and nodded.

"Good one on the yearbook," she said. "I hope she can find it."

32

BALLARD MADE MASSER drive the initial leg back to L.A. so she could get first crack at the yearbook. It was thin with a thick leather binding. Angled across the cover it said *Veritas 1999.*

"*Veritas,*" Ballard said.

"'The truth,'" Masser said.

"You know your Latin."

"I'm a Jesuit boy. They made us take Latin. Came in handy a few times in law school. *Ipse dixit* and all of that."

"*Ipse dixit?* What is that?"

"It means 'He said it himself.' It's an argument that states that if someone of authority said it, it can be held to be true. It goes back to Cicero and the Roman Empire."

"And they still use it in the courtroom?"

"Sometimes. Mostly in rulings by the judge."

"What about *Mortui vivos docent?*"

"That one I'm not familiar with."

"'The dead teach the living.' It's the motto of the California Homicide Investigators Association."

"I get it. Good one."

"I only know it because it's on the challenge coin."

Ballard started paging through the yearbook. The inside covers had no autographs or messages written to Mallory Richardson by other students. Ballard assumed that was because the yearbook had been published after she left school and Pasadena. It was probably sent to her at Smoke Tree and she never had an opportunity to have other students sign it.

Ballard leafed through sections dedicated to sports and class field trips. When she got to the section dedicated to the seniors, she looked at the photos of the boys; two were named Rodney.

"We have a Rodney McNamara and a Rodney Van Ness in the senior class," she said.

"I wonder if they're still around," Masser said.

"We'll find out when I get to my computer. There's a total of twenty-nine boys in the senior class. We'll run them all and see what comes up."

"What's your take on the suicide?"

Ballard was looking out the window at a wind farm they were passing.

"What do you mean?" she asked.

"Well, it feels like a contradiction," Masser said. "What was she depressed about? Was it having to give up the baby? Was she raped and still experiencing trauma? But if that was the case, why didn't she tell anyone, especially her parents? It was like she was protecting the father of the child, but at the same time she goes into a spiral that leads to suicide. You see what I'm saying?"

"I do, but there's no accounting for why people do what they do. And people respond to being raped in all kinds of ways. *If* she was raped, that is. We need to find out more, and hopefully one of these Rodneys will help."

Ballard turned the pages until she reached the tenth-grade photos. She located Mallory Richardson. It was a flattering photo and Ballard understood why her mother liked it. The girl had blond hair that hung down to her shoulders and curved in at the neck, framing her face in a stylish oval. Ballard thought about the friends Robin Richardson had named when she gave them the yearbook.

"Her girlfriends were Jacqueline Todd and ... was it Emma?" she asked.

"Emma Arciniega," Masser said. "But Robin said there was no contact after they moved out to the desert. It was before social media. Nowadays people stay in touch forever. My daughter's twenty-seven and she's still in touch with kids she knew from kindergarten."

Ballard flipped through the pages to look for the friends' photos. Jacqueline Todd was one of the few Black students in Mallory's class and Emma Arciniega was one of the few Latinas.

"A white girl from Pasadena has Black and brown BFFs," Ballard said.

"Interesting," Masser said. "Think they know anything that will help us?"

"Who knows? But sometimes the besties know more than the parents."

Ballard closed the book. The conversation made her think about her mother. She needed to call Dan Farley in Maui to get an update on the ongoing search. She decided she would do it once they got back to L.A. and she could make the call in private.

"You thinking about your mother?" Masser asked.

"Jeez, don't go all Colleen on me, Masser," Ballard said. "How did you guess that?"

"That look on your face. Wistful, I'd call it. I've seen it before."

"You should keep your eyes on the road."

"Yes, ma'am."

"And don't call me ma'am."

"Yes, ma'am."

Before she could respond, her phone buzzed. She didn't recognize the number but took the call.

"Detective, it's Robin Richardson. You were just in my home and left your business card."

"Yes, Mrs. Richardson, is something wrong?"

"Uh, no. It's just that I remembered Rodney's last name. Rodney Van Ness."

"Thank you, that's very helpful."

"Will you let me know what you find out? I really need to know."

"Of course I will. Thank you for calling."

Ballard disconnected and told Masser that the prom date was Rodney Van Ness. She opened the yearbook again and flipped the pages until she was looking at his photo.

"You think it's him?" Masser asked.

"Maybe. That would be too easy," Ballard said. "And so far nothing about this case has been easy."

MONDAY, 9:54 A.M.

33

BECAUSE IT WAS a holiday and she had moved the weekly team meeting to Tuesday, Ballard didn't expect to find anyone on the raft when she arrived at Ahmanson Center with Mallory Richardson's yearbook under her arm on Monday morning. Instead, she found Colleen Hatteras and Maddie Bosch sitting side by side in front of Colleen's large computer screen.

"You guys know it's a holiday, right?" Ballard said.

"I thought crime fighting never took a day off," Hatteras said.

"We found Elyse Ford's family," Maddie said.

There was excitement in her voice. Ballard stayed standing at her desk. She slowly put the yearbook down on an envelope that had been sent from the photo lab.

"What do you mean, you found the family?" she asked.

"Colleen started with the name of Elyse's mother—it was in the newspaper stories back then," Maddie said. "She found a granddaughter online, the daughter of Elyse's little sister."

Colleen said, "She's Elyse's niece. I DM'd her and she responded and said her mother—Elyse's sister—was still living. She's in her eighties but still sharp, according to her daughter, and she agreed to talk to us, so we set up a Zoom."

"When are you Zooming?" Ballard asked.

"In five minutes," Hatteras said.

"Really?" Ballard said. "Last I heard, I was running this unit. Didn't you think to clear this with me first?"

"Uh, we're just going to talk to her," Maddie said. "We'll show her the photo from Thawyer's files. The first shot. See if we can confirm ID."

"Have you ever done this, told a family that their loved one was murdered?" Ballard asked. "Either of you?"

"Uh, no," Hatteras said.

Maddie timidly shook her head. "My partner has," she said. "After a TA. I was there but he did the talking."

"This was no traffic accident," Ballard said. "It doesn't matter how much time has gone by. You tell someone her sister was murdered seventy years ago or seven hours ago, you'd better be prepared. You should have talked to me first."

"I'm sorry," Maddie said. "Should we cancel it?"

"It's too late," Ballard said. "It will be worse to leave her hanging."

"And it's time," Maddie said. "The Zoom's set for ten. Would you rather handle it?"

Ballard shook her head. "No, you do it," she said. "It'll be good for you to get the experience."

Ballard sat down and moved the yearbook off the manila envelope from the lab. She opened it while listening to Maddie and Hatteras get ready for the Zoom call. The envelope contained a one-page lab report paper-clipped to Thawyer's photos of the woman they believed was Elizabeth Short. Her eyes went to the summary box at the bottom of the page. It said that digital analysis of the photographs submitted and the photographs of Elizabeth Short in evidence and available online indicated a 92 percent probability that the photos were of the same woman.

Ballard sat up straight and looked over the privacy wall at Hatteras and Maddie. They had made the Zoom connection and were staring at the screen.

"Mrs. Fanning, my name is Madeline Bosch and this is Colleen Hatteras. We're investigators with the Open-Unsolved Unit of the Los Angeles Police Department. We would like to talk to you about your sister, Elyse."

"Yes, Martha told me. This is Martha. I wanted her here with me."

"That's fine, ma'am," Maddie said. "Your sister was reported missing in Los Angeles in 1950. Do you remember that time?"

"I was a little girl. Elyse was my big sister, eight years older. But I remember those days well. It was an awful time for my family."

"I understand. Uh, it was your parents in Wichita who reported her missing from Los Angeles?"

"Yes. I remember my father went out there to look for her because he didn't think the police were trying very hard to find her. But he didn't find anything and when he came back...he wasn't the same man. He'd sit in the dark by himself a lot. I remember we felt helpless. There was nothing we could do but wait and hope and pray. We thought someday that she would just come home or call and say she was all right. We waited...but that never happened. My mother stopped coming out of her room. I remember having to make dinner for my father and me."

"Martha told us you have photos of your sister from back then. Do you have them now? Could you show us?"

"I have these. This one is the whole family. That's Elyse. She was a beautiful girl. Everyone said she should be in the movies."

Ballard did not have to see the expression on the face of the old woman holding up the photos to know the pain of waiting that she and her family had been through.

"This one my father took when Lysie—that's what I called her—was leaving on the train for Los Angeles. She called it the City of Angels."

"Mrs. Fanning, we're going to arrange to get copies of those photos. We would also like to show you a photo to see if you can confirm that it's Elyse."

Ballard watched Hatteras hold up what was likely the last photo taken of Elyse Ford when she was alive and unscathed.

"Yes," the old woman said. "That's Elyse."

"Are you sure?" Maddie said.

"That's my big sister. I'd know her anywhere."

"Okay. Thank you for confirming that for us."

"Did you find her?"

"No, ma'am, we haven't. But, uh, we believe she was a victim of a man we're investigating. I'm very sorry."

"I guess our waiting is over. Did this man . . . make her suffer?"

"We don't know, ma'am," Maddie said.

Ballard could tell by the looks on the faces of Maddie and Hatteras that the two women on the screen were crying. She could hear Elyse's sister and niece attempting to console each other. There were never enough decades to ease the pain of the murder victim's loved ones.

"Has there been an arrest?" the older woman managed to ask. "How did you find her picture?"

"No, there is no arrest," Maddie said. "We believe the man is dead now. We found your sister's photos in the things he kept in storage."

"There are other photos? Can we please see them?"

Ballard saw Maddie lean her head back as she realized her mistake. "Uh, we can't show you those right now, ma'am," she said.

"If you only have photos, how can you be sure that this man killed my sister?" the old woman asked.

"I'm afraid I can't tell you everything we know, Mrs. Fanning. But we are sure this man killed your sister. We know it was a long time ago, but we're very sorry for your loss."

"I never thought we would know."

"I'm sorry to be the bearer of such upsetting news. We will be in touch through Martha as the investigation continues."

"Thank you."

Martha also thanked them, then they all said goodbye, and the Zoom ended. Ballard got up and walked over to Maddie and Hatteras with the photo-analysis report.

"Good job," she said. "Those are not easy."

Maddie just nodded. She looked a little shaken. Ballard put the report down on the desk.

"The photo analysis came back as a ninety-two percent probability that the woman in the photo is Elizabeth Short."

"That's pretty good, right?" Maddie asked, looking brighter.

"That will be up to the DA's office to decide," Ballard said.

"When do we go to them?"

"Soon."

34

BALLARD SPENT THE rest of the morning running down the names from the yearbook with Hatteras and Maddie. Hatteras worked the social media and genealogy sites while Ballard and Maddie worked the DMV and law enforcement databases.

Ballard split the list with Maddie, telling her to start with the two girls Robin Richardson had identified as her daughter's best friends. Ballard began with Rodney Van Ness, but she could find no current California license or criminal record in local, state, or national databases. From there, she moved on to the names of other boys in the class.

An hour into the project, Hatteras came to Ballard's desk.

"Can I see the yearbook?" she asked. "Are there any pictures from the prom?"

"Yes and yes," Ballard said. "There's two pages of photos from the prom, but I already checked and Mallory isn't in any of them." She handed the book to Hatteras. "Is that what you're looking for?" Ballard asked.

"Not really," Hatteras said. "I just wanted to get..."

"A feel for it?"

"Sort of."

Ballard was tired of trying to rein in Colleen's "feelings." "Have at it," she said.

"I did the math," Hatteras said. "I just think the prom is important."

"The math?"

"Nicholas Purcell was born January twenty-ninth, 2000. You go back nine months from there and you are in April or May of 1999. Most proms are near the end of the school year."

"You think something could have happened at the actual prom?"

"I do."

Ballard was annoyed with herself for not having thought of doing the math.

"That's good, Colleen," she said. "Run with it. After you're finished with the yearbook, see what you can find on Mallory's date, Rodney Van Ness. He's got a clean record, so I haven't found him. His last California driver's license expired in 2009. I think he moved out of state."

"I'm on it," Hatteras said.

Hatteras went back to her pod and Ballard checked her watch. She'd have to leave soon. Dr. Elingburg had texted her to say that she'd decided to keep her office open on the holiday because so many of her clients had expressed concern about missing their weekly therapy sessions and didn't want to have them over Zoom. Ballard was not among those who had complained, but she was relieved when she read the text.

Elingburg had moved her usual noon appointment to one o'clock, so Ballard still had time to run a few names through the National Crime Information Center index. So far she had found only one senior boy with a criminal record, and that was for financial crimes.

After a few minutes Hatteras came back with the yearbook open to the two-page spread of photos from the senior prom.

"Look," she said. "I think this was at the Huntington."

The Huntington was an upscale hotel in a residential section of Pasadena. "Pretty nice for a prom," Ballard said. "What makes you think it's the Huntington?"

"I've been there for weddings over the years, including one about a month ago," Hatteras said. "I remember these arched French doors leading out to the courtyard with the fountain."

She pointed to the French doors that lined the wall behind the slow-dancing couples.

"Okay, so it was at the Huntington," Ballard said. "What's that get us?"

"It goes with the math," Hatteras said. "The prom was at a hotel. Did you go to your prom?"

"Uh, no, I didn't."

"Me neither. But I know that when a prom is at a hotel, the kids — the boys, mostly — get hotel rooms and that's where they sneak back for alcohol, drugs, and other things."

"Like sex."

"Exactly. I think something happened to Mallory at the prom, whether it was consensual or not. I really feel it."

Ballard nodded. She was impressed by the way Colleen was putting things together. "Then we really need to find Rodney Van Ness," she said.

"I already did," Hatteras said. "He's on LinkedIn. He lives in Las Vegas and is a security supervisor at the Cleopatra Casino."

"You found him that quick?"

"Almost all these people have LinkedIn accounts. They're in their early forties and in the business world. LinkedIn's a better starting point than Facebook or Instagram."

"What else does it say about him?"

"He's been there nine years. He worked at Caesars before that."

"What about a home address?"

"It doesn't give that. But it has a work phone for him and a second number that I think might be a cell. Should we call him?"

"No, not yet. We have to think about the best approach to him. We might only get one shot. Did it say anything about him being in law enforcement before casino security?"

"Let me pull up his whole résumé and check."

"If you're locating a lot of these people, are you making a chart?"

"Oh, yes. I'm writing it all down."

Ballard raised her voice so Maddie could hear her on the other side of the privacy wall: "Maddie, what about Mallory's friends? Have you found them?"

"Found one — Jacqueline Todd," Maddie said. "Has a clean record and is still local. By the way, my prom was at a hotel that was in the Galleria in the Valley. A lot of people got rooms, and all I'm saying is there were a lot of drugs."

"That was where the prom was in *Valley Girl*," Hatteras said.

"Love that movie," Maddie said. "Nicolas Cage was awesome."

"Okay, so, on the names," Ballard said, bringing the conversation back to the point. "Let's go see Mallory's friend who stayed local."

"When?" Maddie asked.

"I have a one o'clock appointment for an hour," Ballard said. "Let's go after that."

"What about going to the DA on the Dahlia case?" Maddie asked.

"They're dark today," Ballard said. "We'll think about that tomorrow."

Ballard's cell phone buzzed. She looked at the screen and saw that it was Harry Bosch. "I have to take this," she said.

She grabbed the phone and headed for the evidence room, where her conversation would not be overheard.

"Hey," she said on her way, purposely not saying his name.

"Can you talk?" Bosch asked.

"Yes. Let me just get to . . . hold on."

She unlocked the room, entered, and closed the door behind her.

"Sorry — I can talk now," she said. "What's up?"

"Let me guess," Bosch said. "Colleen was hanging around listening."

"Well, your daughter's here too and she hasn't said anything about what happened Saturday, so I'm assuming you don't want her to know."

"Might not be able to prevent that now. I just heard from a reporter at the *L.A. Times*. That's why I'm calling, to give you a heads-up that somebody in the FBI is leaking."

"Damn. Who was the reporter?"

"Scott Anderson. I neither confirmed nor denied."

"I saw that he wrote a couple of the initial stories. So he's plugged in. What did he ask that you didn't answer?"

"Somehow he knows I was the CI. He asked how I knew about these guys wanting to buy machine guns."

"Ugh. Did he mention me?"

"No, but I didn't give him a chance to. I no-commented and hung up on him. But even if he doesn't know about you, if they run a story about me, there are people in the department who know that you and I are tight. So that's the heads-up."

"Okay, got it. I appreciate the call."

"Let me know if you hear from him."

"I will."

"How's Maddie doing? I thought she worked Mondays at Hollywood."

"She's doing really good. She does work Monday PMs, but she came in today and I didn't even ask why. She's going to be a good detective, Harry. You're gonna be proud."

"I already am."

"Good. Talk to you later, then."

Ballard disconnected and looked at her watch. She needed to leave for her appointment with Dr. Elingburg, but first she put in a call to Agent Olmstead.

"Ballard, how are you doing?"

"I'm good. You still basking in the glow of your domestic-terrorist takedown?"

"Well, you could say that the powers that be around here are my new best friends."

"Good to hear. But what's not good to hear is that the *L.A.* fucking *Times* is calling Harry Bosch about him being your undercover informant on the caper."

There was a pause while Olmstead considered this news.

"When did this happen?" he asked.

"Today," Ballard said.

"I hope he declined to comment."

"Of course he did, but here's the thing — his name should have never gotten to the media. He's a confidential informant, for Chrissake, Gordon. If the *Times* comes out with a story, it could put him in danger. Who knows how many sympathizers and yahoos think that what Dehaven was planning was patriotic."

"I know, I know. All I can tell you is that it wasn't me and I'm going to jump on this and find out who the fuck it was."

Ballard was not sure she believed him. It seemed to her that the feds always had ulterior motives. Her prior experiences with Olmstead made her think that he could be trusted, but if she was wrong about that, it wouldn't be the first time.

"The other thing is that if your leak is giving me up too, you're going to have a PR problem," she said. "Because if I get named, I won't hold back. I'll tell the *Times* that I gave you this on a silver platter after *I* did the groundwork and ID'd Dehaven and his merry band of roaming terrorists. The powers that be won't think you're walking on water anymore when that comes out."

There was another silence before Olmstead responded.

"Understood," he finally said.

"Good," Ballard said. "Let me know when you've shut it down."

She disconnected without a goodbye to emphasize her anger over the situation. She called Harry Bosch back.

"I just read Olmstead the riot act. He might not care too much about you, but he *is* worried about keeping this as a big fat FBI and Gordon Olmstead win. All of that goes down the tubes if you and I get pulled into the media on it."

"I knew you'd know how to handle it."

"Well, hopefully he'll take care of it."

"You think there's any chance he's the leak?"

"I thought about that but it doesn't make sense. Right now he's a hero. If the whole truth comes out, he doesn't look as good. It's probably someone in that office who's jealous of the attention he's getting from this."

"I think so too. But thanks for setting him right, Renée."

"All in a day's work."

After disconnecting, Ballard checked her watch. She needed to get going. She noticed the old-style suitcase on the floor next to the file cabinet holding what was left of the Black Dahlia files. The suitcase, which contained Elizabeth Short's clothes, had been found in a locker at the bus station in Hollywood several weeks after her murder in 1947. The locker's rental time had expired and the janitor was cleaning it out. No one knew who had stored the suitcase there—it could have been Elizabeth or her killer.

Forensic analysts at the time had failed to find any fingerprints or other evidence on or in the case that might lead to a suspect. The suitcase and its contents had not been pilfered over the decades because the case was stored in the department's secured evidence archive, whereas the file cabinet containing the investigative files was kept in the homicide unit offices, to which many people had access.

Seeing the suitcase gave Ballard an idea. She decided that she would follow up on it after the appointment with her therapist.

35

BALLARD WAS FIVE minutes late for her appointment with Dr. Elingburg. When she entered the waiting room, the door to the inner sanctum was already open, and she walked right in. Dr. Elingburg was in her usual spot on one of the couches. There were two glasses of water on the coffee table in front of her.

"Sorry I'm late," Ballard said.

"Busy day?" Elingburg asked.

Ballard sat in her usual spot on the opposite couch. "Wasn't supposed to be," she said. "But, yeah, it got busy."

"No holiday in the pursuit of justice," Elingburg said.

"Something like that."

"I see that you're wearing a badge on your belt. Is that the badge that went missing or a replacement?"

"It's the badge that was taken, yeah. A little worse for the wear, but I got it back."

"Without your superiors finding out it had been stolen?"

"As of now they haven't found out. But that could change. You never know."

"Let's hope it doesn't. Before we get started, is there anything you would like to discuss today?"

"Uh, not really. To be honest, I haven't had a day off since our last session, so I haven't really had time to think about therapy. But I'm here."

Elingburg nodded and picked up the notebook she kept on the coffee table during their sessions. "Well, let's go down our discussion list, then," she said. "How has your sleep pattern been?"

"Uh, good and bad," Ballard said. "I have the usual insomnia some nights and on others I'm so tired by the time I hit the pillow, it's like I'm knocked out. But even after a few hours I'll wake up and not be able to get back to sleep."

"You told me once that you can hear the ocean from your bedroom. That doesn't help?"

"In the winter, it's too cold at night to keep a window open. So lately I don't really hear the ocean."

"I'm going to send you a link to a white-noise machine you can get online. It has various settings, like ocean, wind, leaves blowing across a lawn. I think it could be helpful, but the bottom line is your sleep mechanisms are not working."

"I know that. Isn't that why I came here in the first place?"

"It is and we need to keep trying to figure it out. Is there anything new with your mother?"

Ballard shook her head. "Not that I know of, and that's my fault. I haven't had time to call Farley since we last talked."

"Farley is…"

"Dan Farley on the ID team. He's my contact and he's taken a special interest in my case, probably because I'm in law enforcement. Or, I should say, he's taken a special interest in my mother's case."

"Well, maybe you'll have an update by our next session. We can move on. With this busy week you've been having, have you been on the water much?"

"Not at all. I haven't been on a board since the day my badge got stolen."

"So, a week ago."

Talk of surfing made Ballard remember that she had Seth Dawson's watch and needed to get it back to him.

"Renée?"

"Sorry, what was the question?"

"I don't know if there was one, but you sort of went away there. What were you thinking about?"

"Nothing, really. I recovered a watch that was stolen from a surfer and I have to get it back to him, that's all."

"It seems that you're so caught up in and busy with work that you've had no time for the one thing that you've told me keeps your sanity intact: being on the water."

"No argument there. I miss it."

"What was it you said to me before about the water?"

"It's my salvation. I know."

"If you know that, why haven't you been able to get out there?"

"I've had no time. I see the water when I'm driving to work, but I haven't had the time to get out and on it. But if it will make you happy, I promise to get out there tomorrow morning."

"That would make me very happy. For you."

"I'll do it."

"So, I want to talk to you about something I said last week. The more I think about it, the more I feel like I was wrong."

"About what?"

"Well, I wrote something down and you asked what it was. I had written 'vicarious trauma,' and I proceeded to tell you that I thought it was at the root of the agitation and insomnia you're encountering. I more or less said that you were a sin eater, that you took in all the horrors you saw on your job and kept them inside, and they came out in these symptoms we are seeing: insomnia, agitation leading to a short temper."

"And now you're saying that's not it?"

"It's part of it. But I want to get into abandonment issues with you. Is that all right?"

"I guess so."

"Let me start with a question that might be difficult for you to answer."

"Just what I need."

"Tell me your thinking on this. I know you have this man Farley in Maui who keeps you updated about the search for your mother, and you have a very busy job here, but——"

"Why haven't I gone there to look for her myself?"

Elingburg pointed her pen at her. "Exactly. Sounds like you've thought about this."

"Yeah, I have."

"And?"

"And I don't know. Sometimes I think I don't go there because she didn't come looking for me. You know, after my dad...died, I was left on my own. I was alone and scared and she should have come looking for me. But it was Tutu who came for me. She saved me. And I can't get past that, you know?"

"It's a common response. Abandonment resentment. What comes up for you when you understand that's what's going on?"

"Well, it makes me feel guilty as hell. Like I should be over there looking for her."

"It's a cycle. Lather, rinse, repeat."

"I guess so. That's why I can't sleep?"

"Partly, yes. You're not sleeping because your mind can't rest. This cycle keeps it active. You need to break the cycle. You can't just keep lathering, rinsing, and repeating forever——you have to find the triggers that begin the cycle and deal with them."

"I mean, I see the triggers all the time. I deal with families that have been shattered by the sudden loss of a daughter or son or mother or father. Doesn't matter who it is, I see the loss and it doesn't ever go away. I see how they've been hollowed out by it. All of them waiting for some form of closure they know in their hearts isn't coming. And I think, *Why wasn't she like that? Why was she okay with leaving me and with me dealing with what happened alone out there?*"

Elingburg said nothing. Ballard knew this was a way to keep her talking and revealing herself. She used the same technique with suspects. And it worked.

"This morning we had a Zoom call with a woman whose sister disappeared almost seventy-five years ago. This woman tried to be so stoic, but I could hear the pain in her voice. It never goes away. Never..."

She didn't finish.

"Sorry," she said. "I'm just rambling."

"You're not rambling," Elingburg said. "You're digging down to the core of this."

Ballard smirked.

"What?" Elingburg asked.

"I have a sign on my pod wall that says 'Dig Down,'" Ballard said. "It's from a song I like. That's what we do in cold cases. We dig down into the past."

"And what we do in here."

"I guess so. Maybe that makes me a cold case. Too cold to get on a plane to go find my missing mother. Waiting for somebody else to do it when deep in my heart I know it should be me."

Ballard watched Elingburg write that down.

36

COLLEEN AND MADDIE were still working when Ballard got back to the Ahmanson Center. They showed her the chart they had put together. They had located fifty-two of the sixty-six seniors listed in the 1999 St. Vincent's yearbook. Of the remaining fourteen, five were boys and nine were girls; the girls were more difficult to find because their last names sometimes changed when they got married. Additionally, Maddie had run criminal record checks, but those produced only two former students who had been convicted of crimes, the one for financial fraud that Ballard had also found, the other for indecent exposure.

They spent the next half hour putting together an interview-priority list. The name at the top was Rodney Van Ness, Mallory's date for his senior prom. Although he was first on the list, because he was located in Las Vegas, he was probably not going to be the first interview. Taking a road trip required planning and approvals.

Next on the list was Jacqueline Todd, one of Mallory's two best friends. She was still living in Los Angeles, according to LinkedIn, and working as a screenwriter. Mallory's other best friend, Emma, was third on the priority list, but she had not been located. They hoped that Jacqueline Todd would have her contact information.

Fourth on the list was Nathan Hyatt, the former student who had been arrested for indecent exposure a year after graduation. He was living in Venice, according to the DMV. He had no criminal record since that arrest but was an obvious choice for scrutiny, as the indecent exposure could have been a precursor to more serious sexually motivated crimes. Most serial offenders follow an escalating path of sex crimes, Ballard knew. Her only hesitation about Hyatt was that he had most likely been interviewed by the original Pillowcase Rapist task force. She would have to pull the records, but she knew that the task force had thrown a wide net and interviewed almost all known sex offenders living in the county then.

"Maddie, how much time you got before you go in today?" Ballard asked.

"A few hours," Maddie said. "I have roll call at six."

"Let's go talk to Jacqueline Todd," Ballard said.

"Sounds good," Maddie said.

They took separate cars so Maddie could peel off and go to work if the interview went long or was delayed. Ballard took the lead, working her way to the 405 freeway and then heading north toward the Valley. Jacqueline Todd, according to the DMV, lived in Sherman Oaks.

Ballard's GPS app said it was a thirty-eight-minute drive. She decided to use the time to make phone calls. The first was to Gordon Olmstead at the FBI, but it went straight to voicemail. She assumed Olmstead was avoiding her after the earlier call and left a message: "It's Ballard. Just looking for an update on whether you shut down the leak. Call me back, please."

She knew he wouldn't. She thought about how aggressive she had been with Olmstead earlier and what Dr. Elingburg had said about her short temper. She called Olmstead back and left another message: "Gordon, me again. Sorry about being so testy last time we talked. A lot of stuff is going on and I overreacted. Call me when you can."

She disconnected and drove for a bit, thinking about the interview she hoped to conduct with Jacqueline Todd. She knew the apartment complex she and Maddie were headed to because she had been there on prior cases. It made her think about her mother, so she made her next call to Dan Farley in Maui. It was a holiday but he had told her that MINT members were not taking any holidays off, other than Christmas, because of the urgency of identifying the dead from the fires and informing their families.

Farley took the call and Ballard could tell he was in a car.

"Hello, Renée."

"Dan, did I catch you at a bad time? I thought you'd be working today."

"I am. On my way down to Wailea to make a notification. Members of the family are staying at the Four Seasons."

"Oh, man, that's tough. Not the Four Seasons, the notification."

"Yeah, but I find it's better face-to-face than over the phone. I've done a lot of those and they seem so impersonal. This one's a twenty-two-year-old son. He was bumming around the islands and went to Lahaina. Wrong place at the wrong time."

"Yeah."

There was a beat of silence before Farley spoke.

"If I had any news for you, I would have called, Renée."

"I know. I was just thinking about her today. My mother. Whenever I talk to you, it sort of calms me. I don't know why."

"I understand. You know you can call me anytime. I deal with a lot of families waiting to hear something, whether it's good or bad. But we haven't found her among the dead so far, and that's a good sign, right?"

"I guess so."

"I think that when we find Makani, she's going to be alive."

With all the cases he was working and all the families he was dealing with, the fact that Farley remembered her mother's name comforted Ballard.

"I hope so," she said. "Thanks, Dan."

"Call anytime," Farley said again.

The freeway took her over the Santa Monica Mountains through the Sepulveda Pass, and on the downgrade Ballard transitioned to the 101 and then immediately exited at Van Nuys Boulevard. Jacqueline Todd lived in an apartment complex on Magnolia called the Horace Heidt Estates. It was a very large complex with a distinctive Hawaiian-village feel, with tiki bars and facilities with names like the Aloha Room. Horace Heidt had been a radio band-leader in the 1940s and '50s and had built the apartments so members of his band could live and practice together. There were three pools and an executive golf course. There was also a mini-museum of Hollywood memorabilia that Ballard had toured with Heidt's son, who now ran the place. It was largely photos, costumes, and other keepsakes Horace Heidt had collected during his time as a bandleader.

Ballard drove through the complex and found the building where Jacqueline Todd lived. As she parked, Maddie pulled in next to her. Before getting out, Ballard looked up Jacqueline Todd on IMDb and found her writing credits. Over the past ten years she had written and produced several episodes of various television series. Most of them were crime shows. Her latest credits were on a streaming series called *Apex,* about a squad of LAPD detectives who went after the "biggest predators out there." The unit had a logo that showed a cartoonish great white shark's gaping mouth and double rows of teeth. Ballard noted that the writer went by the name Jackie Todd professionally.

She got out with her leather laptop bag, though she had left the computer at the office.

"Let me do the talking," she said to Maddie. "If I give you the nod, you take it from there."

The knock on the door of apartment 241 was answered by a woman wearing baggy sweatpants and a T-shirt with the same shark logo Ballard had just seen on IMDb. She had short-clipped hair like the lead actress on a show Ballard liked, *Criminal Record*.

"Jackie Todd?" Ballard asked.

"Yes," the woman said. "How can I... help you?"

"I'm Detective Ballard with the LAPD and this is Officer Bosch. We'd like to come in and ask you a few — "

Ballard didn't finish. Todd had raised a hand to cover her mouth and hide a wide smile.

"Is something funny?" Ballard asked.

"Uh, no, I'm sorry," Todd said. "Please, come in."

She moved back so Ballard and Maddie could enter. They stepped into a living room with an old and lumpy couch and three cushioned chairs positioned around a bamboo-and-glass coffee table. A balcony off the living room looked down on a pool. It was a sunny day but February-cold, and the lounge chairs surrounding the water were empty. There was an adjoining dining room with a table holding an open laptop and several scripts and notebooks.

"Are you working today?" Ballard asked.

"I'm a writer," Todd said. "I'm always working. Should I sit down, or how do you want to do this?"

"Sitting is good," Ballard said. "How about over here?" She pointed to the couch and chairs.

"Sure," Todd said. "But I'm warning you, don't stand on the coffee table. It's too rickety."

"Uh, we weren't planning to do that," Ballard said, puzzled.

They moved toward the chairs, and Todd sat on the couch.

"Did you bring your music in that?" Todd asked. She pointed to Ballard's laptop bag.

"Music?" Ballard asked. "No. We just want to ask you a few questions."

"Okay..." Todd said. She smiled again and added a giggle.

Ballard was fully confused now, but Maddie apparently wasn't.

"Do you think we're fake cops?" she asked. "Like strippers or something?"

"Well, yeah," Todd said. "Like a mother-and-daughter thing? Bernardo sent you, right?"

Ballard held up her hand as if to nip that thought in the bud.

"I'm sorry," she said. "We're not strippers and not mother and daughter. And I don't know who Bernardo is." Ballard pulled her badge off her belt as she said this and held it out across the coffee table. Maddie did the same.

"These aren't props," Ballard said. "They're real."

Todd sat straight up.

"Oh my God!" she said. "I thought it was — I'm so sorry. Today's my birthday and I thought the writing room sent you. Like, as a gag. They pranked me last year and ... I just thought ... you know."

"This is the *Apex* writing room you're talking about?" Ballard asked.

"Exactly," Todd said. "I was told to expect a delivery today, even though it's a holiday. I'm so embarrassed."

"Well, I'm glad we cleared that up."

"I don't understand, though. Why would you want to talk to me?"

"Well, we were told that twenty-five years ago, you had a friend named Mallory Richardson. Do you remember her?"

Todd's face took on a serious look.

"Mallory?" she asked. "Why are you asking about Mallory?"

"She's come up in an investigation we're conducting," Ballard said. "What we would like to do is just ask you about the period when you two were friends. Is that all right?"

"Well, yeah. But you do know that Mallory's been dead for a long time, right?"

"Yes, we know."

"Are you saying she was murdered or something?"

"No, we're not. Her death is not why we're here. Can you tell us a little bit about your relationship with her? Like how you knew her and what sort of girl she was?"

"Well, we became friends because we went to school together."

"St. Vincent's in Pasadena?"

"Yes, St. V.'s, as we called it. And we weren't part of the popular clique. We sat at the odd-fellows table in the cafeteria and that's how we met."

"What was the odd-fellows table?"

"You know, for the kids who didn't fit in. That's what we called it. I was one of only three Black kids at the school, and the other two were boys and athletes. I was writing poetry, not playing sports, so I wasn't like them. The odd fellows were the nerds and outcasts. Late bloomers socially."

"I think you just described me in high school. But they called our table the losers club," said Ballard.

"Then you get it. So that's how I knew Mallory. But that was like twenty-five years ago. She left after tenth grade and I never saw her again. Her family moved out to the desert and we lost touch."

"Right. So you didn't have any contact with her the summer after tenth grade or later?"

"No, it was kind of weird. It was like she dropped off the planet. And then, like a year after that, we heard that she'd taken pills and killed herself."

"When you say 'we,' who else do you mean?"

"There was another girl we were friends with."

"Was that Emma Arciniega?"

253

"Yes. Sounds like you already know a lot about it."

"Well, you write cop shows, you know how it goes. Are you still in touch with Emma?"

"On occasion. She's got her life and I have mine."

"What's that mean?"

"Marriage, kids, the whole thing. For her, I mean. I'm not married."

"What's Emma's last name now? Where does she live?"

"Emma Sepulveda. Like the street. She's still in South Pas."

"She work?"

"She's a court stenographer at the appeals court over there."

"And her husband?"

"Randy Sepulveda. He's an actor. Or trying to be. That's when I usually hear from her, when she wants me to get him cast in a show I'm working on."

"You ever do it?"

"You do know that I'm a writer, right? Writers don't make those kinds of choices. I've had to explain that to Emma many times."

Ballard turned slightly toward Maddie and gave her a single nod. Her turn.

"What about Rodney Van Ness?" Maddie asked. "Was he one of the odd fellows?"

Todd paused for a moment to search her memory.

"Rodney—no. He was two years ahead of us—a senior," Todd said. "Odd fellows didn't cross lines like that. You stuck to your own grade."

"He took Mallory to his senior prom."

"If you two already know everything, why come here?"

"We need to know more. Did you go to the senior prom when you were in the tenth grade?"

"I never went to the senior prom, even when I was a senior. Was never asked, and the patriarchy did not allow the girls to ask the guys back then."

There was an undertone of bitterness to that answer that could not be missed, a resentment that had not gone away even after all these years.

"How did Rodney Van Ness know Mallory if they were two grades apart?" Maddie asked.

"The older boys were always checking out the younger girls," Todd said. "I don't think he knew her that well when he asked her to the prom."

"Was she excited to be asked?"

"Sure."

"Did she tell you about the prom afterward?"

"No, she wouldn't talk about it."

"How come?"

"Because — as I'm sure you know because you already know things — something happened."

"What happened?"

"I don't know. I just said she didn't talk about it."

"Did her behavior change? What was the tell?"

"The tell?"

"That something had happened at the prom."

"I don't know if there was a tell. She wouldn't talk about it, that's all. Emma and me, we thought it had just been a really bad date. There were only a few weeks left of school at that point. And then she was gone and I never heard from her again."

"What about when she died? How did you find out about it?"

Todd thought for a moment.

"You know, I can't remember," she finally said. "I think maybe Emma told me. But that's when we started to think that something really bad had happened. Maybe at the prom."

"But you have no idea what that was?" Ballard pressed.

"Well, the obvious thing is that she'd had sex with Rodney and it was her first time and it didn't go well. Or she'd been coerced into having sex. Or even worse. But like I said, at the time I just thought it had been a bad date. Mal gave no indication it was anything else."

Ballard nodded but didn't say anything, waiting for Todd to continue, but she didn't.

"Okay," Ballard finally said. "We have a copy of the yearbook from when you were in tenth grade. I'm hoping you can look at it and tell me if you remember who some of the people in the photos are."

"I can try," Todd said. "But that was like twenty-five years ago."

"I know," Ballard said. "I just need you to give it a try. We're interested in identifying people in the photos from the prom. Also, I assume there were more than just the three of you at the odd-fellows table. It would be good if we could get those names as well."

"You know, you never said exactly what this is about," Todd said. "I mean, if Mallory wasn't murdered, then what are you investigating? Was it rape?"

"Like I said, we're not investigating her death," Ballard said. "But we can't really give more information yet. When it comes together, we will let you know."

Ballard pulled the yearbook out of her leather bag and opened it to the double-page spread of photos taken at the prom. There was a center photo showing the prom king and queen onstage with a cutline that identified the couple, but the four other photos did not have any captions beneath them.

"We're trying to figure out who was at the prom because we might need to speak to them," Ballard said. "Do you remember any of these people?"

Todd gazed down at the five black-and-white photos.

"I don't think I can — well, that's Rodney right there," she said.

She tapped a photo of a group of boys standing around a table where some of their dates were seated.

The individual in the photo she tapped had a beard.

"Really?" Ballard said. "I thought that was a teacher."

"No, he had a beard then," Todd said. "I remember that. Made him look old."

Ballard looked at the senior photo of Rodney Van Ness again and then flipped back and forth between that and the prom picture, doing a comparison between the clean-cut and studio-styled Rodney and the bearded prom-night Rodney.

"I think you're right," Ballard said.

"I know I'm right," Todd said. "He had a full beard by the end of the year. I think he might have been held back a year in grammar school. He was like a grown man by graduation."

Ballard counted six boys standing behind the table and only four girls seated.

"So if that's Rodney, where is Mallory?" she asked.

"She's not there," Todd said. "Maybe she was in the restroom or something."

"And maybe not," Ballard said. "Do you know the names of anybody else in this shot?"

Todd tapped the boy standing next to Rodney.

"That's Victor somebody," she said. "I can't remember his last name. He and Rodney were tight."

"Victor," Ballard said. She turned back through the senior photos looking for a Victor. There was only one. "Victor Best," she said.

"That's it," Todd said. "Victor Best. I should have remembered a name like that."

"He was friends with Rodney?" Ballard asked.

"Yes," Todd said. "He and Rodney and a few other guys used to hang out on these benches behind the school. Down in the arroyo.

The rumor was that they'd get high there during lunch. Seniors were allowed to go off campus."

"You remember the names of any of the other guys in the photos?" Ballard asked.

"No. They weren't really on my radar, you know," Todd said. "They were seniors."

"What about the girls?"

"Same thing. I didn't know any seniors. In fact, I think Mallory was the only sophomore who went to the prom that year. From what I remember."

Ballard pointed to the arched windows behind the photo of the slow dancers.

"Was it at the Huntington that year?" she asked.

"I have no idea," Todd said. "I didn't go, remember?"

"Right," Ballard said. "Well, I think that's good for now, Jackie. Thank you for your help. We really appreciate it."

"Sure," Todd said. "I mean, I guess. If it was useful to you, that's cool."

"It was," Ballard said.

"Would you be able to give us contact information for Emma Sepulveda?" Maddie said. "It would save us some time."

"Sure," Todd said. "If you give me your contact information."

Maddie looked confused but Ballard had a sense of what was coming.

"I'm tired of working on other people's shows," Todd said. "I want to create my own and I need someone to bounce ideas off of. Maybe give me some ideas too. It will be a female lead."

"Uh," Maddie said. "I guess that's okay."

She looked at Ballard to see if she was making a mistake. Ballard just nodded.

After exchanging contact details, including an email address for Emma Sepulveda, Ballard and Maddie thanked Todd and left the apartment. When they got back to their cars, they stood between them to talk.

"Victor Best," Ballard said. "Did you and Colleen run him down?"

"He was one of the seniors we couldn't find," Maddie said. "But Colleen was still at it when we left."

"Well, I want to find him and talk to him. Along with Rodney Van Ness."

"Interesting that Mallory wasn't in that photo. What do you think that means?"

"That's what we're going to talk to Rodney and Victor about."

37

HATTERAS WAS STILL in her pod when Ballard got back to the Ahmanson Center.

"Colleen, what are you doing? You are spending too much time here," Ballard said. "I don't want you to burn out."

"I won't," Hatteras said. "I like being here and I wanted to stay to find out how it went with Jacqueline Todd."

Ballard filled her in briefly on the interview with Jackie Todd and then asked if she had been able to locate a senior from the yearbook named Victor Best.

"No, there's nothing on social on the Victor Best from St. Vincent's," Hatteras said. "There are other Victor Bests out there, but I was able to determine pretty quickly they were not our guy. And you didn't find any criminal record when you looked him up, right?"

"Right. Nothing criminal."

"I could start a genealogy run, if you want."

"Okay, but maybe wait till tomorrow. You've put in enough time today. Anything else come up I should know about?"

"Well, I jumped back on the Black Dahlia case for a while and worked on Willa Kenyon."

"Anything new on that?"

"Yes. I reached out to the site manager at Lost Angels and she called me back. She was intrigued enough by what I told her that she—"

"Wait, what did you tell her, Colleen? I said nothing about this case should leave the raft. You were right here when I said that."

"I know, I know. You don't have to worry. I didn't mention Elizabeth Short or Black Dahlia or anything that would lead her to make a connection. I simply said that while we were working a cold-case investigation, Willa Kenyon's name came up on a genealogy tree, and we wanted to know what they had on her disappearance. That's all."

"Okay, fine. I'm sorry I jumped on you like that. So what did the site manager have?"

"Well, she got curious enough to go into the office even though it's a holiday because she said they have physical files on many of the really old cases. Lost Angels was operating before there was an internet, so there are paper files. She pulled the Willa Kenyon file and it had some family names in it—the parents who reported her missing—and also a boyfriend. I was able to confirm that her parents have long passed and there were no siblings. The boyfriend is dead too, but his name was pretty unique: Adolfo Galvez. I plugged that in on Ancestry and found a son and grandson still here in L.A. Adolfo got married a long time after Willa disappeared, when it became clear she wasn't coming back, and I think maybe there's a chance he talked about Willa with his son or grandson. But I didn't call anyone. I thought you'd want to weigh in, since we sort of jumped the gun with Elyse Ford's sister today."

"Okay, send me what you've got, but I'm okay with you taking it forward and talking to them. You and Maddie handled Elyse Ford's family well. So—your lead, your move. But not today. I want you to start on that tomorrow."

"Okay. Tomorrow."

There was an excitement in her voice, although whether it was due to the compliment or the approval to continue with the lead, Ballard didn't know.

"Was there anything else in the file besides the names?" Ballard asked.

"There was a copy of the police report the family made when she went missing," Hatteras said. "She scanned it and sent it to me."

"Anything stand out?"

"Not really. But, here, I'll pull it up. It's pretty short."

Hatteras turned to her screen and opened a document. It was an LAPD missing person report dated June 21, 1950. The color scanner had picked up the yellowed edges of the seventy-three-year-old document. The missing individual was identified as Willa Kenyon, age twenty-two, and gave her address as an apartment on Selma in Hollywood. The summary said she had been missing two days at the time of the report. Her occupation was listed simply as *singer*.

"That's interesting," Ballard said. "She was a singer. Depending on what that actually means, she could have needed photos for promotion."

"She could have somehow contacted Thawyer and gone to him," Hatteras said.

Ballard nodded, more to herself than Hatteras. She was seeing possible connections coming together. It reminded her that she needed to get into the lockdown room and open Elizabeth Short's suitcase. She had a hunch she wanted to follow up on.

"Send me that report too," she said. "Then that's enough for today, Colleen. I'll see you tomorrow at the team meeting."

"Are you sure you don't need me for anything else?" Hatteras asked.

"Not today. It's supposed to be a holiday, remember? I'm leaving too after I get some paperwork done."

Ballard knew that if she went to the lockdown room now to retrieve the suitcase, Hatteras would never leave; she would stay and look over Ballard's shoulder. So instead Ballard went to her desk, opened her terminal, and started writing a summary of the interview with Jackie Todd to send to Captain Gandle.

It was a waiting game. Hatteras was taking her time finishing up her work and shutting down. Ballard wrote a two-page summary on the interview, and Hatteras was still at her desk. Ballard could hear her keyboard clicking on the other side of the partition.

Once she filed the report and sent a copy to Gandle, she started an email to the captain requesting his approval for a trip to Las Vegas to interview Rodney Van Ness. She carefully outlined his connection to the Pillowcase Rapist case. Van Ness could be a key witness, a person of interest, or even a suspect, and she explained that he had to be approached in person so his reactions and answers could be properly gauged. Ballard wrote that the trip was critical and that money from her unit's NIJ grant would pay for her and Officer Bosch to make the likely two-day road trip to Nevada and back.

"What's that?"

Hatteras had come around the raft and walked up behind her without Ballard's noticing while she was doing a final read of the email. She immediately clicked the send button. She turned to look at Hatteras, who had car keys in her hand. Finally, she was leaving.

"An email to the captain," Ballard said. "You're going home now?"

"Yes," Hatteras said. "But are you going to Las Vegas?"

She had obviously spied the subject line of the email before Ballard sent it.

"I don't know yet, and it's not something you need to worry about," Ballard said.

"I was just going to say I could go with you," Hatteras said. "To help."

"Colleen, it's fieldwork and we talked about that. You need additional training if you want to do anything in the field."

"Then sign me up," Hatteras said. "I'm tired of being a computer nerd."

"Colleen, you're not a nerd. You are a very important part of this unit. Look at all the leads you have come up with in just the past few days. But this is a team, and every member of the team needs to do their part so that we can get the best results on our cases. I'm sorry I have to keep explaining this to you."

"I know, I know. I just wish —"

"Look, you've put in a long day and I want you to go home and rest up. I need your best work when you come in tomorrow. Okay, Colleen?"

Hatteras frowned and nodded. "Are you leaving now? I'll walk out with you."

"No, I still have more paperwork and emails to do," Ballard said. "And this is only delaying it. I want you to go home, Colleen."

"Okay, okay. I get it. I'm leaving."

"Thank you. I'll see you tomorrow."

"Nine o'clock?"

"Right, though we both know you'll be in before that."

Hatteras smiled slightly and nodded again. She turned and finally headed to the door.

Ballard waited, half expecting to see Colleen round the corner by the first row of the murder archives and come back to the raft.

Luckily, she didn't.

When she was sure Hatteras was gone, Ballard stood, opened her desk drawer, and grabbed the key to the lockdown room. She picked up the file containing Thawyer's photos of Elizabeth Short and went to open her suitcase.

TUESDAY, 6:25 A.M.

38

BALLARD CALLED SETH Dawson, hoping he was up and about, maybe even surfing. But when he answered, she could tell he was in a moving car with the windows open. She was in a moving car herself.

"It's Detective Ballard," she said. "Are you going to the water?"

"You guessed it."

"Which break? I'm on my way out too, and I have something for you."

"Zuma. Going with the app."

Ballard had checked the Surf's Up app herself and knew that Zuma was the recommendation. She was already heading toward Venice and she'd have to turn around on the PCH to get back to Zuma. She tried to judge how much time she'd get on the water going all the way up there.

"I'll meet you there," she said.

She finished the call and made a U-turn in front of Pepperdine. Thirty minutes later, she was on her board, waiting for her first wave. There was no sign of Dawson.

She got in two long runs on five-footers before she saw Dawson carrying his board across the beach. She paddled parallel to the shore to meet him on the break.

"Hey," he said after paddling out. "How is it?"

"Not bad," Ballard said. "Fives and sevens. Fives mostly."

She paddled closer and turned her board so they were side by side.

"Got something for you," she said.

She had the Breitling watch on her arm almost all the way to the elbow of her wetsuit. She slid it down and over her hand, then held it out to Dawson.

"No way!" he exclaimed, taking the watch. "You found it?"

"Check the back," Ballard said.

He did, then gripped the watch in his hand.

"That's it," he said. "I told my dad it was gone. He won't believe this. How'd you get it back?"

"Well, I can't tell you everything," Ballard said. "It's part of an ongoing investigation. But the person who stole it took it to a fence that cooperated with us. So we found it."

"Thank you so much."

"Glad to return it to you. I know it means a lot. Now I'm looking for one more wave and then I gotta go to work."

Ballard glanced over her shoulder. The next set was coming in. It looked like more of the same—five-footers. She leaned forward and started paddling. She called back to Dawson, "That's my wave. See you."

Dawson started paddling too.

"Thank you!" he called after her.

They both got up on the wave but Dawson bailed early to go back out for more. Ballard was done for the day. She rode it all the way in, then stepped off the board in the shallows. She turned back to see Dawson holding up his hand, his fingers spread wide—a familiar surfer goodbye. She returned the gesture and lifted her board out of the surf.

39

THE FULL TEAM was there for the meeting when Ballard entered at nine, coffee and computer bag in hand. She put both down on her desk and immediately went to her usual spot in front of the whiteboards.

"Okay, let's get started," she said. "We've got a lot going on."

"How was the water?" Masser asked.

Ballard looked at him, surprised, then realized her hair was the giveaway. It was still wet.

"It was nice," she said. "But too short."

She waited to see if there were any questions from the others. There weren't.

"Okay, let's go with old business before we see where we are on the Pillowcase and Black Dahlia cases."

Ballard turned to look at the whiteboards.

"Tom, you have an update on Shaquilla Washington?" she asked.

"I do," Laffont said. "We got a genetic match to a man who is twenty-two years into a twenty-five-to-life sentence at Soledad. Gerald Grover, a gangster, formerly from Inglewood."

"Well done," Ballard said. "You take it to John Lewin?"

"I did and he's going to file charges," Laffont said. "Grover was

269

probably counting on parole in the next few years, but that won't happen now. He's never getting out."

"Beautiful," Ballard said. "Did you talk to the victim's family?"

"Not yet," Laffont said. "Waiting on John. I don't want to make the call until charges are in place."

Ballard nodded approval. She walked over to what they called the scoreboard. It had been part of a sign for keeping track of consecutive days without injury on the manufacturing floor of the aerospace firm that previously occupied the center. It had been salvaged from the debris left behind when the company moved out and the LAPD moved in. Ballard flipped the number indicating the cases solved since the inception of the unit from 41 to 42, and the team seated behind her applauded, as was the routine.

"Okay," Ballard said as she turned back to the group. "Anybody else? Paul?"

Masser reported that the interview with the now-cooperating Maxine Russell was still being negotiated by her lawyer and Lewin. Ballard decided not to flip over another number yet.

Ballard then went to new business and reported that she and Maddie Bosch were heading downtown after the meeting to present the Black Dahlia evidence to Carol Plovc at the district attorney's office. She also said she was awaiting approval from command staff for a trip to Las Vegas to track down and interview Rodney Van Ness with the hope of getting closer to the Pillowcase Rapist.

"Everyone has done great work on these cases," she said. "But let's keep digging. Thank you."

As soon as the meeting ended, Colleen Hatteras got up from her pod and worked her way around the raft to Ballard. Before she could speak, Ballard beat her to it.

"Colleen, I was thinking you might want to come downtown with Maddie and me," she said.

Hatteras pulled up short with surprise.

"What?" she said. "Are you kidding?"

"No, I think it would be helpful for you to be there," Ballard said. "To explain how we found Elyse Ford's family. You up for that?"

"Of course I am."

"Good. Get your files. We have an eleven o'clock appointment with Carol. We're going in five."

Hatteras hurried back to her pod, leaving Ballard smiling in her wake.

40

THE HALL OF Justice on Temple Street in downtown L.A. was ninety-nine years old. For most of that near century, the building housed on its top floors a jail operated by the sheriff's department. But the incarceration needs of the county outgrew it, and a county jail complex was built, and for many years after that, the Hall's cells were left empty. Eventually, the needs of the district attorney's office, which had a growing staff commensurate with the city's crime and incarceration numbers, led to a renovation that put prosecutors into the cells that were once home to the prosecuted. The office of deputy district attorney Carol Plovc, of the Major Crimes Unit, was in one of the refurbished jail cells on the fourteenth floor. There were no steel bars remaining, but the rear wall of the room received light through a window of thick glass gridded by ironwork into six-inch-by-six-inch escape-proof squares.

In its previous use, the office had likely been a multi-inmate cell, because it was spacious enough for a bookcase, a desk, and ample seating. Ballard, Maddie, and Hatteras sat comfortably across from Plovc while she looked over the photos spread across her desk. She had been given the full files, the ones containing all the photos from Emmitt Thawyer's storage room. Plovc, who was in her early forties and a seasoned lifer in the office, grimaced as she looked through the photos displaying the degradation, torture, and murder of eight women.

"We had the photo analysis unit do a comparison of the Betty pictures to known Elizabeth Short photos," Ballard said. "It came back as a ninety-two percent likelihood that it's a match."

Plovc spoke without looking up from the photos.

"That leaves eight percent," she said. "That's where reasonable doubt lives."

Though Plovc was the sign-off to clear cases where the identified suspect was dead, this was no rubber stamp. To prevent investigators from seeking clearances with only thin evidence, she had a protocol she followed. At the top of this checklist was the likelihood, or not, of a conviction had a suspect been charged.

"We were thinking that the Ford case kind of eliminates reasonable doubt," Ballard said. "Her photos were in the same file cabinet. She disappeared a few years after Short was murdered. Colleen located her family, and they identified her from the photos. Our theory is that the Elizabeth Short murder — the whole Black Dahlia thing and the massive attention it got — made Thawyer go underground. He kept killing but he stopped displaying his kills."

"What did he do with the bodies?" Plovc asked.

"He probably buried them," Ballard said.

"Griffith Park was not so far away from the house," Hatteras said.

Plovc looked up from the photos. "I really only want to hear from the sworn officers on this," she said.

"Sure, I understand," Hatteras said, looking a little cowed.

"The point is that we've identified a pattern," Ballard said. "Multiple women's photos found in the same drawer. Our suspect was a photographer. It's the oldest trick in the book — luring women with the promise of photos that will help them achieve their dreams. Been done a hundred times, but maybe it started with Thawyer."

"You're missing my concern here," Plovc said. "I have no doubt that these photos are legit and that these women were killed in truly horrible ways by this man Thawyer. But the jump to Elizabeth Short has an eight percent hole in it. And with a case of this magnitude...I mean, this case is part of Los Angeles history. There have been movies and books and TV—James Ellroy's book is out there, an ex-LAPD cop who says his dad was the killer is out there, so many theories. So we have to be one hundred percent sure, not ninety-two percent sure."

Ballard stood up.

"Okay, I brought her suitcase, and I want to show you something," she said.

Ballard had left the suitcase by the door when they entered the office. It had tweed sides with a leather handle and edging. It had double snap locks and an ID plate with *Elizabeth Short* handwritten on it along with a Boston address.

"The guy who came up with the idea of putting wheels on a suitcase was a genius," she said. She carried the suitcase by the handle back to her seat and sat down with it across her knees. She popped the locks and opened it.

"This suitcase was found in a bus terminal locker about two weeks after Elizabeth Short was murdered. These were temporary lockers, so they cleaned them out every two weeks. Her name is on the ID, so the janitor called the police rather than putting it in the lost and found. It was checked for fingerprints then. Later, in the nineties, when DNA testing came along, the clothing was checked for foreign DNA, but nothing was found. But if you look at the first photo in the file, where Elizabeth is posing on the stool, you see her bra and underwear match. There is a cross-stitch pattern down the hips and it is repeated in the seams of the bra."

Ballard lifted a matching set of bra and panties from the suitcase. They were encased in clear plastic evidence sleeves. Each item had the same cross-stitch pattern of the undergarments in the photo. Plovc looked back and forth from the photo to the items Ballard was holding.

"You think that those are the same things she was wearing in this photo?" Plovc asked.

"We don't know," Ballard said. "She could have bought multiple sets at the same time. But what's clear is that they match. I think that bumps the ninety-two percent to a hundred."

"It's her," Maddie said. "It's obvious, if you ask me."

Plovc looked at Maddie, and Ballard got ready for her to tell Maddie that her opinion carried no weight in the decision she would make. But instead, Plovc swung her attention back to Ballard.

"So this suitcase was found two weeks after the murder?" she asked. "How long was it there?"

"Yes, two weeks after," Ballard said. "A lot of the records from then are gone. There is an evidence log that mentions the suitcase, but I couldn't find anything that says when it went into the locker."

"Think about it," Maddie said. "She goes to the guy for photos. He probably told her to bring a variety of clothes for various shots. She was a Hollywood hopeful. He could have told her he'd give her a whole album of different looks. Then he kills her, puts all the clothes, including her underwear, back into the suitcase, and dumps it at the bus terminal."

Plovc nodded. "Makes sense," she said. "But we have no proof of that, do we?"

"Well, we know the suitcase was Short's," Ballard said. "And the underwear matches the photo. That is Elizabeth Short in the photos and Thawyer's the guy."

Plovc nodded, but not in agreement. It was more an acknowledgment of how sure Ballard and Maddie were.

"I think I'm going to have to take this across the street," she said.

The main offices of the district attorney, including that of the top prosecutor, were located across Temple in the Criminal Courts Building. Plovc was probably passing the decision to her supervisors, maybe even to the elected district attorney.

"How long will that take?" Hatteras asked.

Plovc looked at her sharply.

"As long as it takes," she said. "There is no hurry on this. It's been seventy-seven years."

"I was just thinking of the Ford family," Hatteras said. "They want answers. Can we talk about that case?"

"Everybody wants answers," Plovc said. "And no, we're taking these as a whole. I will walk all of it across the street and get back to you as soon as a decision is made. Thank you all for coming in today. It's really exciting stuff."

Plovc started stacking the files at the side of her desk, a clear sign that the meeting was over.

WEDNESDAY, 10:22 A.M.

41

THE CLEOPATRA CASINO and Resort on the Las Vegas Strip was a place of withered beauty. Built in the 1980s, it was now dwarfed by the opulent glass towers that surrounded it. Like everything and almost everyone in Vegas, it was slated for a ground-up rebuild. Once owned and operated by mobsters out of Chicago, the casino had long since passed to a corporate conglomerate that invested in hotels and amusement parks. Because its end was near, the casino's interiors were not as polished as they once were. It felt second tier to Ballard. The glass skylight that stretched over the gaming floor had once been a point of pride, but the glass was now dirty with the debris of settling smog and auto exhaust, and several panels that had been cracked by falling liquor bottles from the tower rooms, presumably, had been replaced with plywood. Its signature pulpit, a faux-gold-leaf structure with the face of Cleopatra extending up toward the glass and over the gaming tables, was propped against collapse by two industrial stanchions. The Cleo had clearly seen better times, and this was reflected in the clientele that gathered at its five-dollar blackjack tables and one-dollar-minimum roulette wheels.

It had been a four-hour drive from Los Angeles after a 6:00 a.m. departure from the Ahmanson Center. In the course of those miles,

Ballard and Maddie Bosch had covered the basic topics of casual conversation between two female law enforcement officers, one with most of her service years behind her, the other at the start of her career.

Maddie had expressed a dissatisfaction with patrol work and was hoping that her time with the Open-Unsolved Unit would fast-track her ascent to the detective ranks.

"I mean, I'd work auto theft," she had said. "Anything to get out of the uniform."

"I was the same," Ballard responded. "Couldn't wait to move my badge to my belt."

The conversation was interrupted when Ballard took a call from Captain Gandle, who said he had received her request for the Las Vegas trip and was approving it. Little did he know that they were already going by Zzyzx and were approaching the state line and Nevada. After Ballard disconnected, Maddie started laughing.

"We didn't have permission before we left?"

"Well, I figured we'd get it. I laid it all out for him in the request. I just didn't want to wait around. You'll learn this: Part of being a good detective is knowing your boss and how he thinks."

"Or how she thinks."

"Right. Your dad can tell you a lot about all of this."

"Uh, I don't think my dad did too well in supervisor psychology."

"True."

"I mean, he threw a lieutenant through a glass window in the watch office once. They still talk about that at Hollywood Division."

"Yeah, I'm sure they do."

After they parked in the garage at the Cleopatra, Ballard reminded Maddie to follow her lead during the play with Rodney Van Ness. The strategy they had discussed while in the car was simple: Set him up with questions that would reveal his level of candor. If he lied, that would give them leverage.

There was a line of people snaking through a velvet-roped warren in the lobby of the hotel. They were all waiting to check into their discounted rooms. Ballard scanned the space until she saw a man in a blue blazer with the telltale radio wire coiling up out of his collar and looping into his ear. She tapped Maddie on the arm and nodded in the man's direction.

As they approached, Ballard pulled her badge off her belt, palmed it, and flashed it discreetly to the security man.

"We're over from LAPD on a case," she said. "Can you ask Rodney Van Ness to meet us in the lobby?"

"I don't know who that is," the man said.

"Last we checked, he was a security supervisor here."

"Don't know any Rodney Van Ness."

Ballard nodded. There was no law about lying on LinkedIn. She started to wonder if the trip had been for nothing and blamed herself for not confirming Van Ness's employment before leaving Los Angeles. It wasn't hard to imagine what Captain Gandle's response would be.

"Then could you call a supervisor down to talk with us?" she asked.

"That I can do."

He raised his wrist to his mouth and spoke into a radio transmitter. He asked someone named Marty to come talk to two detectives from the LAPD.

"Marty will be down in five," he said. "Wants you to wait over by the concierge." He pointed across the lobby to a counter that had its own line of people waiting for attention.

"Thank you," Ballard said.

"Hey, are they hiring at the LAPD?" the security man asked.

"These days, they're always hiring," Ballard said.

He looked at Maddie for a moment. "You seem kind of young for a detective," he said.

"She just solved the biggest case in L.A. history," Ballard said.

"Yeah?" he said. "Was it the O.J. case? You found out who really killed Nicole?"

"Funny," Ballard said. "But not quite."

They left him there and walked across the lobby to the concierge desk. They took a position to the side so people wouldn't think they were trying to jump the line.

"It's not officially solved yet, you know," Maddie said.

"What do you mean?" Ballard asked.

"Black Dahlia. The DA has to sign off on it."

"Maybe so, but I consider it solved and a closed case."

"How long will it take them to decide?"

Before Ballard could answer, they were approached by a woman who also wore a blue blazer and had a wire loop over her ear, though hers was better camouflaged by her long hair.

"Are you the detectives from L.A.?" she asked.

"We are," Ballard said. "I'm Renée Ballard, this is Maddie Bosch."

"Marty Branch. Ballard, Bosch, and Branch—has a nice ring to it."

They shook hands. Branch was in her forties. She was short and wide in the hips, and she eyed Maddie the way the first security man had.

"Honey, you look like a baby," she said. "How old are you?"

"Twenty-six," Maddie said. "And I'm a vol—"

"I'm sorry," Ballard interrupted. "We're working on a breaking case. We're looking for a possible witness named Rodney Van Ness. His LinkedIn page says he works here as a security supervisor. Do you know him?"

"Rodney? Yes, I know Rodney," Branch said. "But he hasn't worked here in a good long time."

"How long is a good long time?"

"Oh, two, three years at least."

"Do you know why he left?"

"I know he was asked to leave and I got his job."

"Why was he asked to leave?"

"That you'd have to get from HR — confidential."

"Do you know where he went from here?"

"I heard he went to the Nugget but I don't think that lasted too long. After that, I don't know. I haven't heard anything."

"Do you have any records that would give us a home address?"

"Don't you people have access to the DMV database? I'm sure the folks at Vegas Metro would help you out with that."

"We checked the DMV. This is the address on his license. Do you have an office where we could maybe sit down and talk? We're working a case involving multiple rapes and at least one murder, and Mr. Van Ness may have information that will help us identify a suspect."

Branch nodded as she considered what to do.

"We wouldn't have driven all the way over here just because of a LinkedIn profile if it weren't important," Ballard added.

Branch nodded again.

"Let's go to the security office," she finally said. "You two can wait at my desk while I talk to HR about this. But don't you go flipping through my little black book, now. This way."

She led them through a door at the side of the concierge counter to an employees-only elevator, which they took to the third floor.

"Did you all come over this morning or last night?" she asked.

"This morning," Ballard said. "We left at six."

"That's early. How you fixed for coffee?"

"We could probably use some."

"I can get that going."

"Thank you."

42

THEY ARRIVED AT the address that Marty Branch's little black book had provided for Rodney Van Ness, a run-down apartment building in the Fremont East neighborhood of downtown. The book had also provided a cell phone number and work numbers that were different from the numbers posted on LinkedIn. But the entries in her book were at least three years old, and Branch had told them she could not vouch for the accuracy of any of the information. Ballard was worried. She didn't want to have wasted a day and leave Las Vegas without finding and talking to Van Ness.

The Fremont Crest apartment building was two stories with exterior walkways branching right and left from a center entrance and staircase. It was white stucco with aquamarine doors and accents. The parking lot was located in front of the building, and there had been no effort — at least in recent years — to put any desert flora into the baked brown ground of its unpaved areas.

Prior to arriving, Ballard and Maddie had scouted the neighborhood for a location to take Van Ness to if he agreed to speak to them. The plan was simple. They wanted to take him out of the comfort zone of his own home. Based on a recommendation from Branch, they scoped out and chose a nearby restaurant called the Triple George

Grill because it offered private booths and was favored by local law enforcement.

The apartment building's security gate had not closed and locked after its last use and that allowed Ballard and Maddie to get to the second floor without having to use the call box. Ballard knew it was always better to knock directly on doors and keep the element of surprise.

They stopped in front of apartment 202 and Ballard leaned an ear toward the door. She heard no music, TV sounds, or people talking. She whispered to Maddie, "This reminds me of the sign your dad supposedly kept at his desk," she said.

"'Get off your ass and knock on doors,'" Maddie said, doing a not-so-good impression of her father. "Words for a detective to live by."

Ballard nodded and knocked sharply on the door. After half a minute there was a verbal response from within the apartment. It was a female voice:

"Who is it?"

Ballard looked at Maddie and then responded.

"We're looking for Rodney Van Ness."

"He's sleeping."

Ballard pulled her phone and looked at the time. It was noon.

"Well, ma'am, wake him up," she said. "This is a police matter."

That got no response, so Ballard knocked on the door again, this time hard and loud enough that hopefully she could wake Van Ness herself.

"Hello?" she called. "Open the door, ma'am. This is the police."

The door was finally opened by a young woman wearing a short silk robe and seemingly nothing else. Her unkempt hair and heavy-lidded eyes made it clear she had been roused from sleep

"He's coming," she said. "What's this about anyway?"

"Who are you, ma'am?" Ballard asked.

"Harmony."

"Harmony Van Ness?"

"Shit, no. We're not married. We work together. That's it."

"Where do you work?"

"The Library."

"You're a librarian?"

"It's a club."

Ballard was getting the picture now. When you've been black-balled on the casino security circuit in Vegas, the next tier down was strip clubs, which were plentiful in Vegas and ran the gamut from hole-in-the-wall brothels to high-end nightclubs that catered to rappers and all manner of the rich and famous. It did not take a leap of imagination to guess what Harmony did for a living and where Van Ness would fit in with that.

"How long has Rodney been working at the Library?" she asked.

Before Harmony could respond, a deep male voice came from behind her:

"Don't answer that."

It was a command. Harmony stepped back, and the doorway was filled by a man Ballard recognized from the yearbook as Rodney Van Ness. He was taller than she had guessed from the yearbook photos, but then, a lot of kids shot up in their late teens. He was barefoot and wore board shorts and a misbuttoned Hawaiian shirt with a sailboats-on-water motif, the blue of the ocean matching the door-frame he leaned against. He had the same hair and beard as the kid in the yearbook prom photo. But he had grown into a two-hundred-plus-pound wedge in the twenty-five years since graduation.

"Go get dressed," he said to Harmony.

He turned to watch Harmony go, the hem of her robe not quite covering the lines of her spray-tanned bottom. He turned back to Ballard and Maddie.

"Strippers," he said, rolling his eyes. "What do you want?"

Ballard was not sure if that was a rhetorical question about strippers or a direct question to her and Maddie. But her quick take on Van Ness was that he was not much of a rhetoric man.

"You're Rodney Van Ness?" Ballard asked.

"All day," Van Ness said. "What do you want?"

This time the meaning of the question was clear.

"Mr. Van Ness, we're with the LAPD. We need to ask you some questions in regard to an investigation we're conducting involving crimes in Los Angeles."

He held his hands up. "You got the wrong guy," he said. "I haven't been back to L.A. since my father's funeral, and that was six years ago."

"You're not a suspect in anything, Mr. Van Ness," Ballard said. "But we think you may have information that can help us identify a suspect. That's why we came across the desert to talk to you."

"Well, then, ask away."

"Actually, we want you to come with us. We have a reservation for a booth at the Triple George. It would be best to do this in a quiet spot like that. Away from any distractions."

"Uh . . . I thought this would be like a ten-minute thing. You said I'm no suspect, and I have stuff I gotta do today. You know, like, before work."

"That's okay. We won't keep you long and you'll get a free lunch out of it. Why don't you put some shoes on? I'm sure you want to cooperate with the police, don't you?"

Van Ness said nothing for a moment. Ballard knew he was measuring the implied threat in her words, a simple statement that even a glorified security guard like Van Ness would understand: Those who don't cooperate with the police could very quickly become suspects.

"All right, let me get some shoes," he finally said. "Can Harm come too?"

"Uh, do you mean Harmony?" Ballard asked.

"Yeah, Harmony. You mentioned lunch. We don't have anything here."

"Tell you what — leave Harmony home, and you can order take-out to bring back to her. On us. But it would be better if we spoke just to you."

"Okay, I guess. I'll get my shoes."

He stepped back and closed the door.

Just in case he was staying on the other side of the door, watching through the peephole and listening, Ballard looked at the time on her phone and said, "We get this over by one, we drop him back here, and then we hit the road," she said. "We'll be back in L.A. by five."

"That would be cool," Maddie said, playing off the wink Ballard had given her. "I've got a date tonight."

43

RODNEY VAN NESS had done Ballard a favor by just throwing on shorts and a shirt earlier, and he was wearing only sandals when he came out the door of his apartment. By the time they had walked down the stairs and into the parking lot, she was able to determine that he was not carrying a weapon. His shirt barely reached the top of his shorts, and it would have been impossible for him to have a gun or a knife tucked into his beltline without her noticing.

That was one of three obstacles out of the way. The other two were getting his permission to record their conversation and advising him of his right not to speak to law enforcement. Ballard was confident in her ability to get the first done. The rights requirement was a different story. Nothing ended the cooperation of someone who was straddling the line between witness and suspect like being told that his words could be used against him in a court of law.

The Triple George Grill was not very new but it was designed to look like it was as old as the Tadich Grill in San Francisco and Musso and Frank's in Hollywood. It was all dark wood and light tile with a long bar running down the middle of the room and private booths with floor-to-ceiling dividers and curtains to ensure the visual and audio privacy of conversations. The grill was located near a former courthouse and was originally meant to accommodate lawyers and their clients during lunch breaks. But that courthouse was closed now; it had been turned into the Mob Museum, dedicated to the history of organized crime — specifically its part in the establishment and rise of Sin City — and law enforcement's attempts to fight it.

They slid into one of the private booths, Ballard and Maddie sitting across from Van Ness. A waitress came and Ballard ordered coffee to start; Maddie asked for ice water, and Van Ness went for a Bloody Mary.

Ballard began casually.

"Van Ness," she said. "There's a Van Ness Avenue in L.A. — is that your family?"

"I wish," Van Ness said. "You'd think I'd be running security at a strip club if it was?"

"But you grew up in Pasadena and went to St. Vincent's, right? That sounds like old-school privilege."

"My mother was a dyed-in-the-wool Catholic. I had to go, but technically I was from the wrong side of the tracks. South Pas. Those arroyo kids had all the privilege, not me."

"You never did any of those genetic-heritage sites — Twenty-Three and Me, that sort of thing — to see if maybe ..."

"Nah, not interested. So what's this all about and how do you know I went to St. Vincent's?"

"We're looking for a classmate of yours. But before we start, is it all right if we record this?" Ballard reached into her pocket for her mini-recorder.

"If I'm not a suspect, like you say, why do you need to record it?" Van Ness protested.

"Good question," Ballard said. "New rules. The LAPD has been burned so many times by witnesses recanting what they said, we have a rule now where we have to record every interview. It also helps when we're writing reports to have the recorded version to refer to."

She held up the recorder. Van Ness stared at it but said nothing.

"So, okay?" she asked. "I'll send you a copy so you have it."

"Whatever," Van Ness said. "Go ahead."

Ballard turned on the recorder and checked its small screen to make sure it was working and had enough battery.

"Okay, we're recording," Ballard said. "The time is twelve four-teen p.m. on Wednesday, February twenty-first. This is a conversation between Rodney Van Ness, Officer Madeline Bosch, and myself, Detective Renée Ballard. Now, rule two, we need to advise you of your constitutional rights to — "

"Wait a minute, wait a minute," Van Ness said. "You say I'm no suspect but now you're telling me about my rights? That's not cool. I'm out of here."

Ballard, who had the outside spot on her side of the booth, reached across the table and put her hand on Van Ness's arm as he was trying to slide out.

"No, would you please wait a minute," she said. "These are the rules we have to play by in the LAPD. Every interview recorded, every witness read their rights. That way everybody is protected. I know it's a pain, but it's just…bureaucracy, okay? I can assure you that you are not a suspect in any crime — and I'm saying that on tape."

She pointed at the recorder on the table.

"So now it's even recorded — you are not a suspect," she said. "But we need to talk to you because you can help us. Please let's just get through this so you can go home and we can get back to L.A."

Van Ness stopped pushing his way out of the booth. He sat back and shook his head as if he was thinking about it. Just then the wait-ress parted the booth's curtain and placed a Bloody Mary with a tall sprig of celery and a straw in front of him.

Van Ness looked at the drink and then at Ballard.

"So I can end the interview anytime I want?" he asked.

"Anytime," Ballard said.

"Well, I don't like this. Seems kind of sneaky, if you ask me. But go ahead. Let's get this over with."

"Officer Bosch, do you want to do the honors?"

Maddie recited the Miranda warning and Van Ness responded that he understood his rights. Ballard was pleased that they had succeeded in getting through the pre-interview gauntlet.

"Okay, then, let's start," she said. "We are in the middle of an active investigation that is confidential in nature. So we can't share specifics, but we want to ask you about some people you associated with at St. Vincent's."

"Jeez, that was like twenty-five years ago," Van Ness said.

"Do you remember a girl in your class named Gina Falwell?" Ballard asked.

It was just a random name Ballard had pulled from the yearbook. Gina Falwell had no bearing on the Pillowcase Rapist case, but Ballard wanted Van Ness to think that she was on a fishing expedition.

"Can't say that I do," Van Ness replied.

"No memory of her at all?" Ballard asked.

"Nope."

"Okay. We have a yearbook from St. Vincent's with us. All right if I show you Gina's photo to see if it jogs anything loose?"

"You can if you want, but I don't remember her."

Ballard pulled the yearbook out of her bag. She had marked several pages with Post-its as part of her prep for the interview, and she flipped the book open to the page that had Gina Falwell's senior photo, turned it so Van Ness could see it, and tapped the photo.

"Her. You recognize her?"

"Well, I recognize her, yeah. But I didn't know her. What is the... is she, like, dead?"

"We can't really get into that. What about Mallory Richardson, did you know her?"

Van Ness didn't answer. Ballard could see the wheels turning. He bought time by taking a long pull of his Bloody Mary through the straw.

"I think I remember that name," he finally said. "But I can't really place her."

Ballard flipped the pages to another Post-it and showed him a photo of Mallory.

"Remember now?" she asked.

Van Ness nodded.

"Yeah, I remember her," he said. "But we weren't in the same class. She's the one . . . I heard she died. After graduation."

"Who told you that?" Ballard asked.

"I can't remember. It happened, like, pretty soon after graduation, I think."

"You mean your graduation or hers?"

"Mine."

"How well did you know her?"

"Not very well. It wasn't a big school, and she was . . . I'd see her around, you know. Like at football games and shit."

Ballard nodded like she understood. Van Ness was cagey with his answers, but he had just crossed a line from using the fogginess of memory as a cover to making a statement that conflicted with common sense. How could he forget who he went to his senior prom with? Would a jury believe that? He admitted to knowing she died but couldn't remember that she had been his date?

In crossing that line, Van Ness had also crossed from witness to person of interest. The next stop was suspect. But Ballard had to continue to play the interview as routine. She flipped to another Post-it.

"Okay, here is the important one," she said. "Victor Best."

Van Ness leaned over to look at the yearbook photo. Ballard tapped the page.

"Yeah, Victor, I knew him," he said.

"Were you friends?" Ballard asked.

"Yeah, we were friends. We hung out."

"Still in touch?"

"No, not really. We've got a twenty-fifth reunion coming up and he sent me an email to see if I was going. You know, stuff like that."

"Are you?"

"What?"

"Going to the reunion."

"No, I'm not into that stuff. I told him no."

"So, where's he live now?"

Van Ness paused and took another pull through the straw.

"So, he's the guy you're trying to find?" he said.

"We want to talk to him, yeah," Ballard said. "Do you know where he is?"

"Last I heard, he lived in Hawaii."

"Where? What island?"

"Oahu...I think."

"What's he do in Hawaii?"

"Runs a restaurant in one of the hotels over there. Last I heard."

"He went there from St. Vincent's and never came back?"

"Well, not right away. He went to school. Then he ended up over there as a chef or something."

"When would that have been? That he went over there."

"I don't know. Twenty years ago? We're not really in touch, not since high school."

"What about you? Did you go to college after high school?"

"Me? Yeah, CSUN."

CSUN was in Northridge — the Valley, where several of the Pillowcase rapes had occurred.

"When did you graduate?" Ballard asked.

"I didn't get a degree, if that's what you mean," Van Ness said. "I left school for a job."

"Doing what?"

"Security at the school."

"CSUN?"

"Yeah, my first security gig."

Ballard nodded. She was confident that they had enough leverage on Van Ness to turn the interview into an interrogation. It was just a matter of how long she could keep him talking once he was confronted. As she was considering how to begin that phase, the waitress ducked through the curtain to see if they were ready to order lunch. Ballard asked her to come back in fifteen minutes.

Before the waitress left, Van Ness held out his empty Bloody Mary glass and asked for another. Ballard looked at the straw still in the glass. The waitress took the glass and left. It was an opportunity Ballard didn't want to miss. She glanced at Maddie, hoping she would get it.

"You know what, I need to hit the restroom," Maddie said. "It was a long drive, lots of coffee."

"Sure," Ballard said. She slid out of the booth quickly, and Maddie moved just as quickly to follow the waitress.

Ballard didn't want to continue asking significant questions without Maddie present, so she detoured into questions about Van Ness's move to Las Vegas and his work for casinos.

"We found you through LinkedIn," she said. "But you haven't updated your résumé."

"I never got a bite through LinkedIn," he said. "So why bother, you know?"

"How long have you been at the Library?"

"Just a couple years. I'm waiting for something to open up on the Strip again."

"Why'd you leave in the first place?"

"A bunch of bullshit is why. I don't want to talk about it."

"That's fine. I was just making conversation until—"

As if on cue, Maddie split the curtain. Ballard slid over to make room. Maddie gave a slight nod that Ballard took to mean she had secured the straw from the Bloody Mary glass.

It was time to put Rodney Van Ness in a corner.

44

BALLARD LOOKED VAN Ness directly in the eye.

"You know, Rodney, we have a problem," she said.

"Here we go," Van Ness said, shaking his head. "I knew this was bullshit. Give it to me. What problem?"

"Well, to begin with, parts of your story don't add up. And that concerns me because we came here hoping you'd provide information that would help us find Victor Best. But I gotta be honest, I have problems with what you've been telling us."

Van Ness put his hands flat on the table as if he was about to push himself up to leave. Ballard hoped Maddie would be quick to put an arm out to dissuade him.

"Hey, I'm trying to help you," Van Ness said. "I told you all I know about Victor. I haven't seen the guy in like twenty years. I got an email from him, big deal. Everybody's email was on the thing the reunion committee sent out. That's it."

"You said he runs a restaurant over there," Ballard said. "How do you know that?"

"He said it in the email. He said if I ever went over there, he'd comp me a meal. He was hoping I'd comp him in Vegas. That's it."

"Fine, but that's not where my problem really lies. It's right here, Rodney."

Ballard opened the yearbook again and slid it across the table until it was right in front of him. It was open to the page with Mallory Richardson's photo.

"Her," Ballard said. "You say you didn't know her."

"No, I said I didn't know her *well*," Van Ness protested. "You can check your recorder."

"But did you forget something?"

"No. I mean, yes, I could have. It was a long time ago."

"Did you forget that you took her to your senior prom?"

Van Ness looked up from the yearbook. Ballard knew that if he was smart, he'd slide out of the booth, push past Maddie, cut through the curtains, and be gone. But she was banking on him not having the guts to do that.

Instead of leaving, he put on an amateurish look of surprise.

"Oh, shit, you're right," he said. "I did. I mean, we did go together. But it was a one-and-done date."

"And you couldn't remember that when I first showed you the book and her photo?"

"Look, to be honest, I did a lot of drugs back then. I was high that night and it's always been a blur."

Wrong answer. It opened a door.

"Did you give her drugs?" Ballard asked.

"No way," he said. "I didn't give drugs to anybody."

Ballard reached over and flipped the pages to the Post-it marking the photos from the prom. She put her finger down on Van Ness standing in the group photo without Mallory.

"Why isn't she in this photo, Rodney?" she asked. "Where was she?"

"I don't know," Van Ness said. "Probably the bathroom. How would I know?"

"You're saying she'd ducked out of a group prom photo to go to the bathroom?"

"I told you, I don't know where she was."

Ballard moved her finger over to the image of Victor Best.

"What about Victor?" she asked. "Where is his date?"

"I don't know," Van Ness said. "I don't think he had one. A lot of guys came stag 'cause it was the last dance."

The courts had long ago ruled that police could lie to suspects about evidence they had against them, the thinking being that if the suspects were innocent, they would know the police were lying. Ballard had always used the privilege judiciously because it never went over well with juries. The logic was murky, and at the end of the day, people didn't like their police to lie.

Ballard and Maddie had strategized the interview on the drive from L.A., and they had come up with a lie that Ballard could inject into the interview if the moment called for it.

The moment was calling for it now.

Ballard tapped the group photo again.

"This was at the Huntington," she said. "You know what's a cool thing about the Huntington and really useful to law enforcement?"

"I don't know," Van Ness said. "Cameras?"

"Not back then. But what they have done since day one is keep their occupancy and banquet records."

"So?"

"Well, we went back and found that the St. Vincent's senior prom was held on May twenty-second, 1999. Then we looked at hotel occupancy on that night and we found a room with your name on it."

"That's bullshit. I didn't have a room."

Ballard stared at him. He had called her bluff and now she was scrambling.

"You sure about that?" she said. "If you lie to the police, you know you can get into some deep shit. I'm trying to get you back home, but this —"

"Look, if they put my name on the room, they didn't tell me," Van Ness said. "But I didn't rent the room and I didn't pay for the room. My name shouldn't have been on it."

Ballard nodded as her adrenaline kicked up. She had used the lie, the bluff, to get to a hidden truth, and her instincts told her this was going to lead to something.

"Who is 'they'?" she asked. "Who put your name on the room?"

"Fine, we got a room to party in," Van Ness said. "Lots of kids did. They all shared rooms and most of us were on the same hallway. It was party central."

"I get that. Who did you share a room with?"

"Look, I had no money back then. Remember, South Pas? So some guys added me to their room."

"Okay, sure. Which guys? Show me."

Ballard opened the yearbook to the senior photos. Van Ness leaned in.

"One was Victor," he said. "Then there was Andy Bennett and Taylor Weeks."

He flipped through the pages and tapped on the photo of each senior.

"Okay," Ballard said. "You said Victor didn't have a date. What about Bennett and Weeks?"

"Uh, Andy I think went stag. Taylor had a date. Katie Randolph. I think she was a junior and I heard they ended up getting married."

Ballard nodded. She was in the flow, getting solid new information with every answer, getting names of people who were at the heart of the case. Interviews didn't always go this way, but when they did, it felt like there was no stopping her momentum.

"What happened in that room, Rodney?" she asked.

"The usual, I guess," Van Ness said.

"Don't guess. Tell me. What was the usual?"

"You know, we partied. Got there early and partied before the dance."

"The four boys and Mallory and Katie?"

"Well, I think Taylor and Katie got there late. But yeah."

"Was it drugs or alcohol or both?"

"There was a bottle of gin. So we did that."

"You brought the gin?"

"No, I think it was Andy."

"Did Mallory drink gin?"

"Yeah, she drank. Nobody forced her. She drank a lot."

"How long did Andy and Victor stay in the room partying with you?"

"I don't know. It was a while and then they went down the hall to visit other rooms and get more booze."

"You ran out of gin?"

"Eventually, yeah."

"And you were left alone with Mallory?"

"Just for a little bit."

"Did you have sex with her?"

"Look, I don't know what's going on here but it wasn't rape, okay? She wanted to have sex, so we did."

"Was that before or after she passed out?"

Another bluff, but based on what had been revealed, an informed bluff.

"I'm not like that," Van Ness protested. "She wanted to do it, so we did. There was no rape and you can't prove that there was. This is complete bullshit."

"We are not saying it was rape," Ballard said. "We weren't in the room. I just want to hear from you whether she was conscious when you had sex."

"Yes! She was awake and willing. Yes, goddamn it!"

"Okay, let's keep our voices down here."

"Okay, but you are saying shit that isn't true."

"Look, I believe you, Rodney, but we need to understand what happened. Mallory did pass out, right? That's why she wasn't in the photo, correct?"

Van Ness shook his head as if it were wrong to give up secrets about the dead.

"She got sick from the gin, okay?" he said. "Then she crawled back into one of the beds in the room and fell asleep. And that's it. She never made it to the dance. I had to wake her up to get her home."

"So you went down to the dance without her?"

"Yes, I did. It was my senior prom and I didn't want to spend it in a hotel room babysitting a girl who couldn't hold her liquor."

"Did all four of the guys have keys to that room?"

"Uh, yes. I mean no. There were two keys, so we had to share."

"You had a key?"

"No, I borrowed Andy's or Victor's when I went up. They had the keys. I told you, it wasn't my room. I didn't have a key."

"What about Taylor? He have a key?"

"I don't think so but I don't remember."

"So, I want to be sure I'm clear. When Mallory was passed out in that room, anybody with a key could get access to the room. Is that right?"

"Yes, but I wish you would tell me what is going on here. You're making it sound like we did something wrong and we didn't."

Ballard ignored the plea. She was too locked in on checking boxes with her questions.

"When Mallory got sick, was that in the bed or did she go into the bathroom?"

"The bathroom. She jumped up and ran in there. After a while I checked on her and she was leaning against the bathtub, passed out.

I got her up and cleaned her up a little bit and then I helped her to the bed."

Ballard wanted to say sarcastically that he had shown some real chivalry, but she kept editorial comments out of her questions.

"And this was after you two had had consensual intercourse, correct?" she asked.

"Yes, definitely consensual," Van Ness said.

"What was she wearing at the time? When she got up to go into the bathroom after sexual relations and when you brought her out."

"Uh, well, nothing. She had taken off her clothes."

"When you got her back to the bed, did you cover her up with a blanket or something?"

"Of course. I put her head on a pillow and pulled the covers over her. I'm not an asshole."

"And then you went downstairs to the dance."

"Yes."

"And did you give your key back to the person you borrowed it from?"

"Probably. I don't remember if it was Andy or Victor."

"Could you have given it to anybody else?"

"I mean, I don't know. I doubt it. It was their room; they got the keys."

While Ballard was able to hold her emotions in check, Maddie apparently could not.

"So you left a naked girl passed out in a room that just about any boy at that dance had access to," Maddie said in a heated tone. "Do we have that right?"

"Look, she got drunk," Van Ness protested. "What was I supposed to do?"

"Maybe protect her? Did you ever think once about how vulnerable she was?"

"I covered her up and locked the door. She was safe and nothing happened to her."

"Are you sure about that?"

Van Ness did not answer. He shook his head, then turned his gaze as if looking out of the booth into the distance. But the curtain was closed.

"Are you saying something happened to her?" he asked in a quiet voice.

Ballard put her hand on Maddie's arm to stop her from blasting him again.

"Yes, something happened to her," she said. "She got pregnant and nine months later she had a baby."

Van Ness turned to face them. Ballard could tell this was new information. He was stunned.

"Well, it wasn't me!" he said. "We used protection. I had a rubber and I used it."

"You sure about that?"

"I'm damn sure. She made me use it."

"Then good news, Rodney. If you're telling the truth, you're in the clear. Because the man we're looking for is the father of her baby."

Van Ness's mouth dropped open in surprise. This wasn't remotely how he had anticipated this going.

"Well, it wasn't me," he finally said.

"Then your quickest way out of this is to give us your DNA," Ballard said. "You volunteering to let us swab you would go a long way toward convincing us that you're not the man we're looking for."

Ballard held back on telling him they already had the straw with his DNA on it. Van Ness shook his head like he should have known better than to come with them.

"Why are you looking for him?" he asked.

"A murder," Ballard said. "And several rapes."

Van Ness leaned his elbows on the table and ran his hands through his hair.

"Oh my God, oh my God," he said. "That's not me. You can't believe..."

He didn't finish.

"Then let us swab you and cross you off our list," Ballard said.

Van Ness nodded.

"Where do we go for that?" he asked.

"We do it right here," Ballard said. "Officer Bosch can do it."

Van Ness hesitated, then nodded again.

"Okay, let's do it," he said. "I'm not your man."

45

THEY DROPPED VAN Ness off at his apartment building with a warning not to communicate with anyone from St. Vincent's, especially the men he had shared the hotel room with on the night of the senior prom. Ballard told him that should he alert anybody to the investigation, he would be charged with aiding and abetting murder and rape. It seemed to properly scare him.

Ballard and Maddie then got in the car and headed to the freeway. They didn't start to debrief until the neon glow of the Strip was in the rearview mirror. Maddie was the first to speak.

"I'm sorry," she said.

"For what?" Ballard said. "You did good. We did good."

"I know, but I shouldn't have let my anger go like that. It was unprofessional. You were so good, holding it in the whole time. It kept him talking."

"Maybe, but when you said what you did, it worked. He showed his guilt over how he'd left her that night and that made me think that he's not our guy. Did you feel that?"

"I did, actually. He's definitely a loser and will always be one, but I don't think he's our guy either. He wouldn't have given us the swab."

"Still, we give it to the lab and nail it down."

"Right."

"He was still hiding something he knew."

"How so?"

"He lied by omission at first, supposedly not remembering Mallory was his date. That tells us he knew something had happened that night. When he did that, I thought he was our guy. But then no hesitation about the swab. That means he lied for some other reason. He probably told those guys that she was passed out in the room. He made her an easy target, whether he realized that or not."

"Isn't there some way we can nail his ass for that?"

"Maybe, but we may need him for the bigger picture."

"Which is?"

"Prosecutors hate going into court with just DNA. Too many jurors either don't trust it or don't understand it. They want a person to tell the story, somebody who can connect the dots. Prosecutors want what they call DNA-plus cases. So the bigger picture here is the Pillowcase Rapist, not what Rodney Van Ness did or didn't do the night of the prom. If we make a case on one of these other guys as the Pillowcase Rapist, we may need Rodney as a witness to tell a jury about the room and the keys and who had access."

Maddie nodded. "You think two or three moves ahead," she said.

"You have to," Ballard said. "Do you have Colleen's number?"

"Sure. She's already texted three times today asking what's happening."

"Better you than me. Text her and see if she can start running down Victor Best in Hawaii. I take it you already found Andrew Bennett and Taylor Weeks?"

"I'm not sure about Weeks but I remember Bennett we found. I think he's down in Orange County."

"Not bad. A lot closer than Hawaii."

Maddie pulled her phone and opened the text app.

"You might want to ask her to also do a media search in Oahu or wherever she finds Best," Ballard said. "See if they've had a serial-rapist case in the last fifteen to twenty years there."

"Got it," Maddie said.

She typed the message on her phone. When she was finished, she had more questions.

"You think Taylor Weeks could be the guy? He had a date that night and now they're supposedly married."

"I'd bet on one of the other two first, but we have to nail all of them down. Never give a defense lawyer somebody else they can blame."

"And any of them could have given the key to any guy at the dance. We could be running down names for weeks."

"Don't say that. I want to clear this one bad."

"Sorry. You're like my dad when he was on a case. Driven. Nothing else mattered."

"You might not want to hear this, but that is a great compliment. Thank you."

"No, I meant it as a compliment. My dad wasn't always the easiest guy to live with but when he was engaged in something, he was fucking *engaged*. I hope I can be like that."

"You already are, Maddie. And I am super-happy you joined the unit."

Maddie's phone dinged and she read a text. "Colleen's on it," she said. "I wonder if Mallory knew what had happened to her."

"I think she must have," Ballard said. "If she didn't, she would've tagged Rodney as the father. But did you see his face when we said she got pregnant? That was news to him. I don't see why she would have kept that to herself if she thought he was the father."

"So fucking sad. It makes me angry."

"Yeah."

They lapsed into silence. They were about to cross back into California when Ballard's phone buzzed. It was Gandle.

"Captain."

"Ballard, a couple of things. First, guess what just came across my desk?"

"No idea, Captain."

"Well, I'll tell you. It's the motor-pool record for the car you requisitioned last night. So I gotta ask: Did you go to Vegas before I gave you permission to go to Vegas?"

"Uh, well, I knew you'd approve the request because you want us to solve this case. So I was counting on that, yes, but I did not drive to Vegas last night, if that's what you're asking. I got to Vegas today. After you gave me permission."

Ballard looked over at Maddie, who was watching her, and winked. Before Gandle could respond, she continued, "We're heading back now. We got some solid leads that we're already following up on."

"What about the guy you went to interview? Is he a suspect?"

"We could count him as a suspect but he volunteered to let us swab him, so we're kind of thinking he's not our guy."

"Then the trip was a bust."

"No, not at all, Captain. He gave us some names, leads that I think could be fruitful."

"I hope so, Ballard."

"I've already got the team running them down."

"Let me know what comes up."

"Yes, sir. Did you say you had something else?"

"Yeah, I just got a reject from the DA's office on Thawyer."

"What?"

Ballard glanced at Maddie with distress in her eyes.

"It was rejected. Insufficient evidence for conviction."

"That's unbelievable. Who rejected the case, Plovc?"

"No, this comes from on high. Ernesto signed it."

That explained it. Ernest O'Fallon was the recently elected district attorney. The chief of police had endorsed O'Fallon's opponent in the election and that had led to an ongoing feud between the two. Neither side would concede any victories to the other, and it had resulted in some questionable applications of justice in the county. O'Fallon, nicknamed "Ernesto" by his detractors because of an ill-conceived attempt to claim partial Latino heritage during the election, would never give the LAPD the public relations bonanza of solving the iconic Black Dahlia case. And Ballard was upset with herself for not foreseeing this when she took the case to Plovc.

"That is complete bullshit," she said. "That case is cleared."

"Doesn't matter," Gandle said. "You know the protocol. If the DA doesn't sign off on it, it's not cleared."

"We should go to the media. Reporters will love this story."

"Ballard, think about what you're saying. Don't do something stupid that gets you demoted or worse. You've already been through that. You make a false move on this and you're looking at freeway therapy just as a start. You'll be out of cold cases before the dust even settles."

"It's still bullshit. We have the evidence."

"You're preaching to the choir. But sometimes the choir has to stop singing."

"I don't even know what that means."

"Doesn't matter. Stand down. Stay on the Pillowcase investigation, and if we're lucky we get to stick it up the DA's ass with an arrest, a press conference, and everything else."

"Whatever. I have to concentrate on driving."

"Then I'll let you go. But remember, Ballard, think before you act. There are consequences. For every action, there is an equal and opposite reaction. The laws of politics are the same as the laws of physics."

Ballard said nothing.

"Are you there, Ballard?"

"I'm here."

"I want to make sure you hear me."

"Loud and clear, Captain."

"Good. Get back safe and I'll speak to you tomorrow."

"Copy that."

She disconnected, and Maddie was immediately on her.

"They rejected Thawyer?"

"Not *they*. One guy. O'Fallon—because he didn't want to give the department a big win."

"That makes no sense. It's Thawyer, I know it."

"No argument from me."

"So what do we do?"

"Maddie, how long have you been in the department? Two years?"

"Coming up on three."

"Okay, I know you know a lot from your dad. He got tangled in the politics and bureaucracy of it more than once. But even now, in the so-called new LAPD, you'll learn that the politics of policing are ever present, and never more so than when you get into detective services."

"And so—what? We just roll over because some elected asshole won't close a case we know we solved?"

"That's the point. We know it's solved. We're still going to call the Fords in Wichita and give them final answers. Okay, the DA won't sign off on this because he doesn't want to give our chief the win, but that doesn't matter. We know what we know."

"It matters to me."

Ballard realized that it mattered to Maddie in part because the Black Dahlia case could launch her career and get her into the detective ranks sooner rather than later. Ballard suddenly felt bad about trying to educate her on the politics of the department.

"Look," Ballard said, "people in the department will know what you did. Captain Gandle already does. When we get back, let's see what we've got and what we could still get to make the case so bulletproof that the DA won't have any choice but to sign off on it. We're already close. There's got to be something else. Something we haven't thought of yet."

Maddie responded in a dejected voice. "We already gave them enough," she said.

"True—from our point of view. But O'Fallon's a political animal. We have to think about it from his perspective and bring in something so important that the case becomes a liability to him if he *doesn't* sign off on it."

"Don't you think if there was such a thing, we would have already found it?"

"Maybe. But there were photos of other victims. Let's confirm another one. Or two more, whatever it takes. Then we go back to the DA."

They passed a freeway sign announcing the exit to Zzyzx. Ballard opened her phone contacts and called Carol Plovc. She put the call on speaker so Maddie could hear.

"Carol, what happened?"

"Renée, I'm sorry. It was completely taken away from me. I brought it across the street to Nicki Gallant, and I had no idea she was going to take it up to O'Fallon. I knew as soon as that happened it would be a reject. I'm sorry."

"Did you get anything back? Deficiencies? What can we do?"

"Nothing, and I don't expect there to be any feedback. It's the photo analysis. Like I told you, there's reasonable doubt in the numbers."

"Okay, Carol. Thanks for the effort."

"If it were up to me, I would have signed off."

"I know."

Ballard disconnected.

"If she would have signed off on it, why did she send it across the street?" Maddie asked.

"Politics," Ballard said. "She was in a lose-lose situation. If she signed off on it, O'Fallon would probably have demoted her. So she sent it across the street to die."

The frustration in the car was palpable. Ballard and Maddie fell into silence. They had a hundred miles to go and nothing more to say.

THURSDAY, 9:12 A.M.

46

EVERYONE ON THE team had already fulfilled their weekly time commitments, but Ballard arrived at Ahmanson to find Hatteras at her desk. Hatteras could always be counted on for three to five days a week, but today Ballard had asked her to come in. She knew Hatteras had worked into the night Wednesday to locate Victor Best, Andrew Bennett, and Taylor Weeks. Ballard had been too tired after returning from Vegas to take her report and asked for a morning meeting instead.

"Colleen, sorry I'm late," Ballard said. "I got hung up at the lab."

"You took in the swab from Van Ness?" Hatteras asked.

Ballard put her bag down at her desk.

"I did," she said. "I'm going to go up and get coffee, then we can talk. You want a cup?"

"No, I'm good," Hatteras said.

Ballard opened a drawer at her desk and pulled out a coffee mug. It was a memento from her days in the Robbery-Homicide Division. Printed on it was a familiar slogan: LAPD HOMICIDE — OUR DAY BEGINS WHEN YOUR DAY ENDS.

She headed up to the coffee room on the second floor. While she was pouring, she got a call from Captain Gandle. Reluctantly, she accepted it. Any call with the captain these days felt adversarial.

This one started off no different.

"Ballard, I thought I'd have a report from you on Vegas in my email."

"Sorry, Captain. We got back late yesterday and I was tired. I'm at the office now and I'll be writing it up this morning. Right after an interview I'm in the middle of."

She hoped the lie would keep the conversation short.

"Good," Gandle said. "I want to see what you've got."

"You'll get it before lunch," Ballard promised.

There was a silence, but Gandle didn't hang up. Ballard guessed that another shoe was about to drop.

"Is there something else, Cap?" she asked.

"Yes, I need to talk to you about something," Gandle said. "Something that I don't want to blow up in my face."

"What? Something in Vegas? Did Van Ness file a complaint?"

"No, nothing from Vegas. I got a call from a reporter at the *Times* first thing today. The FBI shoot-out at the beach—they won't let that go because they know Harry Bosch was somehow involved."

"Okay. What's that got—"

"The reporter also sent me a video that was taken on an iPhone by one of the bystanders—some kid who was playing roller hockey. He wants me to ID the woman Bosch is talking to at the crime scene tape. He hugs her and puts something in her pocket. That woman looks a lot like you, Ballard, and I want to know what the fuck is going on."

Ballard was stunned silent.

"Talk to me, Ballard," Gandle said. "Right now."

"Uh, I can't at the moment, Captain," Ballard said. "I'm in the middle of an interview. But I will."

"When?"

"Uh, soon. I just need to finish this. How about I go downtown to see you?"

She was trying to buy time to come up with an explanation he'd accept.

"All I can say is this better not be something that detonates in my hands, Ballard."

"Don't worry, sir, it's not," Ballard said. "But could you send me the video? I'd like to see it before we talk."

"I'll send it. And I'll see you today, Ballard. Today."

"Yes, sir."

Ballard disconnected. She was in a fog and felt a little dizzy. There was a single table in the coffee room with two chairs. She sat down, put her elbows on the table, and ran her hands through her hair. She had to come up with something to explain why she was in the video but could think of nothing to say other than the truth.

"Shit, shit, shit," she said to herself.

She felt a pit opening in her chest. It grew wider as she realized that she had recovered her badge only to possibly lose it again — permanently.

47

STILL IN A fog of misgivings, Ballard returned to the unit to find Maddie Bosch talking to Colleen Hatteras at her station. They both saw Ballard's approach and judged that something was wrong.

"Are you all right?" Hatteras asked. "I thought you were going to get coffee."

Ballard realized she had left her cup on the counter in the coffee room.

"Uh, yeah," she said. "I drank it up there while I took a phone call."

"Well, if you left your cup there, someone's going to steal it," Hatteras said. "I'll get it for you."

"Uh, okay. Thank you, Colleen."

Maddie waited until she was gone before speaking.

"Renée, what's wrong?" she asked. "You look like you've seen a ghost."

"Nothing's wrong," Ballard said. "Anyway, nothing to do with what we're doing. But I thought you were taking today off."

"There's something I want to show you. I think it's another way to take a run at the Black Dahlia case."

"Okay. Show me."

They went to Ballard's desk and Maddie sat down, opened her terminal, waited for the Wi-Fi to connect, then went to a commercial site of something called the Film Forensics Institute.

"What am I looking at here?" Ballard asked.

"This company claims it has the world's best experts in verifying film and video," Maddie said. "They can do a comparison for us and confirm that the victim in the Thawyer photos is Elizabeth Short."

"Or confirm it's not."

"Yes."

"How do we know this place knows what they're doing? Looks like some kind of a Hollywood thing."

"They were recently contracted by CNN to ferret out deepfake videos and photos in the presidential campaigns. I called them and they would love this job. They're getting more and more into law enforcement gigs, the guy said. He could give us police references if we want to check them out. He said that locally, they've worked for Beverly Hills PD."

"And they're located here?"

"The best film experts in the world are here."

"How much would it cost?"

"Well, I tried to get the guy to do it gratis but he said we'd have to at least pay the hourly rate of their techs. Two techs separately evaluate ear images and determine if they belong to the same person, then see if they both reached the same conclusion. A hundred an hour each. We would also have to give them credit in any press release that goes out about the case."

Ballard hesitated.

"I was thinking you could use my pay from the grant," Maddie offered.

Ballard shook her head.

"No, I don't want to get crosswise with the union," she said.

Hatteras appeared and put Ballard's coffee mug down on the desk. It was steaming with fresh coffee.

She must have heard the tail end of their conversation because she looked at Maddie and said, "You get paid?"

"Uh, well..." Maddie began.

"She gets a stipend," Ballard said. "I had to do that or the union would block it, and we needed another badge on the team."

"Oh," Hatteras said.

"I'd appreciate it, Colleen, if you kept that to yourself," Ballard said.

"Sure," Hatteras said. "I always said I would do this work for free."

"And the city and I owe you our thanks," Ballard said. "Let's get back to this. Maddie, what can this private company do with the photos that our own lab didn't do?"

"He said law enforcement lags behind in the use of identifiers that help in cases like these," Maddie said.

"Like what?" Ballard asked. "This just sounds like a sales pitch."

"Like ears," Maddie said. "There are a number of studies out there that say the lines of the external ear — you know, the lobe, the helix, something called the concha, and various other shapes — all combine to be as unique an identifier as a fingerprint. There is this thing called Cameriere's ear identification method that can be used to compare and confirm identity."

"Wow, interesting," Hatteras interjected.

Ballard realized that Hatteras was still standing behind her listening to the conversation.

"You showed me the file of photos you turned over to our lab," Maddie said. "It had photos of the Thawyer victim named Betty that showed her right ear, but all the known photos of Elizabeth Short you submitted were headshots that didn't show much of a side view of either ear. So I don't think the lab did this kind of comparison."

"I think I would have heard about it if they had," Ballard said.

"I went online," Maddie said. "Even the side-view mug shot of Short taken during her 1943 arrest in Santa Barbara didn't have it. Her hair is over her ear."

"So we have nothing to compare?" Ballard asked.

"No, we do," Maddie said excitedly. "I found several, actually. They're all from the crime scene on Norton Avenue where the killer left her body. In those photos, her face is turned to the side in the grass and you see her full right ear. But you didn't include any of those shots in the lab package."

"Because her face was bloodied and her cheeks were cut through like the Joker in that Batman movie," Ballard said. "Horrible. And I didn't think they were good photos for comparison."

"They weren't, not for normal facial comparison," Maddie said. "But now we have clear images of her right ear to compare. I really think it's worth a shot, and the guy said they would jump on it right away."

"I think it's worth a shot too," Hatteras said.

Ballard turned to take in Hatteras again.

"Colleen," she said, "why don't you go to your pod and get ready to walk us through what you found yesterday."

"No need," Hatteras said. "I'm ready to go. I was waiting for you."

"Well, go over there and we'll join you in a minute, okay?"

"Okay."

She said it like a child being sent to her room and walked away with her head down. Ballard turned her attention back to Maddie.

"Okay, go ahead with it," she said. "Quietly. And I want you to write up some kind of confidentiality agreement and get Camerero or whatever his name is to sign it. I don't want word of this leaking out."

"No, Cameriere is the guy who invented the comparison index. The guy I talked to at FFI is named Ortiz, first name Lukas."

"Okay, well, you can tell Mr. Lukas Ortiz to put a rush on it and that we'll pay his people by the hour."

"Okay, cool. I'm excited. I think it's going to work."

"That's only going to be half the battle. Even if they call it a complete match, we'll still need to convince the district attorney," said Ballard.

"If this is as good as fingerprints, he'll have to sign off."

"Maybe. But this was good, you coming up with this, Maddie. Get it going."

"I'll head there now."

48

NO VIDEO FROM the roller-hockey player had come in from the captain. Ballard tried to push the problem she was facing with him out of her mind as she pulled her chair around the raft and sat down next to Hatteras.

"Finally," she said. "Colleen, show me what you've got on our boys from St. Vincent's."

"Well, good and bad news," Hatteras said. "I'm pretty sure I located all three. The bad news is that Weeks is in Hollywood Forever."

"He's dead?"

"Died in a car accident three years ago."

"Where?"

"He hit a tree on Los Feliz Boulevard driving home after a concert at the Greek. I found a story in the *Pasadena Star-News*. I guess because he grew up there and had sort of made good in Hollywood, they ran a story."

"What did he do in Hollywood?"

"He was a producer of independent films. None that I ever heard of, but stuff that made the festival circuits."

"Can you pull up the story? I'd like to read it."

"I have a printout."

Hatteras opened a file folder and took out a sheet of paper. Ballard scanned the story and noted that there had been a female passenger in the car who survived but sustained critical injuries. Her name was not given in the article. At that time, the accident was under investigation by the LAPD traffic division.

"Then there's this," Hatteras said.

She handed Ballard another document from the folder, a printout of a four-page lawsuit against the estate of Taylor Weeks filed by Amanda Sheridan, the passenger in the car crash. Her lawsuit said Weeks was driving under the influence of alcohol and Ecstasy at the time of the crash and had refused Sheridan's repeated requests to pull over and let her drive. According to the lawsuit, an angry Weeks yelled, "How about if I pull over here?" and drove intentionally into an oak tree ten feet off the road, killing himself and seriously injuring Sheridan.

"This is good stuff, Colleen," Ballard said. "They would have drawn blood during the autopsy, and it should still be at the coroner's office if this lawsuit is still active."

She flipped to the front page of the lawsuit to check the court stamp.

"Filed in September of '22," she said. "It's probably still winding its way through the courts. I'm pretty sure we'll be able to get his DNA."

"I was hoping that would be the case," Hatteras said.

"I have to go downtown in a bit. I'll go by the coroner's office and see what they have."

"You have to see the captain?"

"Unfortunately."

"Is something wrong? I feel like there is."

"Everything's fine, Colleen. Nothing for you to worry about."

Hatteras was the last person Ballard wanted to confide in about her predicament. She changed the subject.

"What about Bennett and Best? You found them?"

"Yes. Van Ness had the wrong island—Victor Best is currently the head chef of a restaurant in Kona on the Big Island. I don't have his home address but I have the restaurant's."

She started typing on her computer.

"Good," Ballard said. "Did you look for any news stories on serial rapists over there?"

"I did but didn't find anything. But here is the restaurant."

A website for a restaurant called Olu Olu came up on the screen. It showed outdoor seating with a stunning ocean view. Hatteras opened a pull-down menu and clicked on *Who We Are*. A photo and bio of the restaurant manager appeared. She scrolled down to the next photo, and Ballard was looking at a man wearing a white chef's jacket and smiling warmly at the camera.

"That's Victor Best," Hatteras said. "Head chef and kitchen manager."

Ballard leaned in to read the two-paragraph bio of Best.

"'Nearly twenty years of experience in restaurants in Hawaii,'" she read out loud. "If that's true, he would've been over there when the last attack occurred here. Van Ness said the same thing."

"So we scratch him off the list?" Hatteras asked.

"Not yet. We still need to confirm. Bios like this are exaggerated. And Van Ness was wrong about the island, so he could be wrong about the timing too."

"Got it."

Ballard stared at the photo of Best. He had a shaved head, a wide smile, and a deep tan. She could see how the kid in the yearbook photo had grown into the man on the screen. The eyes were the same, a deep brown so dark that she could barely see the ring around each iris. She wondered if she was staring at the eyes of a rapist-murderer.

Hatteras interrupted her thoughts by asking, "Did you ever live in Kona?"

"Uh, no, I never lived on the Big Island. I lived in Maui, and I went to J-school in Oahu."

"J-school?"

"Journalism. I was a reporter for a while before I was a cop."

"Interesting. I didn't know that."

The mention of her past suddenly gave Ballard an idea for how she might be able to learn when Best left California for Hawaii.

"Colleen, how did you find him?" she asked.

"It was easy," Hatteras said. "I just googled 'Victor Best Hawaii,' and this page on the restaurant site came up. I wish it were always this easy."

Ballard kept her plan for Best to herself and moved on with the report from Hatteras.

"Okay, what did you find on Andrew Bennett?"

"It was not as easy with him. As you can imagine, there are a lot of Andrew Bennetts out there. Again, based on what Maddie said Van Ness told you, I made Orange County one of my parameters and found four Andrew Bennetts in the county. I went through them and locked in on one down in Laguna Beach. He works for a real estate firm that has bios of its sales reps on its website. His bio says he was born in California, and then I just did a comparison to the yearbook. Take a look."

Hatteras pulled up a photo of a smiling Andrew "Andy" Bennett on a real estate firm's website, then put up next to it an enlarged photo she had scanned in of the Andy Bennett from the yearbook. There was no doubt that the agent was the Andy Bennett who had graduated in 1999 from St. Vincent's in Pasadena. Unlike Victor Best, who had lost hair and added sun wrinkles around the eyes, Bennett looked like he had found the fountain of youth or a good plastic surgeon. There were no wrinkles, and he still had a full head of hair. Ballard realized the style had not changed either. His jet-black hair was still parted cleanly on the left. He was smiling broadly and standing by a SOLD sign in front of a house.

"I wonder how old this photo is," Ballard said. "He looks like he's about thirty."

"I know," Hatteras said. "I tried to find more photos but struck out. The California Department of Real Estate database has no record of complaints against him, and he's been licensed since 2007."

"I'll run his DMV and hopefully we come up with a home address. But shoot me his office address on a text."

"I already ran his DMV records and got the address. I'll send it to you."

"How did you run his DMV?"

"I used your password."

"Colleen, how do you have my password?"

"Anders gave it to me."

"What?"

"I think it's yours. That's what he said."

"This can't be happening. Look, whatever he gave you, do not use it again. You understand? That could bring the whole unit down. I'll talk to Anders, but don't use it anymore."

"Okay, sorry. I didn't know it was such a big deal. The other day you had me run a check on your screen because you were still logged in. I didn't see the difference. I just thought you gave it to him."

"No, I didn't. He hacked it and I'll take care of that with him. What you need to know is that the department is very serious about unauthorized users running DMV checks."

"Like what you asked me to do the other day?"

Ballard was getting exasperated.

"Look, that was different," she said. "And I'm not going to argue about it with you. Just don't do it anymore. It's actually illegal. It could get both you and me in trouble."

"Okay, fine," Hatteras said. "No more."

"Send me Bennett's address and then at least it will look legal."

"Will do. Are you going to go down to Laguna to see him?"

"Eventually. Probably. Tell you what, see if you can find out if he has any open houses this weekend."

"Ooh, that would be cool. You posing as a potential buyer to observe him. Before he knows you're a cop."

"Maybe."

Ballard knew what was coming next and was not wrong.

"If you go down, can I tag along?" Hatteras asked. "Wait, don't answer. I know it's a no. Never mind."

Ballard was relieved that she didn't have to lower the boom one more time. Hatteras was self-editing.

"Colleen, you might want to think about taking a break and going home," she said. "You've been here every day this week. I really don't want you to burn out. You're too valuable to the team."

Ballard left Hatteras with that to think about and rolled her chair back to her desk, where she saw her coffee, now cold, waiting for her. That was two cups fallen by the wayside. Before she went upstairs for another refill she might actually drink, she checked her email.

First in the queue was the email that had just come in from Hatteras with Andrew Bennett's DMV record. Though he sold homes in pricey Laguna Beach, he lived in Laguna Hills, a suburb west of Laguna Beach with lower housing costs because of its distance from the Pacific. The driver's license had been issued three years ago, and the photo was of the same man in the one Hatteras had pulled up of Bennett in front of the SOLD sign. Bennett still looked younger than his years.

After writing down the pertinent information in a notebook she kept on her desk, Ballard signed in to the California DMV database. Through the interagency portal, she was able to pull up Victor Best's Hawaii driver's license records. These showed that Best had not been licensed in the state until 2008, with an address first in Oahu and then on the Big Island in subsequent renewals. But Best not getting his Hawaii driver's license until after the Pillowcase Rapist's L.A. rampage had stopped didn't necessarily mean anything. He could have moved there years earlier and simply waited until his California license expired before getting the Hawaii license. The information was useful but it didn't move the needle on Best. Ballard needed to know more precisely when he had left California for Hawaii. Ballard was also aware that no matter when Best moved to Hawaii, it was not a solid alibi. He could have gone back and forth between Hawaii and California and committed the Pillowcase crimes.

To help narrow his location history down, she pulled up the website of the *Pasadena Star-News* and scrolled through its pages until she saw the byline of a reporter named Claudia Gimble. She didn't need to write the name down.

Ballard straightened up to look over the divider and saw that Hatteras was still at her desk. She didn't want to make her next call with Colleen eavesdropping, so she stood up, coffee mug in hand. "You're still here," she said.

"I'm going to go," Hatteras said. "Just finishing up a few things."

Ballard held up her mug.

"I'm going up for a refill, and then I'm heading downtown. So I'll see you tomorrow or maybe even Monday."

"What about Laguna Beach?"

"I haven't decided on Laguna Beach. Going down there and back would take up a whole day and I'm not sure I want to invest that kind of time yet. There's still a lot to do here. I'll let you know when I go."

"Okay, fine."

"I'll see you, Colleen."

"See you."

Ballard went up to the coffee room and found the urn empty. She had to brew a fresh batch. By the time she got back to the unit, there was no sign of Hatteras. She was finally alone. She sat down at her desk, blocked the ID on her phone, and called Olu Olu in Kona. It was three hours earlier in Hawaii, but Ballard was hopeful that as head chef and kitchen manager of a restaurant that was open for lunch and dinner, Best would be there.

The call was answered by a woman who said that Victor was in his office and that she'd put the call through. He answered right away.

"This is Victor."

Ballard quickly put her phone on speaker and pulled out her mini-recorder. As she spoke she started a new recording.

"Hello, Mr. Best. This is Claudia Gimble with the *Pasadena Star-News* in California. I was wondering if you had a few minutes for an interview."

"Interview? For what?"

"As you probably remember from growing up here in Pasadena, we're a small community paper and we're doing a story on the twenty-fifth reunion of the St. Vincent's class of '99. Would this be a good time to ask you a few questions?"

"That's a story? Or is this some kind of a prank?"

"No, sir, not a prank. It's a feature, a where-are-they-now story, which people love to read. And I wanted to talk to you because you living all the way over in Hawaii makes you one of the most far-flung and exotic members of the class of '99. My first question is, what made you make the move to Hawaii?"

"Look, I'm not sure I want to be involved in this... feature. Who else have you talked to from the class?"

Ballard recited three names of female classmates from the yearbook. She knew it was a risky maneuver; Best might be in contact with one of the randomly chosen women. But Best's response didn't indicate that he was.

"All right, I guess," he said. "What do you want to know?"

"Well, let's see," Ballard said. "When did you move to Hawaii and why?"

"Uh, that would have been . . . 2003, and to be honest, I did it for a job. I went to the CIA — the Culinary Institute of America, not the spy agency — and the job here was a referral from the school. It was a sous-chef gig in Oahu and I thought, why not? It's an adventure, right? And I've been here ever since. About nine years ago I moved from Oahu to the Big Island to work at a new restaurant, and it's doing very well. And I can tell you this: I'm never leaving Hawaii. In fact, I'm looking for investors so I can open my own restaurant."

"That's great. Do you get back to Pasadena very often?"

"Hate to say it but no. My parents followed me over here when my dad retired, so there isn't a big reason to go back."

"What about for the twenty-fifth reunion?"

"Uh, I'm thinking about it, yeah. Not sure if I can swing it. We're pretty busy here."

Ballard suddenly heard typing and realized it wasn't coming from Best's side of the call.

"Mr. Best, can I put you on hold for a moment?" she said quickly. "It won't be long."

"Uh, sure," Best said.

Ballard put her phone on mute and paused the recorder. She stood up and looked over the divider. Hatteras was at her workstation, typing something on her computer.

"Colleen, I thought you left," she said, unable to hide her irritation.

"No, I was just putting murder books back on the shelves," Hatteras said. "That is so cool how you got him talking. Like you're undercover. I love it."

"Look, you need to go home. You're throwing off my concentration, Colleen, and this conversation is not something I want you hearing, because that could be an issue down the line."

"Really? How? I'm just listening and learning."

"I don't want to get into it, but if this guy ends up being *the* guy, you could be called as a witness to the conversation. I don't want that, you understand?"

"Okay, I'm sorry. I'll just finish this email and send it and then I'm leaving."

"That would be good."

Hatteras moved her eyes back to the screen and the now-familiar pouting look returned to her face. Ballard sat back down, started the recorder again, and took her phone off mute.

"Sorry about that, Mr. Best," she said. "Where were we?"

49

BALLARD'S FIRST STOP after leaving the west side was Harry Bosch's house up in the hills. She hadn't called, emailed, or texted ahead of her arrival. Any one of those would have left a trail. She had thought about making an end-around play by calling Maddie Bosch and having her check to make sure her father was home, but that would have left a trail of its own. It would also bring Maddie into the matter, giving her knowledge of the badge-recovery scheme that she would be better off without. So Ballard turned her phone off and drove up Woodrow Wilson to the Bosch house unannounced. She knew there would be Ring cameras in the neighborhood and other ways to document her visit, but she counted on Internal Affairs making only a lazy effort from a desk to investigate possible collusion between her and Bosch. They'd check phone and email records but would likely not go out and knock on doors.

She was in luck. Bosch was home and welcomed her in.

"What's going on?" he asked as he closed the front door. "You could've just called instead of driving all the way up here."

"No, I didn't want to call," Ballard said. "And you'll understand when you hear why."

They spent the next half hour working out a story. Then Bosch disappeared into his bedroom to get something from a drawer that he believed would seal the deal with Captain Gandle. Ballard was waiting for him at the door when he put it in her hand.

"Thank you, Harry," she said. "I can't believe all of this happened just because I didn't want to report a stolen badge."

"I'm glad you didn't," Bosch said. "Remember, those guys didn't need your badge to do what they were going to do. The badge was just part of a possible escape plan. But it never got to that point, and people are alive today because you didn't want to report a stolen badge."

"I guess so. I'll take that."

"Nobody else will ever know, but I will."

"And I hope it stays that way."

"Let me know how it goes with your captain."

"No, I won't be able to."

"Right. But if I get pulled in to verify, I'll get the word to you somehow."

"Okay. Be safe."

"You too."

Forty minutes later, Ballard was sitting in front of Captain Gandle in his office at the PAB. He had never sent her the video taken by the roller-hockey player. He claimed he forgot, but Ballard knew that it was probably intentional. He had not wanted her to see it in advance and have time to make up a plausible explanation.

He played it for her now, turning his computer screen so they could watch together. Though the video was taken from a distance, it was clearly Ballard waiting at the police tape when the camera tracked Bosch walking from the center of the crime scene. Then came a short conversation, the hug, and the hand dropping into the pocket of her coat. Ballard was grateful for two things. First, that it was not clear what, if anything, Bosch had put in her pocket. And second, that the hockey player hadn't started taking video on his phone while she and

Agent Olmstead were talking at the crime scene tape. With nothing to connect her to the agent in charge of the op, Ballard saw daylight.

"That is you, right?" Gandle said. "You were there."

"Yep, that's me," Ballard said. "I was there."

"Jesus Christ, and you didn't come forward with this?"

"I was off duty. I was there because Harry Bosch asked me to be there."

"Why? Why would he do that?"

"You said you knew Harry back in the day. So you know he has a thing about the feds. He didn't trust them when he was a cop, and he trusts them even less now. He wanted some sort of backup. Somebody who wasn't an FBI agent who could be a witness if things went sideways and they tried to put the blame on him."

"So you were just an observer. Not part of it."

"You see that on the video. I'm outside the tape. If I were part of what went down, don't you think I'd be inside the tape?"

Gandle didn't say anything as he contemplated that. His next question revealed to Ballard that he was finding her story plausible.

"What did he put in your pocket?" he asked.

Ballard reached into her pocket and took out the medal and chain Bosch had given her at his front door. She held it out to him across the desk and he took it. One side of the medal depicted Saint Michael, the patron saint of police officers. The other side was customized. It showed an LAPD badge with a 6 underneath it. Many officers in the department had side gigs. They sold insurance or real estate or gave self-defense lessons. An officer at Hollywood Division—LAPD's Sixth Division—sold the medals, and Bosch had one from his days in Hollywood Homicide.

"I got that when I worked the late show at Hollywood," she said. "I gave it to him to keep with him because I guess I wasn't so trusting that the FBI was going to watch out for him if shit went down."

Gandle dangled the chain, and the medal swung in front of his eyes.

"Saint Michael," he said. "You never struck me as religious, Ballard."

"When you're on the street in the middle of the night, you take every edge you can get," Ballard said. "If this becomes a full internal investigation, I want to make sure I get that back."

Gandle looked at her for a long moment, trying to get a read on whether she was telling the truth.

"So if I bring Bosch in, he's going to tell the same story?"

"It is the story, so, yeah, he will."

"One last question. On the video, your jacket's all dirty. How come? What happened there?"

It was the one part of the story she and Bosch had not gone over. Though her shoulder was still sore, she forgot to tell Bosch she had fallen out of the FBI van and landed hard on the street. Her mind raced to come up with an answer that didn't knock down any of the previous explanations.

"Oh . . . yeah, I fell."

"You fell? Where?"

"I was up on Ocean Avenue on a bench, watching the meet between Bosch and those guys who wanted the guns. Ocean Avenue is above the parking lot, so that made it a good vantage point. Then when the shooting started, I wanted to get to Bosch. I should have taken the stairs down but they were like a hundred feet to my left. I tried to just run down the embankment and I lost my footing and fell. I got dirty."

"So why didn't you go to Bosch then? Why'd you wait till they were taping the crime scene?"

"Well, I was sort of hurt—I still need to get my shoulder checked out. I can't sleep on it. But the main reason is that there were FBI snipers and they didn't know about me. Only Bosch knew. I suddenly realized that if I ran out there into the parking lot, I might get shot. So I waited until the tape was up and it was safe."

Ballard wasn't completely happy with her quick answer but thought it covered the question. Gandle hesitated, then leaned across the desk and held out the chain, still dangling from his fingers. She opened her palm and he dropped the medal into her hand.

"I don't know, Ballard," he said. "The whole thing sounds sketchy."

"It's what happened," Ballard said. "What are you going to tell the *Times*?"

"Fuck the *Times*. I'm not telling them anything. And if Anderson calls you or Bosch, you both better do the same. Now get out of here. I have work to do and so do you."

Ballard stood up. She felt like she was in the clear.

"Wait a minute," Gandle suddenly said. "Sit back down. What is going on with the case? You said Vegas was good but I don't have a report from you yet."

Ballard sat down again and summarized what she and Maddie Bosch had gotten from Van Ness and told him about the follow-ups being made on the three names he had given them. She said she would check with the coroner's office to see if they still had blood from the late Taylor Weeks.

"Let's hope it's not a match," Gandle said.

"Why?" Ballard asked.

"Because you get no real media traction with a dead suspect. We could use a live one for once. Somebody in cuffs at an arraignment or on a perp walk. A dead suspect just provides answers. A live one provides a shot at justice being carried out. That's what the people want and it makes us look good."

Ballard nodded in agreement. The captain was right.

"Then I hope Weeks is not a match and we find a live one," she said. "Either way, I will close this case."

She stood up again.

"One more thing," Gandle said. "I'm thinking now that bringing Madeline Bosch into the unit was a mistake."

"You approved her," Ballard said.

"Yeah, I know. But now I want you to drop her."

For the third time, Ballard sat down.

"What are you talking about?" she said. "She's great. The Black Dahlia case is all because of her. And she was the one in Vegas who finally got Van Ness to open up and talk. On top of that, she's the only one in the unit other than me who has a badge, and I've been telling you for months I need a second badge in the unit."

"It just doesn't look good," Gandle said. "You and her father and that whole mess at the beach, then you turn around and bring in the daughter. Not good optics, Ballard. Cut her loose."

"It's only bad optics if it gets in the *Times,* and you said you weren't going to talk to them."

"I'm not, but you never know. This could still blow up. So cut her loose."

"Sir—"

"That's an order, Ballard."

Ballard paused before responding. She was trying to think two moves ahead of the captain.

"Understood," she finally said. "Can I go now?"

"I'm not stopping you," Gandle said. "Go make cases."

"Right."

"And have a good day."

Ballard got up. The hollow feeling in her chest had not gone away. The concern about the *Times* inquiry had just been replaced with the order from Gandle to cut Maddie Bosch from the unit. She knew she had merely traded one problem for another. She needed to find a way to make the captain rescind his order and let her keep Maddie.

50

BALLARD DROPPED OFF a blood sample drawn from Taylor Weeks during his autopsy at the lab and she had just gotten on the 10 freeway when her phone buzzed and she saw the name Dan Farley on the screen. She braced herself. He had never reached out to her except for the first call when he had introduced himself and said that her inquiry had landed on his desk at the MINT. All the other times, it had been Ballard calling him to check in and see if there had been any progress.

She wished she could pull over to take the call but it would be dangerous to sit on the shoulder of the eight-lane freeway, let alone try to get back into the heavily congested traffic lanes afterward.

She took the call and tried to concentrate on her driving while she spoke.

"Dan? What's up?"

"I found your mother, Renée. And she's alive."

Ballard didn't respond at first. She had prepared herself for a call confirming the opposite news. For months she had assumed the woman who had birthed her but had done little else as a mother would be among the casualties of the fires in Maui. She had prepared herself for losing her without a chance for confrontation or reconciliation. In a moment that had changed, and she wasn't prepared for it.

"Renée?"

"Yes, I'm here. It's just that...I wasn't expecting this. Where is she?"

"Right now she's at Maui Community Correctional in Wailuku. But they are going to ROR her today."

"She was arrested?"

"Yeah, on warrants. Unpaid traffic stuff, I guess a lot of them. I don't know the details. But I had put a BOLO into the system after you filed the missing person report. I got the heads-up a little while ago and I knew you would want to know."

Ballard went silent again.

"Still there?"

"Yes, I'm just thinking. Did she give a home address?"

"She would have had to give something and I can get that for you. I'm here in what's left of Lahaina, and Wailuku is on the other side of the island. I'm not going to be able to go over there today."

"Sure, I understand."

She was in a daze. She couldn't think of what else to say. She thought about Farley having put the BOLO into the system. Be on the lookout — that said it all about her relationship with her mother. All the early years looking for her, hoping to find her.

"Um, I'm going to close this file," Farley said. "But if you come over to see her, you have my number. I don't know, I could show you around, show you what we're doing here. I mean, if you're interested."

"Uh, sure, Dan," Ballard said. "I'll call you."

Ballard snapped out of her fugue and realized that this man had done so much for her.

"And Dan, thank you," she said. "You went all out for her. For me. She might not have been worth it, but cop to cop, I appreciate it."

"Of course," Farley said. "That's what we do here. And this is one of the better endings, believe me. You take care, Renée, and I hope knowing your mother is still alive leads to something good between you two."

"Yeah, me too. Thank you."

She continued the drive west but passed by the transition to the south 405 that would have taken her back to Ahmanson. Instead, she continued west and took the curve through the tunnel where the freeway became the Pacific Coast Highway.

She headed toward the water.

FRIDAY, 9:00 A.M.

51

HER HAIR STILL wet from a morning surf at Trancas, Ballard entered the unit at Ahmanson, Starbucks cup in her hand. She expected to see Colleen Hatteras in place at the raft, but instead she saw Maddie Bosch.

"Maddie, what are you doing here?" she said. "It's Friday. You have a shift tonight."

Maddie looked up from her screen.

"I know, but I had to come in," she said. "We already got results from the FFI and it's a match. No qualifiers, no percentages. It's a confirmed match. The woman in Thawyer's photos is Elizabeth Short."

Ballard put her cup and computer bag on her desk and walked around to Maddie's station.

"Show me what you've got," she said.

Maddie pushed her screen back so Ballard, who was standing, had a good angle on it. There was a document on the screen with letterhead from the Film Forensics Institute. It was addressed to Officer Madeline Bosch. It stated that Cameriere ear analysis between the photos submitted confirmed a match. It was the same woman in each photo. The letter said that two technicians, Paul Buckley and James Camp, conducted independent analyses of the photos and came to the same conclusion and that both techs were qualified experts who would be available to testify in court about their findings.

"Okay, this is good," Ballard said.

"Who do we submit to?" Maddie asked. "Plovc, or do we go right to the DA with it?"

"We start with Carol. We need to stay in our lane. If it goes across the street to the DA again, she has to take it over."

"Okay."

"Send that to me and I'll send it and follow with a call. I want it in front of them today."

Ballard looked around to check the raft once more. There was no one else in yet, not even Hatteras.

"You haven't seen Colleen, have you?" she asked.

"Not since yesterday," Maddie said. "You need me to do something?"

"No, it's just that she's usually here."

"She's probably at home sulking because you're so mean to her."

"Really? You think I'm mean to her?"

Maddie smiled. "I'm just kidding," she said. "She just gets too in-your-face, you know what I mean?"

"Of course I do," Ballard said. "That's why I'm so mean to her."

Maddie laughed and then got serious.

"Will you let me know how Plovc or anybody in the DA's office responds to the ear match?"

"As soon as I know something."

"I might go, then. I have to do some stuff and I want to work out before I go in."

"Then get out of here. And thank you for sticking with this. We'll see what happens."

"They'd better sign off on it. We fucking solved it."

"We did. You did. But we'll see whether they can see the light. I'll call when I know."

"Thanks."

Ballard headed to her desk. She opened her email to retrieve the FFI letter Maddie had just sent. She then composed a new message addressed to Carol Plovc.

Maddie came by her desk on her way out.

"I forgot to tell you," she said. "I was talking to my dad last night and he said Captain Gandle called him up out of the blue."

"Really?" Ballard said. "Why?"

"I think to see what he thought of me volunteering for the unit. But then Gandle asked about you."

"Me? Why?"

"I guess to see if you were doing okay with, you know, the pressures of the job. Anyway, he said to tell you that Gandle called but that everything is fine."

"Well, okay, I guess. Thanks."

"So, I'm heading out."

"Okay. As soon as I hear something I'll call you."

Ballard watched her go. She knew what Harry's real message was: He had backed Ballard's story when Gandle called. Her only disappointment was that the captain had called Bosch to check the story out, which meant she had not entirely convinced him earlier. At least the whole badge caper was behind her now and she could concentrate on the cases in front of her.

She finished the email to Carol Plovc explaining the new analysis. She sent it with the letter from FFI attached.

Ballard had another reason for urgently wanting to officially clear the Black Dahlia case. She knew that if they cleared L.A.'s greatest mystery, the credit would rightly go to Maddie Bosch and that would make it politically difficult, if not impossible, for Gandle to have her cut from the Open-Unsolved Unit. Ballard wanted it done through official channels, with Captain Gandle agreeing to rescind his order and keep her on. She also knew that if the DA's office failed to sign off on the clearance again, there were other ways to keep Maddie on the team.

Ballard took her mug upstairs to get a second cup of coffee. When she returned, she again expected to see Hatteras at her screen, but the raft was empty. She stepped down the aisle next to the archives and looked into each row of shelved murder books. No Colleen.

As much as Hatteras's nearly constant presence in the office annoyed her, Ballard realized that the room didn't feel quite the same without her. Ballard had explicitly told Colleen to take time off, and now that she had, Ballard had to acknowledge that she sort of missed her relentless hovering and questioning. She sat down, put her coffee to the side, and sent an email to Hatteras asking if she had determined whether Andrew Bennett had any open houses in Laguna Beach over the weekend. She ended the message with a suggestion that they could both ride down and get a look at him, and maybe they'd get lucky and surreptitiously capture a DNA sample as well. As she wrote it, she wasn't sure if the offer was merely to bait Hatteras into responding or a real offer to take her into the field.

She sent the email, sure it would elicit a quick response. While she waited, she opened a Word document and finally started to write the overdue summary report on the trip to Las Vegas. This took over an hour because of the distraction of phone calls from Masser and Laffont, who were checking in to see what was happening with the Black Dahlia and Pillowcase Rapist cases and asking if she needed them to come in before the weekend started. After updating them, Ballard told them they didn't have to come in until the usual Monday team meeting.

It was almost noon by the time Ballard sent the report to Captain Gandle. Hatteras had still not called or responded to the email, and Ballard wondered if her feelings were still hurt by the way Ballard had dismissed her the day before.

She decided to extend an olive branch if that was the case and called Colleen's cell. It immediately went to voicemail. Ballard hesitated but left a message.

"Colleen, it's Renée. I'm at the office today and just wanted to see if you're interested in going down to Laguna to get a look at Andrew Bennett. Undercover, of course. If he's having an open house, we could go there, but even if he's not, we could still look up one of his listings and make an appointment to see it. So give me a call and we'll see what we can set up."

She disconnected, knowing that the word *undercover* was an enticement Hatteras wouldn't be able to resist.

Ballard had skipped breakfast to surf and was now famished. She left the office and drove over to the Melody on Sepulveda. She knew one of their hamburgers would power her through the day and well into the night. Since her return to red meat, she went to the Melody often. The place had been around since 1952 and had been through many transformations as the nearby airport expanded and its runways got closer and closer. Now the jets came screaming in directly overhead, but with its good food and drink and live music at night, the Melody had a loyal clientele.

Ballard ate her hamburger at the bar that ran down the center of the room. She kept her phone face up next to her plate so she wouldn't miss a call from Hatteras while a plane passed overhead.

By the time she finished there still had been no call, and her concern about Hatteras was building. She wondered if she had subconsciously chosen the Melody because it was just on the other side of the airport from El Segundo, where she knew Hatteras lived.

Ballard went out the back door to her car. Once inside she opened her laptop and pulled up the file that contained all the applications submitted by current members of the Open-Unsolved Unit. She plugged the home address Hatteras had put on her form into the car's GPS.

It took her fifteen minutes to cross the airport on Sepulveda and make it to Mariposa Avenue in El Segundo. She pulled into the driveway of a small ranch house with pale yellow walls and rust-colored shutters. She had never been to Colleen's home before and there was something intriguing about seeing how one of her unit's members lived.

There was a double-wide garage with the door up. Colleen's Prius was in there. The other space was filled with storage boxes, bicycles, and a lawn mower. Ballard could see that the door leading from the garage into the house appeared to be ajar. Her curiosity turned to alarm.

Ballard got out of her car and approached the garage. She pulled her phone and called Colleen once more. She did not hear a ringtone coming from inside the house. The call again went immediately to voicemail.

She entered the garage, and as she approached the door to the house, she called out loudly, "Colleen? It's Renée. Are you home?"

No answer.

Ballard opened the door all the way. She saw that it led into the kitchen. She called out once again:

"Colleen Hatteras, are you home?"

Ballard entered the house. The kitchen was neat, the counters clear, with only a rinsed plate and fork in the sink. There was a door to Ballard's left that led to a dining room, and a doorway straight ahead past the refrigerator that led to what looked like a TV room. Ballard went in that direction, scooping her right hand under her jacket and unsnapping the safety strap on her holster. She gripped her gun without pulling it free.

She entered the TV room and found it neat and orderly as well. A flat-screen on the wall was off. On the coffee table, two remotes were lined up next to each other. At the end of the room were doorways on the right and left. Ballard looked through the left opening and saw an empty living room that connected through an archway to the dining room. To the right, the doorway led to a corridor.

"Colleen? It's Renée."

No answer. There was a closed door on her left, and on the right were several open doors to what were presumably bedrooms, closets, and bathrooms. She checked the room to her left first, opening the door and finding what had been a bedroom converted to an office.

She entered and saw a large computer screen that matched what Hatteras had at Ahmanson. It was set up on a desk that was part of a built-in shelving and cabinet system entirely covering two walls. Ballard recognized the room even though she had never been to this house. She had seen the workstation in Facebook videos when she was vetting Hatteras's application to be part of the unit. Colleen had been involved in online sleuthing long before volunteering for the Open-Unsolved Unit. She had even been an integral part of a group that identified a previously unknown serial killer by connecting aspects of murders committed in seven different states. Her work on that case had been the clincher and Ballard had offered Hatteras a position as her volunteer IGG expert.

Closed cabinet doors lined the lower sections of the built-in, with shelving above. The shelves were stocked with books, manuals, DVDs, framed photos of her daughters, and other family keepsakes and knickknacks. On a third wall next to the only window was a framed poster of a Matt Damon movie called *Hereafter.* The fourth wall was dominated by the closed louvered doors of a closet.

Ballard stepped over to the built-in workstation and saw an outline of dust delineating the space where a desktop computer had been.

She turned to the closet. Ballard was now on high alert and looked at the embedded finger pulls of the sliding doors. She wanted to open the closet but was thinking about fingerprints. She turned back to the desk and took a pencil out of a clay mug obviously made by a child. Sloppily painted on it was *World's Best Mom.* She turned to the closet again, pushed the pencil between two of the louvered slats, and slid the door open.

The body of Colleen Hatteras was slumped on the floor of the closet. An electric cord connected to a computer mouse was tied tightly around her neck. Her eyes were open and bulging. She was wearing a long sleep shirt with a faded design on it. There was lividity discoloration on her legs, and Ballard could tell she had been dead for hours.

Ballard dropped to her knees.

"Colleen, no, no, no," she whispered.

Ballard tried to compose herself. She knew she needed to clear the rest of the house. She stood up, pulled her weapon free, left the room, and proceeded quickly down the hallway door by door until she confirmed the house was empty and that whoever had killed Colleen was gone.

In the hall, Ballard holstered her weapon, pulled her phone, and called the LAPD comm center; she identified herself and requested that a homicide team from West Bureau meet her at the address in El Segundo. She then disconnected and opened her text app. There was a text chain she used for sending messages to everyone on the Open-Unsolved team at once. She typed out an urgent message to all of them.

I am sorry to tell you this by text but Colleen has been murdered.

Take all measures to secure yourself and family.

She put away the phone, took a pair of latex gloves from her pocket, and reentered the home office. Keeping her back to the closet, she started looking for anything that might tell her what had drawn death to Colleen Hatteras's door.

52

THE TWO DETECTIVES from West Bureau assigned to the murder of Colleen Hatteras were Charlotte Goring and Winston Dubose. Ballard knew Goring slightly from a loosely affiliated group of the department's female homicide cops that met irregularly at Barney's Beanery in West Hollywood, usually when one had just had a major misogynistic encounter with the patriarchy and needed a therapeutic sharing session or legal advice. Ballard and Goring had both been in that spot and shared but had never worked a case together. The fact was that Ballard had no idea whether Goring or Dubose, whom she didn't know at all, were good at their jobs.

Ballard sat in her Defender outside the house while the detectives took their first survey of the crime scene with the criminalists and the coroner's investigators. As she waited, she took calls from every member of her unit, all of them stunned by the news and asking questions Ballard could not yet answer. Who killed Colleen and why? Most of them said they wanted to come to the scene, but Ballard dissuaded them, saying it would only complicate things. She did tell each to expect a call from the investigators, who would likely be looking for any possible reason for Colleen's murder and would surely want to question her colleagues.

The last to call was Maddie Bosch, and after that conversation, Ballard was left to wait with dark thoughts crashing in on her about her own possible culpability. Hatteras had been a volunteer who gave her all to the unit. Had Ballard not trained her well enough? Had Colleen made a mistake that Ballard missed and that had cost her her life? Had Ballard, through her own actions, somehow caused this?

Ballard knew that the death of a volunteer in Open-Unsolved guaranteed an internal review of the entire unit and the department's decision two years earlier to follow the law enforcement trend of using non-cop volunteers in cold-case squads. The conclusion would obviously be that it had been a mistake. Ballard knew that the whole operation could be shut down because of this. But those thoughts were secondary to the pitiful image of Colleen slumped in the closet. She could not get it out of her head.

Her phone buzzed and she saw that the call was from Captain Gandle.

"Captain."

"Renée, I just got your message. I'm in the car and I'm coming out."

"Uh, okay."

"West Bureau is handling it for now, but I want to be there. This is going to be a shitshow. You know that, right?"

"Yes."

"Have you talked to the detectives yet?"

"Just briefly when they arrived. They're in the house. They told me to wait in my car."

"Good. That's good. I informed the chief's adjutant. I haven't heard back. But this is going to be a shitshow. I guarantee that."

"Yes, you said that."

"Any idea what she was doing?"

Ballard hesitated for a moment. The question raised the dark thoughts again.

"Well, yeah," Ballard said. "She was working for me."

"I know that, Ballard," Gandle said. "But what exactly was she working on?"

"She was on the Pillowcase Rapist case. We all were. I told you. We're looking at four different persons of interest. But none of them knew it except maybe the guy in Vegas, and he wouldn't have done this. Not after we were just there."

"Could it have been something else? Something that had nothing to do with your unit or its cases?"

"Anything is possible at the moment, I guess. But I don't know what else it could be."

"You told me when you wanted her for the unit that she was already working cases on the internet."

"She was, yes."

"Well, maybe it was one of those."

Ballard could see the company line on this forming: Hatteras was killed because of some misstep she had made before she volunteered for the LAPD. That would put the department in the clear.

"I doubt it," Ballard said. "She tripped a wire somewhere while she was working for me."

"We don't know that," Gandle said. "Not for sure."

Ballard saw Goring come through the open door of the house and stride toward the Defender.

"Uh, Captain, I think I have to go," Ballard said. "Detective Goring is heading toward me. I think she'll want to question me now."

"Okay, I'll let you go," Gandle said. "I'm still an hour out. The traffic sucks."

"I'll tell the detectives you're coming."

"Roger that."

Ballard disconnected and watched Goring cross in front of the car and open the passenger door. The automatic step deployed and she climbed in.

"Renée, how are you doing?"

"Uh, not good. A woman I've worked with closely for the past two years is in there dead. Murdered."

"Yeah, not good. I'm going to tape this conversation, okay?"

"Sure."

Goring put her cell phone on the center console's storage compartment. She opened a recording app and pressed the red button. She gave the date and time and named those in the car and then got down to it.

"Let's start with Colleen. Tell me who she was."

"She's a — she was a divorced mother of two girls who are both away at college. I'm not sure where. About three or four years ago, after her kids were in high school, she took some online courses in IGG — do you know what that is?"

"The genetic-tracing stuff."

"Yes, investigative genetic genealogy. She took classes and then started basically being a citizen sleuth online. Her thing was helping to identify unnamed victims of murder. Mostly women. There's a whole network out there of people — mostly women — who are proficient at this. She became part of this network and that's when I became aware of her. I was putting together an all-volunteer cold-case team and I started floating around online looking at some of these people. I reached out to her when I learned she was local. She came in, I vetted her, then gave her the job. She did some really good work for us. Right up to the end."

Goring had taken a notebook out and was jotting a couple of things down, even though she was still recording everything said.

"Okay," she said. "What do you mean, 'right up to the end'? What was she working on?"

"We were all working a case," Ballard said. "You probably are too young to have been in the department at the time, but do you remember the Pillowcase Rapist?"

"Oh, yeah, I was going to Pierce College in the Valley when that was going on. He did a bunch of rapes and then just disappeared, right?"

"Yeah. The last one was a rape and murder. We were on that because we had gotten a solid genetic lead. Our focus was on four men who were all high-school classmates in Pasadena. Class of '99."

Ballard watched Goring's eyes sharpen.

"These four men," she said. "Did they know you were looking at them?"

"It's possible," Ballard said. "We interviewed one in Vegas on Wednesday and he let us take a DNA swab. I felt we threw enough of a scare into him to convince him not to give the others a heads-up."

Goring made a *hmm* sound that Ballard took as questioning her actions.

"He voluntarily gave us the swab," Ballard said. "He wouldn't have done that if he was the guy. I don't see where he'd have any interest in warning the others, even if he knew that one was probably the suspect we were looking for."

Ballard didn't like her own tone of protest and defensiveness.

"You never know," Goring said. "You said 'we.' Did Hatteras go with you over there?"

"Oh, no, that was Maddie Bosch—the other sworn officer in the unit. I wouldn't have taken Colleen on something like that. She worked exclusively in the office, though she was not happy about it."

"In what way?"

"She...wanted to go into the field and follow through on some of the leads she came up with through IGG. I told her many times that that wasn't what I'd brought her into the unit to do."

"And how did she take that?"

Ballard's phone buzzed and she saw that the call was from Carol Plovc. She sent the call to voicemail.

"Sorry about that," she said. "To answer your question, Colleen was frustrated by not being able to go into the field. I told her more than once that she would need more training if she was ever going to go out on an investigation."

Goring waited for further explanation but that was all Ballard offered.

"Okay," she finally said. "Let's go back to what put these four guys on your radar. You said it was a genetic link?"

Ballard spent the next ten minutes explaining the genetic connection between a man arrested recently for domestic violence and the rampage of the Pillowcase Rapist. She told Goring about the 1999 prom at the Huntington, Mallory Richardson's vulnerable position in a hotel room, and the fact that at least four boys and maybe more had access to the room. She said the working theory was that someone used that access to enter the room and have sex with Mallory, leading to the birth of the man who had been arrested twenty-four years later.

Goring just listened and took notes until Ballard was finished.

"So you got a swab from the guy in Vegas—what about the other three suspects?" Goring asked. "Have you had any contact with them?"

"We weren't really calling them suspects," Ballard said. "Not yet. More like persons of interest at this point."

"Okay, but have you made contact with any of them?"

"Well, one is dead. Colleen found that out. He was killed in a car accident a couple years ago. But the coroner's office took blood at the time and still had it because of a court case that came out of the incident. I picked up a sample and the lab now has it for DNA analysis. We think the third guy has been living in Hawaii since before the rapes stopped here. And the fourth—"

"Why do you think that?"

"Well, I talked to him yesterday," Ballard said. "I deked him on a phone call and he told me he moved to Hawaii in 2003. The last Pillowcase rape and murder was in late 2005."

"'Deked'? What's that mean?"

"Decoyed. The twenty-fifth reunion of their class at St. Vincent's is coming up. I told the guy in Hawaii that I was a reporter for the paper in Pasadena doing a where-are-they-now story on the class. He bought it and I did the interview. He was very detailed about his history since St. Vincent's. Went to chef school up in wine country and moved to Hawaii right after for a job."

"And you believed him?"

"Well, we haven't independently confirmed anything yet, but yeah, my feeling is that he was telling the truth. I hit him up out of the blue, and for him to provide the details he did... I'm thinking he couldn't have made it up on the spot."

"And the fourth guy?"

"We haven't approached him yet. He sells houses down in Laguna Beach. The last thing I told Colleen to do was see if he had any open houses this weekend. I thought we'd go down and take a look at him, maybe get a chance to collect some DNA."

"When you say 'we,' are you talking about you and Officer Bosch again?"

"Uh, no, I actually did throw that out to Colleen. Wait, no. I mean, I did make her the offer when I left a phone message today, but I don't think she ever got it."

"Why do you think that?"

"Because I saw the body. I saw the lividity. I think she was dead long before I left that message."

Goring nodded and then looked at the notes she had written. Through the windshield, Ballard saw the two investigators from the coroner's office squeeze through the front door, carrying the body bag containing Colleen Hatteras. Ballard looked down at the steering wheel.

"I'm going to need the names of these four persons of interest," Goring said. "And any reports you've written up."

"Sure," Ballard said. "I don't have a lot. Today was supposed to be my paperwork day. I did write up a summary of the Vegas trip I can give you."

"I'll take it. Let me ask you a question. When you deked the guy in Hawaii, was Hatteras there?"

Ballard hesitated before answering.

"Uh, she was there for part of it," she said. "But she left while I was in the middle of it."

Goring wrote a note. Ballard watched the morgue men put the body bag in the back of their van.

"Okay," Goring said. "Just a couple more things. What made you come here today to check on her?"

"I thought it was unusual that she hadn't come to the unit this morning," Ballard said. "Her husband left her back in September, and with her kids in college, she didn't have much to do. She was at the squad at least three days a week, more often four or five days a week. So I emailed and left phone messages, and when she didn't respond, I started thinking something might be wrong. Nothing like this but that maybe she was upset with me or something. I ate lunch by the airport—at the Melody—and just thought I would drop by. I wasn't expecting anything, but then I pulled in and saw the garage was up and the door to the house was open."

"That set off the Spidey senses."

"You could say so, yeah."

"Did you see anything in the house that could help us?"

"Not really. It looked like her computer was taken. It shouldn't have had anything from work on it. People in the unit use department computers. It's a rule."

"The killer might not have known that."

"True."

"There's a dust pattern on the desk that indicates there was also a backup hard drive taken."

"I didn't see her phone anywhere, and when I called it, it didn't ring in the house."

"It's gone. We're already working on getting her records. But that'll take some time."

Ballard nodded as a thought came to her that she didn't want to share with Goring. "So," she said. "What else can I tell you?"

"Her ex, did she ever talk about him?" Goring asked. "Should we jump on that angle?"

"She didn't talk about the divorce much. She wasn't blindsided by it, I know that. And she never said anything about being in fear of him. He left her the house and he pays for the kids' college and all of that. For what it was, it seemed amicable."

"Do you know if she had a gun?"

"A gun? No. I mean, I didn't know about one. Why do you ask?"

"Just trying to determine whether she might have been shot with her own gun. We'll check ATF—"

"Wait, she was shot? I didn't see that."

"Once behind the left ear. Point-blank. There wasn't a lot of blood, and her hair covered the wound."

"I saw the mouse cord around her neck."

"We're thinking that could have been some kind of control or coercive thing used before the killing. We did find the casing. It was in her hair. A nine-mil Federal Premium. The criminalist in there says the firing-pin stamp looks like a Glock's. We'll get that confirmed by the gun unit."

Ballard just nodded. She was consumed by thoughts of Colleen's last moments. She had been tortured, and Ballard had to wonder what she had told her killer.

"I think that's it for now," Goring said. "I'm sure we'll have more later. Are you going back to the office?"

"As soon as I'm cleared, yeah. My captain is supposedly coming here."

"Who's that, Gandle? He thinks RHD is taking this?"

"He didn't say so."

"Good, because that's been settled. It would be a conflict of interest, since your unit falls under RHD. My LT says it's ours to keep."

"No argument from me."

"Good. We'll want to take a look at the victim's workspace and get into her computer there."

"You may need the tech unit to get into it. It's password-protected."

"Not a problem."

"When are you coming?"

"As soon as we're done here, we'll head over. One of us, at least."

"I'll make sure it's undisturbed. Am I clear now?"

"You're clear. Let me give you my card in case you think of anything else." She picked up her phone, pulled a card from its case, and handed it to Ballard.

"Thanks," Ballard said. "When Captain Gandle shows up, tell him I went back to Ahmanson to protect possible evidence."

Goring turned off the recording app.

"Will do," she said. "And Renée, you look like you're carrying this on yourself. It's not on you. Okay?"

"We'll see," Ballard said. "But thanks for saying that."

"You know, I haven't seen you the past few sessions at the Beanery."

"Oh, yeah, well, been kind of busy. But I'll be back."

"Good. Us girls need to stick together."

"You got that right."

Goring opened her door and got out. Ballard watched her go back up the front walk and through the open door of the house.

She pulled her phone and called Anders Persson.

"Renée? Please tell me they've made an arrest."

"No, not yet. They're just starting. What are you doing right now, Anders?"

"Now? Not much. I mean, I can't believe this, you know? She called me last night and told me you were angry about the password."

"Never mind that now. You know Colleen's cell number, right?"

"Sure, but—"

"I want you to see if you can get into her account. I want to know what calls she received and what calls she made in the last forty-eight hours."

"Uh...isn't that the kind of thing you—"

"I know I told you no hacking, but we both know you didn't listen. And this is different, Anders. This is Colleen. Her phone is missing and it will take the investigators on the case a week to get a search warrant and get the carrier to come across with the account records. I don't want to waste that much time. Can you do it?"

"Uh, sure, I can do that, but...you know..."

"If you don't want to do it, just tell me, Anders. You and Colleen were close. I thought you'd want to help get whoever the sick fuck is who did this."

"No, I do. I do. I can do this. I'm on it. No worries."

"Okay, Anders, thanks. Talk only to me about it and don't leave a trail. You got that? No trail."

"Got it."

She disconnected and started the engine. She knew she was crossing a line with the request to Persson. She had a feeling there were going to be other lines to cross as well. But she told herself essentially the same thing she had just told Anders: *This was Colleen. One of us. And we will cross every line we have to.*

53

THE UNBREAKABLE RULE that command staff had put in place during the formation of the volunteer cold-case squad was that the volunteers could not take murder books, police reports, or any official documentation or evidence home or even out of the Open-Unsolved Unit. To make sure this rule was not violated through digital means, the volunteers were all furnished with desktop computers at their stations. All work was to be performed on the in-house, password-protected computers, which would be randomly monitored and audited by the department's tech unit to confirm that the rule had not been broken. This had all come about because the command staff was concerned that volunteers on the squad might have ulterior motives behind their volunteerism. For example, they might be secret screenwriters or television producers looking for content to pitch at the next studio meeting. Content was king in Hollywood, and its purveyors went to great lengths to get what nobody else had.

Though Ballard had not uncovered such a scheme in vetting any of her volunteers, the rule was one reason Colleen Hatteras had spent so much time in the office at Ahmanson. Her work for the unit was entirely online. She could not transfer her IGG work from her office desktop to her home computer without the risk of being discovered and dismissed from the unit she so loved. So she spent many more hours than any other volunteer at her station in the office.

Still in a fog of confusion, grief, and guilt, Ballard entered the empty Open-Unsolved Unit and went directly to Colleen's workstation and desktop. Six months earlier Hatteras had taken a week off to drive one of her daughters to school. While she was gone, Ballard had needed to print out a genealogical tree that was part of a charging package she was submitting to Carol Plovc at the DA's office. The only way to get the document was to get into Hatteras's computer. Ballard had called Hatteras, who had revealed her password without hesitation: the names of her two daughters spelled backward.

Ballard now had to hope that Hatteras had not changed it upon her return or in the months since. She opened the password portal on her desktop and typed in *eiggaMeitaK,* hoping she remembered it correctly.

The password went through and Ballard was in.

The last thing Colleen had said to Ballard before leaving the office yesterday was that she would finish an email, send it, then go. Ballard wanted to know what that email had been and if there were any other messages to or from her that could have a bearing on her murder.

Once in Hatteras's email account, Ballard pulled up the Sent folder and saw that the last message sent from Colleen's office desktop was to Colleen's personal email account. Ballard opened the message and found an almost word-for-word transcript of the beginning of Ballard's phone conversation with Victor Best in Hawaii. Ballard realized that when she had heard typing during the phone call, it was Colleen typing what she was hearing from Ballard's pod.

Ballard leaned back in the chair and thought about this, then almost immediately leaned forward again and checked both the incoming and outgoing emails on the account. She knew it would not be long before Goring and Dubose arrived.

Nothing else in the email account drew Ballard's suspicion or caught her interest. She then moved to the files Hatteras had kept on her desktop. Most of these were labeled with the names of victims that were on the unit's active list of investigations. Most contained genetic family trees that she had been filling out over time as members of families responded to her attempts to contact them. She opened the file folder titled *Pillowcase24* and saw nothing in it that she didn't already know. There was a file within this file titled *PoI,* which Ballard took to mean "persons of interest." She opened it and found a list of the four St. Vincent's alums — Best, Bennett, Weeks, and Van Ness — the unit had been tracking.

Hatteras had added details on the four men as information came in. Birth dates, addresses, phone numbers, social media accounts, marital and employment status — everything she and the other members of the team had gathered, here in one neat file. She had included the photo of Andrew Bennett standing in front of the SOLD sign. Ballard stared at Bennett's eyes, and it suddenly became clear to her what Colleen Hatteras had done that might have gotten her killed.

Her cell phone buzzed and she saw it was Carol Plovc again. She had forgotten to return the call.

"Sorry, Carol, I was going to call you back."

"I'm leaving early today and I just wanted to make sure you heard that O'Fallon declined again."

"What the fuck?"

"I know, I know. I would have signed off on this but he won't. He called the ear identification you got junk science."

"He's junk science. This is just political bullshit."

"I'm not disagreeing."

"So is there anything else we can do?"

"Outside of finding a signed confession from Thawyer in his files, probably not."

"Yeah, right."

"Please tell Officer Bosch I'm sorry. I think you guys have it nailed. But my hands are tied."

"I understand."

Plovc's voice dropped down to a whisper: "You know there's a recall effort starting, right?" she said.

"Yeah, I heard," Ballard said.

"Well, if it works and we get a new DA, you bring this to me again."

"But when will that be, in a year? Elyse Ford's sister is in her eighties. She's waited all her life to know who took her sister. And now thanks to the politics of this town, she may die waiting."

"I'm sorry. I hope you or Officer Bosch can tell her that it might not be officially closed, but that you consider the case solved."

Ballard was silent as she remembered that it was Hatteras who had been dealing directly with the Ford family. She looked at a photo pinned to the workstation's privacy wall. It was Colleen and her two teenage daughters sitting at a table behind a birthday cake with lit candles. Ballard knew those girls had just gotten or were about to get news that would permanently alter their lives.

"All right, well, I'm in the middle of something here, Carol," she said. "Thanks for fighting the good fight on this."

"Anytime," Plovc said. "I'm here when you need me."

They disconnected. Ballard reached over and unpinned the photo of Colleen and her daughters. She got up and went to her workstation, pinned the snapshot to her own privacy wall, and stared at it for a long moment.

She knew she needed to call Maddie Bosch and tell her the bad news about the Thawyer case, but that could wait. She opened the email Hatteras had sent her with the details from Andrew Bennett's DMV record. She typed his Laguna Hills address into her phone's GPS and saw that the estimated drive time was ninety-three minutes.

If she waited until rush hour, that number would balloon and possibly even double.

She wanted to get on the road but had to wait. She wondered if Goring and Dubose had been held up at the crime scene by Captain Gandle. Though she had put Persson on Hatteras's phone records only an hour before, she called him.

"Anders, you got anything yet?"

"I just got the call records, yes."

"Good, give me the last calls. Give me the time and length."

"The last two were to her daughters. Do you want them?"

"How do you know they were calls to the daughters?"

"They are on her family plan."

"Got it. What time did she make those calls, and how long was she on?"

"She called the first number at seven last night and it was only one minute. She probably left a message. Then the last call was one minute later, and she talked for nine minutes."

Ballard wrote the information down on a fresh page in her notebook.

"What was the call before that?" she asked.

"That was to me," he said. "She said you were mad about the password. I am very —"

"We can skip that one for now. Go to the one before that."

Persson gave her a number with a 714 area code and told her the call lasted twenty-nine minutes.

"When was the call made?"

"It began at four thirty-three and lasted until five oh-two."

Ballard wrote it all down, then flipped back to her previous notes. She found the page where she had written down the information Hatteras gave her about Andrew Bennett. The number Persson had just given her matched the number Bennett listed below his bio on the real estate website.

"Does it say whether this was an outgoing or incoming call?" she asked.

"Outgoing," Persson said. "These are all outgoing calls."

Hatteras had called Bennett and they had talked for almost half an hour.

"Okay, previous to that?" Ballard said. "Any other calls yesterday?"

"She made a call yesterday morning at nine twenty," Persson said. "That was to me too."

"And what was that about?"

Ballard heard the door on the other side of the murder archive shelves open and then a pair of shoes walking on the linoleum.

"One of us called the other every day," Persson said. "You know, just to check in and see what was going on. She called me yest—"

"Uh, Anders, I have to go," Ballard interrupted. "I'll call you back if I need to, but for now you can stand down on that."

"Do you want me to send this to you?"

Ballard saw Goring come out of the aisle that ran along the murder library.

"No, that's fine," Ballard said. "I'll be in touch."

She disconnected the call and greeted Goring. "Where's your partner?"

"I left him in the neighborhood. He was knocking on doors and collecting video."

Ballard nodded. The collecting of video from neighborhood Ring cameras and the like was often more important than finding witnesses. Cameras didn't have memory issues and biases.

"Did you get anything good yet?" Ballard asked.

"The guy came into the neighborhood on foot," Goring said. "Head down, wearing a hoodie. So far, no angles that would give us an ID. He was good. That sound like any of your persons of interest?"

"Sounds like it could be anyone. He broke in? What time?"

"We're piecing together video—that's why Winston is still out there and I need to get back. But we have the guy entering the house at twelve thirty a.m. and leaving just before one. He was quick and it looked like he had a tool that opened the door."

"What kind of tool?"

"You know what a fireman's friend is?"

"Hmm, no."

"You can google it. It's like a T-shaped blade that slides into a door-jamb and pops the lock. Supposedly a guy on the LAFD invented it for getting into burning houses — hence the name."

"Wow."

"When the killer left, he had her computer and the extra hard drive under his arm." Goring looked at the desks on the raft. "Which spot was the victim's?"

Hearing Colleen referred to as "the victim" hit Ballard like a punch to the heart. She stood up and walked Goring over to Hat-teras's workstation.

"This is hers," she said. "Was."

Goring sat down and tapped the space bar on the keyboard. The screen lit up, and the password portal appeared.

"You think anybody on the squad would know her password?" she asked.

"Probably not," Ballard said. "But I could check."

"Don't bother. I'll take it down to the tech unit."

"The guy there who set these up for us is named Chuck Pell."

"Okay, I'll take it to him."

Goring tried the file drawer that was built into the workstation. It was locked. "How about a key for this?" she asked.

"I have one."

Ballard went to her desk and opened the middle drawer. There was a ring of keys that opened the file drawers of every station on the raft. They were marked by number. She handed the ring to Goring.

"Number nine," she said.

Ballard watched Goring open the file drawer, wishing she had thought to check it out earlier. The drawer contained several files with the names of victims written on the tabs. Ballard bent down so she could read some of them.

"Those look like closed cases," Ballard said. "I think when we closed a case, she printed out all the IGG stuff and put it in a file. The active stuff was on the computer. She'd been working on what she called heritage patterns for several active cases."

"'Heritage patterns'?"

"Like a genetic family tree."

"Got it."

Goring closed the file drawer.

"I should get back over there," she said. "I'm going to take the computer and drop it by the tech shop."

"Fine by me," Ballard said. "At some point I'll need to get that stuff back. We have another guy on the squad who can continue Colleen's work."

"I'll return it to you as soon as we're finished with it." Goring reached under the desk to unplug the CPU and detach it from Colleen's oversize monitor.

Persson would inherit that screen, Ballard thought, unless she found another IGG specialist to take Colleen's place. That thought led to another.

"Have you told Colleen's daughters?" she asked.

"Not yet," Goring said. "Too busy running with the case."

Ballard nodded. "You want me to make the notification?" she asked. "I met them once when she brought them here."

"There is nothing I would like better than to take a pass on that job," Goring said. "But I need to interview them, see when they last talked and all of that. So I'll do it."

"They should know soon."

"Don't worry, I'll get to them today."

Ballard nodded.

Goring successfully detached the CPU and slid it out from beneath the workstation. She lifted it, testing its weight.

"You want me to get a dolly to roll it out to your car?" Ballard asked.

"No, I'm strong," Goring said.

She hefted the computer so she could get her hands under it and turned toward the aisle.

"In more ways than one," she added.

Ballard took it as a reference to experiences that had led her to the Beanery meetings.

"Remember, if you think of anything, give me a call," Goring said.

"Will do," Ballard said.

Goring headed to the exit. She seemed to slow her walk and focus on the murder-book archive as she passed.

"All these cases," she said. "Waiting to be solved."

Ballard just nodded and watched her go.

SATURDAY, 8:42 A.M.

54

THE GARAGE DOOR of Andrew Bennett's home on Linda Vista Drive started to rise. Ballard had a good angle on it and locked in with a small set of binoculars. She was parked in front of a house on El Conejo Lane half a block away. Bennett's home was at the top of the T where the two streets met. She could see directly into the garage and watched as a man she was pretty sure was Bennett popped the trunk on a Mercedes sedan. Along the left wall of the garage were a number of real estate signs of all sizes. Bennett chose the ones he needed and loaded them into the trunk. Ballard could see that all had his name and phone number on them. At least a few of them said OPEN HOUSE.

Bennett closed the trunk, grabbed the briefcase and the Yeti cup he had placed on the roof of the car, and climbed into the driver's seat. When Ballard saw the brake lights flare, she put the binoculars down, pushed the ignition button on the Defender, and got ready to follow.

Bennett took a meandering route to his open house, first driving toward the beach, then taking the coast highway north to Crystal Cove. He pulled into an upscale ocean-view shopping center and went into a Starbucks. The place was crowded and Ballard followed him in, knowing the other customers would provide camouflage. She studied him as he filled the Yeti with dark roast, looking for any indication that he was the man who had strangled and then shot a woman a little more than twenty-four hours before. Ballard had studied many murderers up close over her years on the job. She could find nothing in common about them other than a certain flatness in the eyes. But in the Starbucks she didn't want to get that close and possibly tip Bennett off that she was watching him.

After the coffee stop, Bennett went south back to Laguna Beach and made stops at various corners to put up OPEN HOUSE signs that gave an address on a street called Sunset Ridge and helpful arrows pointing the way. The signs said the house would be open from noon till four. It was only ten a.m., so Ballard decided against peeling off and going directly to Sunset Ridge. Bennett had two hours to kill and she suspected that he wouldn't immediately go to the house he was selling.

After the last sign was placed on the last corner of the hillside neighborhood, Bennett took the coast road south through the beachside village before pulling into the parking lot behind the two-level business plaza where Destination Realty was located. He entered through a rear door, and Ballard assumed he would stay in his office until it was time to go to Sunset Ridge and host the open house.

Ballard lowered the windows and killed the Defender's engine, readying herself for a possible ninety-minute wait. But only twenty minutes into it, Bennett came out the back door of the office and went to his car. With Ballard tailing from a distance, he drove north again. The traffic slowed as they went through the village, and at one point, Bennett stopped his car in a traffic lane and put on his flashers. This brought on an angry chorus of horns from cars that got stuck behind him. Ballard thought he had stopped because she had been made, that he had picked up on the single-car surveillance. She quickly switched lanes and passed the Mercedes just as Bennett was opening his door. She cut back into the right lane and checked the rearview mirror. She saw Bennett run around the front of his car, cross the sidewalk, and go into a business she couldn't identify. She breathed a little easier. He didn't seem to know he was being tailed.

Ballard saw an open space in the line of parallel-parked cars ahead and skillfully slid the Defender in, noting that the space was open on a Saturday morning in the beach village only because it wasn't a legal parking spot — it was a red curb in front of a fire hydrant. Nonetheless, she stayed; she hit her flashers and kept her eyes on the mirrors. Within moments Bennett reemerged onto the sidewalk carrying a pink bakery box and ran back around the front of his Mercedes. He jumped into the car with a renewed blare of horns from drivers lambasting him for his selfish move.

The little moment checked a box for Ballard. It showed narcissism, a key trait of psychopaths. She turned off the flashers and pulled her car back into the traffic lane. She was now moving ahead of Bennett on the highway, but that was okay because she knew where he was going.

Sunset Ridge was at the top of a hillside neighborhood of multimillion-dollar homes with staggering views of the Pacific Ocean. Ballard positioned the Defender a block from the house Bennett was hoping to sell. She had an angle of view between two homes that showed her the whitecaps atop the blue-black waves coming ashore below. They were the kind of waves she waited for every time she was on the water.

She lowered the back of her seat so that Bennett would not notice her as he cruised by and checked the time on the dashboard. It was 11:11 — still almost an hour before the open house was scheduled to begin. She saw this as an opportunity to engage Bennett while he was alone.

She started the car again.

55

THE FRONT DOOR was open. Ballard pulled into the driveway, not worried about announcing her arrival. She had already locked her holstered pistol and badge in the glove compartment. She got out and locked the car.

The house did not fit with the architecture of the neighborhood. It was an adobe-style construction with a flat roof and brown clay walls rounded at the corners. It said *desert,* not *beach.* Ballard entered through the open door into a hallway that stretched straight through the house to a rear deck with a view of the Pacific.

"Hello?" she called.

She stepped farther in. The Spanish-tiled hallway branched off to the right into a step-down living room with an adobe-style fireplace and an open wood-beam ceiling. There were no sharp corners, just blunt angles.

The furnishings of the room didn't match the architectural style. The couch and chairs were thickly upholstered in bright blues, yellows, and whites. The coffee table was glass-topped with chrome legs, and beside the couch was a standing lamp with a chrome base and stem. The wall hangings were modern rip-offs of Rothko, not O'Keeffe. Ballard guessed that the owners or prior tenants had moved out and Bennett had staged the house using furniture that didn't quite fit. There probably wasn't a lot of call for staging adobe houses in Laguna, and he had made do with what he had.

She moved farther down the hall.

"Anyone here for the open house?" she called.

The hall led past a staircase going down, and Ballard understood that it was what she called an upside-down house. It had been built into a hillside, and the communal spaces were on the entry floor on top and the bedrooms were down below.

Ballard came to the end of the hall, which gave onto a large living space with a den on the right and the kitchen and dining area on the left. The rear wall was all glass sliders leading to a deck that ran the width of the house. Out there was a built-in grill and plenty of space for outdoor furniture and tables. Every house had a special spot, and this deck with its unblocked view of the ocean was what would sell this place.

On a kitchen counter was a stack of fliers for the property and a sign-in sheet on a clipboard with a pen attached by a string. The box she had seen Bennett pick up earlier was open on the opposite counter. Next to the pastries were paper plates and napkins. Bennett's briefcase and Yeti were on a kitchen island, but there was no sign of Bennett.

"Hello?" Ballard said loudly. "I'm here for the open house."

No response. Ballard looked around and realized the opportunity she had. She quickly went to the briefcase, unzipped it, and opened it to check its contents. What she saw changed the trajectory of her plan. As she reached in, the house started to vibrate, and she knew that someone — Bennett — was opening the garage door. She quickly finished with the briefcase, zipped it closed, and headed for the deck.

Ballard unlocked one of the doors and slid it open. As she stepped out, she heard a door slam and guessed that the ocean breeze she'd allowed into the house had pushed the front door closed. She knew that should get Bennett's attention, wherever he was.

She kept her eyes on the ocean as she stepped all the way out to the deck's railing. She then looked down and saw a sub-deck with similar views that extended from the bedrooms below.

"Uh, we're not open yet."

The voice came from behind her. Ballard turned to see Andrew Bennett standing in the doorway.

"The signs all say twelve to four," he said. "We still have forty minutes till we open."

"I know, I'm sorry," Ballard said. "I was in the neighborhood and thought I'd just sneak in for a quick look. I mean, if you don't mind."

"Well, since you're already here...could you come sign in first?"

"Sure."

She followed him into the house.

"You're down from Los Angeles?" he asked.

"How do you know that?" Ballard asked.

"I was in the garage, tidying up, and I thought I heard a car pull in. When I opened the door, I saw you have a Galpin frame on your license plate. That's the dealership up in Van Nuys, right?"

"Oh, yes, right."

"I'm from up that way. I remember Galpin ads on TV from when I was a kid."

They went into the kitchen and Ballard picked up the pen next to the sign-in sheet on the counter.

"How long have you been down here?" she asked. She wrote *Ronnie Mars* on the clipboard, a nod to a fictional detective hero of hers.

"A long time," Bennett said.

She added the number of a burner phone she used on occasion for personal as well as police reasons.

"Ever go back?" she asked.

"No, not really," Bennett said. "Unless I have to fly out of LAX, but that's a nightmare I try to avoid."

"I hear you on that."

"So, I'm Andrew."

"Ronnie."

Ballard turned from the counter to face him. He was on the other side of the kitchen island, his briefcase on the counter between them. He smiled, and she recognized the expression from the website photo — the wide, practiced, and insincere smile of a salesman.

"So, Ronnie, tell me," he said. "Are you looking for a full-time home or a getaway place?"

"Uh, I'm undecided," Ballard said. "I work from home, so I could have a full-time place down here and the getaway could be up in L.A."

"That would be perfect. What do you do?"

"I'm a writer. TV, mostly."

"Anything I might know?"

"Probably not. It's mostly soft-crime stuff."

"Soft crime? What does that mean?"

"Geared toward women. Female endangerment. Unfaithful husbands. More romance than mystery."

"Interesting. But not believable."

"Yeah, that about covers it."

"No, I mean you, Ronnie. Not believable."

He reached into his briefcase and pulled out a handgun. It was a blue-steel Glock.

"Your friend warned me there would be others," he said.

"Whoa, wait a minute," Ballard said. "I don't know what you're talking about. I — "

"Colleen Hatteras. You housewife sleuths think you're all Nancy Drew, and look what it gets you — a date with the devil."

"I don't — "

"Save it, Ronnie. If that's even your real name."

Ballard raised her hands as she thought about Colleen. At the end, she had apparently not revealed all to Bennett. No matter how badly he'd hurt her or scared her, she had been able to hold back and leave Bennett thinking the threat to his existence was from the amateur ranks of the internet.

"You killed Colleen," she said.

"No, she killed herself," he said. "She got too close to the fire and there was no choice. Blame her, not me. And now I need to know who else you've told about me."

"No one. I swear."

Bennett used his free hand to reach back into the briefcase. He pulled out a plastic bag containing coiled snap ties.

"You expect me to believe you came down here without telling another soul?"

"I had to."

Bennett laughed.

"You had to? Why would you have to?"

"Because I came down here to kill you. For Colleen."

Bennett's laugh rose sharply.

"And how's that working out for you?"

"Pretty well, actually...except all of a sudden, I've changed my mind. I don't want you dead, Bennett. I want you to rot in the living hell of prison. For Colleen and all the women you've killed and hurt."

"Well, there's one problem with that plan."

He waggled the gun he held and smiled. Ballard saw the flat, dead eyes then. She thought about him calling himself the devil a few minutes before. If the devil was a psychopath who had no empathy or other emotions, then Bennett had nailed it.

"No, that's your problem," she said. "Because..."

As she spoke, she casually reached down to the left cuff of her pants, pulled the Ruger from her ankle holster, and straightened up with it pointed at Bennett's chest.

"My gun has bullets," she continued. "And yours does not."

Bennett immediately pulled the trigger on the Glock. It snapped on an empty chamber. His eyes widened, and he pulled three more times, all with the same result. Ballard read his expression as he realized the mistake he had made leaving the briefcase unattended in the kitchen while he prepared the house for showing. He focused on the Ruger, and Ballard read him again.

"It's small but it carries seven rounds and I'm good with it," she said. "You make a move and I'll put both your eyes out."

Bennett made an odd sound as if giving voice to the fight-or-flight impulse taking over his brain. He then calmed himself and offered a half smile of surrender.

"I want you to put the gun down on the counter and slide it across to me," Ballard said.

Bennett complied, shoving the gun hard enough that it would have flown off the counter if Ballard hadn't reached with her free hand to catch it.

"Now get down on your knees, hands flat on the counter," she ordered.

"This will never work," Bennett said. "No one's going to—"

"Do it, Bennett, or we go back to plan A. Is that what you want?"

"Okay, okay, I'm doing it."

He started to sink down behind the counter, his hands holding the edge for balance. Ballard moved quickly past the island to his left, grabbing the bag of snap ties.

"Okay, hands behind your head," she ordered. "Now."

Bennett did as instructed. Ballard opened the baggie and grabbed a handful of ties, regretting her decision to leave her handcuffs in the Defender. She moved in behind Bennett and put the muzzle of the Ruger against the skin behind his right ear.

"Do not move or you're going to have a lead slug bouncing around inside your skull. If it doesn't kill you, it'll scramble your brain. You'll need somebody to wipe your ass for the rest of your life."

"Not moving. Just do your thing."

He said it in a tone that suggested he was bored. A few of the plastic ties had already been looped for quick use by Bennett. Ballard now used them the same way.

"Hold your left hand up. Slowly."

Bennett complied, and Ballard looped a tie over it and pulled it tight at the wrist. She followed the same procedure with the right hand, then stepped back and ordered Bennett to get facedown on the floor with his hands behind his back. After he did, she quickly wove one of the open ties through the loops on his wrists and then pulled the free end through the snap-lock.

Bennett was now secure.

"Don't move," she said. "You move and I'll use the rest of these to hog-tie you like you did to all the women you raped."

Bennett turned his head on the floor so he could look up at her.

"Who the fuck are you?"

"LAPD. And you are under arrest for the murder of Colleen Hatteras, with many more charges to come."

"Bullshit."

"No, you're bullshit, Bennett. You're done. And you know what? She led me right to you. Colleen got you."

Ballard stepped back behind his feet and pulled out her phone. She called Charlotte Goring's cell and the detective answered with an accusation.

"You lied to me, Ballard."

"Don't worry about it. I just——"

"No, I'm worried about it. I just got a call from Chuck Pell and he said Hatteras's computer was accessed yesterday at three fifty-five p.-fucking-m. You were in the office then, Ballard, and you told me you didn't know the password."

"Charlotte, listen to me. I just arrested Andrew Bennett. I've got the Glock and he literally just confessed. I need to transport him from Laguna to L.A. Do you want to come down and get him, or do you want to worry about what I said and did yesterday?"

There was no response at first. Ballard could tell Goring had covered the phone and was talking to someone, most likely her partner, Dubose. Then she finally came back to the call.

"Where exactly are you?" she asked.

"I'll text you the address," Ballard said.

Bennett raised his head off the floor and screamed.

"She said she's going to kill me!"

Ballard stepped over, leaned down, and pulled the plastic band between his wrists up off his back, putting pain and stress into his shoulders. He lowered his head back to the floor.

"You shut the fuck up, Bennett, or I'm going to take your socks off and stick them down your throat. Got it?"

Bennett didn't answer. She yanked on his arms again.

"Yes, I got it," he said.

Ballard stood back up and spoke into the phone.

"Charlotte, are you there?"

"Ballard, we're on our way. He'd better be alive when we get there."

"Then don't take too long."

Ballard disconnected.

"Sounds like this isn't going to go too well for you," Bennett said.

"Maybe not," Ballard said. "But it's going to be far worse for you. You hear those waves out there? This is it. You'll never hear or see or taste freedom again."

"We'll see about that."

"Yeah, we will."

Bennett went silent. Ballard texted the address to Goring. As she did so, she heard someone come in the front door. It was time for the open house to begin. She quickly grabbed more of the snap ties and used them to bind Bennett at the ankles, then pulled his feet up to hog-tie them to his wrists.

"Help," he yelled. *"Somebody call the police!"*

Ballard jumped up and turned toward the hallway. A pair of prospective buyers stood there, eyes wide with shock. The man, the arms of a sweater tied around his neck, raised his hands.

"We don't want any trouble," he said.

"Don't worry, I am the police," Ballard said. "This man is under arrest and the open house is over."

SUNDAY, 12:00 P.M.

56

THE PRESS CONFERENCE on the tenth floor of the PAB started precisely on time. As choreographed by the captain of the media relations unit, Ballard led her full team from the Open-Unsolved Unit into the windowless press room. They were followed by Goring and Dubose and then Captain Gandle and the police chief himself, Carl Detry.

Detry was only two years into the job, having been appointed by the mayor and approved by the L.A. Police Commission after the prior chief's surprise retirement. Detry's tenure had started out rough with the political clash caused by his endorsement of Ernest O'Fallon's opponent for district attorney. He had backed the wrong horse and O'Fallon never missed a chance to take the chief and the LAPD to task for any misdeeds. But Detry had come up through the ranks and knew the importance of the media. He knew how a press conference announcing the arrest of a serial predator could swing the needle of approval toward his department and himself. By city law, a police chief was appointed for a five-year term with a possible second term to follow with the police commission's approval. So far, no chief in the modern era had posted a full ten years in the job. If Detry wanted to buck the trend, he needed to court and keep the media on his side.

Detry moved to the microphone. It was Sunday and a slow news day. That meant every seat in front of him was taken, and the raised stage in the back of the room was crowded with TV cameras on tripods and their operating crews.

Detry was tall and handsome. He wore a uniform instead of a suit with four stars on the collar; he was the image of LAPD pride and progressiveness. He was Black and from the city's south side. He had said that as a teenager, he saw his community burn during the 1992 riots, and he had decided to join the LAPD instead of a gang. And now here he was, thirty years after earning the badge, leading the department that many believed had advanced little beyond those days of discord.

"I'm here today with good and bad news," Detry began. "We have arrested a predator who struck fear into our community for many years. But we lost a good person during the investigation. Her loss is a reminder that to protect and serve this community, there are always dangers, and we must remain ever vigilant."

He got down to business, identifying Andrew Bennett as the Pillowcase Rapist and the killer of Colleen Hatteras, a volunteer with the Open-Unsolved Unit. Detry said that Bennett was linked to Hatteras's murder through ballistics and preliminary DNA results. He outlined how these connections were made and ended with the news that Detectives Goring and Dubose would present the case to the district attorney's office in the morning.

Detry said he would take a few questions, but the overwhelming response from reporters were requests for someone to talk about the volunteer who had lost her life. Detry turned to his left and then to his right and signaled Ballard to the podium.

Ballard stepped forward and lowered the microphone.

"Colleen Hatteras was with us on the unit since we started two years ago," she said. "She played a significant part in every case we worked, every case we cleared, including this one. Colleen's work led to the identification of Andrew Bennett as our suspect and—"

"What went wrong?" a reporter interrupted.

Ballard looked down, composing an answer.

"Colleen did nothing wrong," she said. "She didn't deserve what happened to her. She didn't bring it on herself."

"Then why was she killed?" the reporter persisted.

"I take responsibility for that," Ballard said. "It's my unit and I didn't do enough to safeguard my team. I mean, these are volunteers, and I should have been a better leader."

"But how did this guy get to her?" the reporter asked, insistent. "Did she—"

"We don't know," Ballard said, forcefully cutting him off. "We don't know yet."

Ballard felt a hand touch her arm and saw the chief coming to her rescue. He gently moved her away from the microphone and took over.

"Those details as well as the rest of the evidence will become public when we go to trial," Detry said. "For now, we've said what we can say at this time. With great sacrifice, a grave threat to the community has been removed by the diligent efforts of your police department. Thank you for being here and that's all for today."

As reporters shouted questions, the chief started ushering those behind the podium toward the door to the assembly room. Once they were all back there and the door was closed on the shouting, Detry turned to Ballard.

"Tell me this case isn't going to crash and burn," he said.

"Chief, it's solid," Ballard said. "He's the guy. He confessed. And when we get the DNA back from the DOJ, it will be bulletproof."

Gandle pushed his way past Laffont and Maddie Bosch to get close.

"We've got this, Chief," he said.

"I'm going to hold you to that, Captain," Detry said. "And Detective."

The chief turned and headed to the door that led to his suite of offices.

"Ballard, I'll be down in my office," Gandle said. "Stop by."

He said it in a tone that implied that the invite was not a suggestion but an order.

Ballard nodded. She turned to look for Goring and Dubose. The powers that be had decided that the West Bureau detectives would take the case to the DA's office in the morning. This would allow them to tailor the presentation of evidence around Ballard's questionable actions. Ballard did not object to the decision. It wasn't her case. She would be a key witness for the prosecution, testifying before a judge and jury to what was said and done in the kitchen of the house on Sunset Ridge. Her credibility would be viciously challenged by Bennett and his lawyers, and she would be ready for it.

But Goring and Dubose had slipped out, and after Gandle left, Ballard was alone with her team. She turned and looked at their faces. All eyes were cast down. The victory was hollow.

"All right," Ballard said. "Group hug."

Everyone gathered around and locked arms. At first they were silent, heads bowed. Then Laffont spoke.

"To Colleen," he said. "May she rest in peace."

EPILOGUE: THE KULA LODGE

BALLARD'S PHONE STARTED buzzing before sunrise. It was dark in her room but the glow from the phone's screen helped reacquaint her with the lines of the cottage. She had been in a deep sleep after a long journey. Five hours on a plane followed by three hours in a rented Jeep bouncing along dark roads.

She grabbed her phone off the night table, checked the screen, and accepted the call. It was Maddie Bosch.

"Did you see the *Times?*" she asked.

"Uh, no, not yet," Ballard said. "I've been sleeping."

"Oh, shit. I forgot you're three hours behind over there."

"We used to say three hours, three thousand miles, and three decades behind. What's in the *Times?*"

"They did a story on the Black Dahlia case. They laid the whole thing out. There's going to be a shitstorm."

"What does it say?"

"I'll send you the link. It's all about the DA not filing on our package."

"Well, that's good, isn't it? Maybe it will change Ernesto's decision."

"It names me. They're going to think I leaked this."

"Did you?"

"No way."

"Then you have nothing to worry about. They can't prove it happened if it didn't happen."

"Was it you? Did you — no, wait, never mind, I don't want to know."

Ballard smiled; Maddie understood that it would be best for her not to have any further knowledge of the leak. Ballard swung her legs off the bed and sat up. The deal she'd made with Scott Anderson was that he had to mention prominently in the story that Officer Madeline Bosch was responsible for the break in the Black Dahlia case. Ballard had trusted him, and it appeared that he had made good on his promise.

"Who's on the byline?" she asked, pretending she didn't know.

"It's that Scott Anderson," Maddie said. "He's the one who was asking all the questions at the press conference."

"Right. Is there anything factually wrong in the story as far as you can tell?"

Maddie laughed.

"No, it's right on. It makes the DA look like a petulant asshole holding out on the chief because he didn't endorse him."

"Sounds pretty accurate, then. What's it say about — "

Ballard got a call-waiting buzz and checked her screen. It was Captain Gandle, most likely calling about the same thing.

"I've got another call I have to take," she said. "Send me the link when you get a chance."

"Will do," Maddie said. "And Renée — thanks."

Ballard didn't respond before she switched over to the other call.

"Captain?"

"Ballard, have you seen the *Times*?"

His voice was almost shrill.

"Uh, no, Captain, I'm in Hawaii and not really looking at any news."

"Hawaii? What are you doing in Hawaii when all hell is breaking loose here?"

"I told you I was taking the week. I gave everyone on the unit the week as well. What hell is breaking loose?"

"Somebody leaked the Black Dahlia case to the *Times*. It's all over the front page, the website's home page, everywhere. Now we've got TV people in the courtyard waiting for the chief to make a statement."

"What does the *Times* say?"

"It says we solved Black Dahlia but the DA won't stamp the case closed. It actually says Maddie solved it, and that puts us in a big fucking bind. Did you fire her yet?"

"Uh, no. I was going to wait until I got back next week."

"Thank Christ."

Ballard could hear the relief in his voice.

"So you don't want me to drop her now?"

"Hell no. Just keep her on. We'll look like shit if we fire the officer who broke the case."

You mean you *will look like shit,* Ballard thought.

"Fine with me," Ballard said. "We need the second badge and she obviously does good work."

"Now, Ballard, I'm going to ask you something," Gandle said. "And don't fucking lie because the tenth floor is going to ask me the same thing."

"Okay, ask."

"Did you give this story to them? It cites unnamed sources and you better not be one of them."

"Is it written by Scott Anderson?"

"It sure is."

"Well, he called me about it and all I said was 'No comment.' I even turned on my phone recorder because I knew somebody was feeding him stuff on the case and I didn't want to be blamed. You want me to send the recording to you?"

"Yes, I do. It might be helpful when the chief comes to me and says, 'What the fuck?'"

"The story — it makes us look bad?"

"No, it makes us look good and that can be bad. You understand? O'Fallon's going to shit a brick and he'll know it came from us."

"Tell you what, Cap. If it makes us look good and him look bad, then my guess is that the leak's in the DA's office. It went up the chain over there and they all wanted to close the case, but O'Fallon rejected it. Half the people in that office are working on a recall."

"I don't know. You're probably right."

Ballard nodded as a silence ensued, and she thought she was going to skate on this one.

"Where in Hawaii, Ballard?" Gandle said. "Hope you're on a beach."

"I'm in Maui, up-country near a town called Kaupo."

"That doesn't sound like a vacation. What are you doing?"

"I grew up here. For a while. And today I'm going to see someone I haven't seen in a long, long time."

"Well, good luck with that, Ballard. I'll see you when you get back. If they track you down, don't talk to any reporters. Understand?"

"Yes, sir. I understand."

She disconnected and switched over to her email account. Maddie Bosch had sent the link, as promised. Ballard opened the *Times* story on the tiny screen.

LAPD: BLACK DAHLIA CASE SOLVED
DISTRICT ATTORNEY: NOT SO FAST

By Scott Anderson, Times Staff Writer

The Los Angeles Police Department is ready to close the book on the infamous Black Dahlia murder case, but the district attorney's office has refused twice to accept newfound evidence and mark the city's most gruesome case as finally closed, the *Times* has learned.

The LAPD's cold-case team used new evidence and technology to make the case that a recently deceased photographer was the killer of Elizabeth Short, the so-called Black Dahlia, whose body was found cleanly cut in half in a south-side field in 1947.

The murder of Short became a headline-grabbing story across the nation and has remained unsolved despite efforts over the decades by police and amateur detectives alike. It has been the subject of numerous books, documentaries, films, and television shows.

Short, 22, was described as a Hollywood hopeful who frequented bars and dance clubs in Hollywood and downtown. On January 15, 1947, her severed body was found on Norton Avenue in the Leimert Park area. During the initial investigation, detectives questioned several suspects but charged no one. Taunting letters from an unknown individual claiming to be the killer were sent to local newspapers and the police.

It is not clear if Emmitt Thawyer was ever one of those suspects. Thawyer was named as the killer in the case presented to the district attorney's office last week. Though Thawyer died six years ago, it is LAPD policy that the Open-Unsolved Unit submit all murder cases involving a deceased suspect to prosecutors for review and agreement to close.

However, the *Times* has learned that the review process involving Thawyer was rejected twice for insufficient evidence, even after investigators used a new technology to further substantiate the case against Thawyer.

The latest turn in what may be the city's most famous unsolved case began when Officer Madeline Bosch was given access to a set of photos from Thawyer's abandoned storage unit in Echo Park. Bosch is assigned to patrol in Hollywood Division and is also a one-day-a-week volunteer on the Open-Unsolved team. Bosch had a unit at the rental facility where Thawyer's property was stored. When operators of the business were cleaning out Thawyer's unit, they came across a file containing gruesome photos of several women who appeared to have been tortured and murdered; they turned them over to Bosch. Among these Bosch recognized photos of Elizabeth Short, both before and after she was viciously assaulted and murdered.

According to sources, the LAPD's photo unit confirmed that the paper stock the photos were printed on was from the same era as the murder and that the photos were not props for a Hollywood film. Technicians in the unit concluded that there was a "90+ percent probability" that one of the victims in the photos was Elizabeth Short.

Cold-case investigators also identified another woman who appeared in the photos in both life and death. She was an actress who was reported missing in 1950. Investigators also confirmed that all the photos were taken in the basement of a house in Angeleno Heights where Thawyer lived in the 1940s and 1950s.

Thawyer was a commercial photographer who primarily took photos for equipment catalogs. However, sources theorize that he also ran a side business taking headshots and other photos for would-be Hollywood entertainers. It was likely this work that brought Short and other young women into his orbit.

The cold-case team submitted a charging package to prosecutors a week ago. It was rejected by district attorney Ernest O'Fallon as having insufficient evidence to win a conviction had the case been filed against a live suspect. The stumbling block was confirming without doubt that it was Elizabeth Short in the photos from Thawyer's storage unit.

Investigators then sought to bolster the case by using a technology new to law enforcement involving ear comparison. Earlier photos of Elizabeth Short in which her ears were visible were compared to the Thawyer photos. Paul Buckley, an analyst with the Film Forensics Institute who conducted one of the comparisons, said the tests proved that Short and the woman in the Thawyer photos were the same person.

"No doubt," Buckley said. "Elizabeth Short is the woman in the photos the police found. Ear identification is as good as fingerprints, and one day law enforcement will accept that."

But when the "ear evidence" was presented to prosecutors, O'Fallon rejected the case again, claiming ear comparison was an unproven technique.

Reached at his office Monday, O'Fallon declined to comment on his rejection of the case. He also denied that his decision was linked to the ongoing friction between him and LAPD chief Carl Detry, who endorsed O'Fallon's opponent in the 2022 election.

"We make our decisions based on the law," O'Fallon said. "Nothing else."

But Jacqueline Gaither, who operates a blog called *LAPD-watch,* said the top prosecutor and police chief are locked in a political battle that is detrimental to the cause of justice in the city.

"These guys don't like each other and this Black Dahlia case is a perfect example of how their issues affect the community," Gaither said. "Luckily, the suspect in this case isn't alive and can't hurt anybody else. But there's no doubt that O'Fallon rejected this case because he doesn't want to give the LAPD and its chief the headlines. It's petty and beneath his office."

Gaither, a lifelong resident of Los Angeles, said she was disappointed that the city's most notorious criminal case remains open. "Some say it's a mystery that is part of the fabric of the city and that it should never be solved," she said. "I don't think so. This city has waited a long time for answers. I think we all need answers."

Chief Detry did not return multiple calls for comment on the case and its rejection by the district attorney's office.

Ballard put the phone aside. Anderson had done a good job with the story and she was pleased. It had done the trick as far as keeping Maddie Bosch on the Open-Unsolved team.

Morning light was beginning to creep around the drawn shades of the cottage. Ballard reached over to the table for the map she had bought at the airport the night before. It had been a long time since she was up-country and she wasn't sure of the route. She couldn't rely on her GPS app because cell service was always spotty there. She had to go the old-fashioned way, with a map. She opened it on the bed and smoothed out the sharp creases with her hand.

She found Kaupo and then used a finger to trace the Hana Highway out to Keawa Bay. The address Makani gave when arrested on
traffic warrants was there on Haou Road. It looked like an hour's
drive, depending on the terrain. Ballard knew there were mostly
growers out there, some legal, some not. Some surfers. Few tourists.
She saw that she would pass by the stables where her horse, Kaupo
Boy, had been boarded thirty years before.

She got up to get dressed for the final destination of the trip. She
decided she would head out before she changed her mind. She would
go find the woman who had brought her into the world and then had
left her behind.

ACKNOWLEDGMENTS

Many thanks to all who made contributions big and small to this book. They include Asya Muchnick, Emad Akhtar, Bill Massey, Jane Davis, Heather Rizzo, Betsy Uhrig, Tracy Roe, Callie Connelly, Linda Connelly, John H. Welborne, Dennis Wojciechowski, Shannon Byrne, Tracy Conrad, Sean Harrington, and Terrill Lee Lankford. And many thanks as well to Mitzi Roberts for inspiring Renée Ballard, and to Rick Jackson, Tim Marcia, and David Lambkin.

The author also wishes to thank Michael Pietsch, Craig Young, Terry Adams, and Mario Pulice for their many, many years of support for his work.

ABOUT THE AUTHOR

MICHAEL CONNELLY is the author of thirty-eight previous novels, among them *New York Times* bestsellers *Resurrection Walk, Desert Star,* and *The Law of Innocence.* His books, which include the Harry Bosch series, the Lincoln Lawyer series, and the Renée Ballard series, have sold more than eighty-five million copies worldwide. Connelly is a former newspaper reporter who has won numerous awards for his journalism and his novels. He is the executive producer of three television series: *Bosch, Bosch: Legacy,* and *The Lincoln Lawyer.* He spends his time in California and Florida.